continued . . .

"I loved this book! Bennett delivers a sizzling-hot yet swoon-worthy love story with a mystery that keeps you guessing until the end, all set in the fresh and ultra-cool world of Jazz Age San Francisco. Can't wait to read the next one!"   —Kristen Callihan, author of *Shadowdance*

"Complex and smart romantic leads . . . Expect historical romance authors and fans to eagerly hop on the Roaring Twenties bandwagon, following Bennett's very able lead."
                              —*Publishers Weekly* (starred review)

"Absolutely delightful . . . Stirs intrigue, paranormal activity, and romance into a wonderfully refreshing brew . . . Bennett's fast-paced dialogue, often witty and sharp, as well as her charming characters and detailed setting, will truly captivate romance readers."   —*Booklist* (starred review)

"The combination of sizzling sex, gritty danger, and paranormal thrills adds up to one stupendous read!"
                              —*RT Book Reviews* (top pick)

GRAVE
PHANTOMS

JENN BENNETT

BERKLEY SENSATION, NEW YORK

THE BERKLEY PUBLISHING GROUP
Published by the Penguin Group
Penguin Group (USA) LLC
375 Hudson Street, New York, New York 10014

USA • Canada • UK • Ireland • Australia • New Zealand • India • South Africa • China

penguin.com

A Penguin Random House Company

GRAVE PHANTOMS

A Berkley Sensation Book / published by arrangement with the author

For information, address: The Berkley Publishing Group,
a division of Penguin Group (USA) LLC,
375 Hudson Street, New York, New York 10014.

ISBN: 978-0-425-28076-8

PUBLISHING HISTORY
Berkley Sensation mass-market edition / May 2015

PRINTED IN THE UNITED STATES OF AMERICA

10 9 8 7 6 5 4 3 2 1

Cover art by Aleta Rafton.
Cover design by Lesley Worrell.
Interior text design by Kelly Lipovich.

To the spirit of Mary Tape,
who stood up for her children when no one else would

ACKNOWLEDGMENTS

Many thanks to my agent, Laura Bradford, and to all the people who helped put this book together at Berkley, including my editor, Leis Pederson, as well as Jessica Brock, Lesley Worrell, and Bethany Blair. Kudos to Aleta Rafton for bringing Astrid and Bo to life on my favorite cover in this series.

I'm also grateful for all the kind people and organizations who answered my (hundreds of) research questions, including: John Jung (author of several fascinating books about the history of Chinese immigrants in America), the National Women's History Museum, the Bay Area Radio Museum, the Shaping San Francisco history project, the University of Washington's Seattle Civil Rights and Labor History Project, the National College in Mexico City, radio historian John F. Schneider, and Professor Tak-Hung Leo Chan.

Most of all, I'd like to acknowledge all of the readers, bloggers, and reviewers who championed this series online. Your enthusiasm has meant so much to me. Thank you for reading!

September 15, 1928
University of California, Los Angeles

Dear Bo,

I got your letter in the mail today and was so eager to read it, I completely forgot to attend my history class—no great loss. My professor never smiles and doesn't seem to like me. Besides that, everything is wonderful here. My dorm mate, Jane, and I took a streetcar to Hollywood Boulevard this weekend. Unfortunately, we saw <u>zero</u> motion picture stars.

Sorry to hear someone scratched your new Buick, but not half as sorry as they'll be when you find out who did it. Sounds like you're working too much at the warehouse. Just because Winter promoted you to captain doesn't mean you're his personal slave. Tell him to give you some time off. Perhaps <u>a weekend in sunny L.A.</u> would do you some good!

I have to go. My next class, Physics, starts in ten minutes and I've already missed it too many times. Luckily, <u>that</u> professor thinks I'm cute.

Your friend,
Astrid
P.S.—Don't tell Winter I've skipped any classes.

———❦———

September 25, 1928
Magnusson Fish Company
Pier 26
San Francisco, California

Dear Astrid,

*Your brothers both send their regards. In fact, Lowe
came by the warehouse with Hadley and Stella today.
They have booked a trip to Egypt next month. (All
three of them.)*

*The mystery of the Buick's scratch is solved. It was
Aida. She ran into it with the baby carriage—an
accident, of course. It's hard to stay mad at a pretty
woman. By the way, I'm thinking of naming the Buick
"Sylvia."*

*Sounds like you're having fun, but you need to
stop missing classes. If they expel you, Winter will
blow his top. He's mad enough that his baby sister
isn't going to Berkeley and still moans about your
Southern California campus being a "poor
substitute for the real U.C." And while we're
on the subject, who is this Physics professor?
Old men shouldn't be telling you that you're cute.
Be careful around him. Don't make me worry
about you.*

Your friend (and enemy to lecherous old men),
Bo

October 5, 1928
University of California, Los Angeles

Dear Bo,

*Egypt? Stars above. Please give Stella lots of kisses
for me when you see her again and tell her Auntie
Astrid misses her. I'm not sure how to make the word
"miss" in sign language, but Lowe will know.*

My dorm mate, Jane, and I are not on good terms

right now because her sweetheart asked me to join him and some of his friends last night when Jane was at a sorority meeting. We saw the Bruins play football—that's our collegiate team. I thought it might be boring to spend time with all those boys, but they were cutups, and called me Queen of Sheba, joking that they would be my male harem.

You don't have to worry about dirty old men. Professor Barnes is only twenty-six. This is his first year teaching. He thinks I'm "delightful," and not just cute, so he's not only interested in my good looks. He told me if he has time this semester, he might take his best students to visit Mount Wilson Observatory, to look through the giant telescope there. It's up in the mountains near Los Angeles, so we will stay there in a hotel overnight. More soon. Sylvia is a great name for the Buick!

Your friend,
Astrid

———✥———

October 15, 1928
Magnusson Fish Company
Pier 26
San Francisco, California

Mui-mui,

Your professor is up to no good. Teachers should not be staying in hotels with students. Lowe, being a professor himself, agrees with me. I am very concerned about your well-being. If you need to wire me a message for any reason, please do so. Never mind the train ticket, I will drive down there and come get you. I haven't mentioned this to Winter, *because he would already be down there. Please use common sense.*

Your friend,
Bo

———

October 30, 1928
University of California, Los Angeles

Dear Bo,

I can't believe you told Lowe. That was personal, between you and me. I am perfectly capable of making decisions without anyone's help, you know. And for your information, I had a wonderful time with Luke at the observatory. He is kind and sensitive, and he sees me as none of you do: as a woman.

Your adult friend (not your "little sister"),
Astrid

———

December 5, 1928
University of California, Los Angeles

Dearest Bo,

I am sorry about my last letter. I suppose I was upset with you, but that was silly. It's really very touching that you're concerned about me. It means a lot. I just wish you'd trust me to make my own decisions, even if they are the wrong ones sometimes.

Are you receiving my letters? I've heard on the radio that terrible storms are heading up the coast toward the Bay, so please stay safe.

My favorite wristwatch broke, which was upsetting. I will look for a replacement in S.F. There are no decent jewelry stores here. Oh, I bought my train ticket home and leave in ten days. That's _December 15th at noon_. (Does that date sound familiar?) I can't wait to see you at the station.

Your _true_ friend,
Astrid
P.S.—I'm sorry I got mad about you calling me mui-mui. _I actually miss hearing you saying that. No one here speaks Cantonese._

ONE

———◆———

ASTRID MAGNUSSON WAS MAD AS HELL. SHE FURIOUSLY WIPED
the fogged-up window of her brother's Pierce-Arrow limousine with the mink cuff of her coat, but it didn't help.
The hilly streets were nothing but darkness punctuated by
the occasional streetlight as they drove through more rain
than she'd ever seen in her life.

"I can't believe it's been like this all week," she said to
the family driver over the half-raised window divider
between the front and back seats. "It never rains like this
here. Never."

"*Ja*," Jonte replied in Swedish as they turned onto the
Embarcadero. "You shouldn't be down here with all this
flooding. Winter will be angry."

Whoop-de-doo. She'd been back in San Francisco since
noon and had barely spoken to her oldest brother. Half the
city was barricaded, and she knew that's why Winter was
down here working at nine in the evening—to help sandbag

the warehouse. She also knew that's why Bo was here; however, *him* she wasn't ready to forgive.

She hadn't seen Bo in almost four months, he'd stopped answering her letters, and now that she was home, he couldn't step away from the warehouse for one hour? Not even a telephone call or a note?

At least the staff had made her a nice dinner to welcome her back, and she'd had a little celebratory champagne. A little too much, possibly, but she didn't *feel* very drunk. Then again, she wasn't very good at drinking. A couple of months back, she'd downed five glasses of bathtub gin and ended up with a sprained ankle after falling off the dormitory balcony. But the post-drinking sickness had been far worse than the sprain, and she swore to all the saints she'd never drink again.

But really, that was a pointless promise to make, considering that Winter was one of the biggest bootleggers in San Francisco.

The limousine slowed in front of a long line of bulkhead buildings that sat along the waterfront. Warm light spilled from windows that flanked an open archway marked PIER 26. Magnusson Fish Company's waterfront dock. At least, that's what it was in the daytime; at night, it was a staging warehouse for citywide liquor distribution.

Astrid grabbed her umbrella and began opening the Pierce-Arrow's door before it came to a complete stop. "Don't wait for me," she told Jonte. "I'll get someone to drive me back home."

"But—"

"Good night, Jonte," she said more forcefully and erected the umbrella against the blustery night rain.

Ducking under the building's gated Spanish stucco archway, she splashed through puddles and immediately smelled exhausted engine oil and shipping containers. Familiar and oddly pleasant. Just past a fleet of delivery trucks parked for the night, men stacked sandbags against the warehouse walls, where water ran across the cement floor. Winter was there, talking to someone as he directed the sandbagging.

But no Bo.

Before Winter could spot her and yell at her for coming out here at night, she folded her umbrella and took a sharp right into the warehouse offices. The reception area was empty, but a light shone from the back office. She marched with purpose, head buzzing with champagne, and stopped in the doorway.

The office was exactly as she remembered. Framed ancient photographs of her family lined the walls, slightly askew and dusty: their first house in the Fillmore District, her brothers as small children, and every boat her father had ever owned—even the last one, right before he died in the accident three years ago. Watching over those photographs was Old Bertha, a stuffed leopard shark that hung from the ceiling.

And hunched below that spotted shark was Bo Yeung, stripped from the waist up and dripping wet with rainwater. A soaked shirt lay on a nearby chair; a dry one was draped across a filing cabinet.

A sense of elation rose over the champagne singing in Astrid's bloodstream. He was here, her childhood friend, the person she trusted more than anyone else in the world, and the only man she'd ever cared for.

Stars, she'd never been so happy to see his handsome face. She wanted to rush forward and throw her arms around him, like she used to do when they were both too young to recognize things were changing between them . . . when she was just the boss's baby sister, and he was only the hired help.

No longer.

And with that realization, all her hurt feelings rushed back to the surface.

"So you *are* alive," she said.

At the sound of her voice, he stood and turned to face her, and the sight of his sleek, sculpted chest momentarily took her aback. She'd seen him without a shirt a dozen times before—working outside in the sun, in the China-town boxing club where he sometimes went to blow off steam, or when they'd find each other in the kitchen raiding the icebox at midnight. But as he stood there in front of her now, holding a damp towel as if poised to fight, the elegant sheen of his finely muscled arms seemed almost risqué. Virile. She felt hot all over, just looking at him.

It was unfair, really.

"Astrid," he finally said in a rough voice. Straight hair, normally neatly combed, fell over one eye like a stroke of black calligraphy ink. He pushed a damp lock of it back and stared at her like she was a mirage—one that he hadn't expected to see.

Too bad. Astrid wasn't going be ignored. She'd worn her best fur and a stunning beaded amaranthine dress that showed off her legs, and she'd practiced exactly what she was going to say to him.

Only, now she'd forgotten most of it.

"You didn't pick me up at the train station," she said.

"I was working." He shrugged with one shoulder, as if he couldn't be troubled to lift both of them. "Besides, I'm not the family driver. That's Jonte's job."

As if that were the point? Truly.

"*And* you didn't come to dinner. Lena made almond cake."

"Did she? Sorry I missed that," he said lightly.

"Is that all you missed?"

"Don't tell me she made lemon pie, or I really will be sorry."

Anger heated her cheeks. "I'll give you something to be sorry about, all right. Be serious for one moment, please. I think you owe me at least that for not bothering to say hello to a girl you haven't seen in months."

He snapped the edge of the towel toward the ceiling. "Do you not see what's going on out there? We're nearly underwater."

"But it's my birthday." Even as the words came out, she knew they sounded petty and childish, and wished she could take them back.

"I know," he said.

And that made her *livid*.

"A simple 'Happy birthday' would be the polite thing to say. But I'm not sure why I expected you to even remember, because you haven't answered any of my letters." He hadn't even bothered to write and tell her the disappointing news that her friend and seamstress, Benita—who lived downstairs in the Magnusson house—had left for Charleston two weeks ago to tend to a sick relative. "I suppose you just forgot to write me back?"

Bo grunted and avoided her eyes.

"Don't tell me you were busy working, because I know damn well it hasn't been raining all that time."

"No, it hasn't." He turned away from her, toweling off his hair.

"Then what? Out of sight, out of mind—is that it? Am I that forgettable?"

"Damn, but I wish you were."

"What's that supposed to mean? God, Bo. Is it because you're not being paid to wheel me around town anymore, huh? Is that it? You get promoted and now I'm just a job responsibility you can shuck?"

He tossed her a sharp glance over his shoulder. "Stop being ridiculous."

"*You're* ridiculous."

"You came down here in the middle of the night to tell me that?" He tossed the towel aside and pulled on a dry undershirt.

"What if I did? At least I remembered where to find you after four months, which is more than I can say for your crummy sense of direction."

Swearing under his breath, he snatched up a clean shirt and glanced up at her as he shrugged into it. His fingers paused on the buttons. "Have you been drinking?"

"Drinking?" Astrid repeated, as if it were the most ludicrous thing she'd ever heard.

"You keep squinting at me with one eye shut." He marched toward her. Before she could get away, his fingers gripped her shoulders. She dropped her umbrella and leaned back, trying to avoid him, but his neck craned to follow her movement. His attractive face was inches from hers, all sharp cheekbones and sharper jaw.

He sniffed. Clever, all-seeing eyes narrowed as he tracked her sin with the precision of a bloodhound. "Champagne."

"Only a little," she argued, breathing in the mingled scents of the dusty warehouse and rainwater, and beneath those, the brighter fragrance of *Bo*.

All her anger disappeared for a moment because— damn it all!—she'd missed him so much. She didn't care if his position in the Magnusson household meant they shouldn't be together, or that societal rules regarding their cultural differences meant they *couldn't* be together. If she had to make a vow never to leave him again, she would. And unlike the no-drinking promise, she'd be able to keep this one, because if going away to college had taught her anything, it was that Bo was what she wanted.

Only Bo.

She softened in his grip and dazedly blinked up at him with a small, hiccupped laugh.

"Ossified," he proclaimed. For a moment, the slyest of smiles curled the corners of his mouth. She loved that smile. He was the shiniest, most vibrant person she'd ever known, and she wanted to soak him up like warm sunlight.

His gaze fell to her hand, which had drifted to her neck like a shield, as if it could somehow prevent her runaway feelings from escaping. "I thought you said you broke that wristwatch," he said in a lower voice.

"I did. But my arm feels bare without it."

For a moment, she thought he might reach for her hand. But he merely released her, stepping away to button his shirt. "You shouldn't be drinking."

"So what if I've had a coupe or two of champagne? A girl's entitled to that much, freshly back from college and on her birthday," she said, following him around the desk. Never mind that she'd had five glasses, possibly six. She could still walk straight. Mostly. "Besides, I'm an adult now, if you haven't noticed."

"College magically transformed you, huh? To think I've been doing it wrong all these years, what with this pesky hard work and responsibility."

"You're a jackass."

"So I've been told. By you, several times, if I remember correctly." He tucked in his shirt and donned a leather shoulder holster and gun, a sobering reminder of this warehouse's purpose and Bo's role in it.

"Why are you avoiding me?" she persisted. "Why did you stop answering my letters?"

"I'm sorry—were you waiting on me to answer?" He combed his damp hair back with his fingers, cool as you please, but his words were delivered with tiny barbs. "It sounded like you had your hands full, what with that harem of college boys salivating beneath your skirt."

Her cheeks heated. "I never said that!" Not that crassly, anyway. Sure, the boys at college were a lot more open and forward, which was probably due to the fact that, unlike her suitors in high school, they didn't know she had two older brothers who would pummel anyone who so much as winked at her.

"Not to mention that you seemed pretty busy gazing at stars with what's-his-name," Bo said, snapping his fingers. "Professor Hotel Room."

Astrid was too tipsy to convincingly feign shock over his implication. Yes, she'd told him about Luke and the hotel. But she certainly hadn't said what they'd done there. It was none of Bo's business. Besides, she hadn't spoken to Luke since that night. She merely stopped showing up for class, and he never bothered to track her down.

So much for her sensitive professor.

But it didn't matter. She was a grown woman. So what if she'd made a few mistakes her first semester at college? Well, a lot of mistakes, actually. Luke may have been the worst of those, a lapse in good judgment, but there was nothing she could do about that now. Life went on. And everything else was perfectly fixable as long as Winter didn't find out. Now, as for Bo . . .

Hold on just one second. Her drunken brain oh-so-slowly began piecing Bo's words and tone together. Was he jealous? Her heart skipped a beat.

"Listen," she said as he slipped into his suit jacket, but the rest of her words were lost under a horrific wrenching noise that was so long and loud, it rattled all the family photographs on the back wall for several seconds. Beyond that wall was the northern pier.

They both glanced at each other. Bo drew his gun, and without another word, they raced through the offices and into the warehouse. The workers had abandoned their sandbagging and were running through an open cargo door onto the docks. Cold rain and a howling gale cut through Astrid's clothes as she jogged behind them into briny night air.

Industrial lights lit up the pier. Foaming waves, impossibly high, streamed over the creaking dock boards and splashed over her ankles. No wonder Bo was sandbagging the warehouse; she'd never seen the Bay this high. And it was storming so hard, she couldn't see past the men thronging the edge of the pier. Winter shouted something at Bo, who pushed his way through the crowd. She shielded her eyes with one hand as a bolt of white lightning pierced the sky.

And that's when the source of the noise came into view.

A luxury motor yacht, encrusted in barnacles and draped in seaweed, had crashed into the Magnussons' pier. Inside the main cabin, a group of people stared out the windows, unmoving and silent. And for a dizzying, terror-struck moment, Astrid was convinced they were all ghosts.

TWO

———※———

THE *PLUMED SERPENT* WASN'T PRECISELY A GHOST SHIP, BO
decided, after helping to moor the crashed yacht. But the
strange people who filed off its deck were certainly
spooked. None of them knew who they were. Names, family, homes . . . all forgotten. No one remembered where
the yacht had been or how they'd gotten on it. They all
claimed to have woken up a few minutes before they'd
crashed into the pier.

Six survivors. Six men and women wearing white robes,
and whose cheeks and foreheads were covered with blue
greasepaint, like they'd been staging some kind of theat-
rical performance. They were terrified. Confused. And
yet, apart from looking weak and dehydrated, seemingly
unharmed.

And while the police questioned them, Bo had sent
Astrid back inside the warehouse to safety while he
watched the chaos from a healthy distance, mumbling an
old Cantonese folk saying to ward away evil—along with
a bit of the Lord's Prayer and a line from a popular song
for good measure. Whatever had cursed the yacht, he

wanted nothing to do with it. Granted, the *Plumed Serpent* was a damn fine boat. Only a handful of yachts like it in the Bay Area, and Chief Hambry confirmed this one belonged to a wealthy widow who had reported it missing during an investigation last year.

Lost at sea for an entire year.

A boat doesn't just reappear after being gone that long.

Ambulances carried the stunned survivors to Saint Francis in Nob Hill. And when the hubbub finally died down, Bo shivered in his wet clothes as he watched the police chief's car pull away from the pier.

"I've seen a lot of strange things in this city . . ." Winter murmured from his side as they huddled together beneath a narrow overhang outside the warehouse.

Bo snorted. "I've seen a lot of strange things in your *house*."

The dark-headed Swede chuckled and pressed the heel of his palm against his scarred eye. "True. But this feels wrong. Something happened to those people, and I don't want any damn part of it. We don't need this headache right now."

Winter wasn't just Bo's employer. Five years back, after Bo's uncle (and last living relative) had died, the burly head of the Magnusson clan had taken then sixteen-year-old Bo out of Chinatown and given him a home in Pacific Heights. More than a home. A job. Education. Purpose. A family.

The entire city saw Winter as one of the biggest bootleggers in town—someone respected and feared, no one to screw around with—but Bo knew the man behind the mask. And knowing this man had changed Bo, for good and for worse. Bo was neither wholly Chinatown nor Pacific Heights. Not part of his old life, not fully accepted into all corners of this one, either. He was between cultures and classes. Between worlds. And that was unstable ground.

Bo rubbed warmth back into his fingers. "I'll make sure the yacht's not taking on water and poke around in the engine room. See if she can be started up. If so, I'll move her to that empty pier next door, so that she's off the property and out of sight from the road. Otherwise, I'll get a tugboat over here to move her in the morning."

Gawking reporters and nosy crowds were the last thing an illegal enterprise needed, so the less the public could see of the yacht, the better—at least until the police could track down the owner and get the damn thing off Magnusson property. They didn't need the cops poking around out here, either. Sure, Winter paid them off. But it was one thing for them to look the other way, and another to operate right in front of their faces. Tomorrow night's distribution runs would need to go through their secondary Marin County docks across the Bay, which would mean more time spent in the cold rain.

Bo had little faith he'd ever feel dry or warm again. All of this weirdness with the blue-faced survivors was a bad ending to a bad day, and he was impatient for it to be over.

A lie.

He was just impatient to see Astrid again. After she'd left for college at the end of the summer, he'd hoped time apart would tame his feelings. Instead, the yearning turned him into a deranged man, one match short of combusting with obsession. Absurd, really, that one tiny girl had that effect on him. So he told himself it was merely a case of mind over matter, and prayed when he saw her again she'd appear less dazzling. He would merely look upon her fondly. Platonically. Like the old friend she was, nothing more.

But now that he had seen her, he knew all of that had been a pipe dream. It was so much worse now. Because the truth was, college *had* changed her. He didn't know how or why, only that if it had anything to do with that Luke fellow she wrote about, it would take every man in the warehouse holding Bo back to stop him from driving down to Los Angeles to bloody the professor's face against the classroom chalkboard.

No, time apart hadn't helped one bit. His blood still heated at the sight of her. His heart still ached, wanting what it couldn't have. And no matter how he tried to pretend she was still the same fourteen-year-old, gum-smacking, know-it-all live wire he'd first met years ago, she hadn't been a little girl for a long time. Seeing her tonight did strange, bewildering things to him. The sound of her voice alone sketched a secret road map from his heart to his brain, with a looping detour down to his cock.

Aiya, she made him miserable. Weak. Crazy. Stupid.

He absently glanced toward the light of the office window and spotted her silhouette.

"She's angry with you," Winter said, startling Bo out of his thoughts.

Not half as angry as he was with *her*. But he didn't say that, because then he'd have to explain why. And as much as he confided in Winter, he wasn't dumb enough to admit that Astrid had yanked out his heart and stomped on it with a few careless words in a weeks-old letter. Some lines you just didn't cross, and pining over the Viking Bootlegger's fox-eyed baby sister was one of them.

He tore his eyes away from the girl and stared straight ahead at the yacht. "She'll get over it when she goes back to Los Angeles after the holidays."

Three weeks. He might survive three more weeks of Astrid (devious smile, stubborn chin, blond curls, scent of roses, soft skin) if he stayed busy, out of sight. Found excuses to sleep at his old apartment in Chinatown instead of in his room at the Magnussons'. Kept his cock and balls locked up in some kind of medieval chastity cage . . .

"I'm going home," Winter said in a weary voice. "I haven't had more than an hour of sleep since yesterday, and Aida will divorce me if I stay out another night. She hasn't been sleeping, either. She's had a few unsettling séances lately. Heard strange messages . . ."

"About what?" Winter's wife, Aida, was a trance medium who conducted séances for a living, temporarily able to summon back the dead to talk with their loved ones. Plenty of frauds out there, but Aida was the real thing. "Not about all this, I hope," Bo said, motioning toward the yacht.

Winter shook his head. "No, something else is coming. It's probably . . . well, hopefully she's wrong about it, but it's making her worry."

"Go home, then," Bo encouraged.

"Suppose I should take Astrid back with m—"

"I won't be much longer," Bo said a little too quickly and tried to keep the eagerness out of his voice. "The sandbagging's finished, and squaring away the yacht shouldn't take long. I'll drive her back."

"She's not your responsibility anymore," Winter said softly. "You're my captain now, not a driver, and not her guardian. She can take care of herself while she's home for the holidays. She's a grown woman."

Oh, he'd noticed, all right. But that didn't stop him from worrying over her safety. Hell, it made him more anxious. The Magnussons might be wealthy, and Bo might be better paid than ninety-nine percent of the other Chinese immigrants living in San Francisco, but that money was hard-earned and came with a list of threats so long, he couldn't keep them all in his head at once: rival bootleggers, cheap club owners, crooked cops and politicians. Mobsters from out East. Smugglers hunting new cargo. Disgruntled customers looking to save a buck . . . and hungry, delinquent kids looking to steal one.

He should know.

To someone slinking down dark alleys, trying to stay alive, Astrid Magnusson's blue eyes looked like easy money. A kidnapping waiting to happen. And that's why Bo had been both relived she'd chosen to attend college in Southern California, so far away from all this—yet at the same, time terrified that it was *too* far. That he couldn't watch out for her anymore. That he couldn't protect her.

His absolute nightmare.

"I don't mind taking her home," Bo told Winter, as if it were only a mildly irritating hardship. Casual. "It'll give her a chance to yell at me some more."

"Better you than me," Winter replied with a tired smile and slapped him on his shoulder. Then he bid Bo good night and left the warehouse to drive home to his waiting wife.

Bo sighed heavily.

Before he could punish himself by being confined in a small automobile with Astrid, he had to take care of the crashed boat. He grabbed a chrome-handled flashlight from the warehouse and headed back out into the drizzle to track down the single cop the police had left behind to guard the yacht.

"Officer . . . ?" Bo said, bending down to peer into the cracked window of the black Tin Lizzie squad car.

"Barlow," the man supplied.

"Officer Barlow," Bo said with a smile and a polite dip of his chin. "Sorry to bother you. Just wanted to let you know that I'm going to step onto that yacht to see if she still runs. Boss wants me to move her. We got crabbers coming in tomorrow." Fishing was still the legitimate part of the Magnusson business. Never mind that the storm was moving into the Bay too fast and scattering all their Dungeness pots to hell, filling them with sand; he just needed an excuse to move the damn yacht.

But Officer Barlow wasn't buying it.

"No can do," he said, swallowing a bit of sandwich.

"Sorry?"

"You can't move the yacht. It's a crime scene."

Bo smiled and tried a more jovial tone. "What's the crime? Wearing bad theater makeup? Not bothering to tell their families they decided to sail to some tropical island on a yearlong vacation?"

The officer was too dumb to be charmed by humor. "Magnusson should have cleared it through the chief." He began rolling up the window as if the conversation were over.

It wasn't.

Bo clamped his hand over the rain-streaked glass. "The chief cleared it. You just must not have gotten the message."

"Excuse me?"

Bo held Barlow's dark gaze, measuring the offense in his squinting eyes. It took him all of half a second to know that the man didn't have the balls to physically challenge him.

"The boat's on our property," Bo said matter-of-factly. "We want it off. So you can call someone out here to tow it, or you can let me see if I can move it a few yards to the empty pier next door."

"*Your* property? You people couldn't even vote three years ago."

Bo's vision clouded as a dark urge for violence rose. His hand reached for the car door handle.

But a confident feminine voice piped up before he could open the car door. "Wait for me, Bo! I'm coming on the yacht, too. Oh, hello there, Officer. Are you going along with us? My brother will be glad to know you're concerned about our well-being."

Buddha, Osiris, and Jehovah, Bo cursed under his breath.

Lemony blond finger waves floated beneath an umbrella. Astrid's cunning, foxlike eyes blinked up at him with sham innocence, her previous drunken wink now gone.

I don't need you saving me from this lazy prick, he tried to project to her with a fake smile. Years of living under the same roof had made them good interpreters of each other's body language and expressions.

He's not worth the effort, she seemed to project back at him.

And she was right; he really wasn't. But Bo resented when she stepped in like this and smoothed over the indignity with a smile. Whatever favor she thought she was doing him, he paid two times over with the loss of his pride. But maybe that was a good thing tonight; he needed a reason to stay angry at her.

Anger kept the wanting away.

"Or we can just go on our own," Astrid added.

Officer Barlow opened his car door. "I'm going with

you. Let's make it quick," he said, and without another word, he followed them along the pier.

Lightning streaked over the Bay. The bow of the boat canted in the choppy water. Bo was half convinced that they'd all disappear at sea if they stepped foot on it, but Astrid showed no sign that she shared his worry. When he suggested she go back inside the warehouse and wait, she answered through a stilted smile, "Like hell I will."

"Suit yourself," he answered, and held out a hand.

One after the other, the three of them boarded the aft deck and ducked inside the door to the main salon. Black and blue shadows crossed the spacious room. Without the engine running, there was no power. No lights. And though Bo could make out the general layout by the light filtering through the salon's windows, it wasn't enough to ease his needling anxiety. He popped open the strap of his holster—just in case—and flicked on his flashlight.

"Stars," Astrid mumbled at his side as she folded up her umbrella.

The salon was the pinnacle of class and taste. Expensive furniture. Fine art. A sleek bar in the back near a white baby grand piano. But all of it was wrecked. Furniture lay tipped over, and broken stemware littered the woven Persian rug. The mirror above the bar was cracked down the center.

The police chief had told Winter that there were signs of a party on board, but he hadn't relayed just how recent that party had been. The yellow beam of Bo's flashlight illuminated fresh flowers scattered from broken vases. Fresh flowers and fresh food, not to mention the lingering scents of candle wax, cigarette smoke, and booze.

All this made Bo feel better, actually. Whatever bizarre activities the survivors had been up to, they weren't ghosts or monsters.

He revised that opinion when he swept the flashlight's beam up the walls. Witchy symbols were drawn in bright blue paint. A large ritual circle was painted in the center of the salon floor, around which a dozen or more candles had melted into the wooden floorboards.

"What in God's name were these cranks up to?" Bo murmured.

"They're occultists," Officer Barlow said. "Devil worshippers or something."

"What language is this?" Astrid asked.

"No idea," Bo said.

The officer shrugged. "Who cares? They were probably all taking narcotics. A lot of heroin's been coming into the city this year. Or maybe you knew that already . . ."

Bo did, but only from gossip. The Magnussons didn't have anything to do with narcotics. They only sold alcohol, and not bathtub gin, either. Top quality. And all of it smuggled by ship from Canada, some of which was originally imported from Europe. One of those European imports was a very *particular* brand of black-label champagne— one that no one else in San Francisco sold. Bo would recognize the bottles anywhere; after all, he'd inspected every shipment of it, checking for false labels, evaluating the bottle marks, and tasting the contents.

Several empty bottles of that very champagne lay on the floor of the salon.

He picked one up and sniffed. Definitely Magnusson stock. Only a few speakeasies around town that sold it, along with the occasional special order for a political fundraiser or some socialite's wedding.

He didn't like finding it here.

"Must have been one hell of a party," Barlow said. "Hope it was worth it, because as soon as we can get them identified, they're all going to be locked up for stealing this boat."

"Is that what happened?" Astrid asked. "They stole it?"

Barlow shrugged. "What else would it be? You saw them. They were young—your age, and vagrants, I'd guess. They took the boat for a joyride, got looped up on drugs, probably sailed up the coast and got lost."

"For a year?" Astrid said.

Bo shared her disbelief. He wasn't convinced that vagrants had such expensive taste in hothouse flowers and champagne. And other than the damage to the furniture—which could have been caused by the storm—and the painted blue symbols, the room had been kept up. No piss in the corner. No signs of anyone holing up in here. Hell, there wasn't even dust on the bar. He lifted his fingers to his nose and smelled wood polish.

"The chief mentioned a man who'd claimed to have captained this boat when it went missing last year," Bo said. "Know anything about that?"

Barlow made a snorting sound. "Sure, I heard about him. It was just some geezer with a few screws loose who ended up in a mental institution. Claimed that he'd been hired to pilot the yacht, but a storm threw him overboard and he swam ashore."

"Interesting," Bo said.

"Not really. The yacht's owner had never laid eyes on him. We see that kind of stuff all the time. Lonely people with too much time on their hands read about cases in the newspapers and show up at the station, claiming they can help us. They never do."

Astrid stepped over broken glass and stumbled into Bo.

"Whoa," he said, putting a hand on her arm to steady her. For a moment, he wondered if she hadn't sobered up as much he'd originally thought, but then he realized he was wobbly, too. The storm outside was picking up speed. He leaned against the bar for support and held on to Astrid, relishing the excuse to do so, even for a few stolen seconds.

"All right," Officer Barlow complained when the boat's swaying finally calmed. "I don't have all night. Let's get to the engine room."

"What's this?" Astrid bent to pick up something that had rolled across the floor.

Bo flicked the flashlight's beam near her feet. Bright

blue stone glinted as her fingers reached for it—something about the size of his hand. Turquoise, maybe. When she picked it up, a brief flash of white light ringed her hand like a wreath of electric smoke.

She went rigid, convulsed, and collapsed to the floor.

"Astrid!" Bo cried out as he dropped to her side.

The flash of light was gone, but she wouldn't open her eyes. He couldn't tell if she was breathing. He bent low and listened over Astrid's open mouth.

Breath, thank God. And his shaking fingers felt a pulse at her neck.

"Christ!" Barlow shouted. "What's the matter with her? She having a seizure or something?"

"Astrid, wake up," Bo said into her face, afraid to shake her. Afraid *not* to.

Her fingers still clutched the turquoise object. He pried them open and tried not to touch the thing, but it was unavoidable. The stone was hot, but no light flashed when he touched it—a carved figure, from what he could make out in the dark. Some kind of miniature idol. He pulled out a handkerchief and quickly rolled the figure into the linen before stashing it in his jacket pocket.

What the hell was that thing, and what had it done to her? She was unmoving. Completely unresponsive. She felt limp and fragile in his arms as he scooped her off the floor. Barlow's annoying voice buzzed around Bo's head, suggesting they not touch her because she might be suffering from whatever ill magic had cursed the blue-faced survivors.

And she might be, but Bo would be damned before he sat by and let it kill her.

"Hold on," he mumbled repeatedly as he carried her out of the yacht's salon, doing his best to shield her drooping body from the sting of rain.

"That girl needs to go to a hospital," the officer yelled over the howling wind, dogging Bo's heels. "I can't help you. I'm not allowed to leave my post."

Bastard. Bo would remember that later, but at the moment, he didn't care. He made it to his car and heard Astrid moan as he set her down in the front seat. She still didn't open her eyes.

"You're going to be fine," he told her. "Everything's going to be fine."

He just wasn't sure if he believed it.

THREE

———◆———

ASTRID WOKE IN FITS AND STARTS, OCCASIONALLY SEEING
snatches of the dark city whizzing by a rain-splattered car
window. Though she'd only been inside this car a couple
of times before she left for college, she knew she was
riding in Bo's new forest green Buick Brougham, because
it smelled like dyed mohair velvet upholstery and the
lemon drops he stashed in the glove box. She did her best
to concentrate on those familiar scents, but the bubbling
memory of her dream kept pulling her back under.

Not a dream. It was too strange, too bright and surreal.
And she'd been far too conscious when it was happening,
as if the turquoise idol had opened a door when she'd
touched it, and she'd lifted outside her body and stepped
into another time.

When she finally kicked away the thick haze that held
her under, she was lying in a hospital bed on top of drum-
tight sheets, and a nurse in a crisp white pinafore apron
and pointed hat was taking blood from her arm. "There
she is," the nurse said with a kind smile. "How are you
feeling?"

"A little weak," she admitted.

"I'm Nurse Dupree," she said, removing the syringe and tourniquet from her arm. "Do you know who you are?"

"Someone who stupidly drank too much . . . uh, grape juice." The woman seemed nice, but she might be a teetotaler. Best to play it safe.

"But what's your name, dear?"

"Astrid Cristiana Magnusson," she enunciated carefully.

Behind the nurse, Bo let out a small sound of relief.

"I'm all right," she told both of them. "A little dizzy, but it's passing."

After the nurse bandaged her arm and ran through a list of symptoms that Astrid didn't have, she left with a blood sample and a promise to return shortly. "A lot going on tonight with those boat survivors and the police," she said. "I'll try to get a doctor in here as soon as I can."

Bo's anxious face peered down from the side of the bed. "You scared the life out of me." He blew out a long breath and ran a hand over his hair. A moment later, it was hard to tell if he was genuinely concerned . . . or merely irritated at her for inconveniencing him.

He picked up a pitcher from her bedside table and poured water into a glass.

Astrid looked around and realized they were in a room with three other beds—one of which was occupied by a man in a full body cast, who seemed to be sleeping. Distant commotion and chatter echoed down the spotless white hallway outside the propped-open door. The occasional nurse scurried back and forth.

"Are we at Saint Francis?" she asked. "Are the boat survivors here?"

"Down the hall. Drink," he encouraged, holding out the glass as she sat up in bed.

She took it from him and gulped down the lukewarm water, requesting another glass when she'd emptied it. "Remind me never to get sloshed again."

"I don't think this was from the champagne. I told

the nurse you fell and went unconscious after the yacht crashed into the pier. I didn't tell her why, exactly." He paused and looked at her seriously. "Do you remember what happened?"

"I touched the blue idol and fell out of myself."

"You . . . what? Hold on." Metal zinged as Bo pulled the privacy curtain, separating her from the man in the body cast. "Tell me everything."

Now she had his full attention. Finally. She patted the bed next to her and scooted over to give him room. He hesitated a moment before sitting down. Like it pained him. It was clear he was trying to keep some space between them. She shifted her leg to erase that space, mentally tallying a point in her favor, and began explaining the sensation she'd felt when she'd touched the object.

"It was an electric pain," she said. "A shock. I felt hot."

Then she recounted her strange vision . . .

She'd been on the yacht. In the salon.

It was dim, the room lit by candlelight. Night loomed beyond the band of windows. Nothing was wrecked—no cracked mirror behind the bar, no glass on the rug, or strewn furniture—but the blue symbols were still painted on the walls . . . and on the floor. Standing inside the ritual circle were six people dressed in white robes.

The survivors.

And facing them around the outside of the circle were six additional people. Each of them stood naked in a puddle of rough, brown fabric, wearing nothing put pairs of strange-looking boots.

Bright blue stones glowed in their hands. Miniature idols, like the one Astrid had picked up. Six people, six idols. One by one, each of the expressionless nude participants handed the turquoise statues to the survivors before picking up the brown fabric that pooled around their strange boots. Brown burlap sacks, big enough for a man to stand inside. They pulled the sacks over their heads like cocoons and cinched them closed from the inside.

Lightning flashed in the windows. The survivors stepped outside the circle and embraced the sack-tied people. And as they did, Astrid saw a single person left standing in the middle of the circle. A woman in a deep red robe. Some kind of priestess. She was elderly—her hands were horribly wrinkled, and strands of white hair peeked from her hood—and though her back faced Astrid, when lightning flashed a second time, she could almost make out her blurred face in the mirror over the bar—

And then it was over. Astrid had snapped back into her body. It was the strangest thing she'd ever experienced, and even now, made her shudder.

"Do you think the idol infected me with some sort of magic?" she whispered. "Remember what happened to Winter when he got cursed and started seeing ghosts? I definitely do *not* want to see ghosts."

"Winter was cursed on purpose. There's no way anyone could have known you'd pick that idol up."

"What was it?"

"I don't know, but whatever kind of charge it held seems to be gone." From the pocket of his suit jacket, he retrieved a gray handkerchief embroidered with his initials and unfolded it. Inside the fabric, turquoise winked.

It was definitely a stylized figure. The carving was crude yet beautiful, the bright blue surface covered in a delicate web of cracks. The figure's wide eyes were inlaid with gold, and a strange symbol was embossed on a gold disk in the middle of the idol's stomach.

"You kept it?" she whispered.

"I touched it after you did, but nothing happened." He demonstrated with a finger. "It was hot to the touch before, but it's cooled down. If what you saw is somehow real—"

"It *was* real, Bo. You have to believe me."

"Oh, don't worry, I believe you. You Magnussons are a goddamn magnet for the supernatural."

In addition to Winter's wife being a trance medium, Lowe's wife, Hadley, was a museum curator who'd inherited a regiment of ancient Egyptian death specters from her cursed mother.

So, no, the Magnussons weren't exactly a normal family.

But it was different to witness strange phenomena happening to someone else and a whole other thing to experience it yourself. She hoped Bo was right, and that the vision was merely an unhappy accident.

Bo folded the idol back inside the linen. "Maybe the ritual they were performing on the yacht somehow got absorbed into the idol. Like a magical memory."

"How can we find out?"

"No idea." He sighed heavily and looked at her with a forlorn expression. "Winter is going to murder me for letting you come on that boat."

She handed him the empty water glass. "Does he know we're here?"

"No, but I'll have to tell him eventually, and he's not going to be happy."

"Bo," she said, leaning closer to whisper. "Those other people I saw . . . What if the survivors murdered them?"

"We don't even know if they exist. I believe you saw what you said you did, but let's be practical. The owner of the yacht might be able to identify the survivors. If there are missing people who were on board, she might know that, too."

"The boots . . ." She paused and stared up at him. "There was something funny about them, and I think I just realized what. I know it sounds crazy, but I think the boots were made of metal. Like, iron, maybe."

"Iron boots," Bo muttered. "How could you even walk in them?"

"What if they weren't for walking? What if they were intended to weigh someone down? Think about it. Burlap bags? That's just bizarre. What if the survivors threw those people overboard to drown?"

Quick footfalls approached the hospital room's door.

Astrid looked up, expecting to see Nurse Dupree returning, but two other people stopped outside the door: the police chief and a woman wearing an expensive crimson coat and feathered hat.

For a moment, Astrid's mind jumped to the red-robed priestess in her vision, until she reminded herself that the priestess had been white-headed, and this one was blond and couldn't have been a day over twenty-five.

"I can assure you of that, Mrs. Cushing," the police chief was telling the blonde. "If they are fit to leave the hospital tomorrow, we will release them into your custody until their families can be notified. You are kind to offer them shelter."

"It's the least I can do," the woman replied with a smile. "Whatever happened to them at sea, I can only say I'm thankful they're still alive. And I'm grateful you called me about this matter. I know you'll get everything straightened out."

"That we will, ma'am," the chief said.

The woman nodded and glanced past him. Her gaze connected with Astrid's for a moment, and then the pair continued on their way down the hall.

"I wonder who that was," Bo said as Nurse Dupree strode through the door.

"Mrs. Cushing?" the nurse said, nodding over her shoulder. "That's the widow who owns the yacht."

"Excellent." Bo sprung from the bed and headed toward the door. "I need to speak with her about towing it off our property."

"You can try to catch her, but I think she's leaving with her driver."

"Don't move," Bo said, pointing a finger at Astrid in warning. "I'll be right back."

As he strode away, Nurse Dupree picked up a wooden clipboard and jotted down notes on Astrid's medical form. "Feeling better?"

"Much. I don't think I need to see a doctor, especially since the hospital is so busy with the survivors. Have you seen them yourself?"

"Yes, and if you want my opinion, that poor woman is being taken for a ride."

"Mrs. Cushing?" Astrid asked.

The nurse nodded. "One of the survivors she identified as her former maid, Mary Richards. Mrs. Cushing reported her missing last year, apparently. She'd given Miss Richards permission to use the boat over the weekend, so I understand wanting to help the girl out, but the rest of them are strangers. If you ask me, offering to let them all stay in her home is just begging for trouble. I need to take your pulse again, sweetheart."

Astrid gave the nurse her arm. "Does Miss Richards remember who the rest of the survivors are and what happened?"

"No. She doesn't even remember her own name." The nurse pushed up Astrid's sleeve and looked at a watch pinned to her apron. "Just between you and me, I don't think all of the survivors have memory loss. I overheard two of them talking when Mary was being interrogated, and they sounded mighty familiar with each other."

Astrid perked up. "You don't say?"

"One of the detectives told me he thinks they stole the boat and had no intention of bringing it back—that the engine died and the storm swept them to shore, and now they're playing innocent. That widow believes she's being a Good Samaritan, but I wouldn't be surprised if they rob her blind in the middle of the night."

Astrid spoke in a hushed voice. "You didn't happen to hear if there were others on the boat who are still missing, did you?"

"Mrs. Cushing doesn't know who went out on the boat with Miss Richards last year. You were there when the yacht crashed, right? Did you see other people?"

"No," Astrid said. She didn't actually see them, so it wasn't a lie. But it felt like one, because all her instincts told her that she wasn't wrong.

"Your pulse is too high," the nurse said. "So I think you should stop worrying about all this chaos and get a good night's rest at home. You'll feel better when all the excitement has died down. My advice is to forget it even happened and not make a habit of drinking so much grape juice," the nurse said with a pat on her arm and a wink.

Astrid's thoughts returned to her vision. Twelve people around the ritual circle . . . and the priestess in the middle made thirteen. Thirteen people were on that boat, and only six walked off. She wasn't sure that was something she could easily forget.

And she didn't.

Not when she was released from the hospital half an hour later, and not when Bo drove them back to Pacific Heights while the rain-soaked city slept. The grand homes in this neighborhood sat shoulder to shoulder on tiered streets that belted a steep hill and provided a commanding view of the Bay. Astrid grew up in an immigrant neighborhood across town, but her father moved them here after Prohibition. His decision to take up bootlegging had dramatically changed their lives.

The neighbors had mixed feelings about their living here. Her family was new money, her brother a well-known criminal. They didn't hide their success. Their turreted Queen Anne mansion took up two lots to most of the other homes' one, and several fine cars lined their gated driveway, including Winter's black-and-red Pierce-Arrow limousine. They kept a sizable staff, mostly Swedish immigrants, and Winter employed several hundred workers across the city.

They were not poor, and they were not humble. But whatever the neighbors said about her family behind their closed doors, they were all smiles in public. Astrid had learned the value of holding her head high. And as the silhouette of their imposing home came into view through the light-falling rain, a rush of relief made her shoulders relax and gave her a brief respite from the evening's odd events.

On the car ride here, Bo had told Astrid about his brief talk outside the hospital with the widow, Mrs. Cushing. He said she was polite when he approached her, promising she'd have someone move the yacht in the morning. The police chief, on the other hand, was insistent that no one touch the boat until they'd had a chance to look through it in the daylight.

"And she didn't seem happy about this, not at all," Bo said. "Went from gracious to frosty"—he snapped his fingers—"just like that. Definitely someone who is used to getting her way."

Astrid didn't know what to make of this. She'd told Bo what she'd learned from the nurse, but by the time they'd made it home, she was weary of thinking about all of it.

Bo parked his car behind the others in the driveway, and they quietly entered the house through a side porch. Inside, the Queen Anne was dark. Astrid took off her ruined wet pumps and carried them by the heels as she padded down a chevron-patterned runner. Bo followed. After a dozen steps, a narrow hallway opened up to a large foyer that smelled of orange oil and lilies. Home.

A dog as big as a small horse shuffled across the floor, claws clicking on the hardwood, and greeted her with a wagging tail.

"Hello, Sam," she said, bending to scratch his ear. The brindled mastiff officially belonged to Winter's wife—though Winter treated it like a second child—and was an excellent guard dog. He nuzzled Astrid's hand and then rubbed his head against Bo's leg and left a trail of wiry hair, which Bo complained about beneath his breath—but not without giving the dog an affectionate pat on the rump. Then the mastiff shuffled back the way he came and disappeared into the kitchen, leaving Bo and Astrid alone in the empty foyer.

An awkward silence grew between them. Now that the shock of the night's events was receding, Astrid's mind circled back to where it had all started, and hurt feelings began to reemerge. She didn't want to fight with him any-more. She just wanted him to give her a rational explanation for why he'd been ignoring her.

And an apology. One that he meant.

"Suppose I'm going to head downstairs," Bo finally said in a low voice. The help's quarters were down there, as well as Bo's room. "I guess you better get some sleep, too."

"Are you going to tell Winter?"

"Tomorrow." Which was probably only a couple of hours away. He stuck his hands in his pockets and jingled loose coins. "Not much of a birthday."

"Oh, *now* you remember?"

"You still mad at me?"

"Probably. Are you planning on ignoring me again for no reason?"

"What makes you think I didn't have a reason?"

Her breath stilled. "Do you?"

He didn't answer, and she couldn't see his face very well in the dim light. After a long moment, he just said, "Go get some sleep, Astrid."

If he thought she was going to keep pressing, he was sorely mistaken. Without another word, she strode toward the grand staircase at the back of the foyer. Next to it sat a small birdcage elevator fashioned with wrought-iron whiplash curves—a luxury Pappa had installed before he died. But it made enough noise to wake the dead, so she walked past it to climb the stairs. A hand gripped her arm on the first step.

She spun around and stared at Bo, his face all sharp lines.

"Have you been up to the top of the turret yet?" he whispered.

"No," she said, unsure why he'd be asking that.

"When you go, check the hiding spot." He released her arm and faded into the dark foyer, leaving her speechless.

When she was sure he was gone, she raced up the stairs to the second floor. Her room was on the right. Everything was just how she'd left it when she went to Los Angeles in the fall: pale pink rose patterns on the four-poster bed, the rugs, and the curtains. A little too feminine, she'd decided earlier today when she'd first arrived home from the train station. But she didn't care about that now. She dumped her handbag and ruined heels on the floor and headed down the second-floor hallway in stockinged feet to the back stairs.

This particular staircase was rarely used; after the elevator was installed, most of the house's activity had shifted to the western side, and, consequently, the primary staircase near the kitchen—which began near Bo's room and ascended to the third floor, stopping outside Winter's study. However, the back stairs that she now climbed went all the way to up the attic, a low-ceilinged half story at the top of the house that her father had begun renovating for her mother, and which included the top of the Queen Anne's "witch hat" style turret.

The top of the turret, though stuffy in the hotter months, had the best view of the Bay and the rooftops of Pacific Heights. And it was here that Astrid bent down in front of a window seat, eager to find what Bo had left her.

When Winter first met Bo, he was a fourteen-year-old pickpocket in Chinatown. And because he was so good at it, having successfully stolen from Winter at a boxing gym, Winter hired him to do odd jobs—delivering messages and packages, spying, that sort of thing. But when Bo's uncle died of a heart attack two years later, Winter permanently took in the former pickpocket, and Bo proceeded to live with Winter and his first wife, who later died in the accident with Mamma and Pappa. And after that, when Winter moved back into the Queen Anne three and a half years ago, he brought Bo with him.

Astrid was fifteen when her parents died. And though she'd seen Bo off and on before that summer, when he moved into the Queen Anne with Winter, it was the first time she'd really talked to him—here in the top of the turret, in fact. It was Mamma's favorite spot in the house, and Astrid found solace here, reading.

And chatting with Bo.

He'd lost his mother at an even younger age than Astrid, and it was easy to talk to him. Comforting, even. After school, she'd come up here and he'd teach her words in Cantonese or share childhood memories about growing up in Chinatown. Astrid especially liked the Chinese fables he'd learned from his mother, which he would retell to Astrid with enthusiastic irreverence, mischievously changing the stories to brighten her mood.

It was during one such retelling that Bo found the secret cubby below the window seat, quite by accident when he kicked it open one afternoon. And as their friendship grew, they began leaving small treasures for each other inside it. Notes. Candy. Found things. Pranks.

They hadn't used it in over a year.

Astrid's heart raced madly as she hit the top corner of the panel with her fist, once, twice, and then it popped off. Darkness filled the small hiding spot. Astrid stuck her arm inside, warily feeling around, until her hand touched something.

She pulled out a small box wrapped in rose-patterned silk fabric. The bow was almost too perfect to touch, but in her curiosity she tugged it open after a few reverent seconds. Inside, winking up at her in the darkness, was a silver wristwatch.

It was simple and beautiful. And of course it was, because Bo had excellent taste and was the best-dressed man she knew. But the most important thing was that it was from him. He'd read her letters, and he'd remembered her birthday, after all.

Her breath hitched. Joy flooded her chest. She gingerly picked up the dainty watch and traced the long, rectangular face and the mesh bracelet-style band. The pad of her fingertip felt something on the back plating. She flipped it over and held it up to the thin moonlight that filtered in from the window. Elongated script slanted over the metal. The engraving read:

One day, three autumns.

A Chinese idiom that Bo had taught her years ago. It meant, *When you miss someone, one day apart feels as long as three years.*

Astrid pressed the watch to her breast and promptly fell apart.

FOUR

———◆———

BO DIDN'T SLEEP WELL THAT NIGHT. HE'D KEPT THE DOOR TO HIS
room cracked for an hour after he left Astrid on the staircase, listening to the rain on the narrow window above his
bed, half hoping she'd come down after she found the gift.
In the past, she'd occasionally sneaked down the servants'
stairwell to talk to him at night. There were six private
rooms along this corridor, as well as a community room
and dining area. And though his room wasn't the biggest—
the head housekeeper, Greta, claimed that one—it was, by
far, the most secluded, around a sharp corner from the
stairwell, away from everyone else. Easy enough for Astrid
to manage without getting the attention of other ears.

But she never came down.

Stupid of him to be wounded by that. Hours ago, he'd
worried she might be dead or cursed. Well, he still wasn't
sure about the cursed part, to be honest. But as for the
other, she was exhausted. She probably just went to bed.
It didn't mean she hated the wristwatch.

He'd spent too much money on it. His car had used up

most of his savings, so he needed to be careful. A difficult task when Astrid was involved.

When he'd felt certain she wasn't coming, he'd shut the door and sat up in bed, staring at the bookcase across the room. It was jam-packed with old magazines and books. Forty-two books, to be exact, and one ragged, ancient copy of *Webster's International Dictionary* that he often consulted to improve his vocabulary. Apart from that one, he'd read all the books several times over. Some were missing covers or their spines were broken. Water damaged and dog-eared. It didn't matter. They were his, bought with hard-earned money.

On the top shelf, bookending his five most cherished tomes, was one of the few things he'd salvaged from his childhood in Chinatown: a chipped ceramic white rabbit. His cheap bastard of an uncle said it once belonged to Bo's grandmother, who'd illegally emigrated from Hong Kong at the turn of the century as a bride for sale. She'd given it to Bo's mother, who'd died in the Spanish influenza epidemic ten years back, leaving him orphaned at the ripe old age of eleven—three years before he first spied Winter at a boxing club and picked the big man's pocket.

The day his life changed.

He didn't have any photographs of his mother. Only the rabbit remained. But he did have memories of her recounting old Chinese fables of animal spirits that played tricks on men. He loved those stories. After she died, he used to pretend that her spirit watched him from the rabbit's shiny black eyes. Perhaps he'd pretended so much that he actually believed it now.

"Do not look at me like that, *Ah-Ma*," he said to the rabbit now, turning it around to face the wall so that it couldn't watch him being miserable. "I know I can't have the girl."

Of course he knew this. He couldn't sit with Astrid in all but a handful of restaurants around town. He couldn't walk into a movie theater with her on his arm. Statewide anti-miscegenation laws said it was outright illegal for him to marry her. Hell, he could be thrown in jail for even so much as holding her hand in public.

So, no.

Bo knew he shouldn't want her. Knew he couldn't have her.

But his rebellious heart refused to acknowledge any of this. It tormented him with whispered provocations, urging him to action and kindling hope.

His heart said: when have you ever given a damn about laws?

By some miracle, he finally fell asleep and woke much too late, rushing to bathe and dress at half past nine. His schedule was often nocturnal, but he was accustomed to being up early, no matter how much sleep he'd failed to get. But he especially wanted to be up early today because of Astrid.

And to deal with the yacht. Not Astrid at all, only the yacht. Though, he supposed he needed to tell Winter about Astrid's hospital trip . . . something he relished about as much as a hole in the head.

After shaving and combing back his damp hair with a touch of pomade, carefully arranging an elegant swoop in the front, he grabbed a fresh suit jacket off a wooden valet stand in the corner and raced upstairs to the main floor.

Clinking plates and chatter sounded from the dining room. He made his way there, slipping into his suit jacket as he strained to pick out the female voices. No Astrid. He strode through the arched doorway, half disappointed. The head housekeeper, Greta, was setting a plate of breakfast in front of Winter's wife, Aida, who tended to her wriggling baby in a high chair.

"Morning, Bo." Aida smiled up at him with a sleepy, freckled face. As she held a tiny pewter spoon out of the baby's reach, the wide sleeve of her oriental silk robe fluttering around her elbow. Aida's shop was on the edge of Chinatown, and she often channeled spirits for the women who worked for one of Chinatown's tong leaders—Ju Wong, who owned a sewing factory and ran a small prostitution business on the side; his seamstresses often paid Aida in clothes.

"All this rain must be slowing us down," she said, stretching her back against the chair. "Everyone slept in this morning."

"I did not," a singsong voice with a heavy Swedish accent said. The silver-headed housekeeper held out a clean cloth for Aida; the baby was wearing most of the pureed fruit her mother was trying to spoon into her tiny, smiling mouth. "I was up at dawn."

No surprise there. Greta hadn't slept past five A.M. since Bo had known her. She was proud, efficient, and took her duties *very* seriously. He'd never once seen her smile until the baby came along last spring. Seemed the solemn Swede had a soft spot for children.

He stuck his finger in the baby's bowl and tasted. "Pears," he said, smiling down at nine-month-old Karin, who chirped a nonsensical, happy greeting and reached for him. The infant looked more and more like Aida every day, but when Winter showed them old photographs of Astrid at her age, it was clear that Karin had Magnusson eyes.

"No one wants you smearing your dirty fingers all over them, little beastie," Aida told her as she tried to capture said dirty fingers with the cloth Greta had brought.

"Who knew girls were so messy," he said as he lifted linen from a steaming basket and grabbed a warm biscuit. Greta's jaw clinched. If she had her way, he'd eat all his meals downstairs. He gave her a quick wink, and that only irked her further.

Aida scooted her untouched plate to the empty chair next to her. "Eat before the eggs get cold," she said, tucking the front of her caramel-colored bob behind one ear. "I'll get another plate when Karin's done finger-painting the tablecloth."

"Don't mind if I do." He sat down and settled a napkin on his leg a few seconds before Winter strolled into the room.

"Oh, you're up," Winter said to him, stretching as he passed. "The warehouse just telephoned. The sandbags are holding strong and that goddamn yacht's been moved this morning, hallelujah."

Multiple things went through Bo's head at once. If the yacht was moved this morning, that meant Winter knew Bo hadn't moved it last night. And yet, Winter was in an easygoing mood, lazily rolling up his shirtsleeves as he sat across from his wife and smiled at his daughter. This also meant he probably hadn't heard about the hospital yet. Good.

"You feel okay, cheetah?" he said to his wife, brow wrinkling.

"All this rain makes me a little drowsy," she said.

While Winter frowned at her, Bo asked, "Who moved the yacht?" Surely not Officer Bastard.

Winter settled a forearm on the edge of the table and leaned back in his seat. "The widow who owns it had it towed at dawn. Johnny said no one bothered to inform anyone at the pier—he would've slept through it if it weren't for the officer guarding it, who banged on the warehouse door, accusing them of moving it without his permission. Took several calls for the cop to get in touch with the tugboat operator and find out what had happened."

"Mrs. Cushing had it moved without the chief's permission?"

"Is that the widow's name? I suppose so. Good riddance, I say. Let the police deal with it far away from us." He accepted the morning newspaper from Greta with a nod. "We'll have to wait and see if any reporters are snooping around today. If it looks clear, we'll go ahead and stage tonight's runs at the pier. But either way, I'm probably going to need you to take a runabout to the Marin County dock this afternoon and deal with that new Canadian captain."

"And by 'deal with,' you mean . . . ?"

"See if you can talk him down on the price of that Scotch he's hoarding."

"All right. Rough him up, got it."

"Bo," Aida scolded with a soft smile.

"Oh, *no* roughing up. Let me just write that down so I don't forget."

Winter surveyed the front of the newspaper. "Wonderful. The damn yacht's already making headlines. 'Lost-at-sea Mystery Yacht Reappears,'" he read out loud, then skimmed a short article that had little-to-no information. "Our pier number is mentioned, but not our name, so that's something, I suppose. I take it you couldn't get the yacht running last night?"

Bo's fork hovered over his eggs. "About that . . . Have you talked to Astrid?"

"Haven't seen her."

Aida snorted. "She informed us yesterday that she wouldn't be getting up before noon during the holidays."

That sounded like Astrid, all right. He thought of the gift again and a little pang went through his chest. He ate a bite of lukewarm egg and had difficulty swallowing. Time to get it over with.

"About last night," he began, keeping his eyes on his plate. "Astrid and I ran into a strange . . . situation on the yacht."

Newspaper crinkled. Bo glanced up to find Winter's sharp eyes trained on him. "Why was Astrid on the yacht?"

"A valid question," Bo said diplomatically. "And believe me, I wish she hadn't been—"

"What is wrong?" Greta asked as she set down a carafe of hot coffee.

"Everything's fine," Bo assured all of them.

Bobbed hair appeared in the doorway, blond against the dark polished wood. Astrid's gaze met his for a brief moment, but for once, he couldn't read her. And that made him more anxious than he already was.

"Good morning, everyone." The youngest Magnusson sibling flounced around Greta in a blue and white striped top and a skirt that skimmed her curvy hips. Apart from mildly bloodshot eyes and the dark circles beneath them, which he could just make out beneath a heavy layer of powder, she seemed cheery. Certainly wider awake than the rest of them.

She set down a stack of newspapers and magazines and parked herself in the chair next to Winter, directly across from Bo. "Gotta catch up on all the local gossip I missed while I was gone," she said when Winter looked at her as she was rapping her knuckles on the stack of newspapers. "Did you know that Darla McCarthy threw her husband out of their Russian Hill house in nothing but his underclothes? Good for her, I say. That man is a dog."

"What is wrong?" Greta repeated to Astrid.

"Not a thing," Astrid said. "I'll have what everyone is having. It smells delightful. Oh good. Coffee. Wait, have we got any smoked salmon? I missed that in Los Angeles. The cafeteria breakfast on campus is just dreadful, and—"

"Why were you on the yacht, Astrid?" Winter said, his easygoing mood heading downhill, fast. "And what the hell happened?"

She poured coffee into a china cup with a gilded rim and handle. "Stop being so grumpy. I'm here, aren't I?"

"Astrid fainted on the yacht," Bo said in calm voice. "But she's okay now."

"Fainted?" Winter said, completely abandoning the newspaper.

"I knew it." Greta cupped a hand to Astrid's cheek and frowned. "It was all that champagne."

"It was not," Astrid said, pushing her hand away. Silver glinted on her wrist.

The watch. She was wearing it.

That was good!

And also horrible.

Why was she flaunting it out here, where God and everyone else could see? Bo suddenly felt overwarm and guilty, as if every single perverted, obscene fantasy he'd had about Astrid was on display—and he'd had *plenty* of them.

And yet . . .

She was wearing the wristwatch. That had to mean something. She wouldn't wear it out of pity; he knew that for a fact. He'd worried the engraving on the back was too sentimental—that it said too much about how he felt. About her. About them. About his despair over the possibility of a future together. Oh, for the love of God, why wouldn't she look at him again?

"Bo?"

He blinked. Winter's mismatched blue and gray eyes stared at him expectantly.

"What's that? Oh yes. The yacht. Well, this is what happened . . ."

Bo told the whole story, forcing himself to talk over Winter's rising anger and the suspicion that his boss's twitching fingers were seconds away from strangling Bo's neck. But after Winter was assured that Astrid was, by all appearances, healthy and in one piece, he finally relaxed and ate his breakfast. And no one made any other remarks until Bo mentioned the part about the yacht's owner identifying her maid at the hospital.

"Mrs. Cushing apparently feels so bad about lending out the boat to Miss Richards," Bo said, "that she's offered to house her and the other survivors until they can—"

"Ridiculous," Greta interrupted, her face pinched in disbelief. "What wealthy lady lets her maid borrow a luxury yacht?"

Huh. She was probably right. Bo certainly couldn't imagine, say, Greta asking to use one of Winter's boats for a weekend outing. The proud housekeeper would just as soon set herself on fire.

"Maybe it was a special reward," Aida suggested.

Greta crossed her arms over her chest. "Oh *ja*," she said sarcastically. "I will just please ask Winter"—which she pronounced more like *Veen-ter* with her lilting accent—"if I can borrow the Pierce-Arrow limousine for a big-time champagne weekend with my friends."

Bo smiled to himself. He rather liked it when Greta got

agitated. But she'd made her point, a good one—not to mention that it had temporarily distracted everyone from thinking about Astrid's trip to the hospital.

"The whole story stinks," Astrid said. "Those survivors are lying. And Mrs. Cushing knows something about it, because Greta's ab-so-*lute*-ly right about the maid borrowing that yacht."

"It doesn't make much sense," Aida admitted. "All of them with memory loss . . ."

Astrid folded her arms over her chest. "My nurse said two of them acted like they were familiar with each other. And that Cushing lady got ticked off when the police chief said they needed to inspect the yacht, right, Bo?" Astrid looked at him again for the first time since she'd walked into the dining room.

"Yes, that's right." He glanced at her wrist and made sure she saw his gaze linger there. But she only looked away again, damn her!

Winter sighed heavily. "If anyone cares about my opinion, I think you should just forget all about it. The yacht's gone. We don't know any of those people. And I, for one, am staunchly opposed to anything magical or cursed or haunted."

Aida cleared her throat.

Winter winked his scarred eye at her. "Except you, of course, darling."

"And your daughter," Aida reminded him.

"I'm still hoping that maybe we'll get lucky with her," he admitted with a grin. "One medium in this family is enough."

A maid poked her head into the dining room to inform Winter he had a long-distance telephone call from Canada. "That'll be the captain with the Scotch," he said, pushing away from the table to stand. "But as for you—"

"Yes," Astrid said defiantly. "What about me?"

Winter shook his head. "Just try not to give me a heart attack while you're home. And no more drinking," he called out over his shoulder as he left the room.

Bo slouched in his chair. That went better than he'd hoped. But he wasn't entirely convinced he wouldn't hear more about it later, when Winter and Bo were at work.

Aida straightened the baby's bib. "Well, you heard Mr. Grumpy. But if it were *me*, and I daresay I'm more knowledgeable about supernatural matters than my dear husband, I would certainly want to know what kind of ritual those people were doing on that boat. Magic is a funny thing. You might feel fine now, Astrid, but you don't know what kind of energy you absorbed from that turquoise idol."

"Well, let's hope it's out of my system, because I don't have time for any more weirdness right now," Astrid said. "I have a new dress that looks terrific on me, and I'm meeting friends tonight. We're going to catch up and go dancing before the whole city floods."

Oh, was that so? Bo didn't like the sound of her dancing in a terrific dress. In fact, he damn well loathed it, even though he couldn't get the enticing image out his head. Was she *trying* to make him jealous, or was he so far gone that he'd lost the ability to function rationally around her without his emotions bouncing all over the place?

Aida just smiled. "That sounds nice. By the way, I was admiring that new wristwatch of yours. Wherever did you get it?"

Shit.

Aida knew. He could tell by the careful, teasing way she'd said it. She saw too much. Noticed too much. And now Astrid's response was coming many seconds too late, which would only confirm Aida's suspicions.

"This?" Astrid twisted her arm to look at the watch. If she admitted Bo had given it to her, then it would be out in the open. Casual. Nothing important. It wasn't lingerie, after all, or even a necklace. It was just a damn watch.

However, if Astrid lied about it, that meant she thought of the gift as something more. Because that's when he knew things had changed between them—when the lies started. When she started telling Winter that she'd spent the afternoon with friends instead of strolling along the docks with Bo. When she made up silly errands to run and insisted Bo drive her—only to end up asking him to take her out for subgum in Chinatown, so that they could share a booth in a restaurant together in one of the handful of places in the city at which it was acceptable for them to do so.

Lying meant there was something to cover up.

Bo held his breath, waiting to hear what Astrid would say. Had college changed her feelings? Were all those men she talked about in her letters a ploy to make him jealous, or was it just a spoiled girl wanting attention, unaware of how much it hurt him?

"Isn't it simply gorgeous?" Astrid finally said to Aida, fidgeting with the rectangular dial. "I saw it in a shop in Westwood. It was love at first sight, and I just had to have it, no matter the price. Please don't tell Winter I blew all my pin money on it."

Happiness flooded his limbs, warming the space left behind by his fleeing pessimism. He didn't dare look at her face, just slid his shoe near the side of hers beneath the table and pressed.

She pressed back.

Aida made a choked sound. Bo jerked his foot away from Astrid, but soon realized he wasn't the cause of Aida's distress. Winter's wife stumbled away from the table and raced out of the dining room.

"Watch Karin," Bo told Astrid before he strode after Aida. He found her doubled over the toilet on the floor of the powder room, wiping her mouth on a hand towel.

"Aida?" he said, kneeling down beside her.

"Oh dear," she mumbled weakly.

"You're ill."

"I suppose that's one way of looking at it." A guilty look spread over her pallid face as she whispered, "Please don't tell Winter."

FIVE

———◆———

BY NINE THAT EVENING, THE SLOW DRIZZLE THAT HAD FALLEN
on the city most of the day had turned into a steady rain.
Astrid dodged streaming puddles after Jonte dropped her
off in North Beach, a couple blocks from Chinatown. The
Gris-Gris Club, much like the Magnussons' home, sat upon
a steep hill. Here, cable cars braved the foul weather, climbing Columbus Avenue, but she'd heard on the radio that
tomorrow it may not be running for long: the cable car turn-
around at the bottom of the hill was on the verge of flooding
too deep for service.

The rain was spoiling everything. Only two of her old
friends had agreed to brave the weather to meet her tonight,
and now she wasn't even sure she felt like being out herself.
She'd originally suggested they all meet here at Gris-Gris
because her brother supplied their liquor, and their family
was friendly with the owner; Winter had even met Aida
when she was doing a spiritualism show here a year and
half ago, before he started knocking her up left and right.

Normally the streets would be lined with cars and a

long line would have formed around the unmarked speakeasy. But tonight only the occasional car dotted the curb, and Astrid was able to walk straight up to the door. A tiny window in the door slid open as she shook off her umbrella. "Membership card," the doorman said through it.

"Miss Astrid Magnusson," she answered confidently.

The door swung open and a tuxedoed man with a chest as broad as an icebox greeted her. "Mr. Magnusson's baby sister?"

"I am."

He nodded slowly. "You look more like the younger brother. The treasure hunter."

"Lowe," she supplied.

He snapped his fingers and grinned handsomely. "That's him. If you're here to see Velma, she's busy at the moment. But I can have Daniels seat you, if you'd like. Get yourself out of that rain."

Festive boughs of holly and the muffled sound of hot jazz welcomed her as she stepped inside the speakeasy lobby. A few patrons mingled, smoking cigarettes and chatting near a newly installed coin-operated telephone. Her friends were supposed to be here already, but she didn't see them. And when she asked Daniels about them, she found they hadn't arrived, so she followed him into the dark club to wait.

Gris-Gris was a swank place with a great house band and an interesting rotation of stage acts, from clairvoyants to acrobats to flashy dancers. But the best thing about it was that it was a black-and-tan club. And that meant societal restrictions went unheeded here. You could dine with who you wanted. Dance with who you wanted. No one cared about anything as long as you had cash. Bo came here a lot, so she made sure to mention at breakfast that she'd be coming tonight, hoping he'd get the hint and drop by. She wasn't sure he would. He'd left for work with Winter before she could speak to him alone.

The tables that clustered around Gris-Gris's stage were

half empty tonight, and Astrid didn't see anyone she knew. She certainly wasn't going to sit around waiting for her friends, so she joined the people lined up along the dance floor who were cheering on two couples doing a new dance called the Lindy Hop, with wild swing-outs and kicks. Astrid cheered them on and soon found herself seduced by the infectious beat of the snare drum and joined in when a man offered to teach her the moves. She initially fumbled, laughing at herself, but soon picked up the steps. It was exciting and fun—so fun that she forgot about the rain and her errant friends. She changed partners twice, and then danced with another girl, laughing breathlessly as the musicians onstage sped through another song. And another.

And another.

When the house band took a break, she was ready for one, too, and plopped down at a table to cool off with a glass of ice water.

Her friends weren't coming. Traitors. She wouldn't care so much if an older man a few tables away would stop staring at her. She'd first noticed him on the dance floor, but now he was making her feel uncomfortable—especially when he looked as if he was headed over to talk to her.

Absolutely not.

She took the long way around to the bar at the back of the speakeasy and wasted several minutes ordering a fresh drink and chatting with the bartender before taking another route back to her table. She thought the man was long gone.

He wasn't.

"Your fella leave you high and dry, sweetheart?"

Astrid glanced up to see the older man leaning against a nearby column. He flicked a cigarette into a potted palm and smiled. He had full, fetching lips and an interesting nose with a prominent bridge. He was also twice her age and drunk as a fish.

"Just waiting for some friends," she answered, hoping if she didn't look him in the eye, he'd get the message and move on to another woman. No such luck.

"You've been waiting for a good while now. Think you've been forgotten." He pulled out the chair next to her and plopped down, smoothing his light brown hair. "Pretty little gal like you shouldn't be alone. Especially not during the holidays. Don't worry, Max will keep you company."

His eyes were so glassy, she expected him to reek of booze, but all she smelled was smoke and a fruity cologne. "I appreciate your concern, Mr. Max—"

"That's my given name," he said. "I'm not a stickler for old-fashioned formalities. Everyone just calls me Max. What do they call you?"

"If they call me anything, there's a good chance my brothers will put them in the bottom of the Bay."

His laugh was nasal and lazy. "Where are these brothers of yours tonight, hm?"

She reminded herself that the club was perfectly safe. All she had to do was raise her voice and Daniels or Hezekiah or one of the bouncers would come get her. Hopefully. She glanced up at the big window on the upper tier, where Velma normally watched the floor from her office, but it was dark. Astrid rather wished it wasn't.

"Look," she said. "I'll be straight with you. I don't keep company with men your age."

The votive candle on the table cast flickering shadows on his face that sharpened when he turned his head. "I'm twenty-three, sweetheart."

She started to laugh, but when she took a closer look at his face was surprised to see that, indeed, he might be only twenty-three. Maybe boozing aged him. Her friend Mary's mother drank too much and easily looked twenty years older. And where the hell was Mary, anyway? Astrid thought of the new public telephone in the lobby and wondered if she should try to ring her.

"Let's try this again," he said, flashing her a charming smile. "I'm Max, and you, I believe, are Miss Magnusson."

Her fingers stilled around her glass. "How do you know that?"

"Your family's infamous. And I asked one of the

waiters," he added, hunching over the small table to speak in a lower voice. A gaudy signet ring on his finger flashed in the candlelight when he set his hand on the table, inching closer. "You are the Viking Bootlegger's baby sister, yes?"

The warning bells that had dinged inside her head when he first mentioned her name now grew louder. He was toying with her, and she didn't like the edgy eagerness in his eyes. Maybe he was one of her brother's business rivals. Winter and Bo had both warned her a hundred times to be cautious in public. Being in Los Angeles had made her forget to be guarded. She remembered now.

"If you're hoping for a discount, I'm sorry to disappoint you," she said, pulling away from him while trying to keep her voice light.

"No, no discount. I've got more cash than I know what to do with and plenty of booze back home." His suit looked expensive enough, so maybe that was true. Glassy blue eyes squinted as he smiled down at her. "I'm only interested in you."

"Me?"

"Indeed," he assured her, rapping his knuckles on the table to underscore the word. There was something awfully familiar about the design on that ring, but she couldn't quite place it. "Tell me more about you, Miss Magnusson."

"Not much to tell."

"I doubt that's true. Word is you were at your brother's warehouse last night when that yacht crashed into the pier. That had to be interesting."

She didn't like where this was going. Maybe he was a reporter. Magnussons do not speak to reporters. That was one of Winter's (many) house rules.

"Hold that thought," she all but shouted at Max, pasting on a fake smile as she clinked the melting ice in her glass. "I just decided I need some gin. I'll be right back, and then we can chat."

She all but leapt away from the table in her rush to get away from him and wove around tables looking for Daniels, who was nowhere in sight. She glanced over her shoulder to see if Max was watching her. He was. She waved and darted behind a column. A small crowd of people had descended on the bar. She'd have trouble getting the bartender's attention. She also couldn't make a dash for the lobby, because it was in Max's line of vision. Her anxious gaze fell on the door to the ladies' restroom— out of sight, and that was good enough for her. She stepped inside the bright room, leaving behind the chatter and smoky haze of the club.

SIX

———◆———

BO HELD OUT A CHAIR AS HE STEALTHILY SCANNED THE DIM
speakeasy, looking for the telltale flounce of blond hair.
Gris-Gris wasn't as busy as it should be this time of night,
but there were still enough people to make it difficult to
spot someone across the tangle of candlelit tables and
dancing bodies.

"You owe me for this, Yeung Bo-Sing," Sylvia said in
Cantonese as she sat down in the chair he offered, using
the formal Chinese surname-first pattern to emphasize that
she meant business.

Then again, Sylvia Fong always meant business. The
twenty-year-old switchboard operator lived with her twin
sister in an apartment two floors above the one Bo grew up
in—one he still kept but rarely used—just off Grant on
the northern edge of Chinatown. She occasionally helped
him when he needed to listen in on telephone conversations, and he made sure the building superintendent knew
that he couldn't screw her over on rent or bamboozle his
way out of repairs.

"You said you weren't busy tonight," he told her. The

house band was loud, so they had to practically shout at each other to be heard. "Besides, I'm buying you a drink. Your boyfriend surely won't mind two friends catching up."

"No, he won't." Her ruler-straight short bob swayed as she slowly shook her head. "But no club in the city would make you pay for drinks, and you wouldn't beg me to race over here with you in this nasty weather if you didn't want something."

True.

Thanks to the widow Cushing moving the *Plumed Serpent*, Bo had been able to oversee the loading of tonight's runs from Pier 26 instead of staging everything across the Bay. This saved him a couple of extra hours of work, but it was already past ten. He hoped Astrid hadn't already moved on to another speakeasy—or decided against coming here altogether.

"Only one thing would make you look that nervous," Sylvia said. "*She's* home from college, isn't she?"

Bo sat where he could see the bar and the door. "Who do you mean?"

"Pssh. Don't play dumb. The blond Swiss girl."

"Swedish."

Sylvia widened her eyes and pretended to pant, mimicking small dog paws with her hands. "This is you, wagging your tail and begging for her to scratch your ears."

"A bit lower down than my ears," he said with a smile.

She laughed. "Lucky her."

"You're a boon to my ego, Miss Fong." Bo had known Sylvia several years, and even though things started off lustily between them, it had been quick burning and short. But she was funny and easygoing, and they had not only remained friends but become closer. A rare joy, she was. "Why aren't we together again?"

A stupid question, because they both knew why. She'd been uninterested in being hampered by a serious relationship, and he'd been harboring, well, whatever *this* was for Astrid.

Then, of course, there was the other thing. *That* night. The night he didn't want to think about right now.

But she only said, "Because my mother would just as soon me marry a convicted murderer."

"Mm. That's something I hear a lot," he murmured, half serious as he flagged down a waiter and ordered them two drinks: black-label champagne for her, water for him. When the waiter left with their order, Bo mused, "Maybe I should change my line of work. Do something respectable."

"And give up your fancy new car?" Sylvia said as she took off her gloves and pocketed them.

He smiled. "Good point."

"What did you name it, by the way?"

"I never could decide," he lied. He didn't want to give her the wrong idea—or even the right one, which was that he'd decided to christen it "Sylvia" as a quiet act of petty and irrational retaliation after he'd received one of Astrid's college letters that mentioned that damned professor of hers.

"You should give it a nice Chinese name," Sylvia said. "What about your mother's name?"

"A car is too sexy to be named after a mother."

She huffed and crossed her legs, adjusting the fall of her dress over one knee. "As if mothers can't be sexy."

"Not your *own* mother."

Sylvia squinted over his shoulder. "Don't look now, but I think I've spotted the person holding your doggy leash."

Bo slowly, *slowly* turned his head in the direction Sylvia was looking, and damned if she wasn't right. In the middle of the dance floor, Astrid twisted her curvy hips in a beaded aqua blue dress. Her mouth was open, laughing, while she stomped it up with one of Gris-Gris's regular patrons, Leroy Garvey.

Jealousy, hot and liquid, shot through Bo's chest.

He forced himself to watch her. Penance for dreaming an impossible dream. A voice inside argued: *You could be the one out there, swinging her over the dance floor.*

Dancing with her. Whispering in her ear. Anticipating getting her alone in some dark corner of the club, where people would look the other way.

Could he be satisfied with that? Stolen moments in dark corners, seeing her when he could, between her long trips to Los Angeles and his short trips up the coast to Canada, running booze . . . until she found someone permanent, forcing Bo to step back and accept it? To let her go and watch her spend her life in another man's arms?

He watched her trade partners. Another handsome man, happy to hold on to her, and he, sitting here moping beneath a cloud of nebulous anger and hurt.

The band finally ended their set. As the crowd on the main floor dispersed, Bo tracked Astrid's sparkling dress to a table across the main aisle, where she sat down with her back to him. Alone. Waiting for her friends, he supposed. Or was she? Was that just a fabricated excuse to shake off any protests that she'd be out alone, acting like a spoiled flapper, drinking and dancing with anyone in sight? What the devil was going on here, anyway?

"Oh my," Sylvia said, clucking her tongue and shaking her head. "My-oh-my-oh-my."

Bo's gaze flicked to his companion's face.

She gave him a pitiful smile. "What I wouldn't have given for you to look at me like that."

He relaxed against his seat and tapped his fingertips against the linen-covered table. Casual, cool. Slow breaths. He didn't dare look in Astrid's direction again. In fact, he banished her from his head completely, proud that he actually could.

"But if I'm being honest," Sylvia continued, "I do think I prefer you better as friend. You are less intense."

"You were the one who told me I was coming by too often."

"I got tired of you looking at the clock and hearing you talk about *her*." Sylvia lifted her chin in Astrid's direction.

"You didn't want a commitment," he argued.

She lowered her eyes. "No woman wants to settle for second prize, Yeung Bo-Sing."

"I'm sorry," he said softly, and meant it. "I wish things had turned out different between us. We've never talked about it, but that last night, with—"

"I agreed to it. We were drunk."

"My good sense failed me."

She shrugged with one shoulder. "Amy was always more adventurous."

"It changed things between us, and I can't even look at your sister anymore without feeling guilty."

She dismissed his words with a coy smile. "No need for regret. Amy has long forgotten it."

It may have been two years ago, but her sister still flirted with him shamelessly and occasionally tried to talk him into coming over when Sylvia wasn't around. Which would be a temptation to even the most pious of priests. But he couldn't. Sylvia would be hurt, for one, and he valued her friendship too much. More than that, just thinking about it made him feel like he was cheating on Astrid . . . a woman he'd never even kissed.

He was pathetic. Truly.

"Besides," she said. "I've forgotten it already, too."

"Ugh." He clutched his chest and grinned. "My male pride."

Sylvia swatted his hand playfully. "What about my female pride? You drag me out here tonight for what—to make your little biscuit jealous?"

"No."

Her eyes narrowed with cool incredulity.

"All right, yes." Was she mad? He felt a little ashamed, and hoped she wasn't mad, considering their history. Sylvia was hard to read. Sometimes he felt she was full of light, uncaring about what anyone thought, and other times, he worried that she cared too much and went to great lengths to hide it.

But she only laughed at him right now, and relief washed through him.

"Fine," she said. "But you *really* owe me, and I get to name the price."

They ribbed each other good-naturedly for a while, Sylvia naming off favors that became more and more exorbitant, until she elbowed his arm. "Hold on a minute. Now who is that she's talking to?"

Bo looked. A man sat at Astrid's table. Well dressed, older. No friend of hers that Bo knew—and Bo knew them all. In fact, he'd go so far as to call the mystery man at Astrid's table . . . dangerous looking. An animal toying with its prey. *That's likely your jealous heart talking*, he told himself. But he realized a moment later that his instincts about the man were not based on anything the man himself was doing. Bo was only reading Astrid; she had gone completely rigid in her seat.

Without thinking, Bo pushed away from the table. But before he could stand, Astrid was on her feet and saying something to the man as she dashed away and disappeared behind a column.

"What was that all about?" Sylvia said in a low voice.

Bo wasn't sure, but he didn't like it. And he liked it even less when the mystery man followed Astrid into the shadows.

"Stay here," Bo instructed Sylvia, and strode off after the man.

SEVEN

———❦———

THE RESTROOM WAS EMPTY BUT FOR A SINGLE WOMAN FIXING her hair in a mirror. No attendant. Maybe she was on a break. Astrid breezed past the mirrors, headed to the last of three marble-walled toilet stalls, and closed the door with a sigh of relief.

Tonight was not going well. She sat on the edge of the toilet seat and cursed her friends for not showing up and leaving her here to deal with drunken strangers on her own. Cursed herself, too, for telling Jonte she'd find her own ride home. At least she had money for a taxi. If she could just sit it out here long enough for that shady man to leave, she could make a beeline for the lobby and get her coat.

It will be fine, she told herself as she blew out a long breath. He was just a drunken lout. A nosy reporter trying to get a scoop. So why couldn't she get the image of his garish ring out her head? She was being paranoid, surely, but the ring reminded her of the turquoise idol . . .

What if he wasn't a reporter after all?

A faucet squeaked off. Heels clicked across the floor,

and for a moment the noise of the club filled the tiled restroom. Then the door blocked it out again.

Astrid let out a long breath and heard something else inside the restroom . . . Light footfalls. Not the click of women's shoes. Surely Max wouldn't come in here? Whoever it was, they approached the stalls and stopped. Blood swished in Astrid's temples as she silently waited for the sound of a stall door opening.

It never came. Only a brief shuffling.

Someone was checking beneath the stall door.

A moment later, hinges squealed. The door banged . . . and then the person stepped to the middle stall.

Oh-God, oh-God, oh-God. Astrid lifted her legs and held them up in the air as the same noises repeated only a few feet away, shuffling, hinges squealing, door banging. Why didn't they put locks on these doors? Why—

The person stopped in front of her stall.

Feet shuffled. A shadow fell across the floor beneath the door. Astrid's heart drummed against her rib cage. The hinges began rotating.

She didn't think. Her legs shot forward and she pressed the soles of her T-bar shoes flat against the stall door, pushing it closed with a bang.

Outside the door, a murmur of surprise echoed off the marble. Masculine.

Holy living God, it *was* Max!

Without warning, the door exploded inward. Astrid yelped as her legs folded back like an accordion, and she slid sideways on the toilet seat. She braced her hands on the stall walls and stared up at the dark figure of Max.

"Found you," he said with a dangerous smile.

Survival instincts kicked in. A dozen scenarios raced through her mind at once. The simplest hung on a chain around her wrist: a silver mesh handbag. It was heavier than she preferred, but she'd worn it tonight because it matched the band on the wristwatch Bo had given her. A small bit of fortune. She tightened the chain, and when

Max reached inside the stall to pull her out, she swung the handbag and struck him in the face.

He cried out and stumbled backward a step, more surprised than hurt. One hand caught the casing around the stall while the other touched his cheek briefly and dabbed blood.

"Little bitch," he muttered through gritted teeth.

Inside her head, she heard Bo's voice instructing her how to protect herself if she were ever in a situation like this. *Kick a man straight in the balls*, he'd said. A childish thing to do, she'd thought at the time, but she didn't much care at the moment. She started to raise a leg and do just that. But Max suddenly stilled.

"You're going to want to move away from her, slowly, before I blow a hole in your spine," a familiar voice said behind Max.

Max grunted and raised both his hands as he stepped out of the stall. Bo stood behind him in a long navy coat. The muzzle of Bo's gun was pressed into the man's back.

Relief washed through Astrid's limbs.

"Now, then," Bo said, patting Max's suit jacket with one hand to search for weapons. "You want to tell me just who the hell you are and why you were stupid enough to touch her?"

Max's elbow swung backward and struck Bo in the jaw. Hard.

Bo let out muffled grunt of pain as he stumbled backward. His shoulder cracked against the restroom wall.

Shouting savagely, Astrid jumped out of the stall and tried to whop Max with her handbag. This time he wasn't surprised. His arm shot up and he swatted it as if it were a fly. His signet ring caught her on her wristbone—*the ring is inlaid with turquoise*, her mind realized as pain shot up her arm.

Pain, and something more . . .

Time seemed to slow. In the space of a few rapid heartbeats, Astrid watched Bo shake his head like a wet dog and quickly retrain his gun on Max.

Just not quickly enough.

Max raced through the restroom and was already pushing open the door into the club. Chaos erupted as he plowed through the bar area. Bo growled and took off after him, only to come to a skidding stop when Astrid cried out in horror.

Like an electric bee sting, a strange series of aftershocks radiated from the spot Max's ring had clipped her on the wrist. The shocks buzzed and hummed until they wracked her entire body. The stark-bright light of bathroom dimmed. And all around her, dark water poured from the cracks of the tiled walls.

Dark, odious water.

It flowed down the mirrors. Flooded the sinks and overflowed, cascading black waterfalls onto the floor until it began filling the restroom, rising and rising, covering her feet and climbing her legs. It was briny seawater, reeking of salt and rotting fish, and it quickly rose over her knees.

She tried to wade through the icy water, tried to get to Bo. He looked so confused. Why was he just standing there, staring at her like she'd lost her mind?

Then she realized that she might actually *have* lost it. Out of the floodwater, a dark shape bobbed to the surface.

It was the size and shape of a human body, and it was encased in a burlap sack.

Astrid swayed and fell into blackness.

EIGHT

———— ⚜ ————

BO HOLSTERED HIS COLT AND SQUATTED BY ASTRID'S COLLAPSED
body. His shoulder ached where he'd slammed it against
the tiled wall, but he ignored its protest and flipped her
faceup.

It wasn't like the first time on the yacht when she was
unconscious. Her eyelids were fluttering, the whites of her
eyes showing. He shouted her name, and ice blue irises
rolled back into view and stared up him.

His head dropped in relief.

"Bo," she said weakly before turning her face to survey
her surroundings. "The water is gone? My clothes are dry?"

"Whoa, now. Don't try to sit up."

"Did you see the water? Did you see . . . the body in
the sack?"

"What?" His fingertips skimmed a red spot on her forehead that was already swelling. She flinched and muttered
a weak complaint.

"You hit your head," he told her.

She made a frustrated noise and pushed herself up to sit,
despite his protests. "You didn't see it," she said miserably.

Another vision.

The door to the restroom burst open, and noise from the club blared. One of Gris-Gris's enforcers, Joe, lunged through the doorway. "Bo? What's going on?"

"The man who ran out of here . . ." Bo said. "Someone stop him. He attacked Miss Magnusson."

Joe didn't question him or ask for more information. He just shouted over the clamor and disappeared into the crowd. Bo knew everyone who worked at Gris-Gris, from the janitors to the house band's drummer, and any one of them would pitch in to help.

"What is happening to me?" Astrid whispered. Long lashes, thick with mascara, blinked up at him, a pleading anxiety behind her eyes.

He couldn't bear it any longer. Screw decorum. He gathered her in his arms and pulled her against his chest. She didn't resist. Slender arms circled his back as she lay her head on his aching shoulder and buried her face in the collar of his jacket.

She felt impossibly good, soft and warm, clinging to him. His heart was an overexcited child that raced madly with the thrill of possession, no matter how fleeting.

He heard the door open. Knew Astrid heard it, too. Yet both of them were hesitant to release each other.

"Bo Yeung," a commanding feminine voice called out. "I leave Gris-Gris for two hours and come back to pandemonium. Should've known you'd be involved."

He glanced up to see the owner of the club standing in the doorway, arms crossed over her breasts. Her eyes fell on Astrid and all her irritation turned to worry.

"Lord," she swore. "What kind of trouble have you been into?"

Bo didn't believe the attacker could just disappear into the night after running through a club half filled with people, but he had. According to Astrid, "Max" was the only name he'd given her. It didn't matter. Bo had tracked down people with less information than that, and for far more trivial reasons. He'd find him. No one hurt Astrid and got away with it.

No one.

Following Velma's efficient strides, Bo ushered Astrid through a door behind the bar and into a short hallway. To their right, the club's bustling kitchen gleamed bright behind a windowed swinging door, but they were headed left. A tall painted bookcase was empty but for a small stack of old menus and a metal dustpan. Bo released a hidden latch on the side and swung the bookcase away from the wall to reveal a doorway and a low-ceilinged room. He turned on the lights. Rows of shelves lined with Magnusson-imported liquor bottles led to an open area with a desk, where the club's bar manager did the accounting.

Bo had spent a lot of time back here over the years, unloading crates and taking orders. He turned the desk chair around and urged Astrid to sit while Velma squinted down at her with a troubled look on her face.

"Wanna tell me what this is all about?" she asked, glancing from Astrid to Bo.

Velma Toussaint was a former dancer in her mid-thirties who moved to San Francisco from Louisiana after inheriting the club from her former—and now deceased—husband. She was elegant and beautiful, with pale nutmeg skin of indeterminable ancestry and shiny brown hair sculpted into a short Eton crop. And she not only single-handedly ran one of the most successful clubs in the city, but was also a *hoodoo*—or a root doctor, as she liked to call herself. Her talent was magical spellwork, mostly herbal in nature. She was well versed in curses, hexes, jinxing, and unjinxing.

In other words, you did *not* want her for an enemy.

Bo leaned against the edge of the desk and let Astrid tell the story about the yacht, only interrupting when she chattered too far off into tangential territory, which Astrid often did, no matter the subject. He secretly enjoyed listening to her talk. She had opinions about everything and rarely kept them to herself, even when she was wrong, and he liked that. But Velma didn't share his amusement or patience.

"So this Max fellow knew who you were?" Bo said when Astrid finally got around to explaining what had just transpired in the club's restroom. "But why do you think he had anything to do with the people on the yacht? He wasn't one of the survivors, was he?"

"I'm not sure."

Hard to tell in the rain, with all that blue makeup smeared on their faces. Now Bo wished he'd taken a second look at them at the hospital. "He was probably just a reporter."

"That's what I thought at first," she admitted. "But I started feeling funny when his ring hit my wrist." She quickly rubbed her hand over the spot, as if she could erase it. "The symbol on the ring could have been the symbol on the idol. And, Bo, the inlay was turquoise."

Shit.

"Just where is this so-called idol?" Velma asked.

Bo retrieved it from his coat pocket and unfolded the handkerchief wrapping. "It doesn't seem to have any sort of charge anymore. I've touched it several times without incident."

"No magical energy," Velma confirmed as she peered at it for a moment, and then picked it up. "Heavy," she noted, weighing it in her hand. "Solid turquoise, you think? If it's old, could be worth a pretty penny."

"No doubt," Bo agreed.

"That's it! That's the symbol that was on the ring," Astrid said, pointing to the gold disk on the idol's belly.

"Are you sure?" he asked.

She stared at the bright blue statue, biting her bottom lip. Doubt crept in. "I think. It was dark in the club, and everything happened so fast in the restroom . . . Do you know what the symbol means, Velma? Is it bad?"

The conjure woman gestured for Astrid to move out of the way so that she could switch on a lamp. The three of them hunched over the desk as Velma examined the gold disk under the light. "Sorry. This is no symbol I've ever seen," she finally admitted and turned the idol around to study the back. "What's this?"

"I think that says 'NANCE,' but it's hard to read," Bo said. "I wasn't sure if it was some kind of magical word or part of a larger spell. Maybe the other idols Astrid saw in her vision had other words on them, too."

"I wasn't paying attention," Astrid confessed.

"Strange," Velma murmured. "The figure's overall design looks primitive. Ancient. Asian or South American, perhaps. But these are clearly English letters. It seems like a mishmash of styles. I don't know what to make of it."

Astrid groaned. "So you don't know what kind of magic it would be used for? What about the ritual I described? Have you heard of anything like that?"

Velma absently stroked her collarbone with her thumb. "I can't say that I have, but I don't think you're wrong about the iron boots and the burlap sacks. It sounds like those people were drowned as some kind of sacrificial offering."

"But why?" Astrid asked.

"That, I don't know. And I don't understand why they'd be missing for a year at sea, either." Velma put her hand on Astrid's forehead and held it there, as if testing for fever. When she withdrew it, she tilted Astrid's chin up and studied her face. "However, I think I know where the magical charge in that idol went."

"Where?" Astrid said.

"Inside you. Don't be alarmed, dear, but you have two auras."

Astrid tucked her chin and peered down at herself. "What the hell does that mean?"

"Everything living gives off an emanation," Velma explained, putting her hand on Astrid's shoulder to calm her down. "An aura is someone's personal energy. And your aura has always been red, as long as I've known you. Now you've got a second layer . . . almost like it's a shadow. Something that doesn't belong."

Bo didn't like the sound of that.

Neither did Astrid, apparently. She shook herself like a dog, as if she could rid herself of it. "Am I cursed like Winter?"

"Winter was hexed with magical poison," Velma said. "You aren't hexed. This sounds accidental to me. And it doesn't look bad or evil. It just looks different, is all."

"Can you get rid of it?" Bo asked. "One of the unhexing baths you gave Winter?"

The conjurer's brow furrowed. "Like I said, Astrid's not hexed. I can give her some herbs to drink for purification, and I can pray over her. But unless we know what kind of ritual they did on that boat—and, more specifically, what this symbol on the idol means—I can't offer counter magic. And maybe she doesn't need it. Like anything else, magic fades over time. Maybe this will, too. Might be a bigger risk to stick your nose into these people's business. If you stumbled upon whatever it was they were doing, you might want to stumble your way on out of it. Cut your losses. Return the idol to the survivors and wash your hands of it."

Bo threw a hand up in the air. "And what? Just go about our merry way and hope that Astrid hasn't taken on permanent spiritual damage?"

"Don't get snitty with me, Bo Yeung," Velma warned.

"You're telling me there's a group of people in town practicing some sort of big, dark ritual and despite all the mediums, clairvoyants, and oddball spiritual healers you book at this club, no one's heard a thing about it?"

She settled a hand on her hip. "I'll see if any of my contacts around town have heard rumors about these idols. But you play with fire, you're liable to get burned. Don't say I didn't warn you."

Bo snorted. "If I listened to all your warnings, I'd never leave the damn house."

"Ungrateful miscreant."

"Mean old witch."

"Old?" Velma huffed.

He squinted at her. "Not too old to appreciate an extra case of ten-year-old single-malt Scotch, on the house?"

Velma smiled slowly. "*That's* more like it."

"Now, about those herbs you mentioned . . ." Astrid said.

Velma smoothed a hand over Astrid's back. "Come on upstairs and I'll mix you something up."

Snappy footfalls made them all swing around. Stopping near a shelf of liquor was Sylvia, escorted by the club's master of ceremonies, Hezekiah.

"There you are, Ah-Sing," she said sweetly, using a familiar form of Bo's given name—an intimacy that wouldn't be lost on Astrid. "I was beginning to think you had abandoned me in the middle of our date. Aren't you going to introduce me?"

Bo squeezed his eyes shut for a moment. Long enough for his "date" to take matters into her own hands.

"I'm Sylvia Fong," she said brightly.

Bo winced.

Blond eyebrows shot up sharply. "Sylvia?" Astrid said in disbelief. "*Sylvia?*"

The already-stifling air in the small room seemed to congeal like gelatin and wobble with tension. Well, he'd wanted to make Astrid jealous, hadn't he?

Wish granted.

NINE

———◆———

ASTRID WAS THE VERY PICTURE OF RESTRAINT AND GOOD MAN-
ners. She'd ignored the beautiful Miss Fong while Velma
mixed up a batch of herbs. She'd smiled pleasantly while
Bo helped both women into their coats and led them outside
Gris-Gris just before midnight. He informed Astrid that he'd
not driven "Sylvia" (the Buick) tonight but had instead iron-
ically brought Sylvia (the Glamorous Woman) here by
taxi—which meant now they'd all three be sharing a cab
home, what marvelous fun! Astrid had refrained from
demanding which of the two women would be dropped off
first. Because *that* would sound jealous and petty, and Astrid
was neither.

She merely wanted to club him to death with her umbrella.

Bo sat in front with the taxi driver, leaving her to cozy
up to Miss Fong in the back. He rattled off an address that
sounded an awful lot like his Chinatown apartment building. Was he taking Sylvia there with him? Surely not. And
if so, he would die where he stood when Astrid got
her hands on him. But she didn't say this, of course. She

only sat stiffly, pretending to stare out the window through the rain.

"I like your shoes," she told Sylvia in a calm voice after they'd ridden in silence for a time.

Sylvia turned one shapely ankle and peered down at her pump. "Thank you," she said politely, and then, "Your gown is beautiful."

"Thank you. I think I lost a few beads on the dance floor," Astrid responded lightly, toying with the fringe of her beaded hem.

They continued this too-polite small talk on a too-long ride, which was, in reality, only eight blocks. The conversation went like this: How long have you known Bo? Oh, you live in the same building, do you? Switchboard operator, eh? No, I'm not really sure what field I want to study at college. Yes, Los Angeles is certainly sunny this time of year.

And so forth.

Once they got to Chinatown, Bo escorted Sylvia beneath their shared apartment building's entrance, speaking to her briefly while Astrid waited in the idling taxi. Astrid was in turns relieved (Bo was coming back to Pacific Heights, not staying here) and filled with hurt (he was hugging Sylvia good-bye?), but she waited silently. Remained silent, in fact, when Bo got back in the front seat of the taxi.

Remained silent the rest of the way home.

Bo paid the driver. They entered the Queen Anne together. It was quiet inside, mostly dark. He locked the door behind them as she removed her coat and hat.

"Twice a day?" he asked in a low voice—his first words to her since the club.

She glanced down at the brown paper bag that Velma had given her. So *that's* what he wanted to talk about? All right.

"Twice a day," she repeated.

He began shrugging out of his coat. She didn't wait for him, just went straight to the kitchen and flipped on two pendant lights, which hung over a long butcher-block prep table sitting in the middle of the room. She set down Velma's bag of herbs.

"Need help?" his low voice said over her shoulder. She hadn't even heard him following.

"Think I can manage to boil water on my own."

She strode across the black-and-white checkered floor and looked at the pale green enameled oven. Where was the kettle? Didn't people normally leave those out? She heard a shifting noise and saw it sliding in her direction across a small counter, prodded by Bo's hand.

"Thank you," she said, not looking at his face, and added water to the kettle. Now. The stove. She'd seen this done a hundred times. How hard could it be? The matches were in a ceramic box on the counter. She lit one and stared at the range's cast-iron coiled burner. Right. This didn't look like the stove Lena had taught her to how to light. The pilot light should be . . .

Bo leaned near and blew out the match. "Move."

"I can—"

He turned the handle and a coil magically glowed orange. "The old range needed to be replaced, and Winter insisted the new one be electric," he said, putting the kettle atop a burner. "Lena hates it, for the record. The teacups are in the butler's pantry with the rest of the china."

"I know that," she said, trying to sound insulted and not embarrassed. But when she stood in the wide hallway between the kitchen and dining room, staring too long at the drawers and cabinets that lined the walls, Bo's silhouette blocked the light from the kitchen.

"Middle cabinet."

Right. She turned around and opened it. Bowls. Gravy boat . . .

Warmth covered her back. Bo reached over her shoulder to a higher shelf. "Here," he said. One word, spoken low and deep, just above her ear, and for a moment she forgot all about being angry with him.

His bright scent surrounded her. His suit jacket brushed

the back of her gown, and beneath it a thousand chills rippled over her skin. She was taken aback by the force of it and nearly leaned . . .

If she would just—

If he would only—

The sound of china clinking against the marble counter pulled her back from the deep. He'd set the cup down and was now reaching for a saucer. She spun in place to face him.

He flinched and pulled back an inch or two. Far enough to put some space between them. His arm hovered in the air and then fell by his side as he stared down at her.

"Why were you at Gris-Gris tonight?" she asked in a low voice.

"I was having a drink with a friend."

"Sylvia Fong is too beautiful to be a friend."

"And Leroy Garvey is too debonair to be a dance partner. Where were all these chums of yours that you were supposed to be meeting?"

"Were you spying on me? You were! This is Luke all over again—"

"Luke," he said, spitting it out like it was rotten meat. "Tell me the truth, Astrid. What happened in that hotel? Did he touch you?"

Her mouth fell open. A trembling rage ran up her arms, and before she could stop herself, she swung her hand and slapped him, straight across the cheek.

He reeled backward. The dramatic planes of his handsome face made severe angles. Oh, he was *shocked*.

So was she. Her hand stung. She regretted it immediately and felt like crying. God! Not now. *You will not cry, Astrid Cristiana Magnusson.* You will. Not. Cry.

"I am *not* your little sister," she said through gritted teeth. "Not your *mui-mui*. And if you'd realized that a few months ago—"

She stopped, unsure of what she'd been ready to say. That what? It could have been Bo instead of Luke in that hotel room?

"A few months ago?" Bo said, his words heated with

rising anger. "Astrid, I realized that *years* ago. I realized it before you did. And don't tell me I couldn't possibly know your mind, because I remember the exact day and time and place. I remember how the redwoods smelled, and how the setting sun turned your hair to platinum, and how you looked at me."

He bent his head low, leaning until the tip of his nose was a hairsbreadth from hers, and said quietly, "*I remember all of it.*"

They'd never spoken of it, but she knew the day he meant. Unshed tears prickled the backs of her eyelids. But she did not cry. Did not move. She just dove into the dark pools of his intense eyes and remembered along with him.

She'd been sixteen, he eighteen. She'd harbored something like a crush on Bo long before that afternoon— something that made her giddy at times, but it was sweeter and lighter, tempered with innocence and bound up loosely with the ties of their enduring friendship. But after that day, no longer.

It was the one-year anniversary of her parents' deaths. She went to visit their graves and hadn't expected it to affect her quite as much as it did. Bo had patiently talked her through tears, and to cheer her up, he offered to take her out with him on one of the rumrunners late that afternoon. He was doing some spying on a man who operated a large whiskey still near the Magnussons' Marin County docks, across the Bay from the city. A stretch of coastal redwood forests sat between their property and the still, and Winter had been worried one of his truck drivers was sharing client lists with the still owner.

Astrid was usually kept in the dark about matters like these. When her parents were still alive, the word "bootlegging" was never spoken in the house. After they passed, Winter told Astrid enough to keep her safe, and Bo told her a little more—enough to pique her curiosity. But that afternoon was the first time Bo actually let her *see* things.

It was a spur-of-the-moment, grand adventure. She dressed in pants and sensible shoes, and they went hiking through the majestic old redwoods together, inhaling the clean perfume of the forest. It was a warm, sunny day, and they found a place on a hill to watch the man and his whiskey still. They ate cheese sandwiches and drank Coca-Cola. They sat together, leg against leg, and told stories. About her family. About his. The sun sank into the Pacific behind them, and sometime before dusk, she looked up at Bo's handsome face and something peculiar happened inside her chest.

It was as though, until that moment, her heart had been settled all wrong inside her ribs. And then everything shifted around—organs and muscles and bones and sinews, they all conspired together to make room.

And she hadn't been the same since.

"It doesn't matter," she said angrily, shaking away the old memory. "I'm independent now. I have college and Los Angeles, whether I like it or not."

"You could've gone to school here."

She shook her head. "I needed to know I could do it on my own, without you and Winter and everyone else watching over me and treating me like a china doll. If Mamma were alive, she'd tell me to be my own woman. 'Be bold,' she always told me."

"You're the most daring woman I know," Bo said.

"How come I don't feel that way?" Her voice cracked, and she swallowed hard to get the rest of the words out. "I messed up everything at school, Bo. Everything! You don't even know the half of it. And I . . . God! I was supposed to get over you. All my friends said I'd find someone new—that college would change my feelings."

After a long pause, he asked, "Did it?"

She didn't respond. Couldn't. The answer stuck in her throat.

"I told myself we'd grow apart, too," Bo said softly. "I wanted to believe we could. Because I can't keep hoping and wanting. It is killing me, Astrid. I've been a goddamn wreck since you've left, and now that you're back . . ."

They stood in the transitional space of the pantry, so

close. The dark dining room to one side, the bright kitchen on the other. And them in the middle, in the gray area between. Not dark nor light, not friends nor lovers, this *betweenness* wasn't stable. Crossroads never were. The two of them must choose to go forward or remain as they'd always been. And Astrid was all at once filled with a soaring hope, and yet utterly, numbingly terrified.

"I don't know what to do," she whispered, gripping the marble counter behind her as her fingers trembled. "What do we do?"

His whispered answer came seconds later along with the gentle swipe of his thumb across her cheek, where a stubborn tear was falling. "Let's—"

A clang made her jump. Bo pulled away. They both peered into the glaring light of the kitchen, where Greta stood in her nightdress, silver hair falling down her back. She was moving the noisy teakettle off the burner.

Astrid had never even heard it whistling.

Bo reluctantly left Astrid and Greta alone in the kitchen. Now that the house's resident nosey parker was up and about, he'd get no chance to finish his conversation with Astrid. And maybe that was just as well, because he'd almost gone too far. Been too greedy. Too weak. His pulse pounded like he'd been running up Lombard Street with a sack of bricks, and his head was spinning with possibilities. He prowled through the dark house with her words repeating in an endless loop.

What do we do?

He didn't know. At least, not what they should do. He certainly knew what he *wanted* to do, and that was what had crouched on his tongue, ready to springboard, when Greta had interrupted.

But was it the right thing? Or did he even care what was right anymore?

He just wasn't sure.

One thing he *did* know was that Astrid wasn't safe, and

that was something he could fix. Would fix. He jogged downstairs, but instead of turning right to head to his room, he took a left and stole into the community room. A black candlestick telephone stood on a table in the corner. He picked up the earpiece and waited for the operator to answer. Asked her to connect him to the Saint Francis admitting desk and prayed that a particular admissions-desk nurse he'd talked to the night of Astrid's hospital trip was working the same late shift. He knew her outside of work, vaguely. They'd crossed paths in a small speakeasy near the hospital once before. Her boyfriend was a second cousin of Hezekiah from Gris-Gris; sometimes he thought half the people in this town were related.

And as luck would have it, she was working tonight.

"Nurse Sue, this is Bo Yeung."

"Oh, hello, Bo," she said, cheerful and open. "What can I do for you?"

"It has to do with those survivors of that missing yacht. I was wondering if you could tell me whether they were still at the hospital."

"You and everyone else wants to know," she said in lower voice. "Reporters been calling here nonstop. But no, they were discharged a few hours after we spoke. Police chief allowed them to be transferred into Mrs. Cushing's care. The widow who was making a scene, you remember?"

"I do, indeed. Say, you wouldn't happen to have Mrs. Cushing's address on file, would you?"

Her voice fell to a whisper. "We're not supposed to give it out, but I can probably get back into records after my shift. Won't be until after nine A.M., though."

"Would you? I'd owe you an awfully big favor."

"I like the sound of that," she teased. "Oh, I just remembered something. My coworker told me that she had someone come by earlier today and ask about Miss Magnusson. Wanted to know her name."

"Oh really? Who was this person?"

"The man didn't say. But don't worry, she wasn't stupid enough to give out your address." It didn't really matter;

the entire city knew where to find the Magnussons and therefore Bo.

"Please let me know if anyone else asks about Miss Magnusson. And in the meantime, if you can get your hands on Mrs. Cushing's address, leave me a message at Pier 26, no matter the hour. And I'll be happy to have someone drop off a little thank-you gift for your effort."

"I *am* rather fond of gin . . ."

"Your wish is my command, Nurse Sue. Consider it done."

TEN

———————

IT TOOK A LONG TIME FOR ASTRID TO FALL ASLEEP THAT NIGHT.
The potent combination of Greta's poorly timed interruption and Velma's herbal tea were enough to give any sane person nightmares, and after she'd left the kitchen, Astrid had lain wide awake in bed, replaying every moment in the pantry with Bo.

The things he said. How close he'd been. The way he made her feel, all raw and jumbled up. Anxious. Out of control.

Let's—

Let's what? Let's throw caution to the wind and run away together? Let's end this all now? Let's cool down and discuss this later?

When it came to Bo, she'd done her share of hoping that he might share her feelings—every day, for weeks and months and years. But before last night, she had hoped in a blind sort of way, taking whatever crumbs Bo dropped and fashioning them into some sort of shaky shelter that only partially kept out the bad weather. Now he'd given her more than crumbs. He'd handed over a few pieces of lumber, and her former lean-to was now transformed into a shack: still leaky, but a strong gust of wind might not instantly blow it over.

She'd fallen asleep beneath that shelter, wanting him more than ever. And more fearful that if it *did* fall, she'd be crushed under the weight of it.

No sense in being so nervous, she told herself the next morning. It was only Bo. No matter what happened between them, they were friends, and they would handle it with grace and good humor. Everything was fixable.

And today Astrid aimed to fix two problems at once.

After bathing and dressing, she took the birdcage elevator down and found the house abuzz with good cheer. In the foyer, Greta stood on a tall ladder surrounded with giggling maids who were helping to put up Christmas greenery. And even though everyone had already eaten breakfast—except Aida, who was still pale, still possibly pregnant, still trying to hide it from Winter—Astrid was happy to dine alone, and gulped down strong coffee with a slice of rye toast and a soft-boiled egg. Then she went hunting.

Bo was not on the main floor. And Winter, who carried baby Karin around the foyer to witness the hubbub of the holiday decorating, informed Astrid that his captain hadn't yet left for work.

"Think he's going in later, after a couple of errands," Winter said.

Excellent. Even better, Bo hadn't seemed to have informed her brother about their bad night at Gris-Gris. While Winter bounced his smiling daughter in the crook of his big arm, Astrid slipped away and took the servants' staircase downstairs.

Halfway down, she came to an abrupt stop. She'd nearly plowed straight into Bo.

Her heart pinged.

"Good morning," she said, slightly breathless and nervous. Her gaze flitted over a striking lapis blue suit, expertly tailored to hug lean muscle, with a crisp white collar and cuffs peeking out from the jacket. "Don't believe I've seen that suit before."

"You know me. Vain and frivolous." A lie. Proud and confident was more like it. His gaze flicked to her wristwatch for a moment—*ping!* went her heart again—and then he smiled up at her like everything was normal, and they hadn't done all that confessing in the butler's pantry. Like she hadn't cried in front of him.

All right. Fine. She could act normal. She pasted on a smile.

He scratched the back of his neck.

She shifted her feet and brushed invisible lint off the front of her dress.

"How are you feeling?" he asked. "Did you drink the tea after Greta—"

"Booted you out?" she supplied.

He leaned a shoulder against the stairwell wall. "She probably fantasizes about cracking a whip at my feet while I retreat down here in the dungeon. She'd put bars on my door if she could."

"*Your* door? After you left, she practically accused me of being a manipulative hussy." Astrid did her best Greta imitation, shaking a finger. "Stop bothering that boy, *flicka*. You should be in bed right now. What is this strange tea? You cannot drink this! Velma Toussaint is bride of devil!"

Bo laughed. The low, velvety sound surrounded her like an embrace and sent flutters through her stomach. "Everyone is 'bride of devil' to Greta. Was the tea awful?"

"I got it down by holding my nose. I thought it might make me sick, but I actually think I might feel better today. I wonder if my aura has cleared up."

He squinted and skimmed a finger around her head and shoulder, a phantom touch that never made contact with her, but she felt it nonetheless. "I'm seeing . . . a golden sort of light. Oh wait, that's just wattage from the bulb above you."

Playful. But was that Bo's normal lighthearted playfulness, or something more? He withdrew his hand and stuck it in his pocket, giving her no insight into his feelings. She wanted to scream out: *What were you going to tell me last night, huh? For the love of Pete, what was it?* But doubt made her hesitate.

More awkwardness stretched between them.

When she couldn't take it anymore, she finally said, "Speaking of strange phenomena . . ."

"Yes?" He settled one polished shoe on the step next to hers. Very close. This made her so jittery, she almost forgot what she was going to say.

"I thought of someone who might be able to tell us something about that idol," she finally managed to get out.

His brow lowered. "I don't like the sound of that. Is this one of your schemes?"

"I don't scheme."

"You're a Magnusson. You're all schemers."

That was . . . absolutely true.

"It's nothing risky," she promised. "I'm talking about legitimate academic help. As in, my sister-in-law."

"Hadley?" His eyes scrunched up momentarily and then relaxed. "Actually, that's not a bad idea. She might be able to shed some light on its origins. Either her or Lowe."

They both looked at each other and agreed in chorus, "Hadley."

Besides, Astrid needed her sister-in-law for more than just her ancient history expertise, but she couldn't tell Bo this.

"I have a little free time this morning before I have to head in to the warehouse," he said. "Depends on the flooding, of course, but we could see if we could make it to Hadley. If you're game."

"Oh, I'm game," she said a little too enthusiastically, and cleared her throat. "I'm free, too. My datebook is completely clear this morning."

"No dancing penciled in?"

"None whatsoever," she said. "Will we will be riding in the oh-so-lovely *Sylvia*?"

The corner of his mouth twisted. "Not letting that one go, either, are you?"

"Nope."

"Fair enough. When can you be ready to go?"

It turned out Hadley was not working at the de Young Museum that day, but was instead assisting her husband, Astrid's brother Lowe, at a lecture in a nearby neighborhood that overlooked Golden Gate Park. As long as Astrid got to speak to her in private, she didn't care where they met.

Parnassus Avenue was home to the Affiliated Colleges of the University of California. Driving toward the ocean, Bo and Astrid passed the Romanesque stone facade of the College of Medicine and stopped at building with a large totem pole standing near the front steps: the university's Anthropology annex.

The inside of the building was rather dim and smelled of old stone and dust. No one was there to greet visitors, so they walked around mostly deserted rooms filled with bits of pottery and rusting ancient tools until they found someone who pointed them to the second floor. In a corner room that housed a small Egyptian collection, Astrid heard her brother's cocky voice and peeked inside the open door.

"And *that*, my dear people, is how you defend a dig site from wild dogs."

A ripple of mumbling went through the students attending the class, which was nothing more than a couple dozen wooden chairs lined up in front of a lectern and a rolling chalkboard filled with scribbled drawings and hieroglyphs. Locked cases of broken artifacts sat along the outer walls, as well as a table filled with labeled teaching replicas of Middle Kingdom pottery.

Lording over all of this was Lowe. Several years younger than Winter, he was handsome and dashing and, like Astrid, he shared their mother's blond hair. He was educated, well traveled, and his absurd stories were the stuff of legends.

A student raised his hand. "Will this be on the test next week, Mr. Magnusson?"

"Absolutely," Lowe said, switching off the small light above his notes. "Don't study anything in chapter eight about field methods. That would be a complete waste of your time."

"But—"

Lowe gestured toward the tall, dark-haired woman standing next to him, dressed in black and strikingly attractive, if not intimidating. "And I only brought Mrs. Bacall out here for you to ogle. Disregard everything she told you about Egyptian funerary customs. Sure, she may very well be the most knowledgeable curator on this subject in the entire state, and yes, she holds a Stanford degree *and* a directorship at one of the most prestigious museums in the city, but you are paying gobs of cash to the university for more important matters, like drinking bathtub gin and getting rejected at petting parties."

Soft chuckling followed. The students packed up their things and began shuffling out the door. Astrid moved aside and waited for everyone to leave. Her eyes surreptitiously tracked Bo, who was strolling down the hall and studying photographs that crammed the walls. When the last student exited, he looped around and met up with her, and they headed inside the classroom . . . only to stop short.

Astrid couldn't tell who was the instigator, but Lowe was either pressing Hadley against the chalkboard or Hadley was pulling him against her. Either way, they had their hands all over each other in the least professional way possible.

Nothing like catching your brother with his tongue down his wife's throat.

Astrid was simultaneously unsettled to see them act like randy animals and transfixed by their enthusiasm. She was also a little envious. Lowe said something that made Hadley laugh—a sound more intimate than Lowe's hand, which was most certainly heading to cup Hadley's breast.

And as she watched this unfolding, Astrid was acutely aware of Bo's presence. She wondered what he was thinking. She wondered if he ever thought about putting his hands on Astrid like that.

She certainly had.

She chanced a quick look at Bo's face and found his eyes titled toward hers. She looked away. Heat washed over her cheeks. Bo cleared his throat loudly.

Lowe and Hadley stopped but didn't break apart. Hadley's eyes just peered around Lowe's shoulder, and when she spotted Astrid and Bo, the rest of her face followed.

"The youngest Magnusson has returned to the fold," the black-haired curator said with a warm smile and slid away from Lowe. Astrid strode forward to meet her, eager to get away from Bo and her wild feelings.

"I missed you," Astrid said, hugging Hadley's slender frame.

"And not your own flesh and blood?" Lowe asked. "I'm wounded."

Astrid hugged him, too, clinging a little longer. When their parents died, Lowe seemed to handle everything better. He had Egypt and his friends. He didn't have Winter's burden of being the driver in the accident—or the obligation to take over Pappa's businesses, both legal and illegal. Lowe was the freest of the family, and Astrid always admired that. She longed for his easygoing nature and optimism. His good humor. She'd spent the last few years wishing he wasn't so far away, always trotting off to exotic locations. When he'd settled down with Hadley and Stella, she'd hoped she'd have a little more of him more often, but then she was the one running off to college.

"Hey," he murmured in a reassuring voice, pulling her back to study her face. "Glad to see you, too, baby sister. You look older and wiser. Far too pretty. I thought it had only been a few months. What happened to the towheaded yapper I gave piggyback rides?"

"Funny how getting older works, isn't it?" she said with a smile.

"Ruins all of us," he agreed, and reached beyond her to give Bo a hearty slap on the shoulder. "How's the warehouse, Bo?"

"Still standing and sandbagged deep enough to keep out Poseidon, at least for now. Stella okay?"

"High and dry on Telegraph Hill with her nanny. She's a little sad about the rain chasing all the parrots away, but we've assured her they'll come back and that Number Five hasn't eaten them."

Number Five was Hadley's lucky, death-proof black cat. He used to be Number Four until this past summer; whatever happened, they didn't speak of it.

After small talk about their upcoming trip to Egypt (Bo was right about; Hadley practically glowed at the mention of it), the subject of the idol was raised. Astrid and Bo quickly told the story of the yacht once more. Lowe's concern over Astrid's well-being lessened when she told him about Velma's tea—and then was temporarily forgotten when Bo brought out the polished turquoise figurine for their inspection.

"We think it's solid turquoise," Bo explained. "But we don't know where it came from or what it's for."

Lowe whistled.

"Fascinating," Hadley agreed. "I felt the vibration of it when you walked in."

Lowe slowly lifted his hand away. "What kind of vibration?"

"Velma didn't feel any magic," Astrid argued.

Her sister-in-law shook her head. "Not magic, exactly. Just some sort of energy."

Hadley's ability to feel strange energies stemmed from something bigger. Hadley's mother, a former archaeologist, had contracted a dark Egyptian curse that she passed along to Hadley. Mori specters—*Sheuts*. Shadowy hounds of hell that materialized when Hadley became upset. Few could see them, apparently. Lowe couldn't, but he claimed Hadley's specters had nearly killed him "a hundred times"—which was, of course, an exaggeration, like everything else out of her brother's mouth. Even it were partially true, he likely deserved whatever he got, and it certainly hadn't deterred him from marrying Hadley . . . or keeping his hands off of her in public places.

Hadley now lifted her head and squinted at Astrid. "Huh."

"What?"

"Now that I'm listening for it, I think perhaps the energy is coming from you—not the idol."

"Rats!" Astrid said. "Can you see a shadow on my aura?"

"I don't see auras," she said. "Ask Aida."

"I already did. She only sees ghosts."

"We like our women bizarre and dangerous, eh, Bo?" Lowe mumbled.

Bo stilled. Just for a moment. No one seemed to notice but Astrid. And Lowe was already muttering something else about ancient turquoise mines in California and Mexico. But all Astrid could think was: did Lowe know something about Bo's feelings toward her? She remembered Bo's letter this fall that made her so angry: *Teachers should not be staying in hotels with students. Lowe, being a professor himself, agrees with me.*

Or maybe she was being irrational. Lowe might be making small talk.

But then, why would Bo react like that?

Like *that*, and like this, now, which was to ask a question instead of answering Lowe. "Can you identify what sort of culture the idol comes from?"

"Aztec, I'd say. And it looks genuine. Hadley?"

"Aztec," she confirmed. "Not solid turquoise. It's a mosaic. Small chips of turquoise carefully fitted together and polished."

"Really? I thought it was just cracked," Bo said. "Except on the back, see?"

"Yes, now *that* is a solid piece," Hadley said. "Someone has altered the engraving. What a shame."

Lowe carried it to a nearby table. They all crowded behind him as he sat down and studied it more carefully under magnification. "The gold inlay on the eyes and the disk is real, though it looks odd. Times like this, I wish Adam was still around," he mumbled. His best friend, and Stella's father. Adam died almost a year ago.

Hadley squeezed his shoulder. He patted her hand. And Astrid was once again envious of their bond. She glanced at Bo, but quickly lowered her eyes when she found him already looking at her. *Stars*, there were too many emotions floating around. Or maybe she was overly sensitive. She did her best to brush it all aside and concentrate on the idol.

"Definitely altered," Lowe said when he looked closer. "The flat space has been chiseled down and the word 'NANCE' engraved with modern tools. I can see traces of another engraving beneath it. Another word, perhaps. But it's too fragmented to be able to tell what it was."

"Is it a replica?" Astrid asked.

"Your brother would know nothing at all about treasure forgery," Hadley said with heavy sarcasm.

Lowe let out a nervous laugh and scratched his chin. "Yes, well. That's all in the past. Much like this idol, which seems to be genuine, if I had to guess."

"My straight-and-narrow husband is correct. It does appear to be authentic," Hadley said, giving Lowe the barest of smiles.

"And now the million-dollar question," Bo said. "What purpose does it serve?"

Lowe sat back in his chair and crossed his arms over his chest. "Hell if I know. It's not fertility, and I have no idea about this symbol on the front. I know turquoise was prized by the Aztecs and often used in ritual items. They traded with the Pueblo people, who mined it in the Southwest states. But beyond that, I've got no clue."

Astrid and Bo looked at Hadley. "Hate to say it, but I

don't know, either. This isn't inside our wheelhouse. I can identify some of the major Aztec gods, like Quetzalcoatl, the feathered serpent, for example. But this—"

Bo stopped her. "Hold on a second. Did you say feathered serpent? Would that be the same as a plumed serpent?"

"Why, yes."

Bo looked at Astrid. "The yacht's name. That's a mighty big coincidence."

"Too big. I'd wager that yacht owner, Mrs. Cushing, knows something about the ritual," Astrid said. "What in heaven's name is going on?"

"Whatever it is, stay out of it," Lowe said, handing Bo the idol back. "I'm speaking from experience. Tell them, Hadley."

She nodded. "It's true. You should probably just put this back where you found it. But, in the meantime, if you want to find out more about the symbolism and design—"

Lowe sighed heavily.

Hadley ignored him. "—then the person in town you need to talk to is Dr. Maria Navarro."

"Ah yes. One half of the Wicked Wenches," Lowe said and gave Hadley an innocent look. "What? They love that moniker."

Hadley ignored him. "Both Dr. Navarro and her colleague, Miss King, are experts on Aztec and Mayan culture. Retired anthropologists and friends of my father. Have written several books together."

"How do we get in touch with these anthropologists?" Bo asked.

Hadley smiled. "I can contact Dr. Navarro and see if they'd be willing to meet with you."

"As soon as possible," Bo said, and then smiled back. "If you don't mind."

After lodging his arguments against pursuing more information on the idol, Lowe began probing Bo for mechanical advice about his motorcycle engine. That was Astrid's chance to speak to Hadley alone, and she took it, urging her aside for a private conversation.

Hadley was the single most intelligent woman Astrid knew. The most educated and influential. Hadley was also very rational and had on a couple of occasions backed Astrid's pleas for independence when the rest of the family was busy telling her "no." The two of them weren't what Astrid would call close. Astrid felt a stronger emotional sisterly bond to Aida. But Astrid needed someone who wouldn't let emotions color her advice. Someone who treated Astrid fairly and logically.

Someone who could be trusted not to blab to Winter.

"So," Hadley said, crossing her arms over her chest. "I got your telegram, obviously, and you got mine."

"Thank you for helping me."

"Don't thank me yet. I'm not sure what I can do to help." She pulled out an envelope from the pocket of her skirt and unfolded the letter inside. "The university seems to have successfully changed your address to my office at the museum, so you're safe from Winter finding out. At least for the time being. I received this two days ago."

Astrid scanned the letter. It was a very cold, matter-of-fact letter from the president's office, explaining that she was now on academic probation due to her poor grades and attendance, and if she failed to improve next semester, she would be dismissed from the university. She would also need to meet with an academic counselor to discuss—

"What does this last part mean?" she whispered.

"It means they don't think you have a specific degree in mind, and though they'd like to keep taking your family's money, they have a reputation to uphold."

"They know we're bootleggers?"

"Most likely. Berkeley knows. That didn't stop them from allowing Lowe to attend—or from hiring him, for that matter. But Lowe is an excellent teacher with field experience. And when he was your age, he was an excellent student and graduated with honors."

"Unlike me. You're saying this is my fault for being a dud,

not my family's reputation." Astrid groaned and folded up the letter. "My mother is probably rolling over in her grave right now with disappointment. Please don't tell anyone, Hadley. Not until I figure out how to handle it, all right?"

Hadley sighed heavily. "Want to tell me what happened?"

"I don't know," Astrid said, massaging her palm with one thumb. "I went down there to prove myself. I wanted to do it without Winter's help or Lowe's influence at Berkeley. I just wanted to do something on my own."

"There's nothing wrong with that. Very noble, I'd say."

"Oh sure. Noble. Failing every class really proved my independence."

"You certainly aren't simpleminded, Astrid. But you have to attend class to learn."

"I know. I just . . ." She stared at her hands and let the words spill out. "I hate it there. I hate the city. Hate the school. I don't know what I'm doing there—don't know why I'm even going. Everyone around me seems to know what they're good at. You and Lowe have Egypt, and Winter and Bo have the businesses. My dormitory mate, Jane, wants to be a teacher. I don't know what I'm good at. All my female friends are either engaged, married, or working until they find someone to marry. And everyone at college wants a career. But me? I just feel like my life is spiraling out of control."

Hadley pulled Astrid's chin up with two fingers. "It is not, I promise you. It only feels that way. Perhaps the southern campus is not for you. And marriage isn't something one does with their life."

Easy for her to say. No laws prevented her from being with Lowe. But Astrid didn't say this. They weren't *that* close.

"Don't misunderstand me," Hadley said. "Marriage is a beautiful, wonderful thing, when done for the right reason, but it's not a substitute for finding your place in this world. You are brimming with possibility. You just need to figure out what it is you want to do. That won't happen overnight."

"What if it never happens?"

"Think about it over the holidays. If you want to meet with me at the museum, my door is open. Easier to sit down and talk about it when"—she nodded toward the boys—"no one's listening. But one more thing I have to ask. Have you ever thought about asking Aida to channel your mother? You mentioned that she would be disappointed in you, but I doubt that's true. And you have a rare opportunity to find out."

Astrid stuffed the university letter in her coat pocket. "I don't know. Aida's offered to do that for all of us, but it might be . . . strange. Greta says the dead should stay that way, and maybe the old battle-ax is right."

Hadley gave her a soft smile. "Maybe she is."

ELEVEN

BO SNEAKED A GLANCE AT ASTRID WHEN HE WAS WAITING TO
pull out of the Anthropology annex parking lot. She was
upset, but he couldn't figure out why. Only that she'd been
distressed when she was speaking privately with Hadley . . . and that she'd been speaking privately with Hadley.
Since when had the two of them become confidantes?
Though he'd come to know and appreciate Hadley's cool
demeanor—which was not as cool as she wanted you to
believe—he couldn't for the life of him think what the two
of them were discussing.

"Planning on following in your brother's footsteps and
digging up mummies?"

"What's that?"

"You and Hadley."

"Oh no. That was nothing."

"The same kind of nothing that is bothering you now?"

She nodded and stared out the window.

After several blocks of silence, he said, "You used to
talk to me about those things."

"Yes, well, everything I do or say is likely to be reported to Lowe or Winter, so . . ."

"That's not true. I didn't tell Winter about Gris-Gris last night. And I damn well should have, because a man attacked you, and what would you have done if I hadn't been there?"

"He didn't have a weapon."

"So he couldn't have possibly hurt you."

"Magnussons don't cower. That's what Pappa always told me."

"Cower, no. But chucking caution out the window is just plain stupid. I don't want you going out alone in the city until we find out who the hell Max is and what he wants. It's not safe."

Anger tightened her eyes. "Since when did you become the boss of me?"

"Since when did you stop caring about my opinion?"

Sulking, she turned her head and ran a gloved finger over her fogged-up window. After a long moment she said, "We never finished our conversation last night."

Yes, he knew. He hadn't forgotten for even a moment. "Mm."

"Is Sylvia your girlfriend?" she asked calmly.

"I already told you. She's just a friend."

"Have you slept with her?"

He paused too long. He knew it, and yet . . . he didn't know what to say. She'd never asked him anything so personal.

He slowed at a stop sign and turned the corner. The flooding was worse here, so he drove in the middle of the road to avoid pools of water. "I shouldn't have brought her to Gris-Gris. I was . . . I don't know. There was the wristwatch, but then you were going dancing, and I was confused. You always confuse me."

"You always confuse *me*."

He slanted a glance toward her face and restrained a smile. "Which came first, the chicken or the egg?"

"That depends," she said, adjusting the fit of her glove. "Am I the chicken or egg?"

"I think maybe we're both chickens."

She snorted a little laugh and relaxed against the seat. "You might be right."

Neither of them said anything else until he pulled into the Magnussons' driveway. He put the car in idle and they both stared ahead.

"I guess I better be heading to work now." He considered telling her that the nurse at the hospital had given him Mrs. Cushing's address, but she'd want to accompany him if he admitted that he was heading over there to see what he could find out. The protective part of him worried that it wasn't safe for her to be seen there. So he said nothing.

"Bo?"

"Yes?"

"Let's what?"

"Pardon?"

"Last night you started to say something to me. You said 'Let's,' and then Greta . . ."

The screen door on the side porch slammed. Winter was heading toward the car—probably wanting a ride to the warehouse. Bo cursed the big man's timing.

"Never mind," Astrid said glumly.

"Wait." Bo grabbed her arm as she reached for the door handle. "Let's pretend we're other people. That's what I was going to say."

She stared at him for a long moment, lips parted, cheeks stained pink. His wildly beating heart felt as if it were trying to outpace the quick rise and fall of her chest. And as Winter strolled around the front of the car, she slid her hand over his for a fleeting, impossibly brief moment (soft skin, slender fingers, gentle squeeze).

It was the smallest thing.

It was everything.

Permission.

Bo squeezed her hand in reply, and then she let go and

exited in a whirl of flowing coat and skirt. The last things he saw were the delicate lines that ran down the backs of her stockings.

Mrs. Cushing lived in a grand sandstone-faced manor overlooking the Presidio. An hour after dropping off Astrid, Bo stared up at the manor from his car and knew he had no chance of getting inside. An ornate iron fence and sculpted bushes blocked most of the home's entrance from the street, and standing guard at the gate beneath a gated portico were two bulky men.

Were the guards just to keep reporters at bay? Bo didn't know. He also didn't see any automobiles. No license plate numbers to trace. No sign of anyone at all, except for the guards.

And yet.

One of those guards looked familiar. Bo pulled up to the gate and rolled down his window. "Little Mike?"

A tall, bald man leaned down and squinted into the car. "I'll be damned. Bo Yeung," he said with a wide smile. "What you doin' down here, son?"

"Looking for someone. Thought you were working at Izzy Gomez's speakeasy?"

"Still there. This is just a part-time job. Getting paid well to stand in the rain for five hours and tell reporters to hit the road. You here about the boat that was lost at sea? Heard it crashed into your pier."

"That it did. The owner of the boat, Mrs. Cushing—she employ the two of you?"

"Supposedly, but we've never met her. Fella by the name of Dan hired all of us. Her houseboy, from the looks of him. He tells us where to show up, pays us under the table."

"Ever see a man around here named Max?" Bo asked.

"Is that one of them boat survivors?"

Bo described Max, and the guard's eyebrows shot up.

"Yeah, that could be one of them, but his name isn't Max—it's Kit Manson. Deadbeat gambler who used to stir up trouble at Izzy Gomez's. Had a dope habit. Heroin, I think. Last time I saw him was more than a year ago, but when they brought the survivors in here, I could've sworn it was him. Tried to say something to him, but he didn't remember me. Either it's his twin brother, or whatever happened to them at sea really messed up his mind."

"You don't say," Bo muttered. "Been a year since you seen this Kit Manson fellow . . . You remember where he lived?"

"He didn't have a permanent place. Whatever board-inghouse or room for rent he could find that would take him until he stopped paying. Last time I saw him, he said he got an invitation to a secret club in Jackson Square. Said it was going to change his life, make him rich."

"Jackson Square?" That part of town used to be the red-light district—the infamous Barbary Coast. Gambling, whoring, drinking, dancing. Whatever your vice, the Barbary Coast had it for sale, once upon a time. "That whole area has been a ghost town since Prohibition started and the police cracked down on it."

"That's why I didn't pay much attention to Kit when he said it. He was a dope fiend. He could've dreamed it all up. When he disappeared, we thought he'd finally over-dosed, if you want to know the truth."

"Did he say anything else about it? Where this secret club was?"

"Not really. Oh! He said the club was called Pieces of Eight, or some fool thing like that. Never could tell with Kit. He wasn't always present up here," the big man said, tapping his temple.

Pieces of Eight? Bo didn't know what any of this meant, but it reminded him of a book he owned, sitting on the top shelf in his room: *Treasure Island*. Pirates and cursed Aztec gold. Astrid's Aztec turquoise idol had golden eyes. And if it really was that Max fellow hanging around there, Bo wondered if this was the connection they hadn't been able to fit together—rich widow, strange occult rituals, missing people . . .

He couldn't wait to tell Astrid.

Do not think of her hand on yours. Focus.

Bo tried to pry more information out of the guard, but that was everything the man knew, so he finally asked, "So you never see any of the other boat survivors around here, either hanging around the house or coming and going?"

Little Mike tilted his head toward the other guard. "Jack says he heard from another hired man that they all left last night after dark."

That surprised Bo. "Where did they go?"

"No idea. Dan might. Whether he'll tell you is another story. He's pretty tight-lipped. We aren't allowed in the house, but I can knock on the servants' entrance, ask if he'll come out and talk."

That sounded like a terrible idea. He didn't want Mrs. Cushing to know he'd been snooping around, so he politely declined Little Mike's offer. "I'd rather you never mention I was here. If anyone asks, I was just some hayseed who got turned around, looking for directions into the Presidio, yeah?"

"You got it, Bo." The big man tipped his cap and gave him a smile. "You say jump, half the city asks how high."

The next day, Bo left early to have a look around Jackson Square. Not much to see but several closed-up old dance halls and a few beggars. Two of the dance halls still operated, the Hippodrome and Babel's Tower, but they were dives, constantly being raided. Not playlands for the wealthy. He wasn't sure what he was even looking for—something that looked amiss, maybe. Or a place that didn't look like it was ten years past its prime. But nothing caught his eye, and after he sat in his car, observing the half-flooded streets from afar for a couple of hours, he gave up and went back home to Pacific Heights.

He had plans.

After searching the Queen Anne, he found Astrid in the top of the turret, curled up on the cushioned window seat that housed their secret hiding place, reading a local fashion magazine. And though he knew she must hear him approaching—no one ever came up here except the two of them and the occasional maid—she turned the magazine's pages faster and faster, preening the soft blond waves that were molded against her head and styled back behind her ears, until she could pretend no longer and blinked up at him with those almond-shaped blue eyes of hers.

"Oh, hello," she said.

"Didn't mean to interrupt your literary time."

Her expression shifted to comically feigned reproach as she snapped the magazine shut. "I looked for you this morning at breakfast, but Greta said you took off at dawn. Thought maybe you regretted what you said yesterday."

"Not one bit," Bo said, crossing his arms over his chest as he stepped closer and peered down at her. "Do you? Regret it, that is."

"Not one bit," she repeated. She was dressed in aquamarine today. Long strands of faceted beryl beads hung between softly swelling breasts. *Do not linger here,* he warned himself. He checked her wrist—he just couldn't help himself—and was rewarded with the flash of silver he yearned to see.

Permission.

"What would you say to spending a couple of hours in a jungle?" he asked.

"A jungle?"

He nodded, waiting for her to catch on. "You've been cooped up in here for too long. If we can't enjoy this cheery drizzle outside, we can . . . *pretend* we're outside in a tropical garden."

A slow grin spread across her face. "Golden Gate Park. Wait, what if it's flooded? Hadley said the lake was."

"I telephoned. It's open. And 'deader than a doornail,' according to the woman who answered. What do you say? I'll tell you all about what I was doing this morning on the way over there." He waggled his brows, and said in a low voice, "It involves a pirate club."

Now he had her. She rose to her feet and stood inches away from him. For a moment, his brain went loopy, and he considered pulling her up against him and kissing the daylights out of her. Distant muffled chatter from the floor below them reminded him that this might not be the wisest of plans.

"Take me to the jungle," she said in a soft, throaty voice, and his heart roared with excitement.

TWELVE

———⚜———

SITTING ATOP A HILL STUDDED WITH PALMS, THE DOMED CON-servatory of Flowers was a great, frilly skeleton of white wood and glass. When Bo was younger, and had just started making deliveries for Winter—deliveries that took him into new parts of the city he'd never seen—he'd thought the Victorian-era building looked like an enormous wedding cake. Today it looked decidedly less festive, streaked with rain and bereft of visitors, but just as inviting as ever. Especially with Astrid on his arm.

He huddled under an umbrella with her as they sloshed from their parking space, traipsing past manicured lawns puddling with water. Fields of pansies were flooded, and a display of flowers on the face of a hill that had once been carefully groomed to spell out MERRY CHRISTMAS 1928 now looked like a drowned rat with a head cold.

None of that mattered, though. Because inside the gabled entry it was dry and warm, and the bored docent at the ticket desk who may or may not have discreetly turned Bo away on a busier day didn't even give him a second look. She only momentarily came to life when Bo plopped down a bill five times the entry fee and told her to keep the change. They were given a printed brochure describing the exhibits, and then forgotten. And upon stepping inside the main gallery, Bo quickly realized:

They were the only visitors.

And they were completely alone.

In public.

Buddha, Osiris, and Jehovah were all smiling down upon him.

"Ooaf," Astrid said, peeling off her damp coat in the steamy heat that dripped water onto ferns and primeval jungle plants. "I forgot how warm it is in here. Feels marvelous. And it's so beautiful. I don't know what to look at first. Can you imagine living in a world like this? I can practically imagine dinosaurs hiding behind that . . . whats-a-doodle. Oh, the sign says 'philodendron.' Fifty years old! How marvelous . . ."

Bo couldn't hold back his smile. For maybe the first time since she'd come home, Astrid was spilling words faster than she could think. She was radiant, head tilting this way and that as her gaze scanned the thousands of glass panels circling the conservatory's dome above and the lush tropical foliage below.

She was happy.

And in Bo's proud mind, he gave all of this to her—him, Yeung Bo-Sing. It didn't belong to the city; it was his. His to share with her. To provide escape from the all the nastiness of the turquoise idol and the gruesome visions, all the anguish and uncertainty they'd faced in reuniting. All the long months they'd spent apart.

It all just lifted away with the tropical steam.

"What's the plan?" Astrid said, running her hand over a fern frond.

"Plan?"

"Well, you said no more talking about the idol and the survivors and the pirate club once we got here. You said it was an adventure, and you said yesterday we should pretend we're other people, so we must be playing roles. The real Bo would never ask me out on a date."

She had that wrong. The real him *would*. The real him would have already married her and whisked her off on a yearlong honeymoon around the world. Society and circumstance did not allow him to be himself.

"Let's see. If we didn't already know each other, how would we have met? I think it must have been at Gris-Gris," Astrid said, deciding upon their story. "You were staring at me dancing. I was so enchanting, you couldn't take your eyes off of me."

Bo strolled next to her, his coat over one arm. "That's true enough. It was your smile that did it. I knew you were a girl who liked adventure when I saw that smile." It was an unruly, disruptive kind of smile, and was the entrance to Astrid's unruly and disruptive mouth, which had a way of saying whatever flitted through her brain without filter. And Bo liked this quite a bit.

"My smile, huh?" she said.

"And your hips."

"What about my hips?" she said defensively, moving her coat to cover herself. "You know I hate them."

"Too bad, because I don't. They are so shapely, I was instantly magnetized. And that's why I had to meet you when I saw you at Gris-Gris. Smile and hips, a one-two combination."

"Shapely," she said, like it was ridiculous, but blue eyes slid toward his, and Bo did not miss the delight hiding beneath their surface.

"Like a professional dancer's," he assured her. "But what would a beauty like you see in someone like me?"

"The most dashing, handsome bootlegger in the entire city?"

"Well, when you put it *that* way . . ."

"But it was your wicked tongue that did me in. You made me laugh, and you didn't give a damn what anyone thought."

"Is that right?"

"Maybe it's my Viking blood. Mamma used to say she fell for Pappa because he never hesitated to take what he wanted, and if a mountain got in his way, he wouldn't just walk around it—he'd move it."

Bo had spent a good bit of time with the Magnussons' father before he died. He knew the old Swede had balls of steel to build the bootlegging empire he'd passed along to Winter, but the last couple of years, the man had struggled with a mental illness that greatly affected his moods and decisions. Bo didn't say this to Astrid, though. She'd been through enough. Let her keep that image of her father. It was a good one.

"So that's why you agreed to let me call on you," Bo said, leaning against a wooden railing along the conservatory path, where Astrid had stopped to read an iron plaque that marked an old tree.

She nodded. "Because the world is filled with boring people, but you are not one of them. I knew right away you were the kind of man who'd move mountains," she said, giving him a confident, firm nod of her chin.

And it struck him then: they were both being truthful. This wasn't playacting. It was truth in the guise of a story. He *had* first been attracted to her smile. She really did think he could move mountains.

Could he?

"Anyway, we saw each other in Gris-Gris, and you marched in like a knight and drove away an unwanted suitor who was pestering me. That's how we met. How could I resist when you asked for my telephone number?"

"You had no chance, really," Bo said. "I was more dashing than Douglas Fairbanks."

"And you look even better than he did without a shirt in *The Thief of Bagdad*."

"Oh really?" Slowly Bo turned his head to find her staring intently into the tropical flora.

"Those arms, whew!" she whistled. "It's going to be hard to pretend I haven't seen those already, but I'm willing to try."

He could practically feel his ego doubling in size. Something a little farther south would be joining in if he didn't get control of his racing feelings. "I've seen some things I can't forget, either. Like that afternoon last year in the dressing room at the department store."

Five seconds of time Bo mentally had dubbed the Fitting Room Incident, which occurred after driving Astrid to one of her weekly shopping excursions. One moment he'd been waiting with her seamstress, Benita, while she tried on clothes, the next he'd looked up to see her stepping outside the dressing screen without a stich on.

"That was an accident!" she whispered, face turning a pretty shade of pink.

She'd argued that a thousand times, but part of Bo had never believed this. Either way, it had been a gift—one he'd never forgotten.

Astrid quickly looked around behind them before sauntering down the path. "Oh, look. Here's the Highland Tropics gallery. Let's go inside."

He followed her swaying, shapely hips through the door and felt the temperature drop as they entered a misty gallery that housed plants from higher elevations. He doffed his cap to an elderly lady sitting on a bench. Her small dog stretched its leash and yapped at him as he passed. No longer alone. That was disappointing, to say the least. But Bo's hope soared again when he heard Astrid mumbling that it was too cold in this room. They sailed down a long stone walkway that led to the last gallery on this side of the conservatory, the Aquatic Plants room.

Higher, humid temperature. Completed deserted.

The door swung shut on the dog's high-pitched yaps.

The rain that drummed a gentle rhythm against the conservatory's glass was reflected in a curving pool of water, the surface of which was covered in giant lily pads from the Amazon River.

"The lily pads grow to six feet across and can support the weight of a small child," Astrid remarked as she sat along a low wall that hugged the indoor pond and set her folded coat down beside her. "I wonder if anyone's tested that."

Bo sat next to her and peered over the edge. "Would you like to try?"

"You'd really like to see me sink, wouldn't you?"

"Would I get to see you naked again?"

"You might see something new. I daresay some parts of me are much nicer than they were a year ago."

"Believe me, I've noticed."

Her eyes glittered as she pulled off her gloves and reached over the water to skim the raised, scalloped edge of a giant lily pad and encouraged Bo to do the same. It was strong, but they both decided that she would, indeed, sink. "So, Mr. Yeung, since we're on this fine date, I think you should tell me more about yourself before suggesting I jump in a pond for your entertainment—which I will not do, so don't hold your breath."

"Damn. What would you like to know?"

"You are single, I assume, or you would not be here."

"I am very single."

"Have you ever been in a serious relationship?"

"I've been in a seriously *deranged* relationship for years with someone who left me behind for higher learning in the Hollywood Hills."

She clucked her tongue. "You poor thing. Maybe you should have given her a reason to stay instead of putting her up on a pedestal where she couldn't be reached."

"It's very complicated. Or, I thought it was. She has these two brothers, you see. And one of them adopted me when I was younger, and if he knew I so much as touched her, like this—" He ran a finger along the side of her hand. Once, twice. He stroked over her delicate wristbone and traced along the inside of her arm, back and forth, watching goose bumps spread across her skin. "He might smash my head into a sticky pulp. Or he might do something else, like send me away from the house in which I now live. I would lose my job and my family."

"He would not," Astrid whispered. "If he did, I would— I mean, I'm sure this girl you speak of would pack her bags and never speak to that brother again."

"It's easy to say that now, but what would she do for money? Where would she live?"

"With you, of course."

With him—*him!* He couldn't believe they were talking about this, no matter how remotely. It was like everything that hadn't been spoken over the last few years was suddenly out in the open. Or was it? He couldn't tell. All he knew was that his pulse was pounding in his temples and his mouth was dry.

He licked his lips. "What would I do for money? And I don't think she'd want to live in my old apartment in Chinatown. This girl likes the finer things in life."

"She's not the only one," she said, slanting him a critical look. "And the two of you could temporarily live with her nicer brother on Telegraph Hill."

"You're assuming he wouldn't stand behind his older brother's wishes. And even if he took them in, that might risk dividing the entire family, and this family has already been through a lot of tragedy. I am certainly not worth the injury this could cause."

"You should let her be the judge of worth," Astrid said, brow lowering.

"It's not the only complication, I'm afraid." He continued stroking her arm; touching her was like the patter of rain above them, seductive and relaxing. As long as he could continue touching her, their Pretend Conversation would continue. "Even if the family could be mended, there are other things dividing them. She is high class, and I am low. She is college educated, and my uncle forced me to drop out of school when I was thirteen so that I could earn him money by robbing people—"

"Lazy bastard."

"—but most of all, she is a privileged white woman. I am Chinese."

She leaned closer. "I've heard from a reliable source that the xenophobes plaguing our society have got it all wrong—that the Chinese are beautiful, resilient people with a rich cultural history that spans thousands of years. And that they came here to Gum Shan—"

"Gam Saan," he said, correcting her pronunciation as he leaned closer.

"Gold Mountain, then. The reason they came to California was the same reason my parents came here from Sweden. Because life was hard at home, and though they loved their land, they came here to seek their fortune. How were they supposed to know that a bunch of idiots with power were already out here, and that they'd be jealous of their hard work and make life miserable for them?"

Bo chuckled. "Your reliable source seems to have strong opinions about history."

"He's smarter than every single one of my professors." She tucked a lock of misbehaving blond hair behind one ear at the same moment her knee moved and touched his. "He knows a hundred Chinese fables. Do you know any, perhaps?"

"I know a few."

"Tell me one about a cunning fox spirit. Those are my favorite. I like that all the female fox spirits are beautiful seductresses and make men do stupid things."

"You just described my life."

She laughed.

"Let me think of one I haven't told you." He paused to think and said, "I know one that doesn't have a fox spirit outsmarting anyone to make them do stupid things, but she's still quite extraordinary," he assured her. "So extraordinary, that it's believed she must be descended from the old foxes."

"Tell me about her."

With his knee touching hers, he leaned closer and told the story.

"A young scholar in a small village pined away for his

childhood sweetheart for many years, but he didn't dare touch her because her family was wealthy and respected, and his family was poor. When she was finally old enough for them to be together, he spent his savings to buy fine clothes and a horse and went to her family home to ask for her hand in marriage. But when her father answered the door, a loud celebration was going on behind him. The scholar asked what they were celebrating, and the father told him that another man from a respected family had proposed to his daughter and they were to be married."

"That's awful," Astrid murmured. Her hand dropped between them and settled on the stone wall.

His hand followed hers. He continued.

"Heartbroken and sick with grief, the young scholar left his village and went to the capital to find work. On the hilly road there, he heard the sound of someone running behind him and found his childhood sweetheart had raced two miles up the hill to catch up with him. She loved him, not the other man, and was willing to run away from home to be with him."

"I like her already," Astrid said. Slender fingers slid over his. Her thumb rubbed circles into the heel of his palm. "Was he happy?"

"He was happy beyond belief," Bo told her. "They went to the capital together, where they were married. He found work in the emperor's library. It didn't pay much, but he still had all his savings, so he was able to buy them a meager home—"

"I thought he spent all his money on fancy clothes and a horse."

"He sold those to some dupe in the village for twice what he paid."

"Very savvy. I like this scholar. What happened next?"

"He and his new wife were living out their dreams. Good work, a roof over their heads, and a nice big bed where they spent all their free time—"

"Oh my." Her circling thumb moved a little faster.

"—and they had five children."

"Five? That must have been one very big bed."

"The biggest."

"Stars." Pink dots swelled on the apples of her cheeks. "How did they have any free time with all those children running around? One or two sounds nicer to me. And I'd think that maybe the wife was a famous dancer in the emperor's court, because she isn't going to sit around the house all day. So they should probably have a nanny, too."

"All right, maybe they only had two children. A boy and a girl. And the wife dances, and they have a nanny. And even though the scholar worries how they can afford all this, they somehow make it work, and for five wonderful years they live a joyful, humble life together."

He slipped his fingers around her wrist and stroked the tender skin there. All this closeness and touching and talking of big beds was funneling all of his blood down between his legs. He vaguely thought he should be careful before he embarrassed himself, but another part of him didn't care.

"One day, the happy couple decided to return to their village to introduce their families to the children, so they gathered up their kids and traveled the long road back home. On the last stretch of road, the scholar set out ahead to meet her father, because he was afraid the man would be upset and wanted to prepare him. But when he got to their home, her father was not only surprised to see him, he called the scholar a liar."

"Why?" Astrid's cheeks were very pink now.

This gave Bo a little thrill.

"Well, you see," he told her in a low voice, "the father took the scholar back to his childhood sweetheart's old bedroom. And there, the scholar sees what the old man was talking about. His childhood sweetheart had been sick for the last five years, lying in bed, nearly dead. At this moment, his wife walked into the house with their children, and saw her sick body lying in bed, and they merged together."

"I don't understand," Astrid whispered.

"His childhood sweetheart had loved him so much that five years before, her spirit left her body to meet the scholar on the road to run away with him."

Astrid's mouth curved into a little O shape.

He rested his forehead against hers. "Sometimes, while you were in Los Angeles, I'd lay awake at night and imagine my soul breaking away from my body and flying across the state to be with you."

She made a small noise and squeezed her eyes closed.

At some point, all the gentle stroking they'd been doing had stopped. They were now gripping each other's hands so tightly, he worried he was crushing her fingers. But she wouldn't let go. And he *couldn't* let go. Because if did, some part of him worried that he wouldn't be as lucky as the scholar, and that she would float away like a lost balloon, never to be seen again.

Beyond the gallery door, he heard the muffled sound of the yapping dog. Astrid heard it, too. And they both knew what it meant. Their private jungle was being invaded. How long before the door swung open and broke the bewitchment that had Astrid clasping his hand like he was the most important thing in the world?

"Bo," she whispered. Damp eyelashes fluttered and left small streaks of mascara on the skin beneath her eyes. And those eyes were now fixed on his mouth.

He heard the yapping dog.

He felt his heart hammering wildly.

He saw Astrid looking at his mouth.

And then he saw nothing.

One hand instinctively lifted to cup the back of her neck as he pressed his mouth to hers. It wasn't a sensual kiss. Not skilled or erotic or knee-weakening. He kissed her like he was the heartbroken scholar in the fable and she'd just appeared on the road to run away with him. He kissed her like it was all he'd been dreaming about doing for the past few years.

He kissed her like the man that Pretend Astrid wanted him to be—like a man who could move mountains.

And the way she kissed him back (warm mouth, fingers digging into his arms, desperate moan, scent of roses) . . . it made the Real Bo believe he actually could.

THIRTEEN

———— ❧ ————

HOURS AFTER THE KISS, ASTRID CONTINUED TO WALK AROUND in a daze. She could still feel the thrill of it cascading over her, and was halfway afraid Bo had rewired her nervous system, because everything she touched—her coat, the car door, the silverware at the dining table—set off small fireworks beneath her skin.

Bo had kissed her.

She'd kissed Bo.

This repeated inside her head, over and over, as though her brain was afraid she might forget. Impossible. She'd never forget. It was a desperate and crazy kiss, and when his lips touched hers—lemon bright and frighteningly sultry, all at once—she struggled with the shock of it. He was so sure of himself and she was not. She worried she felt awkward and inexperienced to him. Worried they'd waited too long or built up too many expectations.

But her body had known better than her brain in that moment, and when she'd let it take over, it had roared up like a beast and devoured Bo. Maybe there was some truth to his fable about souls separating from bodies, because she wouldn't be surprised if her beast of a soul had taken a big bite out of his.

She saw him differently now. There was the Bo who drove her to the conservatory, and there was the Bo who drove her back home and dropped her off while he went to work. The new Bo was far more dangerous to her erratic feelings, because now that she'd had a taste, she wasn't sure she could go back.

Stars. One kiss and she was free-falling off a cliff and floating over the clouds. He'd barely touched her. She'd done more petting years ago with the boys in her high school. Done a lot more than petting with Luke.

How could a simple kiss make her feel a thousand times more than any of that? She knew the answer, of course, and she was asking the wrong question. The right one was: what could Bo make her feel if it were more than a simple kiss?

"What is wrong?" Greta had asked her at dinner, when it was just Astrid and Aida dining alone with the baby.

"Nothing at all," she'd said dreamily. "Nothing at all."

Astrid wasn't awake when Bo got home that night, and it wasn't until lunch the next day when she finally saw him again. Everyone was home—Aida, Winter, Greta, baby Karin, and the baby's new part-time nanny. So when Astrid heard Bo's voice in the foyer, she couldn't race to him and jump into his arms. She couldn't do anything at all but try to look as if her heart wasn't bouncing around inside her rib cage like a rubber ball.

When he finally strolled into the dining room and walked by her, the entire length of his arm brushed against hers as he passed.

"Sorry," he mumbled, as if it had been an accident. The apology fluttered wisps of hair near her ear. He put his hand on her arm, and pretended to steady her, lingering a second too long.

It was a wonder she didn't liquefy and drop into a puddle at his feet.

And after that, lunch was torture. She ate but did not taste. Bo's gaze was daring and evasive, just out of reach. She felt it searing her, but when she tried to catch it, he was always looking somewhere else. He talked openly to everyone around the table, but not directly to her. It wasn't until lunch was finished and he was about to leave with Winter to return to work that he caught her in the foyer alone.

"Hadley telephoned," he said in a guarded voice. "We've got an appointment with the Aztec experts at four this afternoon. I should be finished with work by then. No runs tonight. I could go alone—"

"Absolutely not."

"It's just that I won't have time to come get you."

"Jonte can drive me."

"The last time he drove you, Max followed."

"Magnussons don't cower."

"*Aiya*," he murmured, passing her a torn piece of paper with a Nob Hill address scrawled across it. "Just be vigilant and do me the favor of waiting in the car until you see me drive up, all right? I'll be there as close to four as I can."

"Count on it, Captain Yeung," she said with a little salute.

Satisfied with her answer, he started to turn away but changed his mind at the last second. And after glancing around the foyer to ensure they were alone, he lifted her hand to his lips and pressed a kiss to her knuckles. A flurry of chills raced up her arm.

"I can't stop thinking about you," she whispered desperately.

"Then don't," he whispered back with a glint in his eye. "See you at four."

Later that afternoon, Astrid waited in the car with Jonte until she spotted Bo's Buick, and then Bo himself, his navy suit dotted with raindrops. She hopped out to meet him in the cool, gray drizzle. And while traffic rushed by, they dashed toward their destination—a grand French-style Beaux Arts building on California Avenue—and took shelter beneath the entrance's awning.

Bo's dark eyes sparkled as he squinted down at her beneath the brim of his newsboy cap. "Hello again, Miss Magnusson," he said seductively, drawing her closer with a gentle hand on her back.

Her heart leapt. Her nerves jangled as if they were old keys.

She didn't know how to do this. How to go from friends to . . . whatever they were doing. She'd wanted him for years. Wanting Bo was as familiar to her as breathing. Nothing had changed. And yet, *everything* had changed.

She'd had a taste.

She'd bitten off a piece of his soul.

And now she didn't know how to act. Every move she made felt magnified. Her clothes fit differently. What was she supposed to do with her hands? Could she touch him now? He was touching her. It seemed easy and natural to him, while she was frazzled and awkward. But also happier than she could ever remember being.

She was a damned mess.

"Did you miss me?" she asked.

Before he could answer, the front door swung open. A well-heeled middle-aged couple breezed out and huddled beneath the awning, crowding the small space as they waited for their driver to pull up to the curb. When the woman noticed Astrid and Bo, she gaped at the two of them together and gave Bo a nasty look. Then she pulled her fur coat closed and moved away from him to stand on the other side of her companion.

Over the years, Astrid had witnessed plenty of small indignities. People poking fun at her parents' accents. Greta being ignored at the market while someone less foreign was served ahead of her. But none of that came close to what Bo had to suffer.

In the past, when Bo used to take her shopping or

accompanied her on errands, he often avoided confrontation by either sliding into the background or using charm as a distraction. She became accustomed to aiding him, cheerfully reassuring department store clerks that he was there to carry her bags, or whatever lie they wanted to hear to make them look the other way.

Astrid now stared back at the wealthy woman beneath the awning. It would be easy to pretend it didn't happen. To look away. Maybe it was Astrid's already taut nerves, but she wasn't in the mood to let the affront slide. They'd been standing there first. They weren't doing anything wrong. And really, how dare this woman look at them that way?

Astrid was suddenly *livid*.

"What's the matter?" she said to the woman in challenge.

"Pardon?"

"You have a problem?"

The woman's head jerked back in surprise, but she recovered quickly. "If you want to make a scene, I suggest you cross Stockton," she said, waving a hand toward Chinatown.

"You want a scene? Oh, I'll make a scene, all right. Right here, right now."

"Winston," she snapped at her companion. "Are you just going to stand there and let her talk to me that way? Go get the building manager."

Winston hesitated.

The woman muttered something about "trash" and "immigrants" overtaking their apartment building.

Astrid had the violent urge to rip the woman's hair out by the roots. But before she could say or do anything more, Bo herded her inside the building. "Come on," he told her in calm voice. "We're already late."

Astrid didn't take her eyes off the woman until Bo pulled the door shut behind her.

"What have you told me before?" Bo murmured. "It's not worth it."

"I was wrong," she said, only half aware that her voice

was echoing off the walls. "It's not fair. Why should a stuck-up bitch like that get away with that kind of rude behavior? If people are going to act like goddamn jack-asses, they ought to have the decency to do so in private."

Bo cleared his throat. Astrid spun around to find herself standing in the middle of a marble-floored, chandelier-lit lobby, facing an amused attendant behind a raised desk.

Astrid's cheeks warmed. Her anger deflated.

"Mr. Yeung and Miss Magnusson here to visit Dr. Maria Navarro," Bo said.

The attendant consulted a large book with handwritten notes and winked at Astrid as he confirmed their appointment. Dr. Navarro's apartment was on the top floor.

They were pointed to an elevator behind them, where a handsome elevator operator in a burgundy uniform greeted them. He was almost as big as Winter and looked a little like the famous boxer Jack Johnson. Astrid suspected he'd also heard her profanity-laden outburst, but he was too polite to comment. He just closed the scissor doors and pulled the lever to take them up to the top floor.

She blew out a long breath and summoned her dignity. Though her embarrassment was abating, she was still trying to tamp down the irritation caused by the woman outside. On top of that, she was more than a little frustrated that she didn't get any time alone with Bo.

"The answer is yes," Bo said over the clack of the rising elevator, surprising her.

She raised her head. "What's that?"

"You asked me earlier if I missed you. And I did. Terribly."

Oh. Well, then. Astrid flicked a glance to the elevator operator. He looked straight ahead.

Bo wasn't finished. "I thought about you the entire time I was at work last night. I went to sleep thinking of you. I even dreamed about you. About us. Together."

"Stars," Astrid murmured breathlessly.

The elevator operator slid her a sideways glance of approval. He was impressed with Bo's daring, too. It was thrilling to hear Bo say any of this at all—and in public? Well. That knocked her for a loop.

How did Bo do this? And so effortlessly? In a matter of seconds, he'd erased all her negativity. Anxiety, anger, frustration . . . it all just faded away. And, for once in her life, words failed her.

The elevator operator pulled the lever and slowed their ascent.

"Also, you look stunning today," Bo added as the elevator came to a stop. His gaze fell down her legs and leisurely rose back up again. "Whatever fashion genius decided to raise the hemline even higher this year has my full appreciation."

As the operator opened the scissor gates, Astrid recovered her wits. "A girl pays five bucks for imported silk stockings, you can't blame her for wanting to show four dollars and fifty cents of them."

Bo laughed and tipped the grinning operator while she exited, chin high.

Dr. Navarro's penthouse apartment was luxurious and jammed full of expensive art. The grimacing statues, stonework disks, and ancient woven cloth decorating the cream walls of her high-ceilinged rooms made it look as if she'd raided a Mexican temple. Astrid couldn't stop gawking. Plush rugs cushioned their feet as they followed a stiff butler to a receiving room with a stunning view of Huntington Park. And it was here, in front of a fireplace, that two women lounged.

The Wicked Wenches, as Lowe had put it.

Both appeared to be in their fifties. One looked like a pale English rose, as though she'd be comfortable hobnobbing with Queen Mary, and the other, wearing a floral-embroidered shawl draped over her shoulders, looked like a blazing goddess sprung to life from one of the paintings that crammed the walls.

Dr. Maria Navarro.

She was an attractive woman, with long bones and a good figure. Her dark hair was shot through with white and pulled back into a neat pile of braids at the back of her neck, and when she stood to greet them, she seemed to take up all the space in the room, which impressed Astrid quite a lot.

"Dr. Navarro," Bo said, removing his cap and inclining his head politely. "Thank you for taking the time to meet with us."

"You are Hadley's new family—of course we will meet with you, my darlings," she answered with a grand smile and a grander accent that rolled along her deep, rich voice. "This is my friend and colleague, Miss King."

"Please call me Mathilda," the second woman said.

"Delighted," Astrid said, shaking both their hands.

After exchanging further pleasantries, Dr. Navarro led them all to the fireplace, saying, "Please, sit with us." She dismissed the butler in Spanish while Bo and Astrid relaxed together on a long leather sofa facing the two ladies.

"I have known Hadley's father for many, many years," Dr. Navarro said. "A great man, very intelligent. But not as intelligent as his daughter. That brother of yours is a lucky man."

"We spend summers at a small villa in Spain, so we missed the wedding, unfortunately," Mathilda added.

"Spain," Astrid said. It sounded warm and exotic. Probably wasn't gray and dreary and flooding there.

"Maria's first husband was filthy rich," Mathilda remarked casually. "Ricardo Navarro was a bastard of the highest rank, but I thank him daily for having the decency to die quickly—and with his enormous will intact—before I was tempted to do the deed myself."

For the first time, it struck Astrid that the two women were lovers, and her face heated. She wondered if Bo had caught on. Probably long before now. He always had better instincts about people. It also struck Astrid that the two women weren't unlike her and Bo: two cultures, two classes . . . a union unsanctioned by society. And yet, they were living together in a posh apartment building in Nob Hill. Lecturing in Mexico. Vacationing in Europe.

Pretending they were other people.

If they could do it, could she and Bo?

A dangerous thought, and one that struck a match inside Astrid's mind.

"Anyway," Mathilda continued, pushing a lock of delicately waving white hair away from her face. "We finally met your brother a few months back—during a dinner at Hadley's family home in Russian Hill. Lowe was *most* entertaining."

"And he gave us a wonderfully potent bottle of akvavit," Dr. Navarro said. "But I suppose we have you to thank for that, don't we, Mr. Yeung? You work with the older brother, Winter, yes? Bootlegging must be *fascinating* work."

Bo scratched the back of his neck as he struggled with a smile. "That wouldn't be the word I'd use to describe it, but I'm not complaining."

"Indeed." Mathilda gave him an appreciative once-over. "They say noble work should stimulate the mind, but *whose* mind is never specified. I would imagine you've stimulated thousands of minds all over the city."

The corners of Bo's mouth curled. "I'll remind Winter of that when I'm asking for a pay increase."

The women laughed and raised invisible glasses while Mathilda toasted, "Here's to noble work."

Astrid found herself pulled down meandering conversational paths as the two ladies spoke about their career, and how they had lived and worked together in both Mexico City and San Francisco for thirty-odd years, and had finally decided to retire and share this penthouse. "To the eternal disappointment of a few tenants in the building," Mathilda said with a wink.

"Yes, I believe we met one downstairs," Bo said. "She had strong opinions about immigrants."

"Mrs. Humphreys," the two women intoned together.

"Her husband's a state senator," Dr. Navarro said.

"He receives calls from ladies of the evening when his wife is away at their ranch," Mathilda added. "Why he married that cow in the first place is beyond me."

Bo and Astrid glanced at each other with twin expressions of delight.

Mathilda shrugged. "Maria owns the building"—*The entire building? Good God!*—"so they pay us rent, and being able to raise it whenever we damn well please is no small satisfaction, let me tell you."

"I can only imagine," Astrid said with a smile.

"Enough about us. I know you didn't come here to listen to two old ladies gossip," Dr. Navarro said. "Hadley told me you had something interesting to show us."

Bo unwrapped the idol. Dr. Navarro slipped on a pair of glasses that hung from a chain around her neck amongst long strings of beads. A small folding table was set up between her and Mathilda, and it was upon this that she inspected the turquoise figure. While she did, Bo gave them a very condensed explanation of how the idol came into their possession, smoothly leaving out all the details about Astrid's visions. In Bo's story, in fact, the idol mysteriously turned up on the pier when the yacht crashed into it.

Upon doling out this lie, he gave Astrid a look that said: *I know, I know. But how am I to account for why we haven't returned a priceless artifact to the yacht's owner?*

And she gave him a look in return that said: *I am absolutely, positively crazy about you and don't give two hoots about what you tell them.*

And in answer to *that*, Bo gave Astrid's legs a bold perusal that sent a quick thrill through her chest.

Unaware of their silent communiqués, Dr. Navarro studied the idol, turning it over carefully before giving Mathilda a turn. They looked it over for a long time, and when they were both done murmuring small exclamations and pointing things out to each other in Spanish, Dr. Navarro took off her glasses and smiled up at Bo and Astrid. "Hadley was correct, as usual. This piece was certainly made in a style that was common in the fifteenth and sixteenth centuries."

"*Teoxihuitl* is what the Aztecs called turquoise," Mathilda added. "It's a Nahuatl word that means 'stone of the gods.' It was used in special religious and ritual items, and no one was allowed to wear it as casual jewelry, like they do today. That would have been sacrilege. Therefore, this is not an everyday object."

"Do you recognize the figure?" Bo asked.

"I believe it's meant to be Ometeotl, who is a little mysterious. Many believe he was a supreme creator deity with a dual nature not unlike the Holy Trinity. Other scholars think he has been confused with another earlier god who makes life from bones—the Bone Lord, he was called. In fact, I wouldn't be surprised at all if we'd find a bone armature beneath the turquoise, were we to remove it."

"Someone has already altered it," Bo pointing toward the word "NANCE."

"Yes, that is a disgrace," Mathilda said, shaking her head. "No museum will buy it, of course. And I'd wager that's someone's name. Names have great power. Tell them, Maria."

Dr. Navarro stretched out her legs and lay back against her chair, pulling her shawl over her arms. "When Mathilda and I lived in Mexico City, we occasionally heard a legend from other anthropologists about a group of royal soothsayers who advised the Aztec nobility for almost two hundred years. They weren't native. They were said to have come from a foreign land—where, exactly, was unknown. But the interesting thing about them is that they supposedly performed a secret ritual once every decade in order to extend their life."

"Immortality?" Astrid said.

"More like . . . a Fountain of Youth to give them extra time," Mathilda . . . explained. "It was a ritual performed over water—over Lake Texcoco, which was the home of the Aztecs. They established their empire on an island in the middle of that lake. Mexico City was later built on top of it, and the lake was drained."

Ritual performed over water. Astrid thought of the *Plumed Serpent*.

"And how is this legend connected to our idol?" Bo asked.

Dr. Navarro leaned closer, as if someone might overhear them, and spoke in an exhilarated tone. "Because the soothsayer's ritual involved the use of ceremonial turquoise idols purported to be very much like this."

"Very much," Mathilda agreed.

Bo frowned at the idol, and Astrid wondered if he was thinking about the ritual in her vision. She certainly was. "Would this ritual also have involved human sacrifice?" she asked.

Dr. Navarro shrugged. "Perhaps. Sacrifice was common in pre-Columbian cultures. They believed life was cyclical—birth, death, rebirth. Death was not the end of life, but part of it."

"Your Viking ancestors were known to sacrifice a few souls themselves," Mathilda said to Astrid. "And your Chinese ancestors, too, Mr. Yeung. We are all descended from barbarians."

"Barbarians and lovers of grandiose drama," Dr. Navarro said "The Mayans sometimes anointed their sacrifices' bodies with blue pigment and shot them through with arrows."

Blue pigment . . .

Excitement made the hairs on Astrid's arms rise. The yacht survivors were performing a ritual to extend their lives. The people she'd seen in the burlap sacks were human sacrifices. Sacrifices! Could this really be possible in this day and age, here in San Francisco?

Dr. Navarro pointed to the idol. "All of that aside, the symbol on the front is not Aztec. It's not Central American at all, which is very odd. If we entertain the notion that this actually might be one of the ceremonial idols used by the soothsayers of legend, then perhaps it is proof that the soothsayers were, indeed, foreigners."

When pressed, neither woman had a guess as to the cultural origin of symbol on the golden disk. Its style was both too generic and, at the same time, unique enough for them to rule out anything either of them had seen before.

Which was utterly disappointing.

"Is it possible the entire idol isn't Aztec at all?" Bo asked.

Dr. Navarro shook her head. "I say at least most of this is genuine, and the style matches other known turquoise work from that period."

Mathilda gave the idol another close inspection. "In the legend, the soothsayers died off when their ritual idols were stolen. I suppose they did not see the future very well that day," she said with a mischievous smile.

Dr. Navarro snorted. "They must have been terrible oracles altogether not to see the Spaniards coming nor the outbreak of smallpox that would ravage the Valley of Mexico."

"You said the idols were stolen," Bo said. "Stolen by whom?"

"Spanish explorers, most likely," Dr. Navarro said. "When the Aztecs were conquered, their temples were looted."

Mathilda crossed her legs and leaned back in her chair. "And then, of course, there was a French privateer by the name of Jean Fleury. He famously captured two Spanish galleons carrying Aztec treasure back to Spain. Most of that treasure was given to the king of France, but who can tell where all of it eventually ended up?"

Bo made a small noise and stared at Astrid with a look of amazement widening his face. He said only one word. "Pirates."

FOURTEEN

———✦———

UPON LEAVING DR. NAVARRO AND MATHILDA, BO AND ASTRID excitedly talked about the Pieces of Eight Society while they called for the elevator and waited for it to ascend. The more they talked about how it might fit in with the ladies' legendary soothsayers, the more electrified Astrid got—and in no small part because she now knew *ab-so-positively* that her visions hadn't been mere figments of her imagination.

Not that she had much doubt before today, but it was good to be proven right.

"Do you think the survivors are actual pirates who've been keeping themselves alive for hundreds of years?" she murmured to Bo. "One of the survivors was a woman. Imagine that—a female pirate. God, Bo. This is exciting. I feel like we're gumshoes who've stumbled upon the case of the century. Oh! What about Mrs. Cushing? And none of this explains where the yacht disappeared to for an entire year, and—"

"Christ, slow down, Typhoon Astrid," Bo whispered, but he wasn't really irritated. He struggled to control a smile and his face betrayed his excitement. "Let's think for a moment. All this talk of human sacrifice is making me nervous. If it weren't for your visions and your . . . unhealthy aura, I'd just return the idol to Mrs. Cushing and be done with it."

"And let her and her cronies sacrifice more helpless people in the future?"

"These people may be more dangerous than we originally thought."

"Pfft. Max didn't even have a weapon. What kind of pirate doesn't carry a weapon?" she said, wrinkling her nose.

"This is serious, Astrid. There's a chance the idol's done permanent damage to you—not to mention that you could have died that night on the yacht."

"But I didn't. Velma said it might not necessarily be bad. Maybe I should just stay away from cursed turquoise and I'll be fine."

He shook his head with quick, deliberate movements. "Too dangerous to take that chance. I won't risk your well-being on a 'maybe,'" he said, ever the protector.

She tied the belt of her coat around her waist while the clack of the approaching elevator grew louder. "I'm more concerned that these people got away with murder—for God knows how many centuries."

Bo groaned, but Astrid's mind was turning too fast to put on brakes. Mrs. Cushing and the survivors could very well be killers, but Astrid and Bo couldn't take their theory to the police. What would they tell the chief? *I had a magically induced vision and I think six people may have drowned in the Bay, but I don't know who they are, and it's just my word against some high-society dame who's probably ten times richer and a good deal less infamous than my family.*

As much less infamous as centuries-old murdering pirates could be, anyway. But even if it didn't sound utterly insane, when did Magnussons go to the police for help? Never, if they could help it.

And they'd already told everyone in the family about

it, and none of them wanted any part of this. If they were going to do anything more about it, they'd be on their own. Maybe it wasn't worth the trouble, but what if Bo was right? What if she truly *were* damaged from her initial contact with the idol? Velma said she couldn't perform a counterspell without knowing the nature of the original magic. They knew at least part of it now, but they still didn't know the origin of the idol's strange symbol . . .

No, there was no way around it. They had to see this through. Together. She just needed to convince Bo of that.

The elevator clunked to a stop and the scissor gates opened. Astrid heaved a long exhalation and stepped inside with Bo following. It wasn't until the gates were shut that she realized their previous friendly Jack Johnson–look-alike operator was no longer working the elevator. And it wasn't until he pulled the lever too fast that she smelled a very familiar fruity cologne.

She glanced toward Bo and saw his eyes widen. Saw him reach inside his jacket, but his hand froze halfway through the motion . . . at the exact moment she felt something cold and sharp pressed to her throat.

"Nuh-uh-uh," the man warned Bo. "Hands up, please. I'd rather not get blood on this suit, but I will slit her open like a fish if I have to. This knife has felled large beasts, soldiers, and thieving whores. It will easily slay a tiny woman."

Bo complied.

Astrid didn't move her head, just her eyes.

She saw the ornately carved ivory handle of the knife that pressed to her neck. And to her side, she saw Max's full lips and wide-bridged nose.

"Hello, again," he said with a dark smile that didn't climb to the blue eyes shadowed by his fedora. He looked awful. Sickly, with a strange grayish pallor. Dark circles like day-old bruises hung beneath his eyes.

He used his free hand to pull the lever and bring the elevator to a jarring stop between the second and third floors. The movement caused a sharp sting on her throat and a warm trickle below the knife's blade.

"You just made the biggest mistake of your life, friend," Bo said in a low, dangerous voice.

"Now, now. We seem to have gotten off to a bad start." Max quickly swapped out the hand holding the knife and grabbed Astrid's arm roughly to pull her in front of him. She didn't like his body pressed behind hers. It made her feel trapped. "All I want to do is have a private conversation with Goldilocks here, and you'll never see me again."

Astrid barely heard him. She was too busy scanning his hands out of the corners of her eyes. Though she didn't relish the idea of having her throat cut, she also wanted to avoid his touching her with his turquoise signet ring again. It should be on his knife-wielding hand, but she couldn't see it from her precarious and very limited angle.

Bo spoke again, and this time he sounded approximately two seconds away from ripping Max's throat out. "If you want to talk, take the knife off her and put it on me."

"No, I think I'll leave it where it is," Max said. His strong cologne made her brain shrivel up and ache. "Miss Magnusson, I believe, has something of mine. And I want it back."

"I have *no* idea what you're talking about," Astrid said.

"You were on the yacht after it docked, and you stole something that didn't belong to you. A small blue statue. Sound familiar?" His voice was graveled and weary. Was he sick? She hoped it wasn't contagious.

"Not really," she said.

"I had a little chat with a police officer down at the pier who says differently."

Officer Barlow. Dirty little rat.

"Does that jolt your memory, Miss Magnusson?" Max asked.

Bo gave her a guarded look. He didn't want her to answer. Fine, she wouldn't. But she really didn't care for the way he slowly leaned to one side of the elevator car. He'd better not be trying anything heroic. It was far too cramped in the elevator, and there weren't many directions a bullet could go. Two of those directions she wanted to avoid completely—hers and his.

Max could go hang himself.

"I don't know what you think you'll do with it," Max continued, speaking against the side of her head. "It's not worth anything in the antiquities market. If you want it for any other reason, you'll find it's quite useless if you don't know what you're doing. And I promise that you *do not*."

A handful of thoughts popped into Astrid's mind at once. The Wicked Wenches talking about human sacrifice. The burlap sacks from her vision. The old priestess in the red robe inside the ritual circle. Mrs. Cushing stopping to stare at Astrid when she was in the hospital bed. The Pieces of Eight Society.

Pirates.

God in heaven, just how old *was* Max? She knew he looked older at Gris-Gris! And for the first time, in her mind's eye, she now saw him with blue paint smeared over his face.

Panic slithered down her scalp.

"You were on the yacht," she whispered. "I saw you with the other survivors . . . and with the people in the burlap sacks."

She had his attention now. He put pressure on the blade and forced her head back on his shoulder to peer down at her. She now saw the turquoise gleaming on his finger. She also saw Bo moving in the corner. Her fingers began to tremble.

"We don't have access to it right now," Bo said suddenly. "But we're going to need something in exchange. Tell us what the symbol means and you can have the idol back."

Max shook his head. "This isn't a negotiation."

"Not now, maybe," Bo said darkly. "But wait until your back's turned. I'll see if I can't change your mind."

A loud noise outside the elevator made Astrid flinch. Running footfalls echoed in the hallway and someone shouted, "Here! I found him!"

Max mumbled under his breath as a dark figure squatted in front of the third-floor scissor gate and peered inside.

"Jesus Christ!" the real elevator operator swore through the metal grating.

Bo started to lunge but stopped short when Max swung the knife toward Bo's stomach, quick as a snake. Metal gleamed. Bo dodged the strike, grunted, and feinted left to dodge another. But when Astrid tried to shove Max off balance, he grabbed her hair, pounded the heel of his knife-wielding hand on the lever, and pointed the tip of the knife against her ribs. The car jerked upward with a loud jolt, and her Jack Johnson operator disappeared from view as they rose.

There wasn't even time for Astrid to draw in a shaky breath before Max used his elbow to push the lever again, this time slamming to a stop between floors three and four—mostly on four. Reaching up, he kept the knife on her while using his free hand to slide open the fourth-floor gate.

"I want what's mine returned," he said to Astrid. "This is not a game. If I don't have it in my hands by the end of the week—"

More noise from outside the elevator. Astrid wasn't sure which floor it was coming from. Max had to step up to the fourth floor. He put a hand on the open elevator doorway and peered down at them over the bloodied blade of his knife—*my blood*, she thought. And so much of it!

"By the end of the week, Cushing Manor, Presidio Heights," Max said. "Or things are going to take a nasty turn."

Max pushed away from the elevator, and as he turned on a heel, Bo spat out a string of angry words in Cantonese that sounded positively filthy. He pushed Astrid toward the floor and drew his gun on Max's retreating form. Astrid covered her head as a shot exploded inside the cramped elevator car and spent gunpowder filled the air, along with a single, soft sound of success from Bo: he'd gotten him.

Astrid jumped to her feet and peered down the hallway. Max had been hit in the leg. But it wasn't slowing him down much. He just pressed a hand over his thigh and launched into a hobbled run.

Bo wasn't giving up. The elevator groaned as he leapt onto the fourth floor and took off after Max.

They'd kill each other!

Astrid stepped up onto the fourth floor to follow him. Damn, but he was fast. She saw Max disappear around a sharp corner down the hall directly in front of her, Bo trailing several yards behind, but gaining speed. A posted sign told her that Max was headed toward the stairwell exit. She sailed down the corridor, inverted triangles of light from chrome wall sconces blurring in her peripheral vision.

Bo was nearing the corner. He stopped suddenly, hugged the wall, and poked his head around it. Another shot exploded from his gun. Astrid reflexively swerved sideways and ducked as Bo's angry bellow echoed down the hallway. She lifted her head, throat tight with fear, and saw him stumble away from the corner.

He made a strangled noise as his back hit the wall.

She heard the distant slam of the stairwell door as Max escaped, and behind her, apartment doors flying open as she pushed away from the wall and barreled toward Bo. When she came to a stop in front of him, his chest heaved as he clutched himself on his side, near his ribs.

He pulled out his hand from beneath his jacket.

It was covered in blood.

FIFTEEN

———————

ASTRID CRIED OUT IN HORROR. "BO!"

"Fuck," he swore, clamping his hand down over his jacket. Then louder, "Fuck!"

Shock chilled the blood in her veins. If her hands were trembling before, they were positively convulsing now. Memories of overheard conversations sprung up in her head—of Winter saying the worst two places to get stabbed were the stomach and chest . . . but at least you'd live if it were the stomach.

She reached for Bo and spoke in fragments. "Where? Are you . . . ? How? What do I . . . ?"

"He must have gotten me in the elevator," Bo muttered in disbelief.

His blood on the knife—not hers. How did she not notice? How did *he* not notice?

Behind her, the elevator operator was yelling at everyone to shut their doors and stay inside their apartments, but she blocked it out.

Bo grimaced and pulled the right side of his jacket open. Blood blossomed like a poppy flower over his white shirt. A gaping slash in the fabric marked where the knife had gotten him. Astrid's mind went into a strange, detached place and temporarily muffled her manic emotions. The wound was too high to be the stomach, she thought. That was good.

"Bastard only got my side," Bo confirmed. His eyes went to her neck. "Are you—?"

She wiped away the blood with her fingers. "He nicked me. I'm fine. You're bleeding all the way through your coat," she said, a fresh wave of panic washing through her as she noticed the dark spot on the red-brown wool.

He glanced down and clamped his hand around his side. "It's not deep. I don't think."

What if some vital organ was pierced and leaking into his body? What organs *were* on that side of one's body? Spleen? Appendix? She didn't even know what those were for, much less if they were vital. Not for the last time, she regretted that she'd been such a terrible student.

Education or no, she had sense enough to know they couldn't just stand around watching him bleed.

"You need to keep pressure on it," she said, and then turned around to the elevator operator, who was marching toward them, asking if Bo was all right. "Call an ambulance."

Bo shook his head and holstered his gun over his uninjured side. "No ambulance," he told the man, and then said to Astrid, "Downstairs. I need to see where he went. I only got him on the first shot. The second missed, but the man looked sick to me. He'll tire out."

Astrid didn't give a damn about Max's whereabouts. They knew where to find him when they needed him— Mrs. Cushing's manor. But at this point, the man would be long gone, and she wasn't eager to chase him down just to jump back into a fight. Especially when Bo was gripping his side and sucking in sharp breaths with every step.

"I'm fine," he assured her.

He was not.

She had a lot of experience learning from her family how to avoid police involvement, so she talked fast—her best talent—as they were rushed down a secondary out-of-sight service elevator, giving half-truth instructions to the elevator operator.

"I'm sorry, what's your name?" she asked.

"Mr. Laroche," the operator answered.

"Well, Mr. Laroche, I'm Miss Magnusson, and this is Mr. Yeung. And here are the facts." She told him that the police, if they were called—and really, did they need to be?—should look for a man named Max rumored to be living with a Mrs. Cushing in Presidio Heights. Let the police knock on Cushing's door looking for him. That would keep dear old Max temporarily occupied.

Mr. Laroche was as eager to get rid of them as they were to leave, and by the time they exited onto city streets that were now dark and rainy, Bo was in no mood to pick up Max's trail.

"Think I need stitches," he admitted weakly, telling her what she already knew.

"There's your Buick over there. I'll drive you to Saint Francis."

"*Aiya*," he bemoaned. "I must be bad off if I'm considering letting you get behind the wheel of the Buick. But you can't take me there."

"Why the hell not?"

"Because I'm Chinese."

Her stomach knotted. She hadn't been thinking. But she was too worried about him to dwell on it. "Where do we go?" she asked, vaguely remembering hearing Winter speak of a doctor who treated a lot of his bootlegging employees and dockworkers.

"Jackson Street," he said as she opened the Buick's passenger door and helped him into the front seat. "Take me to Chinatown."

It had been months since Astrid had driven a car. Aida had taught her how to drive in Mamma's old silver Packard. She had an operating license, but only because Winter frowned at the man working the desk at the motor vehicle office after she failed the driving test the second time. The problem was that she got carried away with the thrill of driving and forgot how fast she was going. She didn't think she'd get carried away now, but she was too worried about Bo to be careful.

Lines of headlights jammed the street. During a small break in that line, she peeled away from the curb and zipped across both lanes of traffic, turning sharply onto California Street.

"Chinatown is the other way," Bo said.

"Dammit. I've never driven at night."

She felt Bo's eyes on her. "Please tell me you're joking. Whoa!"

The car seemed to fly over the pavement when she pulled it into a sharp U-turn to get them turned back around. For a moment, she was terrified she'd lost control of it, and the horrible squealing noise was disconcerting, but the wheels finally obeyed her insistent yank on the steering wheel and she got traction.

"Oh my," she said breathlessly. "How in the world did I do that? Rats. I can't see!"

He reached out, groaned, and turned a knob. The Buick's wipers began swinging back and forth over the top of the windshield. "Much better, thank you. I don't think I've ever driven in the rain, either."

"Buddha, Osiris, and Jehovah," Bo mumbled as he braced a hand on the dash. "I've changed my mind; pull over. Just let me die."

Not happening. In the cramped air of the car, she could smell coppery blood and a mild tang of sweat, and that doubled her panic.

"No, no—it's flooding down there," Bo said. "Turn here, now!"

She spun the wheel, plowed over the curb, and barely righted the Buick in time to avoid a parked Tin Lizzie. "Sorry!"

He was either angry or in a lot of pain, because he didn't even shout at her for the near miss. The windows were fogging up, and he shook his head like a wet dog, as if he were trying to stay awake. A slash of light from the street fell over a spot of bright red on the front seat, and Astrid realized with a start that it was Bo's blood.

"We're going to make it, I promise. Just stay awake, all right?"

"How could anyone sleep through your driving?" he grumbled. "Stay on this street!"

"It's not my fault that I don't know where we're going!" she shouted. "And if you pass out and die before you have a chance to kiss me again, I'm going to be furious."

He laughed. Laughed! Stubborn man's liver was probably hanging open inside his body and all he could do was laugh. "It was that good, huh? Just north of Grant."

"Yes, it was that good, and I wish we'd been doing that today instead of running around shooting people and getting stabbed, so I'm pretty mad at you right now, if you want to know the truth." She rubbed her hand across the fogging windshield. "How the hell can I tell which one is Grant in the dark?"

"Just look for the dragon streetlamps. Up there, on the right. The building with the balcony. If you can park the Buick without killing us both, I promise to do more than kiss you before the night's over."

Stars. She nearly ran off the road. "Will that be before or after you've bled out?" she said, braking hard at Grant while she impatiently waited for traffic to pass. "Are you still putting pressure on it?"

"I'm running out of dry clothes. Maybe you should let me borrow something of yours to stanch the blood." Was he serious? Alarmed, she gave him a quick look. He was smiling at her with half-lidded eyes. "How about patching me up with one of those five-dollar stockings?"

"How about I strangle you with them instead?"

"This date is not going well."

"This is not a date!"

"Then I just ruined my best wool overcoat for nothing."

"Pressure!" she reminded him.

Following Bo's instruction, she crossed Grant and swung into a tight space between two four-story buildings—

And slammed into a wrought-iron fence with a sharp *bang!*

"Shit," Astrid said, gritting her teeth. The front bumper was dented, that much she knew; they both winced as she backed up a few inches, only to hear the disconcerting squeal of metal on metal. "Where did that fence come from?"

Bo gaped above the dash at the headlights' screwy angle. Then he closed his eyes tightly. "You . . ."

"Got you here in one piece," she reminded him. "You can thank me later. Stay there and I'll come around, then you can tell me on which floor we'll find this doctor of yours."

SIXTEEN

———— ❧ ————

GRANT AVENUE WAS QUIET. CHINATOWN'S DISTINCTIVE PAINTED lamps with their golden intertwining dragons stood sentry over a handful of tourists crowded in restaurant entrances, waiting for streetcars. The occasional umbrella darted beneath strings of rain-drenched red lanterns and blazing signs advertising CHOP SUEY and IMPORTED GOODS FROM THE ORIENT.

In other words, it was a good time to be bleeding freely on the sidewalk without attracting unwanted attention.

With Bo leaning on her shoulders, Astrid helped him through the rain and inside a white building with blue metal balconies. The inner stairwell was dim and a little dingy, but she was more concerned with how to get an injured bootlegger with a body as heavy as a sack of rocks up two flights of stairs. They took it slowly, but it wasn't easy. He was solid muscle, slick with sweat, and his gun poked into her ribs. But as they climbed, his head dropped against hers and he murmured, "You're doing great. Only five more steps."

Him spouting blood like a geyser, giving *her* encouragement.

"Damn you," she whispered. "Why do you have to be so wonderful? Couldn't you just be stupid and mean? It would make my life so much easier."

"And I wish you could be a nice Chinese girl from a humble family, but apparently we are cursed. There's the door."

She heaved him up the last step and pounded on a wooden door with peeling red paint and Chinese characters painted above the number seven. A young Chinese woman wearing a butterfly-patterned apron answered. She was about Astrid's age, and when she saw them, she emitted a small squeak.

"*Nei hou*, Le-Ann," Bo said cheerfully.

"Bo-Sing!" she said in a scolding tone, and then she called out something sharp in Cantonese over her shoulder and waved them inside, chatting the entire time. Astrid had no idea what she was saying, but Le-Ann clearly was familiar enough with Bo; she wondered how many times he had been here with injured employees.

Astrid helped Bo into a tiny hallway, where they were greeted by the woman's husband, who rushed toward them in rolled-up shirtsleeves, pulling suspenders over his shoulders. He was quite handsome, possibly in his thirties, with small creases gathering on the outer corners of his eyes and mouth. When he saw Bo, he made a low noise of disapproval and shook his head at the bloodied coat. Then he looked into Astrid's face, and she saw the surprise in his eyes.

"Magnusson," he whispered.

"Yes, well, first things first, I seem to have been stabbed by a sharp knife," Bo said in English.

"Of course you have," the man said, resigned.

"Now that we have that out of the way . . . yes, you are right. This is Winter's sister, Astrid Magnusson."

"Miss Magnusson," the man said with an incline of his head. "I am Dr. Moon. Did you do the stabbing?"

"No, but there's still time," she answered.

The doctor nearly smiled and pointed to an open door. "Bring him in here."

The room was a small office crammed with books and shelves lined with bottles and tins. It appeared to also serve as an examination room and, from the looks of the narrow metal table, a surgery. Bo discarded his coat and suit jacket before Dr. Moon helped her get the patient into a chair.

She gathered up Bo's cuff links and necktie and put them in his suit pocket—next to the wrapped-up idol—while he dropped his bloodied dress shirt on the metal table. When he carefully peeled off his damp undershirt, his arms corded with straining muscle, Astrid told herself not to get too excited about seeing his bare torso again. She needn't have worried: a moment later, she was too busy being horrified by the size of the slash on his side.

"Bo!" she said mournfully.

"A scratch, right, Doc?"

Dr. Moon rolled his eyes to the ceiling, let out a long-suffering breath, and turned to Astrid. "Go with Le-Ann. It will take a little while."

With one last look at Bo, Astrid reluctantly followed Dr. Moon's wife into a sitting room across the hall. One of the blue metal balconies that Astrid had seen earlier overlooked the rain-slicked street below, and a pair of arm-chairs sat in front of it. Astrid plopped down on one of them while Le-Ann mumbled something in Cantonese and rushed off.

The room was cozy and well-appointed with lacquered furniture and paintings of mountainous landscapes. A small statue of Buddha sat on a high shelf across from the door. Astrid stared at it, trying not to think about Bo's wound—and failing miserably—until Le-Ann came back several minutes later with a tray that she set down on a table between the armchairs. Hot tea. Astrid accepted it gratefully, happy to have something to calm her nervous stomach.

As she inhaled the fragrant steam, she took notice of

other scents for the first time. Scents of things cooking in the kitchen.

"I'm sorry we showed up like this," she told the woman, who was turning to walk away. "We're interrupting your dinner. It smells wonderful, by the way—*hou hou*. Very good. At least I think I'm pronouncing that right. You probably have no idea what I'm saying, do you?"

Though Astrid knew the woman didn't speak English like her husband, she kept talking, nonetheless. Out of nervousness, perhaps. A need for comfort.

"If your husband takes care of my brother's men, I bet you have a lot of people showing up at odd hours. I hope he pays your husband well. It looks like you both do okay," she said, waving her hand around the room. "Your home is very nice. A lot nicer than I imagined from the state of the building. Bo's old apartment is like that, too. His building looks sketchy from the street, but it's nice on the inside."

Le-Ann crossed her arms over her butterfly apron and tilted her head, murmuring a question in Cantonese.

Astrid tried to imagine what she'd be asking. "Oh, I've only been inside Bo's apartment once, just for a few minutes when I was younger. It was nothing improper. Unfortunately," she added under her breath. "I recently found out he's got an old girlfriend who lives in that building. Her name is Sylvia Fong. I don't suppose you'd know her?"

Le-Ann lifted a slender black eyebrow.

"I didn't think so. Well, anyway. She's beautiful, and Bo won't tell me what happened between them, but I have a feeling it wasn't innocent. A woman can tell about these things, don't you think?"

Le-Ann shrugged and asked Astrid another question in Cantonese.

Astrid tried to interpret it. "Maybe you're wondering why I'm here this time of night with Bo—er, Bo-Sing," she corrected. "It's a long story, but I'll be straight with you. I've been positively moonstruck over him for years. And I'm fairly certain he feels the same way about me, but there are so many obstacles. I don't know what to do about it, but I can't do *nothing* anymore. Would you do nothing if you were me? If Dr. Moon were a French man, say, would the two of you be together now?"

Le-Ann ran a hand over her dark, sleek hair as she answered in Chinese. It sounded sympathetic.

"Whenever I've asked my friends for advice, they've been positively scandalized and told me I'm going through a phase. That I'll get over him. But I can't, because my feelings for him are . . . sempiternal. That's probably the only word I learned my entire semester of college." Angry tears welled. "And I have to go back to that stupid school after the holidays, and it won't stop raining, and there's some crazy occultist chasing after us, and Bo's getting stabbed, and all I want is for us to be left alone for ten minutes. Is that too much to ask?"

Le-Ann made a soft snort.

"All right, ten minutes isn't long enough, but you get my meaning. Or you don't. Ugh. I wish I knew more Cantonese. I wish . . ." She glanced toward the room where Bo was getting doctored. "He's going to be fine, right? Your husband is a good doctor? Winter says half the doctors in San Francisco are quacks. What if Bo is bleeding on the inside? I heard about a boy at school who was in a train accident and they thought he was fine, so he came back to school and attended classes, but he didn't know he was bleeding inside and d-died a week later."

It was humiliating to cry in front of a stranger, but Le-Ann, being a doctor's wife, was either used to it or she was just a kindhearted person, because she knelt down in front of Astrid and patted her legs, speaking in a steady, low voice that calmed Astrid's overflowing emotion. She offered Astrid a white handkerchief embroidered in the corner with a small blue butterfly, which Astrid accepted and used to dab her eyes and wipe her running nose.

"*M'goi*," Astrid said. Thank you. One of the first phrases Bo had ever taught her.

Le-Ann smiled, flashing pearly teeth, and gave her hand

a little squeeze at the same moment that a shadow fell across the room.

Astrid looked up to see a bare-chested Bo leaning against the doorway with a large white bandage wound around his midsection. Seeing all that skin took her breath away. Just for a moment. Then worry crashed down like a cold bucket of water over her head.

"Bo!"

"Good as new," he announced with a dopey smile.

She jumped to her feet and stopped in front of him. His eyes looked a little funny, as if he were exhausted. He smelled of antiseptic and the soap he'd used to wash up. His black hair was damp and looked as though it had been loosely combed back with his fingers.

Dr. Moon walked into the room, wiping his hands on a towel. "It was a clean cut, not too deep," the doctor reported. "He's had seven stitches and lost a fair amount of blood. The morphine will wear off in a few hours, and then he'll be sore as hell."

"In a few hours?" Bo said. "I'm sore as hell now."

"That's your own fault for being too stubborn to accept a shot. The pills aren't as strong."

"I don't trust you not to put me to sleep," Bo argued. "But if you *want* me hanging around and spending the night on your sofa, go right ahead and shoot me up."

The doctor ignored Bo and handed Astrid a small envelope. "There's two more tablets in here. Give him one if he can't sleep later, and another in the morning. No lifting anything heavy for a couple days or he'll tear it right back open. No boxing, either. Make him rest tomorrow and change the bandage. With his luck, he'll be back to normal by the end of the week."

"Good as new," Bo repeated.

Dr. Moon shook his head. "Stupid, lucky bastard. If that knife had hit you an inch to the side, you might be dead."

"He's exaggerating," Bo assured her. "He always sees the worst in every situation. Everyone calls him Dr. Doom."

Le-Ann chuckled at this. Maybe she'd heard it before.

Bo looked at the doctor's unhappy face and recanted his statement. "All right, maybe I'm the only one who calls you that, but you have to admit—you *are* always telling me people are about to die and they never do."

"Next time I won't answer the door," Dr. Moon said in a huff, but Astrid didn't think he really meant it. "Meanwhile, you've made me late for my shift at the hospital. You need iron, and there's beef broth in the kitchen, so feel free to enjoy my dinner until you're able to walk out of here without tripping down the stairs. But if you are still here when I get back, I will stab you on your other side."

"Your bedside manner is deplorable," Bo said, and Astrid noticed just how hard he was struggling to stand.

Stupid man.

She slipped her arm around his uninjured side, touching the warm skin of his back—Bo's bare skin! And stars, he really *was* nothing but muscle—and encouraged him to put his arm around her shoulder like he had outside. He didn't reject the help.

"By the way, Mr. Han was asking about you yesterday," Dr. Moon said. "He brought up the tuna fishing again, and he has a point, you know. Everyone's talking about all the gang violence and how Prohibition might be repealed. You should think of your future, and not the present."

"And the future is bluefin?"

The doctor gave Bo a smug smile. "Mr. Han's car is nicer than yours."

"Ooaf! You know how to hurt a man's pride, Moon."

Astrid thought of the dented front fender downstairs and winced. Bo didn't bring it up, but that was likely due to the morphine clouding his mind.

"I've heard little things about you over the years," the doctor said in a softer voice, and Astrid looked up in surprise to realize that he was speaking to her. He had? *Was it from Bo?* she wondered. "I am glad to finally meet you. My door is always open, day or night. Any friend of Mr. Yeung's is welcome here."

And with that oddly affecting proclamation, the doctor shrugged into his suit jacket, kissed his wife good night, and left the small apartment.

Well. That was interesting.

Le-Ann invited them into a bright kitchen, where they sat at a table and she served up Dr. Moon's amber-colored soup in beautiful lotus bowls with stout porcelain spoons. Rice noodles and bits of beef gleamed beneath the surface. Astrid thought she was too keyed up to eat—she kept watching Bo's bandage for more blood to appear—but when the steaming perfumed broth was set down in front her, and Le-Ann disappeared, leaving them alone at the table, she changed her mind.

"Tonight we dine like royalty," Bo said from her side. "This is liquid gold, by the way. Been cooked all day by Le-Ann and her father. He lives upstairs."

"Are you all right?" Astrid whispered.

"I'm starving, so that's a good sign, don't you think?" Bo said with a small smile.

She did, and upon tasting the soup, found that it *was* liquid gold, and that she was famished. She wolfed it down.

While they ate, Astrid struggled with chaotic emotions. She longed to stare at his skin, and was unnerved by her body's curiosity and complete disregard for his injured state. She wanted to memorize the chiseled lines of his muscles and add it to pictures of him she had in her head. She wanted to touch him. To measure his warmth with her fingertips. To assure herself that he was okay. To cover him up so that Le-Ann couldn't see his beauty.

Want. Want. Want.

Her attention fell to his bandage, and it made her stomach clench so hard, she had to put her spoon down. He caught her looking and met her gaze.

I'm so worried about you, she told him with her eyes.

You don't need to be, but I'm glad you are, he seemed to reply. And that made her feel a little better.

Le-Ann hurried back and forth behind them, washing

out Bo's clothes—quite effectively removing most of the blood—and pressing all but his wool coat dry with an iron.

"Is this the 'good Chinese girl' you were hoping for when you said that earlier?" Astrid asked in a low voice. She thought of her own poor housekeeping skills and wondered if Bo thought her spoiled. "Someone to clean your clothes and feed you? Because after that soup, I'm thinking I might want to marry her myself."

"Did you hear that, Le-Ann?" Bo called over his shoulder. "She's ready to fight Dr. Doom for you."

"I heard her," Le-Ann said.

In perfect English.

Astrid's head shot up.

Le-Ann smiled and shrugged. "Sometimes you don't need to know the same language to communicate. But your Cantonese pronunciation was very good. Keep practicing and I might show you how to make the soup one day."

"Oh," Astrid said weakly, remembering everything she'd confessed to the woman earlier.

"By the way," Le-Ann said, shaking out Bo's pressed shirt after he excused himself from the table to use the telephone. "The answer to your question is yes. If Dr. Moon were French, it would not matter."

Astrid glanced at her silver watch when they finally left the Moons' apartment and found it was already almost midnight. Bo had spoken to Greta and asked her to inform Winter that they were both fine, but she didn't relish going home to face her brother. She didn't relish going home at all, actually, because that would mean the end to their evening. And as much as she wished to erase the bloody part of it, she was grateful to have spent it with Bo.

The street was dark and quiet; the rain had slowed to a misting drizzle. Bo had watched from the balcony for a long time before they left, scanning the shadows to ensure they hadn't been followed. He continued to do that now, hand on his gun as he hurried her into the nook between the buildings where his car was parked. Nothing stirred. No one jumped out at them wielding a knife. The only potentially dangerous thing they encountered was Bo's own impending anger when he inspected his dented fender.

"I'm really sorry," Astrid said, peering into the dark space between the car and the fence she'd rammed. "Lucky for you, my family's loaded. Sylvia will be repaired good as new."

"Lucky for you, that morphine pill the doc gave me has not worn off, because I don't much care at the moment."

She laughed nervously. "Well, I'll try not to do any more damage on the way home. Let me help you get inside the car." She knew he'd walked down the stairs without aid. She only wanted an excuse to touch him again. But when she opened the door, he tossed his bloodied coat into the back and climbed into the passenger seat without her help.

Mildly disappointed, she shuffled to the driver's side and slid behind the wheel.

His hand reached out before she could start the engine. "I'm sorry this was a terrible date," he said, curling his hand around hers. His fingers were cool and strong, and she relaxed in his grip, letting him pull her around in the seat to face him.

"It wasn't a date," she insisted. "Dates don't include stabbings. Of that, I'm almost certain."

One corner of his mouth tipped up. "Makes things more exciting, though. Don't you think?"

"No, I do not! It was very upsetting. Are you sure you're all right?"

"I can't even feel it right now, I promise. It's not the first time I've had stitches and won't be the last." His palm glided over the sleeve of her coat and rubbed her upper arm, up and down, while he watched her face. She had trouble looking at him when he was this close. She worried he'd be able to read her thoughts through her eyes, and right now those thoughts were dangerously jumbled.

"If this really was our second date, do you think you'd never want to see me again?" he asked. "Would you be sorry you saw me in the speakeasy that night and wish for a man who was less trouble?"

Were they pretending again? Just the thought of it made her pulse galloop. His hand molded the curve of her shoulder and stole beneath the fur collar of her coat. Currents of energy zipped over her skin as he stroked the tiny hairs at the nape of her neck.

"There's one thing you should understand about me, Mr. Yeung. I am a Magnusson," she said, trying not to melt into his touch. "We are not easily frightened. In fact, we're rather stupidly brave."

He chuckled. His fingers sneaked under the bottom of her bob and traced up the back of her head. She shivered.

"Now that you mention it, I think I've heard that about your family." His words were low and spoken near her cheek. "I'm a bootlegger, too, you know."

"Is that so?"

His hand ghosted down her back and urged her closer. "We travel in the same circles. God, you smell nice. You always smell so good. I used to think it was that fancy French soap you use, but now I'm sure it's just the scent of your skin. It's intoxicating."

"How do you know what soap I use? I only met you last week, remember?"

"Oh, that's right. I haven't been shopping with you about a thousand times, and I don't remember every brand, color, size, and store you like, do I? So I'll just assume it's some bewitching perfume. Let's pretend you're wearing some."

Let's pretend.

Her heart exploded like a spinning Catherine wheel, shooting off sparks.

"All right," she whispered. She wanted to touch him. Badly. His shirt collar, too thick for the iron to dry, was still damp. It lay open and partially unbuttoned to expose the cords of his neck, and she could see that he hadn't put his undershirt back on, nor had he tucked the tails of his shirt into his pants. He looked wild and unkempt. A dangerous rogue. And she couldn't stop herself from tracing the dip in the center of his clavicle with one thumb.

His nose grazed her ear. The sensations this stirred in her traveled down both arms and through her chest. Her stomach. And lower. She sucked in a fast breath and pressed her thighs together in a poor attempt to stanch the sudden heat gathering between her legs, but that only made things worse.

"Has anyone ever kissed you here?" Bo said, voice barely above a whisper.

Where did he mean? Before she could ask, his lips parted over her ear. He began kissing her there—short, heavy, lingering kisses that rocketed though her body. They were so intense, she wasn't certain if she could stand it, and her shoulder automatically rose to either push him away or trap him inside the crook of her neck. Undeterred, he sucked her earlobe into his mouth and did something wildly immoral with his tongue.

Stars! Where had he learned to do that? She'd never felt anything so pleasurable. She sucked in a sharp breath and pressed her thighs together again in an attempt to stanch her body's overexcited response. Terrible idea. That only made things worse.

"Should I try the other side?" he asked in a teasing voice. He didn't wait for an answer, just trailed open-mouthed kisses along her jaw, down the front of her throat where Max had nicked her with the knife hours before, and around to the other ear. She shamelessly bared her neck to give him better access, and he repeated the same slow, erotic maneuver on her other ear, ending with a leisurely lick around the outer shell.

"Good . . . God," she said between breaths. Was she panting? That might be the cause of her light-headedness. She was only vaguely aware she had balled up the front of his shirt in her fist and couldn't quite make her fingers release it. One more kiss and she'd slide off the seat, right into the floorboard.

When she opened her eyes and caught a fleeting look between them, she could see that she'd pulled up enough of the fabric to reveal a golden patch of his stomach above his belt, and below that, angled and askew, a substantial bulge in his pants. More than substantial.

"Astrid," he said on a long exhale against her hair. "I've wanted to do that for a long, *long* time. Would you like to know what else I've wanted to do?"

At that point, she lost her mind a little.

She wasn't sure whose mouth found whose first. All she knew was they were kissing, and it wasn't the same as the first time. It was rough and desperate, and she wasn't nervous. She was ravenous. Aching. Feral. She couldn't get enough of him.

His tongue pushed between her lips, thick and wide, and it rolled against hers, testing. Asking. She answered the call and deepened the kiss as his hands roughly cupped the back of her head and held her in place. No one had ever kissed her like that. No one. She wasn't young and fragile. Not made of glass. Not weak. Not in need of protection. She was strong, and he wasn't afraid to push back against that strength.

That felt glorious. Dizzyingly so.

"Bo," she said, almost a moan, when he pulled back.

"Come here," he whispered. "I need you here."

He needed her. Stars, that was exciting. Before she understood what he was asking, he'd wrapped an arm around her back and was pulling her onto his lap. Her brain wasn't working. Did he want her to sit? No, he didn't. She felt his hand on the inside of her knee as he rearranged her, pulling one leg over his lap until she straddled him.

"Your stitches . . ." she whispered.

"Damn the stitches."

"I don't want to hurt you."

"You make the pain disappear." He ran both hands

down her back and urged her closer. So close, her skirt hiked up above her knees. Her legs made a vee around his hips—around the tented fly of his pants that made her heart pound wildly. He was looking, too. He didn't seem to care that she was staring, but then, it was a sight he got to see all the time. For her, it was novel: he wanted her, and he didn't care that she knew.

But he wasn't the only one not caring. Her legs were wantonly exposed to his heavy gaze, and she didn't bother to pull down her skirt. His hands left her back to smooth up her thighs, fingers splayed. Slowly. Touching the silk like he was savoring the feel of it on his palms. Like he was the one receiving pleasure instead of giving it.

"Make me stop," he murmured.

"Not on your life." Did he really think she would? Why was he going so slow? He was killing her. Tormenting her on purpose.

God help her, but she loved it.

She couldn't believe this was happening. It was a dream, and yet it was real.

He got to the rolled band of her stockings and stopped before he touched bare flesh. A muscle jumped in her leg. He hooked his thumbs beneath her garters. Tugged them. Wound them around his thumbs until they tightened sharply. As if he were imprisoning himself. Or her. Both of them.

If he wanted to punish himself, she would help. His hands were bound, but hers weren't. She kissed him again, holding his face in her hands. Small kisses on the ever-merry indented corners of his mouth that often curled up when he was being playful. A lick across his bottom lip, which was full and swollen from kissing hers. He trapped her tongue and briefly sucked it into his mouth. As he did, her hand dropped away from his face.

She followed his shirt buttons, one by one, fingers lightly grazing over the bump of his bandage. She didn't want to hurt him. She just wanted to find skin. There. Where his shirttails split. His stomach was warm and smooth. She traced the furrows between his muscles, the dip of his belly button. The trail of dark hair that arrowed down into his pants. And then she ran her open hand over his fly.

Beneath her fingers, he was hot, thick, and exceptionally hard. She stroked him through the fabric and was amazed. He moaned into her mouth, which made her feel powerful, so she kissed him harder and gave him another long up-and-down pet, and then pulled her hand away.

His breath came out slow and shaky against her lips.

Her stockings tightened, biting into her thighs. Then with a snap, he released them. He slung strong arms around her waist and roughly pulled her closer, until the damp center of her silk tap pants pushed against his fly. His hips thrust up; his arms pulled her down. He dragged her over the length of him—so hard, she could feel every button in his fly *pop! pop! pop!* against her most sensitive flesh.

"Astrid," he murmured. "My little *huli jing*."

She had no idea what he'd said. Something in Cantonese, and it sounded positively bawdy, so she'd have to ask him later. But not now, because she was reeling from the sudden toppling of all the power she'd wielded over him. She wanted it back.

Without thinking, she let her head drop to the space between his damp collar and his neck, opened her mouth, and bit him. Not hard, but hard enough. His hips jerked upward, pushing his erection against her. Making her shudder. Making her feel powerful again. And at the same time maddeningly desperate.

"Mghm," he murmured, inhaling sharply as his muscles seized.

She drew back. "Oh God."

"It's . . . all right," he said, wincing. "Just got a little carried away, perhaps."

Perhaps? She lifted up his shirt to check his bandage. A tiny of circle of blood showed through. The sight sobered her enough to shift off his lap into the driver's seat.

Their surroundings zipped back into focus. The

windows were completely fogged up, and they were parked in Chinatown in the middle of the night. A few seconds more and she'd have been tearing off her own lingerie. He'd just had seven stitches and was high as a kite on pain pills. What was the matter with her?

"Let's just . . ." she started, and then blew out a long breath and put both hands on the steering wheel, as if it would anchor her buzzing body to the ground. "Let me just get you home before we have to call the doctor to repair what he's already done."

There. That sounded sensible. Responsible.

He lay his head against the back of the seat and looked at her sideways, chest heaving, hand gripping his side. His eyes were nothing but dark slits. Those merry mouth corners she'd kissed now lifted in tandem. "All right. But let's get one thing straight. We're not finished pretending."

SEVENTEEN

———⟡———

AFTER A LONG, UNRESTFUL SLEEP PUNCTUATED WITH MORPHINE-
crazed dreams, Bo was still sore the next morning. But it
was a good kind of pain, one that cleared his head and
made him decisive. Ready to move ten mountains. Which
is probably why he was now standing beneath Old Bertha
the shark in the warehouse office, letting Velma rub an
herbaceous magical poultice over his stitches.

"That should do it," she said, accepting a towel from
Winter to wipe the dark green sticky substance off her fingers. "Now, over the next few hours, you might notice a
strange itching sensation. That's the muscle knitting back
together. The wound should be completely closed by tonight.
With any luck, you can cut out the stitches tomorrow."

"Why do all of your cures smell terrible? I hate mint."

"It's not mint, and I didn't beg you to let me speed up
your healing," Velma reminded him. "Did I mention it'll
leave a nasty scar? Winter can attest to that. This is the
same poultice I used on his eye a couple of years ago."

"Scarred me up good, but I didn't lose my eyesight,"
the bootlegger bragged, tapping the break in his eyebrow,

a reminder of the automobile accident that had killed the Magnusson parents and left Winter with mismatched eyes.

"I don't give a damn about scars," Bo huffed. "I just need my full strength back as soon as possible." Being injured was not an option. Not when there was a wild man with a knife out there, eager to cut Astrid's throat.

The first thing Bo had done this morning was tell Winter everything that had happened with Max and the idol—wisely leaving out the part about putting his own hands all over the man's sister . . . and her putting her hands all over him.

But.

He did confess everything else, and to his great surprise, Winter did not rip off his arms. All he had said was, "Just keep her safe. If that means we need to pay Mrs. Cushing a visit, say the word."

Winter's visits were never genial, but Bo didn't want his help. He could take care of it himself. And he suspected that the reason Winter was so forgiving about the whole situation was because the man was convinced something was going on with Aida. But if she hadn't told Winter about the potential pregnancy, Bo damn sure wasn't going to. None of his business whatsoever.

But he'd take whatever distraction he could get because he had things to do. Calls to make. Witch doctors to see with their cloyingly minty-smelling sticky cures. Astrid to follow . . .

He'd heard her voice before he woke that morning. She'd been in the stairwell, arguing with Greta. From the sound of things, she'd been trying to get down to see him and give him one of Dr. Doom's morphine tablets. Greta had no idea he was hurt and was too busy being aghast that Astrid wanted to stroll inside his quarters while he was still in bed. If she only knew what they'd been doing in the car last night, her head would surely rotate on her shoulders and explode.

His head might do the same if he kept thinking about

the way Astrid melted in his arms when he kissed her ear. The way her legs pressed together. He could still see it now, the beautiful Y shape made by the dark crease of her skirt trapped between her clenched knees and how it ran between her legs and molded the apex of her thighs. And to feel that Y rub against his—

He really must stop. His cock hadn't stayed down a solid hour all morning, and he'd already had to pleasure himself twice. So much for honor.

The first time was upon waking from a morphine dream in which Astrid was a blond fox who cornered him in an elevator that never stopped ascending. She stood upright like a human, but what started with her licking his wound ended up in a confused coupling that had him waking in sweat-soaked sheets before dawn.

The second time was after he'd woken for good. Upon forcing himself to shake off the druggy haze of the pain pill, he'd remembered a word he overheard Astrid saying when she'd been confessing to Le-Ann in the Moons' parlor: *My feelings for him are sempiternal.*

He had no idea what that meant. But like anything else he didn't know, he sought the education he required between the pages of his humble library. He was able to sound the word out and find it in his battered *Webster's*.

Sempiternal: eternal, everlasting.

My feelings for him are sempiternal.

That did it. He was probably the only man alive to masturbate after reading the dictionary. Clearly his self-control was in shambles.

Perhaps Velma's foul-smelling cure would help to restore it.

He'd found out not a half hour ago that Astrid was on her way out—as in, going out in the city alone, when she damn well knew that Max could be anywhere. Sure, Bo had put one beautiful bullet right through the man's leg. Two inches lower, and he'd have shot out the man's kneecap—which is what he'd been aiming for and had unfortunately missed.

A bullet in the leg wasn't as devastating. Max could be up and about today. Not likely, but who knew what kind of weird magic animated the son of a bitch.

It just wasn't safe. Astrid wasn't alone. She'd gone out with Jonte. And Jonte, like Greta, took care of the Magnussons like they were his own flesh and blood, but he was sixty-two and had a bum leg. The old Swede also refused to carry a gun. At least he had the sense to telephone Bo and warn him that Astrid had asked him to drive her around town. When Bo found out where they ended up, he was going to give her a piece of his mind.

"Bo?"

He glanced up from the fresh bandage that covered his minted stitches and found Velma and Winter staring at him like he'd lost his damn mind. Maybe he had.

"I was asking you about that disk," Velma said, pointing to the piece of gold that sat on the handkerchief spread over Winter's desk. "That looks an awful lot like the symbol on the front of that idol you showed me."

Winter frowned. "You've already shown her, too? And Lowe? Am I the last person to see it?"

He was, because right after Bo had confessed everything to Winter that morning, he'd taken his dinged-up Buick over to the Presidio, found Little Mike on guard duty, and handed him a parcel containing the turquoise idol.

Minus the gold disk with the symbol.

No longer giving a damn about preserving either an archaeological treasure or a magical object, he'd taken an ice pick and a hammer and pried the thing off in about ten minutes. Funnily enough, he'd discovered that the "disk" was actually a gold coin that had been melted down on the front and engraved. The back of the coin was still mostly preserved. It was very old. Spanish. A doubloon, he thought. If he had time, he'd take it to Lowe and Hadley or possibly to the Wicked Wenches for verification.

"This is for Mrs. Cushing," he'd told Little Mike when he'd handed over the parcel. "I ended up tracking down that man I was looking for last time I was here. He asked me to return this."

He'd included a friendly note inside the package that said:

You'll get the gold coin back when you tell me what the symbol means. When you're ready to talk, send a note along to Pier 26. And if any of you comes within a hundred feet of Miss Magnusson again, I'll burn your house to the ground.

Straight to the point, Bo felt. And it wasn't an idle threat. He didn't care whether these people were magical pirates or murdering occultists, they could be buried like anyone else walking around on two legs. Bo's patience for bullshit was at an end.

The telephone rang. He waved Winter off and walked around the desk to answer it, re-buttoning his shirt. "Magnusson's," he said into the mouthpiece.

"It's Jonte again," a Swedish-accented voice said over the crackling line. "I just dropped her off and am waiting outside for her to return. So far, no trouble. I can see the building entrance from here and no one is following."

From the dings and clangs in the background, it sounded as though he was calling from inside a restaurant. "Where are you?" Bo asked.

"I am inside Golden Lotus. Miss Astrid is across the street in your old apartment building in Chinatown."

Bo stared at the telephone cord as if it were a snake, and hoped he wasn't having a heart attack.

Jesus H. Christ.

Astrid was visiting Sylvia Fong.

Astrid smiled at the wary eyes that peeked through the cracked apartment door on the fourth floor of Bo's building. "Hiya," she said. "Not sure if you remember me, but I met you at Gris-Gris."

No acknowledgment.

"We took a taxi together," she clarified. "I was with Bo."

Never mind that Sylvia had actually arrived with Bo; Astrid went home with him. Sort of. Her life truly was a mess, wasn't it?

"Bo?" the woman looked very confused. She turned around and spoke to someone over her shoulder in rapid Cantonese. The answer came back in another feminine voice. "Yeung Bo-Sing."

The door opened. Standing inside the apartment was a beautiful woman dressed in a smart coat and hat. A woman who looked just like Sylvia Fong . . . were it not for the fact that her hair was much longer. Astrid's brain was having trouble making sense of this.

Footfalls raced toward the door, and seconds later, Sylvia's bobbed head poked around her shoulder. "Miss Magnusson," she said with a smile.

Stars, there were two of them. Two!

"This is my twin sister, Amy," Sylvia provided helpfully. "Amy, this is Astrid Magnusson."

"O-oh," Amy said, looking her up and down with greater interest, and then checking behind her—as if she expected Bo himself to be there. Astrid could practically smell the disappointment when the twin found the hallway empty. "Nice to meet you, but I'm late for work. Tell Ah-Sing I said to call. I miss him."

Astrid's smile faltered. She would absolutely not be telling him that. But before she could think of a response, Amy was sidling around her and racing down the hallway. Astrid watched her leave, and then turned to Sylvia and cleared her throat. "I was wondering if you had a few minutes to chat."

Sylvia eyed her with suspicion for a moment before making a sweeping gesture with her arm. As she did, the bell-shaped sleeve of her silk pajamas swung gracefully. "Come inside, won't you?"

Astrid stepped into a narrow entrance filled with tiny shelves lined with knickknacks—figurines, souvenirs from the San Francisco Seals baseball team, and several decks of playing cards—and followed Sylvia's slender figure into the main room. It looked much like Bo's did on the second floor, with its small kitchenette on the back wall and the living and dining area in the front. They passed between two rolling racks of clothes and sat together on a small sofa facing a window. Soft gray light filtered in from the dreary sky outside along with the sounds of midday traffic.

Sylvia tucked elegant feet beneath her and fitted a cigarette into a shiny black holder. "Would you like one?" she asked, holding out a silver case. Astrid waved it away and crossed her legs, waiting for her to strike a match and light it. "This is a most unexpected visit. What brings you here today? Did Bo send you?"

Astrid shook her head. "He doesn't know I'm here." *And he won't be happy when he finds out.* I had a favor to ask, but while we're on the subject . . . How long have you known Bo?"

"Let's see," she said, blowing out a cone of smoke. "Three years, I think? Yes, I think we moved in here that winter. It took me several months to get to know him because he rarely stays here. He says his room at your family's home is as big as a bread box, but I guess a fancy bread box is better than a run-down palace."

"He always said he stayed with us for the home cooking," Astrid said.

"The boy loves to eat," Sylvia agreed, smiling. "Not an ounce of fat on him now, but wait until he's fifty." She puffed up her cheeks and mimed rubbing a rounded belly.

Astrid chuckled.

"With his luck, he'll probably still be devastatingly handsome and that will just make me mad."

Sylvia thought he was devastatingly handsome? Well, of course she did. Isn't that what Astrid had come out here to discover? Since the wound had already been opened, she dug a little deeper. "Were you and Bo . . . ?"

One dark brow lifted. "Were we . . . ?"

Fine. Astrid said it. "Lovers."

Sylvia held her gaze for a long moment. "He hasn't told you anything, I assume," she finally said, flicking ash into a silver ashtray surrounded by bottles of fingernail polish. Sylvia's nails, much like Astrid's, were perfectly manicured, the middle of each painted ruby red beneath curved white crescent tips.

"He says you're friends," Astrid said.

"We are," Sylvia confirmed. "He's terrific fun, and I'd do just about anything for him."

"You haven't answered my question." She hadn't meant to sound so accusatory, but there it was. She leveled her gaze at Sylvia and held it.

Sylvia bristled. "What do you want to hear? Yes, we were lovers. Is that what you came to find out? We had sex right here on this sofa. Many times."

A sharp pang knifed through Astrid's chest. Her ribs cracked open and she bled like Bo had, all over the sofa, until she was nothing but a hollow shell of bones and skin and a dried-up heart. Nothing but two empty eye sockets staring blankly at Sylvia, but not seeing.

"I knew it," Astrid whispered. A woman always knows.

"It was a long time ago," Sylvia admitted in a softer voice. "I adored him. But he was almost never around, and when he was, it was only for an hour here, an hour there. He was too busy working, always gone to Canada or running all over the city in the dead of night."

The perils of bootlegging. Astrid had spent most of the last ten years of her life getting used to this. First her father, then Winter. Now Bo.

Sylvia puffed her cigarette and stared out the window. "I began to feel like I was just a last-minute diversion. That maybe I wasn't exciting enough to keep him. It was never sentimental between us, but I wanted more than he was willing to give, so I resorted to risky tactics."

"What do you mean?"

"It was Amy who suggested a way to grab his attention. She was always more adventurous than me. And at the time, I was willing to try anything to keep him—even sharing him."

Astrid stilled. "I'm not sure I follow."

"Don't you?" Sylvia said, pulling her knees to her chest, allowing the implication to hang between them like a threat.

"At the same time?" Astrid asked in a small voice.

She only heard bits of the next few sentences. *Three of us. Drunk. One night.* Her mind scribbled out the rest while her already-pained chest withstood the battering blows of conjured salacious images.

Sylvia. Amy. Bo.

Bo. Amy. Sylvia.

It sounded like something in a stag film. Astrid felt light-headed and queasy. And curious . . . but mostly queasy. Her hands were trembling.

"When?" was all Astrid could get out. God help her, she had to know.

Sylvia shrugged. "Summer of '26."

Astrid let out a shaky breath. Two and a half years ago.

"That's when I lost him for good," Sylvia was saying. "For someone who helps to run a criminal empire, he is strangely honorable. He said he couldn't see me, that it wasn't right. That we could remain friends, but nothing more. And when I pressed him, he said—" She laughed bitterly and screwed up her mouth. "Imagine thinking that the man you're crazy about has fallen for another woman. Now, imagine finding out that he wasn't even seeing that other woman, only looking at her from afar."

"There was someone else?" How many girls had Bo been with? Had he slept with half the city? He never told her any of this, and they used to share everything; apparently he'd been leaving out the juiciest details.

"Yes, there was someone else." Sylvia lifted her hand in frustration. "He refused me for the *fantasy of you.* You! A little girl still in school. You were, what? Sixteen? How insulting is that?"

Astrid wasn't sure how to answer. Emotions roiled and abated inside her—jealousy and indignation, anger and surprise. Relief and sadness. Bo had ended things with Sylvia in the summer of 1926.

That's when he'd taken Astrid to the redwood forest.

Part of her wanted to press Sylvia, to make her tell exactly what day this little erotic triumvirate occurred among the three of them. To find out if it happened before or after the redwood forest. But another part of her didn't want the answer. Didn't want to know. And did it really matter now?

"So, yes," Sylvia said. "Bo and I were . . . and then we weren't. But it is over, so you can stop looking at me like you want to claw my eyes out."

"I—"

"Don't worry. I've wanted to claw your eyes out, too." She gave Astrid a tight smile. "The only thing that made me feel better all this time was knowing that you were an unreachable dream that he could never have. That was my small consolation. But now here you are, asking me these questions, so I think maybe I was wrong. And that makes me sad."

She was sad? She'd had his body. His affection, too, obviously. God only knew what secrets they'd shared. Had he kissed her the same way he'd kissed Astrid? Had he said the same things?

And if Sylvia thought Astrid would feel sorry for her, she could think again. Had Sylvia spent years living off nothing but incidental touches and hope, knowing that none of it could be made public? Did *she* have to pretend like she was someone else?

Angry tears threatened. "Bo and I can't just run off into the sunset. You must know that. So if you want to keep feeling smug about your past victories, don't let me stop you. Because you've had more of him than I've had—maybe more than I ever will."

Sylvia frowned at her and looked away. Neither of them said anything else for a long time. Outside the apartment's windows, rain pinged against the fire escape, and a horn honked as rumbling cars sped over wet streets.

"I'm not smug," Sylvia finally said. Dark eyes slid toward Astrid's. Humor stirred behind them. "But I'm proud, and I see that in you, too. We aren't so different, I don't think."

Astrid let out a slow breath. "Perhaps we aren't."

"Besides, I'm seeing a wonderful man now, so I don't sit around pining for Bo. And I'm not the type of gal to try to take what's not mine."

"That's good. Because I like you, but you were right earlier. If you try to take him from me, I *will* scratch your eyes out. I come from barbaric stock."

"Mm. I'll keep that in mind. I doubt Bo thinks of me as anything but a friend anymore, so you're wasting your time worrying about it."

"I don't know about that," Astrid mumbled. "He named his car after you."

Sylvia's eyes widened. "The Buick? You're kidding."

Astrid wished she weren't. But as crazed and numb as she felt after absorbing all this news, something else was bothering her. An insistent guilt niggled and poked at her from a dark space inside her head. It was easy to ignore her own indiscretions when she was busy raging at Bo's. Easy to forget that she wasn't innocent, and her own indiscretions had occurred a lot more recently than two and a half years ago.

Sylvia stubbed out her cigarette. "You said earlier that you had a favor to ask."

"Yes," Astrid said, shaking off her self-reproach. *Focus on right now,* she told herself. She would deal with Bo later.

"You're a telephone operator," she said to Sylvia.

"I am."

"So that means you have access to private addresses?"

"Yes." Sylvia's brow lowered.

"Bo and I are . . . well, we're caught up in something. You remember the man who tried to attack me at Gris-Gris?"

Sylvia nodded.

"We're looking for someone to help us with that."

And after last night's chaos—Bo getting stabbed, the trip to Dr. Moon's . . . and every delicious thing that happened in the front seat of the Buick—Astrid woke up with an idea about a small detail they'd forgotten. On the night the yacht crashed into the pier, when Bo and she went on board, she'd remembered Bo talking to Officer Barlow about a man who'd claimed to have captained the yacht a year ago when it went missing. A man the police had dismissed as mentally unstable—just someone who'd seen mention of the lost luxury yacht in the papers and woven a fantastical story about swimming ashore.

What if his story wasn't so crazy after all?

"This morning I called the police to ask about someone who'd been involved in a case related to the mess that happened that night at Gris-Gris," Astrid told Sylvia. "They gave me his name, but they say he doesn't have an address on file. He spent some time in a psychiatric hospital last year, and since then, he's changed addresses and occupations. Honestly, I think the cops know where he's living, but they won't tell me. They'd probably tell my brother, but I don't want to get him involved. And Bo says telephone operators know all the city's secrets, so . . ."

Sylvia stared at her as if she thought Astrid needed to be in a psychiatric hospital herself—as if she couldn't believe Astrid had the nerve to ask her this after all the wounds they'd both just reopened. But whether she'd realized that their conversation had created a strange bond between them, or whether she, like Astrid, refused to wallow in misery for too long, she relented with an exasperated sigh.

"What's the name?"

"Marty Haig. He used to be a boat captain from Oakland."

A black candlestick telephone sat on the table next to all the fingernail polish. Sylvia sighed heavily and grabbed it, pulling the tail of the cord that stretched across the room. "Let me ring Amy. She's an operator, too. If she's not too busy at her station, we can track him down."

"Thank you." Astrid rearranged her skirt over her

crossed legs as Sylvia set the telephone base in her lap and picked up the earpiece. "By the way," Astrid asked. "Do you happen to know what *huli jing* means in Cantonese?"

One finger held the telephone hook down. "*Huli jing,*" she repeated, enunciating slowly. "It's . . . slang for a seductress. It literally means 'fox spirit.' It's a supernatural creature from old Chinese folktales."

Astrid sank farther down into the sofa cushion and smiled to herself as all the wounds she'd opened up in Sylvia's apartment began healing.

EIGHTEEN

———◆———

BO PARKED BY THE CURB ON MARKET STREET. AFTER EXITING the car, he pulled down the brim of his hat and strode down the sidewalk, passing in front of a six-story building with two steel radio towers atop it that both read "KPO." Hale Brothers department store. He'd escorted Astrid here a dozen times over the years. He knew the floors by heart. One floor in particular . . .

This was where the Fitting Room Incident had occurred last year.

But he couldn't think about that. He had worse things to worry about right now, like the possibility of Max jumping out to stab him again. And that Astrid had just been visiting Sylvia. Alone. Why in God's name did she have to go and do that?

Umbrellas crowded the wide sidewalk. It was only drizzling, but the damp air made Velma's minty nightmare poultice feel uncomfortably cool beneath his bandage. He ignored the pain and pulled up the collar of his coat, giving Jonte a little wave as he passed the familiar red-and-black Pierce-Arrow limousine. The Magnussons' driver grinned and saluted Bo as he started the engine and pulled out behind a streetcar.

Yes, I've got her now, Bo thought with a mix of alacrity and dread. He watched Astrid's fur-trimmed coat breeze through the department store's glass doors and followed her inside.

The store was abuzz with shoppers happy to be out of the rain, browsing for holiday presents under boughs of festive greenery. He wove past shelves piled with towers of wrapped jewelry boxes and wood-trimmed glass cases filled with fancy bottles, ducking in time to avoid being spritzed with French perfume. Just past an enormous trimmed Christmas tree strung with glass-blown ornaments and silver tinsel, he spotted Astrid's bell-shaped cloche and the blond curls peeking beneath it. She was heading for the stairs at the back of the main floor.

The thought crossed his mind that perhaps she really was only Christmas shopping, as she'd told Jonte before he excused himself to telephone Bo. But then he saw how fast she was taking the stairs and knew it was a lie. Astrid never rushed shopping.

Ever.

He stalked her through the millinery salon and the shoe section, where she paused to look at some pumps before resuming her whirlwind path up the stairs. Third floor, past the dresses—she *really* was intent on her goal not to stop here—and fourth floor, past the men's clothes . . . and then fifth floor, past the cafe and the fur room. She was headed all the way to the sixth floor.

Nothing was on the sixth floor but the executive offices and—

KPO RADIO, a sign read on the wall. 680 ON YOUR DIAL. ALWAYS LIVE!

The National Broadcasting Company affiliate radio studio.

Breathless, stitches sore from all the stairs, Bo watched her breeze into the station's front office and speak to a secretary. A few moments later, the secretary flagged down a silver-haired man who was walking down the hall. Station manager. That was who Astrid wanted to see, apparently. She shook the man's hand, smiling prettily, and began chatting. Bo moved closer, just out of sight, so that he could better hear them.

"—and anyway, I'm sure you don't have time to listen to little ol' me."

"On the contrary. I like your patter, Miss Magnusson. Anyone ever told you that you've got a pleasant voice?"

"Talking is my gift, sir."

Bo smiled to himself. That was one way of putting it.

"If you ever were interested in putting that voice to work, we're hiring voice actors all the time. Radio melodramas are the next big thing, mark my words."

"You don't say?"

He shook her hand again and she thanked him for helping her before he said something to the secretary and left them, breezing past Bo. What the devil was she up to? The secretary, given some sort of permission from the station manager, was now escorting Astrid two doors down, where she knocked on a door marked: CONTROL ROOM A.

Enough. Whatever she was doing, Bo wanted in on it. He sailed down the hall, quietly stepped next to Astrid's side, and stared ahead with her as the secretary got another man's attention—some sort of engineer—who was working inside the control room.

Astrid jumped and put a hand over her chest. "*Je*-sus!" she hissed in a sharp whisper. "You scared the life out of me. Where did you—how? What?"

The secretary turned around and gave Bo a bewildered look.

Astrid cleared her throat. "This is Mr. Yeung," she announced smoothly. Bo removed his hat and waited for her to finish with her normal cover-up—that he was there to carry her packages or that he was her driver or assistant. But she simply held her chin higher and smiled at the secretary as if she didn't owe her any further explanation.

And maybe she didn't.

"You're in luck. Mr. Haig's free now," the secretary said, and moved aside.

Bo held out a hand. "After you."

Astrid's eyes flicked down his body. Back up. Her gaze met his and it was a searing jumble of indignation and rage. Rage . . . and a flicker of something he'd never, *ever* seen so baldly from her: raw lust. He knew it when he saw it. In no more than a single heartbeat, he felt the flame leap from her and catch him on fire. But just as quickly as it sparked, anger snuffed it out.

His head spun. Why was she mad at him?

What had Sylvia told her?

The door shut behind them, and Bo tried to quell his rising panic as he glanced around at the small, dark room. The walls were stuffed to bursting with large pieces of electrical equipment—amplifiers and switchboards, dials and wires. A small window looked out into the adjoining brightly lit room, which appeared to be the main studio; a small orchestra was playing in front of a live audience of twenty or so people crammed into folding chairs.

But here in this room, standing up on a cane from where he'd been sitting at a narrow desk, was a silver-haired man in his fifties wearing an ill-fitting navy suit. His eye twitched as he looked over Astrid, and then Bo. He was quite obviously confused as to why they were here.

Bo was wondering the same thing.

"Mr. Haig," Astrid said, extending a gloved hand. Mr. Haig leaned on his cane and accepted the handshake with trepidation. "My name is Miss Magnusson, and this is my associate, Mr. Yeung."

Associate. That was quite a demotion from last night's erotic petting session in the front seat of his car. Was she punishing him for something she'd learned at Sylvia's or merely being professional? He couldn't tell.

"Thank you so much for agreeing to talk," she said. "I know you're a busy man, but we are investigating a minor incident and were hoping you might be able to help us."

"Investigating? Like detectives?"

"Why, yes," she said brightly. "Quite like that."

Oh, this was straight out of her brother Lowe's play-book. This was . . . so very Magnusson. But she didn't have Lowe's keen ability to lie with a straight face. The man would never believe—

"A young lady detective?" Mr. Haig said with the look of a man smitten. "I'll be. That's remarkable. Please sit and let me know how I can help."

Bo rearranged two folding chairs in front of the man and waited until Astrid sat before he settled next to her. Then he crossed his arms and waited for what she'd say next. This was ten times more interesting than the show behind the window.

"It takes all of this to make those broadcasts come out of my radio, huh?" she said, glancing around. "How fascinating. Have you been doing this long?"

"About six months," he answered. "Not as fascinating as it looks, I'm afraid. I'm good with machines. I used to repair ship radios—used to sail. But since this," he said, tapping his cane against his stiff leg, "I'm better on dry land."

"Actually, that's what I wanted to talk to you about. We are investigating the reappearance of a yacht that was lost at sea, and we understand that you once captained it."

Now Bo understood. He snapped his head toward Astrid and stared at her, feeling just as awed as the engineer. How in the world had she tracked the captain down? With everything that had happened, Bo hadn't even thought to do that. He now remembered talking to that pig Officer Barlow about a captain coming ashore last year.

He tried to give Astrid a pointed look but was distracted by the pallor that had fallen over Mr. Haig's wrinkled face. The man was upset.

"I don't want to talk about that," he said. "Please leave. I have work to do."

"I didn't mean to upset you."

"Who sent you? Was it her? The widow? She said she'd leave me alone if I kept my mouth shut!"

"Mrs. Cushing?" Astrid shook her head. "Absolutely not. We're not here on her account. In fact, we suspect she's not a very nice woman."

That was one way of putting it. And after assuring Mr. Haig several times that Mrs. Cushing didn't know about this "investigation" or that they were even here, the old captain finally stopped trying to push them out the door. Astrid's pretty smile certainly didn't hurt. Neither did her confession.

"You have my word that no one will know about this conversation," she told him. "But I fear that there is something dastardly going on with Mrs. Cushing. I am going to tell you something very private, Mr. Haig. I boarded the *Plumed Serpent* when she came ashore last week, and I experienced a very strange vision. It was so bizarre and chilling, I can't get it out of my head. But I think something terrible happened on that ship, and I fear several people who boarded it a year ago did not come back."

Mr. Haig stared at Astrid with a haunted look, and after a long silence said, "No one believed me."

"I believe you," Astrid said, reaching to put a hand on the man's knee.

He flinched a little and looked down at her brown leather glove. She withdrew it and gave him an encouraging smile.

Bo spoke up for the first time. "We both believe you, sir. And we'd like to prevent it from ever happening again. But we need to know what happened."

Mr. Haig's eyes watered. He swallowed hard and crossed his arms over his chest, knobby fingers still clutching his cane in one hand. "It all started the summer of '27. I used to run a charter service to Marin County, carrying private parties across the Bay. But during a storm, I tore the hull on some rocks and couldn't afford to get it repaired. I was out of work for several weeks and a friend took me out to a club to cheer me up."

Bo perked up. "Which club?"

"A place down on Terrific Street."

Terrific Street wasn't marked on any map. It was something locals used to call a stretch of Pacific Street in the old Barbary Coast red-light district. Bo thought about Little Mike's story of the dope addict striking it rich at the Pieces of Eight club.

"Where, exactly, Mr. Haig?" Bo asked.

"An old dance hall called Babel's Tower. It's a black-and-tan, just down from the main drag, so it doesn't get raided as much as the others. Back before the war, I used to go to Spider Kelley's and the Jupiter and pay ten cents to dance with the most beautiful girls you've ever seen. Present company excluded, miss," he said, giving Astrid a small smile.

"Babel's Tower is still open?" Bo said.

Mr. Haig nodded. "Not every night, and it depends on whether the cops are in a mood to jump it. But you couldn't pay me to go back there. Especially not upstairs. That's where they recruit you."

Babel's Tower, the captain proceeded to tell them, was a two-story dance hall. Anyone could pay the door fee and enter the bottom level, otherwise known to regulars as Hell. Dancing, drinking, music, gambling—Hell had all the normal attractions one would expect to find in an old Barbary Coast establishment. It also had a little something extra: its "taxi dance hall" girls. You could buy a ticket to dance with a girl.

"One song," he said with a shy smile. "Ten cents for a dance to one song."

Astrid inspected her nails. "If you felt greedy, would they let you buy two tickets so that you could dance with two girls at once?"

Realization was a tingling sensation that crawled down Bo's spine and constricted his stomach. Astrid knew. Sylvia had told her. *She knew!*

Bo furiously scratched the back of his neck, as if he could wipe away the shame, and fought the dueling urges to either bury his face in his hand or cart her off somewhere private so that he could explain.

He glanced at her and saw pursed lips, one arched blond brow, and two almond-shaped foxlike eyes slanted in his direction. Those eyes said: *Oh yes. I know everything.*

Shit.

Gritting his teeth, he silently cursed Sylvia. He supposed this was her little revenge against him. No doubt he deserved it, but he damn sure wished he'd told Astrid himself. In about ten years. Or possibly when she was on her deathbed and had lost her hearing. Or possibly never, *never* at all—ever.

Unaware of the current crackling between Astrid and Bo, Mr. Haig just coughed into his fist and said, "Uh, no, but you could buy several tickets to watch them dance in private booths . . . err, burlesque style."

Mr. Haig didn't dwell on the details, and his face turned redder than a cooked lobster as he apologized to Astrid for speaking frankly.

Astrid unbuttoned her coat, clasped her hands, and settled them on her knee as her foot bounced a steady rhythm. She couldn't possibly sit up any straighter.

"Anyway," the man said, "there was a girl there who first told me about Mad Hammett. He's in charge of the dancers. And he's the one who can get you into Heaven."

Mad Hammett was judge and jury over who was allowed in the coveted second floor of the club, where the wealthy and poor rubbed elbows. Mr. Haig was allowed upstairs after Mad Hammett discovered he could pilot boats.

"It's a different world up there," he said. "Everything's fancy. The booze is better. And to get up there, you have to either be beautiful or interesting—that's what my friend told me. But I think now that I know better; it's that you need to be useful. Because that's where Mrs. Cushing's people find their marks."

Mr. Haig began frequenting Heaven and found there was a private area up a secret set of stairs where a society of rich socialites met once a month.

"Pieces of Eight, they call themselves," Mr. Haig said, and all the hairs on Bo's arms rose as a terrible chill ran through him. "None of the members use their real names, and you can't enter until you've put on a mask. They throw wild parties. I'm talkin' *wild*. Things I've never seen or experienced before. Things I can't talk about in front of a lady."

Astrid started to protest, but Mr. Haig refused to budge on this. Bo was grateful, honestly. He didn't want to hear about, talk about, or remember anything in the least bit wild. "Please continue," he encouraged, nodding at Mr. Haig.

The man coughed into his hand again. "Yes, well . . . all I'll say is that I was going through a rough time, and these people made me feel like I was part of something big. And when they asked me to pilot a yacht last December, I was in no place to refuse the kind of money they were offering, so I didn't question why anyone would pay that much for a nighttime trip across the Bay. And it was the biggest mistake of my life."

Six fresh-faced recruits were taken aboard the yacht with six Pieces of Eight members. "And that's when I met Mrs. Cushing. She told me where to take the yacht, out near the coast between Muir Beach and Tennessee Cove. I was to kill the engine and stay put until she came and got me. I had to promise not to leave the pilot room. But they'd given me . . . well, I wasn't quite sober, you see. And a terrible squall came up. After my accident with my own boat, I wasn't all that keen on piloting the yacht in the middle of a storm—especially after one of the windows blew out."

The glass cut up his face. He deserted the pilot room seeking first aid and found the main salon covered in blue symbols and his passengers in the middle of the same ritual Astrid saw in her vision.

"I'd seen a lot of strange things in Babel's Tower," Mr. Haig said, shaking his head and staring out at the radio orchestra beyond the engineering room window. "But these recruits . . . It looked like they were going to drown them. Cold-blooded murder. And there was a strange white light coming from Mrs. Cushing, and it was like a rope, pulling me in. I felt like the whole boat was collapsing on itself.

Like . . . like we were sitting on a whirlpool that would take us all down. And then Mrs. Cushing saw me, and I felt like I was looking into the devil's own eyes."

"What happened next?" Astrid asked, her own eyes wide with alarm. Bo felt something warm on his arm and realized that she was searching for his hand. He wrapped his fingers around hers and was surprised by the strength of her grip. She wanted comfort; he squeezed back, happy to provide it. Happy she wasn't mad at him, however momentarily.

Mr. Haig shook his head before he answered her question, looking blank and haunted. "I panicked. The cabin's doors were open to the deck. I ran outside and jumped overboard. Hurt myself on some rocks, but managed to swim to shore," he said, nodding toward the stiff leg. "Almost didn't make it. Thought I was surely dead, but I reckoned it was better to die in the water than on that cursed boat."

The dim room was quiet for a moment, but for the crackle of electricity coming through the amplification equipment and the soft strains of the orchestra beyond the window. Bo finally asked the question at the forefront of his thoughts.

"Did you see what happened to the *Plumed Serpent*?" he said, studying Mr. Haig's troubled eyes. "Do you know where it went for the last year?"

Mr. Haig stared at him for a moment and said, "I don't know where it went, but I can tell you what I saw when I got to shore. Lightning struck it—a great big white streak from the night sky. And when it did, the damned yacht disappeared into thin air."

NINETEEN

———⚓———

SHAKEN UP AND ANXIOUS, BO MATCHED ASTRID'S QUICK STEPS
back through the executive offices. They didn't speak until
they were heading down the stairs, out of earshot of the
people working on the sixth floor. And even then, she was
only focused on what they'd just learned from Mr. Haig.

"That had to have been Mrs. Cushing in my vision,"
she said, her heels click-clicking as she trotted down the
stairs. "She was the woman in the red robe. She was elderly
then, but that ritual must have restored her youth. That's
the only thing that makes sense. But how come she wasn't
on the yacht with the rest of the survivors when it crashed?"

"I don't know, but the police chief said she helped with
their investigation last year after the boat went missing.
So she had to have gotten off it somehow." Astrid glanced
back at him, eyes fixed on where the gold coin jingled in
his coat pocket. He'd taken out the coin and showed it to
Mr. Haig before they left the radio station. Astrid had been
surprised but didn't say anything until now. "So it's a
pirate coin, not a disk? Where's the rest of the idol? Did you
destroy it?"

"I sent it along to Mrs. Cushing's house," he said, and then briefly told her about prying off the coin and his reasons for doing so. Though Mr. Haig hadn't been able to identify the symbol on the gold coin, he'd vaguely remembered seeing the turquoise during the ceremony on the yacht. And even if he couldn't help them with the exact nature of the ritual, he'd at least been able to point them toward Babel's Tower. It could be dangerous for Bo and Astrid to show their faces there, especially after the threatening letter Bo sent along with the idol. But as long as they didn't run into Max or Mrs. Cushing, no one should recognize them, and Bo believed that the benefit gained would outweigh the risk. Maybe he'd try tomorrow, if they were open; tonight he had bootlegging runs to manage.

Astrid came to a quick stop on the fifth-floor landing and spun around to look at him as shoppers filed out of the cafe. "How did you find me? It was Jonte, wasn't it? I knew he was up to no good. 'I have to telephone Greta,'" she mimicked in Jonte's low Swedish accent. "That dirty liar."

She swung around and started to head down the next flight of stairs but stopped again. "You shouldn't even be out! Dr. Moon told you to stay in bed today and rest. You're probably tearing those damn stitches right back open, but you don't even care, do you?" She waved dramatically at his side, squinting at his coat as if she were checking for blood. "And why do you smell like gum?"

"Velma came by the pier," he said. "It's one of her remedies. Speeds healing."

And at the moment, it was itching terribly, so he supposed what Velma had told him about the wound knitting itself together was true. At least the pain was lessening.

Pale blue eyes blinked at him, big and round. "Are you feeling better?" she asked in a softer voice.

He nodded once. "Been worse. Good job with Mr. Haig. That was smart, tracking him down."

Astrid shrugged off his compliment and descended the stairs at a brisk clip, fur-trimmed coat flying behind her like a cape. She passed the fourth floor and kept going.

He jogged to catch up. "In a hurry to get somewhere?"

"Maybe I am," she said, lifting her chin.

"I see. Where would that be?"

Her mouth twisted up. She clutched the handbag dangling from her wrist and, instead of continuing her descent, made a sharp turn onto the third floor. Women's dresses. She strode past a holly-decorated column to browse holiday gowns displayed on headless wirework mannequins.

He trailed behind her, sighing heavily. When she stooped to inspect the beads around a gown's hem, he finally said what they were both surely thinking. "So . . . you went to see Sylvia this morning." His voice sounded calm. He quickly wiped away the sweat blooming on his forehead while her head was turned.

"Uh-huh." She stood and ran her fingers along the dress's neckline.

"That must have been interesting."

"Uh-huh."

"Lots to talk about."

"Uh-huh." She squinted at the price marked on a hanging manila tag.

He tore off his hat and ran his hand over the crown of his head. "Why did you go to her?"

"I needed her help tracking down the captain. You always say telephone operators are . . . helpful."

He didn't like the way she enunciated "helpful."

"So that's all?" he pressed. "She just gave you the radio station address?"

"We may have discussed some other things"

Dammit. "If you wanted to know something, all you had to do was ask me. Have I ever held anything back when you've asked?"

She whipped around to face him, her face livid with anger. "No, but apparently I haven't been asking the right questions, have I? Twins? At the same time?" She whacked him on the arm with her handbag. "What's"—*whack!*—"the matter"—*whack!*—"with you?!"

When she reared back to hit him again, he grabbed the handbag. "Stop it."

"I will not! How am I supposed to feel about that? Is this your typical Saturday night entertainment?"

"No! Jesus, Astrid!" Shoppers began watching them, so he lowered his voice and let go of her handbag. "That was not typical. That was absolutely *a*-typical. I've never done anything like that before, and damn sure haven't done it since."

"Not even two women, but"—she looked around, lowered her brow, and whispered hotly—"*sisters*? Honestly! That's the most perverted thing I've ever heard."

His coat suddenly felt like it was made of bricks; his shoulders dropped under the invisible weight. "I wasn't even supposed to be there. Sylvia called me at the warehouse and caught me when I was about to head home. I'd just unloaded a shipment of rum and I was tired, but she made me feel guilty . . ."

"I'll bet," Astrid muttered beneath her breath as they waited for a nosy woman to pass. "Then what? They stuck a gun to your head when you walked in the door?"

"No." Bo leaned closer and spoke in a low voice. "Sylvia was already half cut when I got there. Amy poured us all drinks. I had a couple."

Oh God. Was he really telling her this? One look at her squared jaw and he wanted to race out of the store like a coward. He put his hat back on.

"I won't lie. It was exciting—for all of ten minutes."

"My, my. Virile *and* efficient. Aren't you just the epitome of manhood."

"The truth is, I didn't actually go through with it, not with both of them. Only Sylvia. Amy was just . . . a bystander. Do you understand?"

"I don't know if want to."

"Look, I sobered up the minute it was over and couldn't get out of there fast enough. It took months for Sylvia and me to get back to acting normal around each other and just be friends. And I haven't so much as kissed her hand since—hers or anyone else's. There's been no one for years. *Not. One. Single. Kiss.* I swear it, Astrid."

She considered this, her face softening slightly, but he could see her fighting it. He ducked his head lower to look into her eyes. She turned a haughty cheek toward him but didn't pull away, so he spoke in her ear. "Can you say the same?"

The accusation vibrated between them. Her face twisted up. She tried to turn around, but he grabbed her shoulders. A nearby shopper gasped, and he looked up to see someone talking to a matronly store manager and nodding in their direction.

That's all he needed, to get thrown in jail for accosting a blond woman in a department store. He grabbed Astrid's hand and dragged her through round racks of clothes, behind the mannequins, searching for privacy. Three curtained doorways lined the wall, and a memory flashed back to him of Astrid's naked body stepping from behind the changing screen.

He'd never been able to get that damned image out of his head.

Red curtains were drawn on two of the three fitting rooms. A white-haired attendant with a measuring tape draped around her neck was standing guard, waiting to help customers who needed tailoring. Someone called her, and she turned to answer. Seizing the moment, Bo pulled Astrid into the last fitting room and yanked the curtain closed.

It was spacious here, bigger than his own room back at the Magnussons' home. Gilded floral wallpaper and two stuffed chairs circled a long mirror.

He released his grip, shook away the memory, and pinned her with his eyes. "Go on. Fair is fair. I told you about Sylvia and Amy. Now *you* tell *me* about Professor Luke."

A low whine buzzed in the back of her throat as she backed away, heading toward the changing screen. "Bo . . ."

"Three months ago. You were practically bragging about it in your letters, throwing it my face! How do you think that made me feel? I prayed to every divinity in the universe that I was wrong—that nothing really happened. But now that I see your face, I know it's true. You lost your virginity to a college professor you barely even knew!"

"I didn't lose anything. It was mine to give." She pointed a thumb at her chest. "My decision."

"And you gave it to *him?* While I was stuck here, making myself sick imagining another man's hands all over you?" And unable to do anything about it. He was angry now, remembering how impotent he'd felt. How panicked.

How devastated.

"I was trying to get over you!" she snapped.

A distant part of his brain raised a warning flag, but he ignored it and charged Astrid in two strides. "You will never get over me. Do you hear me? Never! You will never be free of me, because I won't let you go. I will put a bullet in any man who touches you. I will go to jail for you. I will die for you. My ghost will haunt you from the grave."

Her pupils expanded, black overtaking all but a ring of blue around the edges. Her breasts rose and fell rapidly. She made a tiny noise that his body recognized: surrender. A switch flicked inside his head. His ability to reason shut down. He flung an arm around her waist, roughly pulled her against him, and captured her mouth with his.

It was a punishing kiss, full of violence. And she gave it right back to him, digging her nails into his neck, knocking his hat off to grab the short hair at the back of his head. A fireball of lust rocketed through his body, tightening his balls and making him uncomfortably hard. He shifted his hold, grabbing handfuls of her coat to feel the swell of her buttocks beneath, and pulled her hips to his. He thrust against her below and licked into her mouth above. Trying to get closer. To get inside.

She let go of his hair, and he felt her hand dive between their crushed bodies a second before it palmed his erection through his pants. Her grip bordered on brutal. His cock was hot iron pressing against her possessive fingers. He groaned beneath her touch.

"No one else," she whispered angrily against his lips. A threat and a vow.

He doubled her hand with his own to reinforce it for a moment, helping her hold him, and then released it to cup the curving mound between her legs through the fabric of her dress. The whimpering noise she made was intoxicating.

"No one else," he whispered back.

Her hand slid away and she threw her arms around his neck. A second later, he was encouraging her legs to part and lifting her off the floor as she jumped upon him, thighs circling his hips, dress hiked up. He stumbled one step as she clung to him. Reached out for support and toppled the changing screen, which clattered to the floor with a muffled bang.

He winced at the sound, but Astrid just gave a little gasping laugh, her eyelids heavy with lust, breath coming fast. It only made him want her more. He walked her two steps to a single narrow shelf, knocked off a pincushion and a wooden hanger with one hand, and set her down with her back against the wall.

She didn't quite fit. Her coat was too bulky. He wanted it off. He wanted everything off. Wanted to take her right here, right now. Years of wanting could be erased in a blink. His mind and body roared for it. Demanded it. The intensity of his feelings was terrifying.

Trying to slow himself down, he slapped both hands on the wall to either side of her head and let his forehead drop against hers. His chest heaved. The stitches in his side protested. His cock ached.

"Astrid," he begged, but he wasn't quite sure what he wanted. For her permission? For her to stop him? For her to assure him that everything was going to be all right between them—that their passionate vows to each other weren't empty promises?

"You belong to me, Ah-sing," she whispered. "You have always belonged to me."

His heart lifted right out of his chest and soared.

He dropped grateful kisses on her nose and eyelids,

tasting kohl and the salt of her skin. He paid attention to everything, so that he could remember it later: the fluttering of her pulse when he pressed his lips to her temple, the warm promise between her legs as he nestled his erection against the silk of her chemise. The crack of the wooden shelf beneath her backside . . .

The shelf snapped off the wall.

She fell and pulled him down on top of her.

They tumbled to the floor with loud *bang!*

Everything hurt. He'd surely torn his stitches and ruined all the progress Velma's poultice had made. But he really didn't give a damn. He could bleed all over the floor as long as she was in his arms.

"Are you all right?" he asked, but she was already laughing, and that only made him want to kiss her again.

The fitting room's heavy velvet curtain flew open. They turned their heads in unison to see the white-haired attendant, frumpy store manager, and three wide-eyed customers gaping at them.

Not missing a beat, Astrid smiled and smoothly said, "You can put that on my charge account."

TWENTY

———◆———

THEY KNEW BABEL'S TOWER WAS OPEN THE FOLLOWING NIGHT
when they saw the cars lining the street and golden lights
twinkling from a two-story brick building. Astrid didn't
think it was the kind of club that had a coat check, so she
stashed her fur in Bo's trunk and hopped over the curb.
Despite threatening clouds and gray skies, it hadn't rained
all day, so even though water still ran through the streets,
the sidewalks were fairly dry.

She didn't know what to expect to find in the club
tonight. Mission or no mission, she chose to think of this
as a rare night out with Bo, and had dressed accordingly
in a two-piece amethyst tunic dress with chalk white beads
and a scalloped hem. The dropped waist covered up hips
that were a touch too full, and the latticework design of
the beading plumped up a bust that was a touch too meager.
A silver clip held back the waves of her blond hair on one
side and matched Bo's watch on her wrist.

He eyed her with open interest and settled a warm hand
on her lower back as they fell into step on the sidewalk.

"It's like we're on an actual date," she said, unable to

stop herself from smiling. On the way here, he'd pulled the car over a block away from home and kissed her thoroughly. Her lips still felt swollen, and the warmth that had spread through her center hadn't subsided. Looking at his handsome face with all its sharp lines made her feel a little buzzed. He was a thousand times better than champagne.

"Here? This is the last place I'd take you," he said, humor lurking in the corners of his eyes. "We'd go somewhere swank, like out to the theater to see a play or a concert."

"I'd settle for a picture show."

"Never settle," he said, and his merry mood turned sober.

"Don't plan to." She put her hand behind her back and pulled his arm to her side. Threaded her fingers through his. "I know exactly what I want, and I aim to get it, no matter the cost."

He squeezed her hand tightly and sighed. "Have I told you lately how much I enjoy your company, Miss Magnusson?"

"No, you haven't."

"Remind me to do just that if we make it out of this dump alive."

It was easy enough to get inside the club. The thug who guarded the door was ten steps down from the tuxedoed bouncers at Gris-Gris and couldn't have cared less who they were, as long as Bo was putting money in his open palm. And it didn't get much better inside.

"Hell" was an appropriate name, Astrid decided, when she scanned the packed main floor. It was dark and smelled of cigarette smoke and beer. The floor was sticky and covered with peanut shells. And though they had a stage, the jazz band playing on it was less than spectacular. Only a few couples bothered to dance. Everyone else seemed to be more interested in hiding in the shadows—and there were plenty of those.

Bo ordered them sidecars from the bar, and they found an empty table with a good vantage point. Astrid flicked peanut shells off the table and stealthily wiped down the rims of their glasses while Bo surveyed their surroundings.

"Don't drink it," he told her as he looked around the room. "From the smell of it, it's probably bathtub hooch. And from the looks of the regulars around here, it might kill a few brain cells."

He didn't have to tell her twice. She trusted Bo's nose when it came to booze, and he was right about the regulars, if that's who these people were. Most of them were men, and though no one gave Bo a second glance, several people were eyeing Astrid in a hungry sort of way, and it made her feel uncomfortable.

"I don't see any dance hall girls or burlesque booths," she said. "Maybe things have changed since Mr. Haig was here. Maybe the secret society shut down while the yacht was missing this year."

"Perhaps, but I don't think so. Don't be obvious, but take a look at the door in the corner by the billiards tables. Two bouncers there, but only one at the door outside? That seems strange. Also sounds like there's different music coming from back there."

He was right. Two men making their way to the inner door stopped, paid one of the bouncers, and received tickets in return. That's where they needed to be.

Bo agreed. They slowly made their way to the inner door.

"How much?" Bo asked.

One of the bouncers looked him over. "Ten cents a ticket. One ticket to dance. Five for the private burlesque shows. That's five apiece if she wants to watch, too," he said, nodding toward Astrid.

Bo handed him a bill. "We'll take ten tickets."

The bouncer gave Astrid a knowing look that made her feel positively dirty. It was all she could do to smile and not shout out, *It's not what you think!*

"By the way, any idea if Mad Hammett is in tonight?" Bo asked as the man pocketed his money and counted off ten paper tickets from a roll around his wrist.

"You and the dame lookin' to get upstairs, eh?"

"Maybe."

"Ask Henry at the carousel." He handed Bo a string of

red tickets and gave Astrid a slow smile. "Enjoy yourselves."

Not likely. Astrid hurried through the open door with Bo and was glad to hear it shut behind them. But not for long. The backside of Hell was just as crowded as the front. Men, and a few women, sat at tables along the front wall, waiting their turn with the "taxi dancers." Most of the dancing girls seemed bored, and some of the men were holding them a lot closer than any dancing Astrid had ever seen. A few even seemed to be giving out more than dances.

But that was no concern of Astrid's. Bo grabbed her hand and pulled her toward the center of the dance floor, where a large circular hut was covered in carnival lights and paintings of frolicking nude angels. A velvet rope and another bouncer stood watch over the door here.

"You Henry?" Bo asked, holding out their tickets.

"Maybe."

Bo added a dollar bill to the tickets. "Fellow out front said you were the guy to ask if we wanted to see Mad Hammett."

He looked at Astrid and took Bo's money. "Yeah, all right. Booth four."

"No need. We just want to talk to Hammett," Bo said.

"You want to talk, you go into the booth. If Hammett likes the look of ya, he'll stop by."

"But—"

"Not my rules, buddy. But I can tell you this much. If you're gun-shy about this in here," he said, nodding his head toward the carousel, "you ain't gonna last five minutes upstairs."

Was this some sort of test to weed out the weak of stomach? Two more men were approaching the carousel, and Henry already had his eye on them, ready to hand Bo's tickets and money back. He plainly didn't care whether they went in or not.

"Let's go inside," Astrid told Bo in a loud voice, putting on a good show of enthusiasm for Henry and hoping she sounded braver than she felt. "It'll be fun."

Bo lifted a brow and hesitated briefly. "You heard the lady. Guess that means we'll be taking booth four."

Henry shrugged and pocketed the cash. "To the right. No touching the dancer."

No touching? Was this a common problem? Astrid's palms suddenly felt overwarm.

"What about Mad Hammett?" Bo asked.

"Yeah, yeah. I'll tell him. Whether he wants to talk to you is his business." Henry opened the velvet stanchion and allowed them to go through. They passed under the carnival lights and into a cramped circular passageway that bounded around the edge of the structure like thread on a spool. Tattered curtains were pulled shut over arched doorways on the inner wall, and each one had a number scrawled above it in peeling paint. Astrid spied light through the edges of the curtains and heard music and laughter, but they ran into no one until they found the doorway marked 4.

Bo lowered his head and spoke into her ear. "We don't have to do this."

"And quit now? Absolutely not. How bad could it be?"

"Anywhere from uncomfortable to downright horrifying," he said, looking anxious about the prospect of either as he pushed back the half-open curtain.

Her stomach twisted anxiously.

Inside was a cramped space with two squat stools and a low bar counter. The counter looked out over a narrow stage whose view was blocked by another curtain. It smelled like bleach, which was good and bad. Good, because someone had recently cleaned the floor and counter. Bad, because it needed to be cleaned. Astrid certainly wasn't eager to sit on the stool.

"Forget the dancer. Don't touch *anything*," Bo warned.

That didn't make her feel any better.

Holding her hand, he perched on a stool and urged her to sit sideways across his lap. "There," he said, tucking her closer, arms encircling her waist and back as she slung her own arm around his shoulder. "How's that?"

"Better," she said as her misgivings subsided considerably. It felt decadent to be held by him, despite their seedy surroundings. His face was so close she could feel his breath on her cheek . . . and when he moved, that breath tickled the flyaway curls that had escaped the silver hair clip over her ear. This sent a shower of chills down her neck. "See, this isn't so bad," she said, speaking as much to herself as to him. "Rather exciting, I'd even say, in a dangerous sort of way."

"Everything involving you is."

She relaxed a little more and glanced at the closed curtain. "That man said Mad Hammett would stop by if he likes the looks of us," she whispered. "But how does he get a look at us? Is he behind the curtain?"

"Was wondering that myself. Maybe—"

Whatever he was going to say was cut off by the movement in front of them. The curtain was opening. Music flooded the small room as a single bright bulb came to life over the tiny stage. Not more than three feet away from them, a pale woman with long brown hair smiled down at them. Her scuffed black T-strap heels were level with the counter, and her dark stockings bore a long run down one knee. In lieu of clothes, she wore five playing cards—one over each breast and three fanned out below her belly button.

The dancer didn't seem put off by Astrid's presence, and after a brief moment of discomfort, Astrid decided she wasn't all that put off by the dancer, either. She'd seen worse things in that hidden collection of pornographic postcards her brother Winter kept in his study—one he didn't think anyone knew about, but, in fact, everyone did. Probably even Greta. The dancer in front of her, who was now half-heartedly swaying to the music, was nude, yes, but she wasn't particularly becoming. Never one to be falsely modest, Astrid felt her own body to be quite superior, which made her feel a little better about Bo looking.

That is, until the woman removed the card over her right breast to reveal one nipple with a large brown areola. The dancer flung the card over her shoulder and winked at Astrid.

Astrid wanted to laugh. Maybe this wasn't so bad. Maybe it was even a little fun. The way Bo was muttering under his breath made it clear that he was uncomfortable and regretting having agreed to all this, and Astrid rather enjoyed that.

"What do you think?" she whispered near his ear, nudging the brim of his hat up with her nose.

"I think there's no way in hell I'm answering that question."

"Boo, hiss," she complained.

He chuckled a little and tightened his grip around her waist. "I think I'd much rather see you on that stage."

"Much better," she said, smiling against his ear. She thought of what he'd done to her own ear in the car that night in Chinatown, and on an impulse, took a little swipe around his earlobe.

He sucked in air.

She did it again.

The dancer removed the card over her other breast.

How in the world did she get them to stick to her skin? Maybe it was best not to know. Astrid placed several soft kisses around the edge of Bo's ear and felt him growing hard against her thigh. She felt the corresponding pleasurable sensation burgeoning between her own legs, and when she pulled back slightly to find his eyes closed, not even watching the dancer, her corresponding sensation became a warm flood.

The arm circling her waist dropped. Bo's hand slid beneath her dress's tunic, fingers moving up her ribs. Slowly, his palm rounded the curve of her breast and molded it through the delicate silk of her chemise. A thumb stroked one tight nipple, causing a cascade of delightful shocks to shoot down her center. She gasped.

The dancer was right there, and Astrid didn't know if the woman could see Bo's roaming hand, but just wondering if she *could* had Astrid caught between panic and thrill. It made her face warm and her breath come faster.

Only three cards left, and as the dancer moved, they

barely covered the woman's dark curls. She made a teasing gesture to remove the cards. Once, twice. Bo was paying attention now, Astrid noticed. It was hard to blame him. Much like seeing a fistfight or an automobile accident, it was difficult to look away. And after another feint toward the cards, the dancer spun around, bent over at the waist, and smiled at them through her spread legs.

There it was, everything, right on display.

The first thing Astrid thought was: *Lord, that's an awful lot of hair.* The second thing she thought was: *I hope I look a lot better down there than that. I'm bending over in front of a mirror to check when I get home, just to be sure.* And the third thing was: *She'd better flip back over soon or all the blood's going to rush to her head.*

"Stars," Astrid murmured, unable to stop blinking. Unable to look away. When the woman wiggled her backside, it was just too much. Astrid clamped a hand over Bo's eyes.

Laughter rumbled through his chest and under her hand—under *his* hand, too, which was still holding her breast. She laughed with him, brimming with an odd medley of joy and arousal and sheepishness. Then she gave the dancer an apologetic look, hoping the woman didn't think they were laughing at her. But the woman didn't seem to mind, and since the blood *had* rushed to her head, her face was redder than Astrid's burning cheeks when she finally stood upright, turned around, and gave a little bow.

Astrid released Bo's eyes and applauded enthusiastically, still laughing a little. Bo's hand slipped out from her tunic to pull out a bill from his pocket. He gave it to Astrid, who passed it up to the dancer. She accepted it with grace and blew them both a kiss before tottering backward as the curtain drew closed.

"My, that was . . . interesting," Astrid said, still mildly embarrassed but unable to stop smiling.

"Not half as interesting as you. *Aiya*, Astrid. You amaze me."

"I do?"

"Every day." His hand ghosted over her stockinged knee and softly squeezed the inside of her thigh. Oh, that was nice. Very nice, indeed. Her blood was hot and she wanted him to squeeze a little more. Everywhere. But when she shifted in his lap to give him better access, his head tilted toward a beam of unexpected light. All his muscles stilled at once.

His hand slipped out of her dress as she turned around to see what had startled him.

"Don't stop on my account," a lilted voice said.

The curtain was open, and a middle-aged man in a suit the color of a fresh bruise leaned in the doorway, crossing his arms over a broad chest. If his face was a wall, his dark handlebar mustache was an overgrown hedge sitting in front of it. The growth was so thick, when he gave them a slow smile, it barely moved.

"Enjoyed Bebe's performance, did ya?" he said. Mr. Haig told them at the radio station that the person they'd be looking for was Cornish, and from the sound of this man's accent, he fit the bill.

"Mad Hammett?" Bo asked as he rotated Astrid along with him on the stool.

"In the flesh." The man's dark eyes roamed over Astrid's legs. She pulled down her dress and started to stand up from Bo's lap, but his arm locked around her middle like a steel bar. Whether it was due to possessiveness on his part or instinct about Hammett, Bo certainly didn't want her to move, and that made her nervous. It only got worse when her head began to clear and realization hit: *This man could be one of them. Like Max.*

"We were interested in getting up to Heaven," Bo said.

"Henry told me. And I liked your show almost as much as Bebe's," he said, jerking his chin upward. Astrid followed with her eyes and spotted a dark circle on the ceiling of the booth. A hole. He'd been watching them from above. Astrid didn't like that. At all. "So I thought I'd pop down and introduce myself."

Astrid stared at his extended hand for a beat too long and finally gave hers. "Mary, uh, Johnson," she said.

Hammett bent low and kissed her hand. The stiff hairs of his mustache made her skin crawl, and she held her breath, terrified of having another vision of drowning bodies. But he wore no ring, and though she didn't want him touching her, nothing supernatural occurred. "Delighted, miss. I quite liked seein' ya laugh. We need more of that around here. How old are ya? Eighteen? Nineteen?"

"Thereabouts," she said, trying to act casual as she gently pulled her hand from his grip.

"And who is the lucky chap gettin' all your affection?"

"Charlie Han," she said, inventing a name for him as fast as she could.

Hammett eyed him with almost as much interest as he had with Astrid. "Young and handsome. You speak well. They'd like that. But I'd feel wrong if I didn't admit that they got a fondness for Nordic blood in Heaven. No offense."

"None taken," Bo said in a low voice, but Astrid knew damn well that was a lie, even if she hadn't felt his legs turn to marble beneath hers and the menacing vibration running along his bones like electricity through wire. She silently told herself to keep her eyes down and not give her own aggrieved feelings away, praying Hammett didn't notice. And he didn't.

"The two of you attached or looking to play?"

What in the world did that mean? Astrid could only guess, and it didn't sound good.

"We might be open to adventure under the right conditions," Bo replied casually.

A small noise of protest escaped the back of her throat. Bo hugged her tighter and she cleared her throat.

"That's fine," Hammett said, smoothing down the edges of his mustache. "Well, I can't promise anything, considering their preferences. Mary here, yes. They're fond of dames like her. But you? I don't know. I might be able to get you up there for a trial . . ." His brow wrinkled. "What do you do for living?"

Astrid remembered Mr. Haig's words. *You need to be useful.*

Bo remembered them, too, apparently, because his answer came fast. "I fish. I . . . pilot fishing boats."

It was halfway true. He did fish, sometimes. But not so much the last few years, though he certainly knew his way around a boat. Astrid did, herself. All Magnussons did.

"A fisherman, eh? Yes, that's not bad. Might be of interest to them." He sniffled and scratched his nose, thinking, and then smiled broadly. With the flick of his fingers, he'd reached inside his suit and withdrawn two small business cards printed on gilded stock. "You'll need these to get in," he said, handing them to Bo. "New Year's Eve, 9 P.M. We're having a party. Come to the carousel and ask for booth seven."

New Years Eve? That was so far away—a week and a half. She couldn't tell if Bo was discouraged by this, but she certainly was.

Before she could stop him, Hammett picked up Astrid's hand again and kissed it a second time. Once again, no vision haunted her, but something else was there. Something dark that made her feel as if a nest of snakes wriggled beneath her skin. It was all she could do not to snatch her hand away.

"I'll be looking forward to it, my dear," he breathed over her hand, eyes jumping from hers to Bo's. Then, without another word, he stood, turned around, and exited the booth.

"Oh God," Astrid murmured, letting out a shaky breath. She wanted to set fire to her hand and burn off the place he'd kissed.

"Hold it together," Bo whispered. "Let's get out of here, yes?"

She nodded and pasted on a smile as they left the way they came in, circling back around the carousel, through the taxi dancers, and back into the front room, where they crunched over peanut shells and headed through the front door.

Once outside, they strode down the dark sidewalk and didn't stop until they got to the car. Bo started the engine and pulled out the gold cards. Astrid leaned closer and they inspected them together under a slant of streetlight beaming through the windshield. The cards were identical. They each said:

> THIS CARD ADMITS ONE CHOSEN SINNER
> THROUGH THE PEARLY GATES INTO HEAVEN
> COURTESY OF THE PIECES OF EIGHT SOCIETY
> ——PREPARE FOR JUDGMENT——

Embossed in the bottom right-hand corner was something vaguely familiar to both of them: a variation on the mysterious symbol from the turquoise idol.

TWENTY-ONE

———— ❦ ————

BO SPED AWAY FROM TERRIFIC STREET FEELING SPOOKED YET
cautiously victorious. They had the gold symbol from the
idol as leverage. They had their tickets into Heaven. And
they'd made it out of Hell without getting stabbed or having
any dark visions of midnight rituals. Now all they had to
do was wait.

"Where are we going?" Astrid said from the passenger
seat as the Buick's wheels spun waves of water over sidewalks as they passed.

Bo wasn't sure. His first instinct—*Get the hell out of
here, fast!*—was now cooling to a simmer, and something
new was taking its place. He had no bootlegging runs
tonight. The warehouse was empty. The docks were empty.
There was no one to track down, meet, or haggle with. No
errands. Nothing.

"You listen to me, Bo Yeung. You will *not* take me
home."

Her words shot straight through him, getting the attention of something primal and beastly that crouched in
the corner, waiting to be loosened. All their touching in the

carousel had left an erotic buzz in his veins. And Mad Hammett touching her had stirred up a dark possessiveness with gnashing teeth and a hunger to claim.

The two of you attached or looking to play?

He'd wanted to break the man's nose for that. He'd wanted to drag Astrid out of there, slung over his shoulder, and mark her with his body, like some feral dog. Wanted to take her away from all of this—her family, this city, their restrictions . . . their past.

He was nearing a breaking point. He could finally admit that to himself. His restraint was running on fumes.

His eyes shifted sideways. Astrid was hugging her arms around her middle, trying to stay warm—they'd left so fast, he'd forgotten their coats in the trunk. He quelled his dark thoughts and switched on the heater. "Better?"

"Yes. Did you hear me?" she asked.

"I heard. Think hard about what you're saying. It's close to midnight and there are few places we can go together, if you're asking me to take you out somewhere . . ."

He tried to sound cool and matter-of-fact, but his fingers would snap the steering wheel in two if he gripped it any harder. He kept his eyes on the road, waiting for her answer. Had he made things plain enough for her? Did she understand? *Tell me to take you home*, he begged silently.

"I don't want to go out," she said. "I don't want to go home. I want to be alone with you."

A tense breath whooshed from his nostrils. He licked dry lips and swallowed hard. She understood, he had no doubt now. They looked at each other and a silent agreement passed between them. The crouching beast in him stood and roared triumphantly. It was all he could do to keep the car on the road.

"Your apartment?" she asked after a few moments, almost shyly. Almost.

No. The walls were paper-thin and there was the possibility of running into Sylvia. Neither woman deserved that. Where else? They couldn't go home. Couldn't go to a hotel, unless she paid for the room and he sneaked up later, and damned if he was doing that. He had his pride, after all.

Where could they be alone?

Was this actually happening, after all these years?

He was driving, but not really seeing. Spinning through thoughts, but not really thinking. His mind was bright with anticipation, teetering precariously. One wrong word, and he feared he'd lose everything at once. But there were practical matters to consider. "I need to stop by a drugstore. If we hurry, there's one that stays open late in—"

"No, you don't."

"Astrid—"

"I have something. I got it in Los Angeles. It's a little rubber dome. A tiny cap. Jane told me about a doctor near school . . ." Her cheeks flamed—even in the dark car, he could see them color.

"I know what you mean." He'd never seen one, but he'd heard about things like that. They were illegal to obtain under Comstock laws. He was surprised and impressed by her courage to seek it out. She was fearless, and he loved that.

She smoothed her dress over her lap. "Anyway. I have it in my handbag. Just in case we . . . Well, I was hoping, I guess. This was after Luke—I didn't . . . Stars! I mean to say that, uh . . . I've practiced putting it in, but I haven't used it," she said quickly, biting her lip. "And then you wouldn't answer my letters, and I thought I'd ruined everything, but I kept it, hoping, you know, maybe. Oh God. Why can't I stop talking?"

He put an arm around her shoulder and pulled her against him, kissing the top of her head and smiling. "I'm happy you were hoping."

"You are?"

"Hell yes."

She relaxed and curled up against his side. "Where can we go?"

At that moment, Bo realized a solution to their problem. He knew where to go.

Ten minutes later, he'd parked the Buick inside the warehouse at the pier and Astrid was doubting his vision. "Here?"

"Not here," Bo said, helping her into her coat. "Oh ye of little faith. Put on your gloves, too. It's going to be cold as hell." He smiled down at her, unable to disguise his eagerness. "But I'll warm you up when we get there."

Astrid followed Bo onto the pier. The Bay wasn't as choppy as it had been the first night she came home—the night the yacht crashed. And though water still threatened to spill over the creaky dock boards lining the warehouse, it wasn't raining.

"Look, Bo," she said, pointing out over the Bay. "Fog! I'd never thought I'd say this, but I couldn't be happier to see it."

"Hm, I might just agree with you on that. Better than stormy water. Come on."

All their crabbers, rumrunners, and trawlers bobbed in the water, asleep for the night. Bo stopped in front of a long, skinny runabout that looked like the tip of a spear pointing out of the water, sleek and long. The varnished mahogany hull gleamed in the moonlight. He removed a blue tarp near the rear that covered a two-person cockpit fronted by a low windshield.

Excitement bubbled up and mixed with the nervousness that was churning her stomach. "Where are we going?"

"Where no one will find us." The white of Bo's teeth showed when he smiled.

"All right," she said, smiling back. "I'm game. Let's go."

Hand on hers, he helped her step inside the cramped seat. It had been nearly a year since she'd been on a boat like this. Her balance faltered, and the runabout rocked. She squealed and awkwardly settled down, slipping her legs under a wooden dash covered in round glass dials.

After Bo detached mooring lines from the pier, she felt the boat dip lower into the water with his added weight as he slid into the other side. His leg was warm and solid against hers. A turn of a key, a flip of a switch, and a pressed button started the rumbling motor. He turned on a bright fog light that shone out over the bow and cut over the dark water. Then he handed her his hat to hold on to, and just like that, they were gliding away from the pier.

A terrible exhilaration came over her as the runabout shot forward, whipping her hair around. The pungent scent of salt water filled her nostrils. Her stomach dropped. Lights of the Embarcadero blurred as Bo accelerated, steering them around the curved coastline, past piers stretching out like spokes of a wheel. Normal conversation wasn't possible over the roar of the engine, but Bo glanced at her every so often. He looked like the boy she'd fallen for years ago—sharp cheekbones, intensely eager eyes, and a tireless enthusiasm that was infectious.

The runabout zipped through the water with its nose tilted upward as they sped north of the coast, away from the city. A quarter hour passed, maybe more, and San Francisco's twinkling lights began fading while distant coastal cliffs to the north stood black against a purpled sky. They crossed from the Bay waters into the Pacific proper and made their way toward those cliffs, around the western side of the Marin County peninsula, and that's when Astrid knew exactly where he was taking her.

The Marin County docks.

Ten miles or so up the coast, the Magnussons owned a few acres of land surrounding a small cove. The entrance to the cove was hard to find in the day, and nearly impossible at night. It was once a military camp, and supposedly a smuggling spot for pirates. Astrid now hoped those pirates didn't include Max and his ilk at the Pieces of Eight Society; it wasn't far from here that Mr. Haig said the *Plumed Serpent* had disappeared.

Bo slowed the runabout when they spotted the cove entrance, a narrow channel between two rocky cliffs. It felt a little ominous when they entered. The boat's headlight shone into shifting fog, and the motor's sputter echoed off jagged rock, where gulls and murres nested in the crags. But it wasn't long before the cliffs parted to reveal a circle of private waters a quarter mile in diameter, ringed by beach in the middle and rising cliffs on the sides. A long warehouse stood along the beach behind a wide dock, where four stubby piers stretched into the cove.

Bo pulled up to the farthest pier, cut the engine, and threw a mooring line, then helped Astrid onto the dock while he anchored the runabout. It was strange to be there so late at night, when everything was dark and deserted.

"Do you remember the last time I brought you out here?" He glanced up the cliff overlooking the cove, where a long set of stone stairs led upward.

Her heart thudded inside her chest. "That afternoon . . . the redwoods."

He nodded. "Too cold and wet out there now, but there's someplace warmer."

They ascended the dizzying cliff stairs in the darkness. When they crested the top of the cliff, a strong coastal wind whipped strands of hair into her eyes. She held them back and stared at the lone building in the distance.

The lighthouse.

Ringed in fog, it stood black against the night sky, in disuse since the turn of the century. Connected to the side of the tower was a small cottage, where, at one time, a lighthouse keeper lived, ensuring the beacon light stayed lit. Her father had used the cottage for an office when he'd worked out here for the fishing business. Now Bo and the Marin County warehouse foreman used it a couple of times a month when they unloaded big shipments of liquor from Canada and needed to guard the warehouse overnight.

After fiddling with the lock, Bo entered the cottage and switched on a lamp. Astrid stepped inside, and he bolted the door behind them. It had been years since she'd been here. The furniture in the living area was sparse but tidy, and they'd recently added an electric icebox in the kitchenette. Bays of low windows ringed the outer wall, providing a clear view of the coast from multiple angles. The Pacific was a dark blanket that stretched out and met the stars at the horizon. No city lights, no boats. Nothing at all but the two of them.

She shivered. Bo mistook it for the temperature.

"Hold on and I'll get the wood-burning stove going," he said, and went outside to fetch wood. While he was gone, she rushed into the cottage's spartan bathroom and rummaged inside her handbag for the small cervical cap case. It didn't take long to wash her hands and get the thing inserted correctly, but Bo was already back by the time she flung open the door.

"Everything okay?" he said, striking a match to light the balled-up newspaper he'd stuffed under logs and kindling inside a squat cast-iron heater.

"Hunky-dory."

He looked up at her and smiled, and that made her feel less anxious. Neither of them said anything while the fire slowly worked its way from the kindling to the logs. After a time, during which Bo fiddled with the damper, heat began to radiate from the old grates. "I am suitably impressed with your masculine ability to provide fire," Astrid said, warming her hands near the potbellied heater.

"Is that so?" he said, leaning a shoulder against hers. "I can also head out into the woods and hunt down something with fur if you'd like."

"I was just hankering for a nice piece of . . . bear?" She grinned. "I don't know what's out in those woods this time of night, and I don't think I want to know."

"A fox?"

"No!" She elbowed him, laughing. "No foxes. They could be fox spirits, and all your stories show what a terrible mistake it is to cross them."

"Especially golden ones," he said, flicking his eyes toward her hair. He slipped out of his coat and laid it on the back of a rocking chair near the heater. "Getting warm, little fox? Your cheeks are rosy."

She was burning up, yet unsure if it was due to the

heater or her vibrating nerves. If she was being honest with herself, she was terrified. Too many what-ifs plagued her thoughts. What if they were terrible together? What if it changed their feelings about each other? What if he found her boring? What if it was as disappointing for her as it was with Luke? She'd never spoken to Luke again, and Bo had ended things with Sylvia after . . .

What if this was the beginning of the end?

"Hey," Bo said in a soft voice, grasping her shoulders. "It's just me. Just us. Forget about all of that."

"Why can you always read my thoughts?" she murmured.

"Because I've spent far too much time looking at your face," he said, tugging her coat over her shoulders and guiding it down her arms. "And I know the way you rub the first joint of each finger with your thumb when you're worried about something. And the way the way your eyelids lower when you're coming up with a terrible scheme."

"I don't *scheme*," she argued weakly as he draped her coat atop his. But what she really meant was: *I love the way you notice everything.*

"Not very well." But what he said with his eyes was: *I adore even the less-than-admirable things about you.*

She tried to respond, but he was taking off his suit jacket, and she was suddenly very, *very* nervous. Her throat wasn't working correctly. She didn't seem to be able to swallow, and her mouth was dry.

He removed the leather shoulder holster that held his gun and stepped closer. He didn't take his eyes off her as his hand went to his necktie. He wriggled it back and forth to loosen it and then tugged until it fell apart and slid off his neck. After tossing it aside, he opened the top two buttons of his shirt and dipped his head to speak into her ear. "I know you're nervous," he said sympathetically, but with no hint of compromise. His nose grazed a few strands of hair, and that tiny motion sent a single chill down her neck, like a lone scout riding out to survey a battlefield.

His hand cupped the side of her face, and he spoke in a

low, calm voice. "Just because we came all the way out here doesn't mean you can't change your mind. If you want me to take you back home, tell me now."

"No," she said softly. "I haven't changed my mind."

"Do you still want me?"

"Yes," she whispered.

He placed a small kiss on her temple and released her face to remove the silver clip from her hair. He threw it on their growing pile of discarded clothing and combed her hair out with his fingers, sending more chills through her. A little warmth sparked low in her belly. Her shoulders relaxed.

"This is what's going to happen," he said in voice that sounded like the low purr of a big cat. Like someone who was calculating, very certain of himself, and unconcerned with trying to hide it. "I need to be in charge now. You've got to let go and give me the reins. You've got to trust me. Whatever I say, you do."

"Are we pretending?" she said in hushed voice.

"No," he said, shaking his head slowly. "No more pretending."

She was confused. "Why, then?"

He exhaled slowly through his nose and made a small contemplative noise in the back of his throat. "I can't explain it, but whatever things are like outside this room . . . right now, when it's just us, I just need to be in control. And I think maybe you need that, too."

Maybe she did, because she thought she might just understand what he meant. Out there, he conceded and compromised every day. Bit his tongue when he wanted to speak. Bowed his head when he wanted to fight. Out there, he did it because he had to. Alone with her, he wanted to be himself.

As for her, and what she needed . . . well, the idea of yielding to him was oddly pleasing. A relief, even. And a bit thrilling. "All right," she said.

"Yes?"

"Tell me what you want me to do."

Dark pupils dilated. He nodded once, the matter settled, and stuffed his hands in his pants pockets. The way he looked at her now was predatory. Startlingly so. She fought the urge to back away from him and felt her heart gallop inside her chest. He didn't say anything for a long moment, and when he finally did, it staggered her.

"Take off your dress."

TWENTY-TWO

———— ❧ ————

THEY STOOD TOGETHER FOR SEVERAL MOMENTS, AND HE DIDN'T lower his gaze. Didn't offer her a way out or ask if she wanted to change her mind again. No quarter whatsoever. The cottage was quiet but for the distant waves crashing against the cliff below the lighthouse and the crackle of wood in the heater.

"Take off your dress," he repeated.

A little shudder went through her. He meant it.

And she meant to comply.

She pulled the top of her tunic dress over her head, unbuttoned the skirt, and let it drop in a puddle on his shoe. Goose bumps rippled over her arms. Her nipples pebbled beneath the silk of a shell pink step-in chemise that was lacy and frothy and very, *very* expensive—but not nearly enough armor to shield her from the intensity of his heavy gaze. Her head felt light. She wasn't sure if she had the nerve to do this . . .

Until she heard the change in his breathing.

Her eyes dropped. An intimidating erection strained

the front of his pants. Like an echo, heat bloomed between her thighs.

"Very good," he said in a steady voice that had a new layer of huskiness that wasn't there before. "Now the rest."

She slipped off the outer silk garters at the tops of her stockings and wiggled off the elastic roll garters beneath; without support, pale pink silk slipped down her thighs and fell to her knees. Her fingers trembled as she bent to push them off her feet along with her heels.

When she stood, Bo undid the buttons on his vest and tossed it aside.

"Get those off for me." He extended a cuff toward her as his free hand tugged the hem of his shirt from his belted pants. She unfastened a silver cuff link engraved with a dragon, a task that was both intimate and mindless, all at once. She was glad for it, because it settled her nerves. After repeating the process on his other cuff, she dropped both cuff links in his waiting hand.

He pocketed them. Rolled out of his shirt. Pulled his undershirt up his back and over his head. A slash of black hair swung over one eye. He pushed it back and unbuckled his belt and left the ends dangling like an invitation while he tugged off his shoes.

She surveyed the elegant bone and hard muscle of his body. The lines of his stitches were railroad tracks across his side. The cut was now a raised, reddened scar, slightly puffy and still smelling faintly of mint, but looking much better than Astrid expected. Velma's magical poultice was a small miracle. Astrid longed to touch him—there, to make sure he was okay, and other places. She wanted to feel his skin beneath her fingers, but when she reached for him, he stopped her.

"Not yet," he said, and nodded to her chemise. "Continue. Everything but my wristwatch," he added with a wicked curl of his lips.

They held each other's gaze for several beats.

She would be naked; he would not.

He wanted control; she would give it to him.

Her tongue was heavy in her mouth. In two quick motions, she tugged down her chemise's straps and removed the last bit of silk covering her body, and then kicked it away and stood in front of him.

His eyes took their time looking her over as he stepped closer and lightly, delicately ran the tip of his middle finger from the center of her collarbone down between her breasts, and didn't stop until he'd circled her belly button. Her breath came faster.

"*Leng*," he murmured. *Beautiful.* "I must have thought of your body a thousand times since that afternoon I saw you in the fitting room mirror. Maybe ten thousand. But memory is a poor substitute for the real thing, and you were right. You've changed . . . here," he said, running his fingers over the slopes of her shoulders to show her. "And here"—over the flare of her hips—"and here." His palms cupped her bare breasts.

She inhaled sharply and bowed her back as he rolled her nipples between index finger and thumb. It was too much and not enough, and she was very aware of the wetness surging between her legs. Just when she thought she couldn't take it anymore, he bent low and replaced his fingers with the suction of his mouth. The flick of his tongue. The gentle scrape of his teeth. First one nipple, then the next.

If what he'd previously done to her earlobe had been wicked, this was positively satanic. Her fingers dug into his hair. Her hips swayed forward. But when she rose up on her tiptoes, he took one last lick and released her. Cool air rushed over the puckered tips so fast, the sensation bordered on painful.

She whimpered and tried to draw him back, but he made a clucking sound with his tongue and pulled her hands between them while he waited for her to submit. Then he gave her another command.

"Finish undressing me."

She glanced at his open belt buckle and took a deep

breath. The buttons of his pants were a struggle until she gave up on delicacy and pulled them open with force, gaze locked with his as she did. He looked back at her with a barely restrained wildness that was dark and hungry and vibrating with delight. She'd never seen him look like that. Ever. And she loved it. With one last pop of a button, she got his fly open and tugged everything down over his hips and looked at what she'd revealed.

The ridges of his stomach dipped over lean hips. The trail of black hair she'd touched in the darkened car trailed down to a cock that stood long and proud, curving upward from wiry black curls. It was thicker around the base and a darker shade than the rest of his skin, and she was astonished, and possibly a little bit intimidated. She was no expert by any means, but she reasoned the matter wasn't much different from evaluating a finely made gown; she knew quality when she saw it.

"Stars," she murmured.

He chuckled low and deep. "Pretty good, I think."

"It's impressive."

"It's yours. Go on and claim it, *huli jing.*"

Delight surged through her when he said that. She hesitated, just for a moment, but long enough for him to guide her hand forward with his. Her fingers wrapped around him. He was shockingly warm and silky, heavy in her hand. She stroked upward and saw his stomach muscles flinch. Stroked downward and pulled back the foreskin to reveal a glistening dark pink tip, beaded with fluid.

He sucked in a sharp breath and shivered. She glanced up to see his head tilted back, eyes shut. A thrill shot through her, and she continued stroking him, slowly. While she did, Bo's hand wrapped around the back of her neck and kneaded her tense muscles. Just that—just him touching her while she touched him—seemed to complete an electrical circuit between them. To put things in motion that couldn't be undone.

Bo's hands ran down her back, fingers splayed. He rounded over her backside and palmed her with a slow, proprietary squeeze. Then he reached a little farther. Warm fingers slid beneath her buttocks and between her legs, dipping into the wetness there and stroking.

"You *do* want me," he murmured, equal parts smug and surprised.

She couldn't answer, because his roaming fingers slid away, only to be replaced by another hand in front. Skimming damp curls, he traced her swollen flesh, making lazy rotations until one finger dove through and found her clitoris, brushed it, testing. A touch like a whisper. The pleasure this caused was an avalanche that made her lose track of her strokes on him and weakened her knees. They wobbled a little and then gave out completely; she might have fallen to the floor if Bo hadn't sensed it in time and slung an arm around her waist.

She grabbed his hips and fell against him. And with her breasts pushed to the solid wall of his chest, his hot erection trapped between them, he urged her backward, repeating, "I've got you."

A single bed was pushed against the cottage's outer wall, beneath the band of windows overlooking the ocean. The mattress was thin; the blanket, tucked military tight around it, was old and worn. Bo pushed the pillow aside as they sank into it together, his mouth covering hers. His kiss was achingly soft. Erotic. And all at once nakedly hungry. If she was hot before, she was burning now. His hands drifted over her with abandon while his knee wedged between hers. She needed no urging. Her legs parted shamelessly, and this time, when his fingers found her center, his stroke wasn't experimental, but sure and steady. He touched her like she touched herself when she thought about him too much before sleep. He touched her like he'd had all the time in the world to imagine how it might best be done. He touched her like it was his own body, and he was pleasing himself.

After he slid two fingers inside her, it didn't take long. She'd worried she couldn't let herself go in front of him, but somewhere along the way, between his murmurings against her cheek—*You're so soft here. Make that sound again for me. Like this? Tell me you want me*—her hips arched off the mattress and she knew she was close.

He knew, too, and when her body began shaking, he moved between her legs. Hovering over her, his weight on one arm near her head, he continued touching her and whispered, "Do you want to know a secret? I was already in love with you the afternoon I took you to the redwoods." And with that, he replaced his fingers with his cock, and drove himself into her in one unrelenting push.

One pump of his hips and she lost her breath. Two, and she regained it, along with her voice, which was making the most bestial noises she could possibly fathom and she *didn't-care-couldn't-stop*. Three, and her mind emptied.

The orgasm ebbed and flowed, lifting her out of her body and pulling her back down again, pleasure and relief in equal measure. When the last pulses of it slowed, she wanted to wrap her legs around his and pull him down under, but he wasn't finished with her.

His body bowed above hers, every muscle taut and tightened like a finely tuned cello. Dark hair hung over his eyes and tickled her face when he dipped his head to taste her lips. "Hold on to my arms," he said, and she obeyed, wrapping her hands around his stony biceps. He lifted himself higher and tucked his chin to his chest, staring between them to the place where they were joined. To where he pinioned her, pushing into her, slow and steady, hips like a machine that showed no signs of tiring. Dark curls, blond curls. The root of him glistening with her wetness. He pulled out completely and then slid back inside with a shudder.

"Look at us," he whispered. "We are beautiful."

His words were a match combusting into fire as they struck over her skin. And she soon felt herself involuntarily clutching around him a second time. How could that be?

"Again," Bo ordered, groaning with pleasure as his

rhythm grew fiercer, steadfast, faster. "And this time, we'll come together."

She felt her climax gathering speed. She breathed in the scents of their bodies. And when his arms shook and his head tilted back, she watched Bo's face straining (mouth open, eyes squeezed shut, dark brows lifted high at the inner corners), and crashed along with him.

Her heart beat slow and forceful, and when he pulled her closer, she felt his own heart pounding in the same unhurried way. The pleasure he'd given her still pulsed in her blood. She was slack, spent, and felt a bone-deep satisfaction of both body and mind. He shifted onto his back and drew her along with him until she was sprawled across him, limbs tangled. She fitted her cheek in the hollow at the center of his chest, sighing heavily.

"Still alive?" he whispered into her hair with an earthy sound that was almost a chuckle.

"Mm . . . not sure." Her voice was broken and sleepy. "I feel like I've been drugged from my knees to my stomach."

This time he did chuckle, and she felt it through his chest. "When have you ever been drugged?"

"I haven't, but I imagine this is what it would be like. I'm all warm and loose. It feels amazing. How long does this last?"

The fingers that were trailing through her hair, lazily combing it back over one ear, stilled for a moment. "Are you saying that this is a novelty?"

"Well, it's a hell of a lot different from doing it yourself," she said.

"I meant—"

"Yes, yes. I know what you meant. This is the first time that's happened for me with anyone else, and was . . . *marvelous*." She sounded inane and a little drunk, but she didn't care. Nothing felt this good. Nothing at all.

She felt his smile against her hair.

"Don't get cocky," she said, curling her toes around his feet.

"Too late." He forced her to look up at his face and squinted down at her with heavy-lidded eyes. His smile was dazzling. "You were loud."

"Oh God." She tried to hide her face, but he wouldn't let her.

"I knew you would be—when I imagined us together. I hoped you would be." His hand smoothed over the skin down her back.

"You were loud, too," she pointed out. Almost alarmingly so.

"Mmm-hmm. You made me feel wild. Are you proud? You should be."

"Not proud, no. Just happy." She sighed with pleasure.

His bare foot danced with hers, toes tracing the curve of her arch and over her heel, and then hooked around her ankle to pull her leg closer. "And if I'm being honest, I'm usually dressed and gone by this time, so this is a little new for me, too."

She twined her leg harder around his. "You aren't leaving, and we're not going home tonight."

"You couldn't make me if you wanted to. I would tie you to the bed."

"You would?" She didn't mean to sound so eager, but the image of it raced through her head and made her chest warm.

"I still might." He shifted onto his side and rolled her with him, capturing both of her forearms together at the small of her back. He pinioned her and smacked her buttocks with his free hand.

She squealed and broke free, rubbing her stinging cheek. "O-ow," she complained, laughing. A grin split his handsome face as he tried to spank her again, and when she was too fast to catch, he wrestled her facedown on the bed and made her whoop with laughter when he threatened to tickle her. "Don't do it," she said into the bedcover, mildly hysterical and breathing heavy. "Do *not* do it, Bo Yeung."

"Looks like you are in no position to tell me what to do."

"I'm begging," she said, trying to blow hair out of her eyes as she twisted around to look at him, but he only pinned her legs down with his and blew the hair back.

"Well, well," he said. "That's different. What can you offer me?"

"Umm . . ." She couldn't stop smiling. Her heart raced madly inside her chest. "I'll let you be in charge one more time."

He snorted and smacked her bottom again, this time more playfully—but it made her jump, regardless. "That was going to happen anyway. *Every* time," he said, and joy shot through her. Every time. More times. Meaning: this wasn't an anomaly.

"Try again," he said, nipping the back of her neck with his teeth. "What can you offer me?"

"I have heard—I mean, I don't know, but I have it on good authority—that some men might enjoy the feel of . . . well, that is to say, when a woman uses her mouth instead of her hand, you know . . ."

"You don't say? And where did you hear such a thing? I don't think it could possibly be true." She couldn't see his face through her hair, but he sounded like he was trying not to laugh.

"Are you teasing me?" she asked indignantly.

"Maybe." He pushed his hips against her backside, where her skin still stung, and she was shocked to feel his erection. "And I accept your offer; though, to be fair, we were going to do that anyway."

"Hey!" She tried to buck him off of her. "No tickling!"

"But for now, I'll settle for another trade," he said, tracing the cleft of her buttocks with one teasing finger that made her gasp. "Because *I* have it on good authority that some women enjoy the feel of a skilled tongue between their legs, and I know Greta says it's a sin to brag, but I am most definitely skilled at this task—"

"Stars," she murmured.

"—and if you're very, *very* good, I might lick you a little before I put my cock inside you again."

TWENTY-THREE

———— ◆ ————

BO WATCHED THE PACIFIC SLOWLY CHANGE FROM BLACK TO BLUE as morning broke. The cottage's windows were ablaze with sunlight, and he could see for miles over the calm water. But it only held his attention for a moment, because his attention was focused on the golden girl in his arms.

He lay on his side behind Astrid, spooning her with one arm curled around her waist, his hand cupping her breast.

Her heart beating in his hand.

They shared the bed's only pillow, and though he'd dozed for a while, his body was aware of the rare gift afforded him—her bare body sleeping next to his—and that had exhilarated him too much to stay asleep for long. He watched her breathing openmouthed on the pillow, limbs entwined with his. He was far too happy.

And far too satisfied for his cock to be thinking about rising again, but there it was. He'd come four times already—the last time, inside her mouth, which was shockingly new to both of them. Neither seemed to have any boundaries, and the realization that her eagerness to explore matched his own was more thrilling than Christmas and New Year and a birthday all rolled up together.

Something in the back of his mind told him to slow down and think of the future. To have a care that they were setting themselves up for heartbreak. But he had listened to that voice for far too long and all it had brought him was misery.

Not today.

He wasn't thinking about consequences, rules, or impossibilities. He was only thinking of the present. And right now, the present was yawning and stretching in the most adorable, sexy way possible.

When her eyes cracked open, he said, "Good morning, *huli jing.*"

"Bo," she said in a sleep-rough whisper as she rolled around to face him. "Tell me I'm not dreaming." Her voice was small and fragile, and hearing it did something funny to his heart.

"If you're dreaming, I must be dreaming, too," he said, pushing back the blanket to look at her.

"Oh good." She kissed him lightly on the lips and winced, slipping a hand between her legs. "I'm sore. And you . . . are not," she said, eyes widening as she looked down between them.

"Don't pay any attention to that. I have to piss like the devil, and until that goes down a little, it's going to be nearly impossible. I'm sorry you're sore."

Her brows lifted. "You don't sound sorry."

"Mmm." He fought down a smile. "Not sorry for what we did, but I don't like you being in pain."

"It's a good pain. I feel like I've been fighting in a battle."

She looked like it, too. Rosy spots were scattered across her neck and breasts, and three small bruises, impressions left by his fingers, darkened the pale skin around her hip bone. Shameful, perhaps, but he bore her brand on him, too: an angry red scratch down his thigh, a bite mark on his forearm, and stinging claw marks on his back. She inspected him, looking rather pleased with herself, and then blinked rapidly and twisted around to peer outside the windows.

"Bo! The sun! It's not raining."

Morning sun gilded the surface of the ocean and reflected back a dazzling light so bright, it made him squint. Not a cloud in the sky and no wind battering the trees along the cliffs. How long had it been since the storms began? Three weeks? He hadn't seen the sun in three weeks.

"Oh, Bo," she murmured. "It's like it's just for us. A sign that everything is right. Let's go outside. I want to feel it."

"The fog's still rolling back down toward the city, and it's early. Give it a little time to warm up out there. How about a nice hot bath first? Might make you feel better."

"Together?" she said.

"It's an old tub, but it's big."

She smiled her consent, and they spent the better part of an hour in the big bathtub, mostly lounging and exploring each other's bodies. She was too sore for anything else—that quickly became obvious to Bo. He forced her to take aspirin, and they helped bathed each other, which was a small but satisfying pleasure, then groomed themselves as best they could with what meager supplies the cottage provided.

After dressing in last night's clothes, they scrounged the small kitchen for a breakfast of soda crackers, peanut butter, and hot tea. The tea was Bo's private stash of *Longjing* Dragon Well tea, imported from China, and for which he'd traded Canadian whiskey. The teacups were mismatched and the plates chipped, but Astrid didn't seem to care. Dressed in their coats, they took their meager meal outside in the briny morning air to a small stone table that overlooked the ocean, and with the blanket from the bed wrapped around them, ate while the sun continued to rise.

Astrid curled her fingers around the hot teacup and inhaled deeply. "This is perfect. Let's stay here and never leave."

"And what would we do for money?"

"That *is* a problem, isn't it?" She lay her head on his shoulder and tugged the blanket tighter around them. A seagull sailed in front of them and landed on the cottage roof with a loud squawk. When the bird settled down, she said, "Bo? I need to tell you something."

His heart skittered inside his chest, but he tried not to let any panic show. "You can always tell me anything, unconditionally."

"I know. It's just that I'm a little ashamed of this. Well, a lot. Do you remember when we went to the Anthropology annex to see Lowe and Hadley, and you asked me what Hadley and I discussed privately?"

"And you refused to tell me. Yes, I remember."

"Well . . . the thing is, I'd asked for her advice because I'm doing poorly in school. My grades are terrible across the board, but Luke, that is, Professor Barnes, failed me."

Bo felt a flush of anger in the center of his chest. "That rotten, dirty pig. He lures you into sleeping with him and then turns around and fails you?"

"He didn't lure me. I'm not defending him—"

"That man should be suspended from his post. And I'm not just saying that because I want to choke the life out of him for touching you."

She put a hand on his wrist. "I know you do. But the fact of the matter is that I stopped going to class. So they are threatening to expel me."

Oh. That wasn't good. At all.

Bo didn't know how to feel about this, but he could see plainly that Astrid was anxiously avoiding his eyes. "Maybe Lowe could talk to somebody," he suggested. "After all, he works for U.C. Berkeley."

"Another reason not to raise a stink. He's trying to build a life with Hadley that doesn't rely on illegal activities. His reputation is precarious, especially considering the family business. I'm not putting his job in jeopardy over my poor grades and attendance. That's not fair to him."

As much as he wanted to argue, she had a point. But he

damn sure wished she hadn't put it that way, because it only made him feel that Lowe was doing the right thing, and here Bo was, on the illegal side of the family business with Winter.

She scratched her forehead and looked out over the water. "I have one more shot in January. One semester to bring my grades up before they expel me. And I guess that's what I'm struggling with. Do I go back?"

"Of course you go back. Do you know how many women in this city would love to have that opportunity?"

"I know, but what if I'm not a scholar? And what about us? Being apart nearly killed me, and that was when I only had hope. Now I have this," she said, putting a hand on his chest. "How am I going to go back now?"

He sighed heavily. No matter how hard he'd tried to avoid that negative inner voice, there it was, saying, *I told you so. You thought happiness would be easy? Think again. There's always a price.*

"We will find a way to make it work. I can take the train down to see you."

"When? You work six days a week. I'll bet you have runs tonight, don't you?"

He did. "Winter will give me the time off," he said, but as soon as it was out of his mouth, he knew it was a lie. Once Winter found out what Bo had been doing with his sister . . .

All his old worries tumbled back. Winter would disown him. Bo would lose his job and wouldn't be allowed to go near Astrid. He could see it all in his mind, playing out like a picture show in a theater.

He tried to shove them all back into the dark corners of his mind and busied himself spreading peanut butter on a cracker. He handed it to Astrid, but she didn't eat it. He took a big gulp of hot tea and attempted to clear his head.

"If I didn't go back to school . . ." Astrid said softly. "And I'm not saying I'm giving up, but I can't help but wonder why I'm doing something that makes me miserable, and that maybe there's something else out there for me. Hadley says I just need to find out what that is."

Bo didn't know how to help her find that. He didn't know how to find it himself.

"I'm not asking for you to help me with that," she said. "But what I'm wondering is . . . what will we do? How can we be—"

"Together," he finished. It wasn't as if he'd never entertained that fantasy. Of course he had. But he could never quite get the puzzle pieces to fit correctly. He could try to find a legitimate job, but nothing would pay enough to keep her in the style she was accustomed to living in. And even if she was willing to make some sacrifices, where would they live? In his old apartment? Not likely.

As if she'd picked out his thoughts, she said, "Aida lived on that end of Grant, and she wasn't the only white woman in her boardinghouse. Besides, I went to Sylvia's apartment, and it was perfectly fine. The building isn't run-down."

"No, but my apartment doesn't even have a proper bedroom. It's not a place for families. I should know. I slept on a pallet in the corner when I lived there with my uncle before he died."

Neither of them said anything for a long while. In the distance, he could see the dark shape of a large ship cutting to the north of them, heading up the coast. The wind picked up and blew golden strands of her hair across his jaw. He tucked them behind her ear and smoothed a hand over the back of her head.

"You know," she said. "I was thinking about the night I drove you to Dr. Moon's. Don't say it—I know I need to get your fender fixed." A small smile lifted her mouth, and that made him feel a little lighter. "Anyway, I was thinking how Nob Hill and Chinatown border each other, and how you can drive a few blocks from the Wicked Wenches' million-dollar apartment and be on Grant."

"That's true of any neighborhood."

"But I was thinking of the incident outside their apartment

building with that horrible woman and her husband, the state senator. The Humphreys. Remember them?"

How could he forget? It was the first time Astrid hadn't tried to smooth things over for public appearances, and like everything Astrid set her mind to, she did it with gusto. He smiled to himself as she continued.

"Anyway, she was upset because the 'immigrants' were invading her neighborhood. And I was thinking, yes, of course they are. Because neighborhoods aren't hard lines. There are those blocks between, where you can still find Nob Hill money living next to a Chinese merchant. Or there's someone like Ju, who owns that small house on the edge of Russian Hill."

Which had been vandalized repeatedly, despite the fact that Ju traveled with thugs wherever he went. "Where are you going with this?"

"I'm just saying, there are those gray areas between the neighborhoods, and that makes me think maybe that's a place for us. We aren't the first people to do this. Love crosses streets. It doesn't realize it's supposed to stay confined to one neighborhood."

Tell that to the old WASPs who would be happier if people like him didn't look them in the eye, much less stepped on their sidewalks. He pulled her head to his chest and laid his own head upon hers, tucking her tightly under his arm.

"What can we do?" she said.

"I could save up money while you go to school—or while you figure out what you want to do."

"Or maybe I could figure out what I wanted to do here. Maybe I could work. I could, you know. Hadley said I could work in the de Young Museum offices. I could be a secretary, or assist her with paperwork."

It took Bo several blinking moments to process just how far her conspiracy with Hadley had gone. He was surprised. And impressed. As for Astrid working with Hadley . . . well, that remained to be seen. But he tried to focus on the larger picture. Astrid could live at home and work—thereby allowing them to see each other—but if she did that, he couldn't stay at the Magnusson house. He'd have to stay at his old apartment building and maybe find new work. New work meant less pay. But if she went back to school, perhaps they could keep things secret from Winter for a while longer—a thought that gave him such a pang of guilt, his stomach twisted. But if he could manage it, he might be able to save money faster. The price, however, was not just lying to a man who'd been like a surrogate father to him; it meant also not being able to see Astrid but twice a year.

And then there were always the deepest worries. The ones about class and race, and how he could not legally marry her. That if she got pregnant, their children would be under similar restraints. Where would they go to school? Would he take them to Dr. Moon if they got sick? Would they get treated with the same indignities that he'd faced? Or would it be worse for them, because they wouldn't be accepted in either community?

He didn't know the answers, and his heart grieved under the burden.

As the sun continued to climb a sky free of rain clouds, Bo urged Astrid to eat and began to think of less weighty problems in their immediate future, like the fact that the Magnusson household would already be awake and soon someone would notice that they weren't home. He'd have to telephone the house and concoct a story. Pray that Greta or Aida answered the telephone, and not Winter. Sneak Astrid into the house.

Whatever he had to do, it had been worth it. All those years of wanting disappeared when he looked at the sun shining on the softly curving planes of her face and saw the joy he felt in his heart reflected in her eyes. It had been worth it all.

"This can't be impossible, Bo," she said as she swirled tea leaves at the bottom of her cup, peering inside as if she could read their future. "We have to make a plan. I can't go back to a life without us."

TWENTY-FOUR

———◆———

THREE NIGHTS AFTER THEY LEFT THE LIGHTHOUSE, ON CHRIST-
mas Eve, Bo stood in the living room of the Magnusson
house, surrounded by twinkling candles, the biggest
Christmas tree in Pacific Heights (surely), and twenty or
so people—most of whom were Swedish and on the verge
of being drunk on tulip-shaped glasses of akvavit spirits
and mugs of cardamom-scented mulled glögg. And amidst
the merry shouts of *God Jul!* and the lingering smells of
the holiday smorgasbord—overloaded with ham, sausage,
herring, potatoes, and the precious few Dungeness crabs
Winter and Bo were able to catch that morning—Bo was
experiencing a wealth of conflicting emotions.

Though few in Chinatown actually celebrated Christmas, he'd spent the last third of his life developing a taste
for yuletide presents and singing "Jingle Bells" around a
piano. And he was experiencing that familiar buzz of happiness now, watching Lowe and Hadley's adopted five-
year-old, deaf daughter, Stella Goldberg, grinning as she
ran from Aida's one-eyed mastiff, who was attempting to
confiscate the almond cookie the girl carried in her hand.

But in the back of his mind, he was also worried that he could lose all this if his relationship with Astrid caused a family schism, and wondered wistfully if this was the last time he'd sit in this room watching Greta loosen her staunch Lutheran morals and get tipsy while Winter played horsey with his infant daughter on his knee.

And somewhere between the joy and worry was Astrid, who wore a dazzling sleeveless red gown that bared half her back, and was now working in tandem with Lowe to help the mastiff chase the merry, pink-cheeked Stella. How could two people live in the same house and never see each other? He hadn't been able to skim more than a couple of passing kisses from Astrid since the lighthouse—what with the combined roadblocks of work and hovering family members who always seemed to show up at the wrong times. He'd come *this* close to stealing into her bedroom last night when he'd gotten home after midnight, but Aida had been up, and she'd stayed in the kitchen with Winter talking seriously until Bo gave in to sleep, waiting for them to go to bed.

It didn't help that every time he looked at Astrid she was staring back at him with those fox eyes that left him grinning like an idiot and forgetting to keep his feelings masked. Watching her now made him want to drag her into his arms and feel her smile against his neck . . . and then haul her off somewhere private, find a pair of scissors, and split that red gown of hers right down the back.

He was in agony.

After little Stella finally tired, he made his way back over to the fireplace and stoked the logs, inhaling the fresh cedar and eucalyptus branches that decorated the mantel. Behind him, Jonte was coaxing Lena to take off her apron and dance; Christmas was the one time of the year that Greta allowed the staff to celebrate with the rest of the house.

"Meant to tell you earlier, Sylvia's fender looks shiny and new."

He glanced up to find Astrid smiling down at him,

flames from the fire dancing across her face. "They did a good job. I would thank you for having it repaired, only you're the one who hurt her to begin with," he said, standing to brush off his pants and replace the fireplace stoker.

"You make it sound like I socked your best friend in the face."

"Didn't you?"

She tried to stifle a laugh and pinch his arm, but he grabbed her hand before she managed it. "I'll throw you in this fire," he teased. "Burn you right up. We'll toast marshmallows over your hair."

This time she laughed, loud and vibrant, but quickly covered her mouth.

"Tsk, tsk. You've had too much glögg, Miss Magnusson."

"I've had no glögg whatsoever, Mr. Yeung. I'm the picture of tolerance tonight."

He peered into her eyes—an excuse to lean closer to her face, really. "Why, you're telling the truth. I think you and I might be the only sober people in the house. Hell, I wouldn't be surprised if someone slipped akvavit into baby Karin's cup."

"Pfft. Winter hasn't let go of her the entire night."

He nodded slowly. "I asked him if he was going to start breast-feeding her, too, and came *this* close to being flayed like a fish."

"Aida says he's getting sentimental," Astrid said. "Maybe he'd only paralyze you."

"As long as it's from the waist up."

"Now *that* I'd drink to."

He smiled down at her and rubbed his thumb over her knuckles. "I'm worried I might accidently paralyze myself from all the self-abusing I've been doing the last couple of days."

Her cheeks flushed. She furtively glanced over her shoulder and murmured, "Now that's a picture."

"I'll give you a theater-worthy performance if I can just find a way to be alone with you for five minutes."

"Is that all it would take?"

"Honestly, I wish I could say otherwise, but yes. Maybe even two."

Mischievous eyes slanted sideways toward his. "We could race."

He sucked in a quick breath and was thankful his suit jacket was buttoned over the front of his pants. "Christ, I need you," he whispered.

"I need you, too," she whispered back.

Upon realizing he was still holding on to her hand, he reluctantly let go and checked to see if anyone was watching them. Not a soul. People were too sozzled to notice, anyway, so he slipped a couple of fingers between Astrid's wrist and the bracelet-like band of her watch and tugged her arm closer. He was just about to suggest they accidently bump into each other somewhere in the house where there were fewer people when Winter stepped in front of the Christmas tree and got everyone's attention.

Bo heaved a dramatic sigh and released Astrid's wrist.

"I wanted to take a moment to thank Lena and Julia for working so hard on the *julbord*," Winter said in a booming voice. "It might be the best meal we've had all year, and it certainly was the most bountiful."

Cheers and applause roared through the living room. When it died down, Jonte spoke up from the piano. "And that goes for the holiday bonus, too. *Tack så mycket!*"

More applause, and Bo clapped along with them. He was shocked when he'd opened up the red envelope from Winter. It was too much—more than he earned in two months' time, and that made him feel grateful and guilty at the same time. *If he only knew*, a negative voice in his head chastised. He pushed it away.

"It was a good year," Winter said. "Pappa always said, 'Shared joy is a double joy.' We are all part of this household, and we all share in its successes. And that's why I wanted all of you to know that, God willing, we'll become one member bigger next year. Little Karin's going to have a baby brother or sister."

A cascade of surprised noises, cheers, and whistles

went around the room, and while Astrid hugged Aida, Bo shook Winter's hand and slapped him on the shoulder. "Good job. Keep it up, and you two will have those five empty bedrooms filled in no time."

"Smart aleck," Winter murmured, but anyone could see he was pleased. And when Bo moved to congratulate Aida, her freckled arms swept him up in a hug as she whispered, "Thanks for keeping my secret. Road goes both ways."

Flustered, he pulled back to see her face, and she smiled at him surreptitiously before the rest of the clan descended upon the fertile couple. As Bo sidled out of the crowd, Astrid caught his arm and said in his ear, "Meet me at the top of the turret in five minutes. I want to give you my Christmas present."

Bo sneaked out of the merry crowd and climbed the back stairs to the upper story. No lights shone. Two of the low-ceilinged rooms were bare and closed off. He passed a powder room with a severely slanted ceiling and pushed open the door to the turret.

"It's only me," he said softly, in case she hadn't heard him come upstairs. "I thought we agreed we weren't giving each other presents this year, so—"

He stopped in the doorway and stared at the windows banding the rounded wall. She was waiting for him, perched upon the window seat of their hiding spot, wearing nothing but stockings and garters. Above her head, a stem of mistletoe hung from a ribbon.

"Merry Christmas," she said.

"*Buddha-Osiris-Jehovah,*" he mumbled. He shut the door and leaned back against it for a moment to take it all in. The inky sky dotted by starlight. City lights like pow-dered sugar sifted over rows of streets that ended at the foggy Bay. The soft panes of moonlight spilling over her shoulders and lining the tops of her breasts. The red dress strewn on the floor by her feet. He took a mental photograph and filed it away under *Things I'll Never Forget as Long as I Live.*

He exhaled a calming breath, adjusted the angle of the growing bulge in the front of his trousers, and tried to sound causal. "Did I ever tell you the story of the fox spirit that climbed over the rooftops at night to sneak inside a young scholar's bedroom window?"

"No," she said, a slow smile spreading over her face. "Tell me."

He fumbled around in the dark and found a chair to wedge under the door handle. "She came to his room every night for a month and aroused him to three orgasms."

"Every night?"

"She was a remarkable fox."

"I'll say. He must have been a little remarkable himself."

"He wasn't one to brag, but he was bigger than the average scholar and had spent many years studying books about pleasuring women." He began stripping off his suit jacket and necktie. "He gave her two orgasms for each one of his."

"I'll bet she was happily surprised about that," she murmured with a smile. Her hands glided over the tops of her thighs and rolled her stockings a little lower. "What kind of books taught him these tricks?"

"You'd be surprised what you can find in the back room of your average bookstore in Imperial China. The scholar had a boss who collected . . . interesting drawings that he thought no one knew about"—Astrid snorted a soft laugh—"so the scholar got an early education in rare books when he went into town to pick up the boss's special-order packages." Bo unbuttoned his shirt. How much time did they safely have? Half an hour?

"He probably should have taken the fox spirit with him on these trips," she said. "They might have realized earlier how much time they could have spent on orgasms all those years."

"The fox spirit was much too young."

"I seriously doubt that," she said as one hand lazily skimmed over her breast. Down, and then up. "Why did the fox spirit only come to his window for one month?"

"Because the scholar's father was superstitious of supernatural creatures. He caught her sneaking in one night and was afraid she was siphoning his son's vitality, so he nailed the window shut."

"The bastard." Her knees slowly opened. The hand that was on her breast dipped down between her legs, shielding his view. Teasing his imagination as it made slow movements. "I hope that didn't stop them."

"Not a chance. They had already fallen in love. So the scholar climbed up the chimney and met the fox on the roof," he said, stopping in front of her. "Spread your legs a little wider and let me see what you're doing," he murmured, enjoying the thrill that careened through his chest when she complied without hesitation—and the way that thrill echoed in the tightening of his balls and the jumping of his cock.

"What happened on the roof?" Astrid asked in a breathy voice as her fingers tentatively dipped lower. She slipped a finger inside herself and he nearly lost his mind.

"He was covered in soot, so she didn't recognize him at first, but he knew a way to prove his identity to her." He stopped in front of her and unbuttoned his fly. His cock sprang free. "And she instantly knew it was him."

"Oh," Astrid said, shyness and daring warring on her face. The daring won out. She leaned forward and ran her tongue up the ridge of his cock, root to tip, forcing a contented sigh out of him before she drew back again. "Quite right," Astrid murmured. "I'd recognize that anywhere."

He cupped the crown of her head and urged her forward. "Again," he murmured. "And this time, take it inside your mouth. And keep your hand between your legs."

Gripping the open fly of his pants as an anchor, she set to the task without hesitation. He watched her gazing up at him, her indrawn cheeks, and then closed his eyes as his head lolled back in bliss. He could only stand it for a moment, and then it was too much. "Any more and this will be over in thirty seconds," he said. "Lean back against the window."

Her eyelids were heavy with lust. "What happened to the scholar and the fox?"

"It wasn't easy for them, because not only did they have to worry about his father catching them, the entire town was superstitious and would watch the rooftops, ready to shoot any fox spirits with arrows. So every night she came to him, she risked her life."

He dropped to his knees, cock glistening as it bobbed in front of him. Then he wrapped his hands around the underside of her thighs and scooted her closer. "Open for me," he said. Beneath the nest of blond curls, he could see the flesh of her sex, plump and slick, unfurling like the petals of an exotic orchid. He trailed kisses on the insides of her thighs, one on each side, back and forth, until he got to the tender crease where her leg met her torso and licked there.

"Have you missed me?" he said, looking up at her.

"Every minute," she whispered.

"I missed you, too. Let me show you how much." He breathed in her scent, inhaling deeply, and swept his flattened tongue against her hooded clitoris. He went slow at first, but her clean, salty taste and soft moans made him harder. He licked and suckled. Kissed and kneaded. Flicked and rubbed. And as her stomach tightened, he dropped a hand to his cock and gave himself a few strokes, just to pacify it.

But when he felt her feet digging into his shoulders and her hips began pushing upward—and when her soft moans increased in volume—he settled his forearm over her stomach to give her something to buck against. "No . . . screaming," he instructed her between licks, and then paused. "Or I'll stop right now."

She roughly pushed his head back into position, and he laughed a little and took up a steady rhythm as she fisted the edge of the window seat cushion in both hands. It gave him joy to watch her as he worked: eyes squeezed shut, open mouth, contorted face, a deep flush of red spreading over her upper chest and neck as she strained. And when she switched her straining grip from the seat cushion to his bracing arm, he watched her face turn to the side as a silent scream floated from her open mouth.

"Good girl," he said when the tremors slowed and her legs tried to close around his head. He gave her one last lick, a lingering kiss, and then released her.

He wanted to feel her skin. As her breath steadied, his palms drifted over the smooth silk of her stockings, up her calves and thighs. He continued exploring, molding her curving hips and the flat expanse of her stomach. He skimmed over the tips of her breasts and savored the way his touch made her jump. The way, when he caressed her breasts, she came back to life. The way her legs parted once more, inviting him closer. And it was then that he realized, with no small amount of excitement, that the window seat was the perfect height. He could take her like this, kneeling between her thighs, framed by the lights of the city winking over a dark sea of rooftops.

"Are you ready for me, now, *huli jing*?" he whispered as her damp curls tickled the head of his cock.

"Yes," she whispered back. "I want you."

He didn't bother to take off his pants—they didn't have the luxury of time—so he only pushed them down below his knees so he could find better leverage on the woven silk rug that covered the floor.

"You know," he said, momentarily sucking her nipple into his mouth because he couldn't resist, "I think I've heard if two people come together beneath mistletoe, you'll both have good luck for ten years."

She choked out a laugh, and then her eyes became serious and glossy. "Have I told you how much I love you?"

"No," he admitted, pushing back a wave of emotion so strong, it made goose bumps spread over his arms. "But tell me afterward if you haven't changed your mind."

He drove himself into her as far as he could, allowed a

moment for the overwhelming pleasure of it to pass (hot, wet, tight, mine-mine-mine), and then gripped her hips and picked up speed.

If the newness of her body was a pleasure during their night at the lighthouse, then the familiarity of it was its own grand reward now. He knew how to angle himself to hit the spot inside her that she liked, right at twelve o'clock. He knew how hard to push her, and when it was too rough. He knew if he kissed her now, with the taste of her sex still on his lips, the taboo of it would excite her and she'd squeeze around him a little tighter.

But most of all, he knew when that pleasurable squeezing started and stopped, started and stopped, started and *didn't* stop, that she was racing toward climax.

He raced for it with her.

They dug their nails into each other. He felt the silken soles of her feet leave the ledge of his buttocks to scrabble for foothold on the edge of the window seat. Heard the rhythmic squeak of wood keep time with his quickening thrusts and the lush sound of their flesh smacking together, the finest symphony ever composed. And when she opened her mouth against his neck to stifle her scream, the gathering warmth in his balls shot forward and he came— quietly, muscles quaking, heart stopping, soul bursting apart into a million points of light.

When he pulled out, still hard, he was so spent, he wobbled on his knees. "Come here," he murmured, summoning the strength to hoist her onto his hips while he repositioned them. He sat on the window seat with her across his legs, and wrapped her in his arms.

"Look at that," he said, gazing through the window. The rooftops of Pacific Heights rolled down the hill toward the Golden Gate. "If you look close enough, I'll bet you can see the lighthouse past the hills."

"No, you can't," she said with a husky laugh and pressed her hand against the windowpane. "But it's beautiful, isn't it? And it's ours."

Their city. For it seemed at that moment to have been painted across the landscape just for the two of them.

He sighed, wholly content. Another minute, perhaps, and they'd have to leave. If they stayed gone too long, someone would notice. He thought of Aida's words in his ear: *Thanks for keeping my secret. Road goes both ways.* If she knew, how long would it be before she confessed her suspicions to Winter?

"Bo?" Astrid asked. "What happened to the young scholar and the fox spirit?"

He rested his chin on top of her head, stroked over her bare shoulder, and then gently grazed his nails down her arm, memorizing her anew.

Impossibly soft.

Scent of roses.

Voice that made his heart warm.

"I don't know," he said. "I'm afraid I just don't know."

TWENTY-FIVE

———✦———

THE WEEK BETWEEN CHRISTMAS AND NEW YEAR'S DAY WAS,
bar none, the happiest in Astrid's life. Firstly, it didn't rain
a single day; the historic storm was finally, truly over.
Secondly, they didn't catch even a glimpse of Max and his
knife, nor did Astrid experience any disturbing visions—
though a visit to Velma told her that the tea she'd pre-
scribed wasn't helping; the unwanted shadow on Astrid's
aura was still very present. But despite this disappointing
news and the fact that Bo and Astrid's impending date at
the carousel of Babel's Tower was quickly approaching,
they were able to put it out of their minds.

Easy to do when you're basking in bliss. Because Bo
made time every day to steal away and visit her at the top
of the turret. And one morning he even sneaked her into
a taxi and took her to his apartment in Chinatown, where
they spent two glorious hours wearing out the springs of
his single bed before walking a block to eat dim sum at
Golden Lotus.

"I remember you," the restaurant owner, Mrs. Lin, had

said with a kind smile after she'd kissed both of Bo's cheeks and seated them at a table with a view of Grant Avenue's bustling sidewalk. "You are Mr. Magnusson's sister. You and another young girl came to visit Aida when she boarded with me upstairs."

"Benita," Astrid said, remembering fondly and wishing her old friend was here to share her secret about Bo. She'd almost written her about it, but changed her mind; it felt too intimate a thing to share in a letter. "She was my seamstress. We'd brought Aida a new coat that afternoon. That was right before the fire in her room."

Mrs. Lin's face darkened for a moment, but she quickly shook it away. "Mr. Magnusson paid for the repairs and now everyone wants to rent that room because it has the shiny, new private bathroom. I charge big dollars for it. What do they call that? Silver lining," she said with a grin.

The old restaurant owner had then proceeded to command every dim sum cart to make a beeline to their table with hot food straight from the kitchen, and Bo fed her steamed pork dumplings from the tips of his chopsticks until she nearly burst—from both the abundance of food and the sheer happiness at being able to sit beside him at a public table while he laced his fingers through hers.

Astrid carefully preserved all of these moments in her mind and tried to be grateful for today, and today only. But the morning of New Year's Eve, she found herself unable to stop the future from leaking into her thoughts. And after some deliberation and self-honesty, she finally made a plan for what she was going to do about school. What she was going to do with herself.

What she wanted.

It was a risky plan—*not a scheme*, she told herself indignantly—and one that required a little more faith in herself than she was absolutely sure she had, but there it was. Her plan for the future.

She decided she would tell Bo after the clock struck midnight. A new year, a new plan, a new, more serious

Astrid. No matter what happened, she would be able to say that she tried, and that was a small boon to her heart. Evening fell, and though Bo and Winter had worked until dawn the previous night, delivering the last of their liquor runs to all the hotels and clubs around town hosting big New Year's parties, they were both taking the night off. Winter planned, he told Astrid, to be asleep with his wife and baby when the city was counting down the new year. And Bo, of course, planned to get into Heaven with Astrid.

Deciding against parking his newly repaired Buick in a sketchy part of town, Bo paid a taxicab to drive them to Babel's Tower dance hall a few minutes before nine. The surrounding neighborhoods were lively with revelers, but Terrific Street was dark and gloomy. A few drunken people shambled down the sidewalks. Music blared from a dance hall down the block. But the area in front of Babel's Tower seemed . . . subdued.

"The streetlights are out," Bo said as he gripped her hand a little tighter.

"What?"

"Four of them, look. And they're all right here."

He was right, but Astrid wasn't sure why he was so bothered about it. This wasn't the best part of town. She doubted the dance halls had a civic group fighting to keep the potholes fixed and was far more concerned that the club didn't look half as busy as it had the first night they'd been there. Maybe everyone was already inside.

Bo shook his head. "I don't have a good feeling about this. Maybe we should ask the taxi driver to wait while— hey!" He slammed a hand on the cab's flank as it peeled away from the curb and left them stranded. Bo said something sharp in Cantonese and looked up and down the street for another cab. It was hard to spot much of anything with the streetlights out.

A stumbling man stinking of gin approached Astrid, muttering something under his breath. Bo put a steely hand on her shoulder and pulled her away, yelling at the bum to leave them alone. "Let's just get inside," Bo said as the man shuffled away and crossed the street. "We can use their telephone and call another cab. We're giving up on this. I'll find another way—"

"How?" Astrid said. "We're already here and you're armed. We didn't go to all this trouble tracking this down just to abandon it. And you heard Velma. That shadow is still on my aura. Whatever that idol did to me, I want it fixed."

Bo exhaled heavily. "All right, but if things look suspect upstairs, we're leaving. And if Max is here—"

"I know." Bo had drilled her on this already several times. "I stay behind you and remain aware of my surroundings. I am a Magnusson, and no one messes with me and gets away with it."

He smiled at that. "You are a Magnusson, and you are mine. Don't forget it."

Not a chance. He pulled her closer, and they hurried to the club's front door, where the same doorman from the first night allowed them entrance. But once they were inside, Astrid understood Bo's reservations. No band played. Most of the tables were empty, and as they crunched over peanut shells, the dozen or so men that were scattered through the bar area all seemed to look up at them with hostile faces.

Astrid told herself she was only imagining this, and when everyone's eyes fell back to their drinks, she breathed an inward sigh of relief. Any number of reasons why it wasn't busy tonight. The establishments in this area got regularly raided by both the cops and the Prohis, and New Year's Eve was prime time for a raid; maybe most of their regulars stayed away because of this. Or perhaps Hell wasn't busy on nights when Heaven was active upstairs.

"No bouncers," Bo mumbled as they headed to the inner door that had previously been guarded by two beefy men. "No one selling tickets."

"Maybe they stepped away." Music sifted through the

walls, so clearly the back dance hall was open for business. Astrid glanced around, looking for the bouncer while Bo tried the door handle. Unlocked. She saw him reach inside his suit jacket for a moment and felt sure he was opening his holster for easy access to his gun, and that made her nervous.

"Stay behind me," Bo said as he pushed the door with one hand. Mid-tempo jazz, tinny over the speaker, flooded the open doorway. They entered the back dance hall, following a short, dim corridor for several steps until it opened up into the main floor. Everything was as it was the first night: seats, dance floor, roped-off carousel with its bright carnival lights and nude angels.

Only, there were no people.

The music played over the phonograph to an empty hall. Deserted. The hair on Astrid's arms rose. Bo grabbed Astrid's elbow. "Something's not right. We're leaving. Now."

They swung around to find the two missing bouncers and gilded flintlock pistols pointed at them. Max stood in the center of the gunmen, a smile spreading over his face.

If Max had looked sick before, he looked positively wretched now. His eyes were jaundiced, the circles under his eyes were nearly black, and one side of his face was peeling and covered in ugly sores.

"Happy New Year," he said in a garbled, raspy voice. He coughed once and pointed a finger at Bo. "Nuh-uh-uh, my friend. Show me your hands, or they'll blast two holes in your chest and have their way with your woman while you bleed out on the floor."

Bo took his hand out of his jacket and mumbled, "Get behind me."

Astrid did exactly that.

"Do you have the missing doubloon from my idol?" Max asked Bo, hacking up another cough.

"Maybe," Bo said. "Are you willing to tell me what the symbol means?"

"I'll do more than that, friend. We'll be hosting a little demonstration for you. See, you both have something that belongs to me. You, the doubloon, and her, my missing vigor."

Vigor? *The shadow on my aura.* Astrid ran a hand over her arm, trying in vain to clean it away. "I don't want your damn vigor, you dirty pig. Get it off of me and you can have your stinking gold doubloon back."

Max coughed again, this time into a dirty handkerchief that was splattered with dried blood. "If it were that easy, I would have taken it back when the bastard here shot me, wouldn't I?"

He hobbled a step, and now Astrid could see that he was still having trouble with his leg. She hoped the bullet festered.

"My doubloon," Max demanded, waving forward one of the men, who stuck the pistol against Bo's head. Bo hesitated for a moment and started to reach inside his jacket, but one of Max's goons stopped him and began searching for the gold himself.

Astrid's heart raced. Two guns, but one of the men was busy patting Bo down. Could she do something to give Bo time enough to get to his own gun before they took it away? Her mind flipped through possibilities—anything at all. A distraction. A scream. A kick in the balls. But before she could decide, a chill slid down her neck.

Someone was behind her.

She spun around to find Mad Hammett smiling darkly beneath his heavy mustache. He was holding something over her head. As her eyes rotated upward, his hands came down like the blade of a guillotine, fast and unavoidable, sheathing her body. Dark. Rough cloth. Loose weave. Strong, earthy scent . . .

Visions of the sacrificial victims in burlap sacks floated inside her head as she screamed and flailed. Arms like steel bands wrapped around hers. She kicked. Struggled. Heard chaotic shouts around her right before an explosion went off, so loud it made her ears ring. The scent of gunpowder drifted through the rough cloth that smothered her.

"ASTRID!"

She tried to answer, tried to shout back, but a pain shot through her legs—so sudden and forceful, her knees buckled.

And then everything turned upside down.

TWENTY-SIX

———————

BO SMELLED THE OCEAN BEFORE THEY PUSHED HIM OUT OF THE car. They'd blindfolded him, and whoever had brained him with the pistol had knocked him hard enough to make the world go sideways. Blood had begun to crust over his ear, and he winced as they jostled him onto his feet and shoved him forward.

He did his best to fight the throbbing headache that threatened to obliterate rational thought and concentrated on his surroundings. Traffic in the distance, and a lot of it, but the sound was muffled by . . . buildings, perhaps? And boats. He heard rigging and groaning hulls and mooring ropes. They were at a pier, but it wasn't his pier. He could tell by the feel of the boards upon which they were now shuffling. Too much bounce.

"Where's Astrid?" he said, his voice sounding weak and not quite right. His lip was split. It hurt like hell to talk.

The two thugs who were shoving him along, hands gripping his arms, guns pointed into his back, didn't answer. But when he asked again, louder, one of them punched him on the back of his head, and somewhere under the fresh jolt of pain, he heard Max's coughing.

"You do what I say, you just might get to see her again," the man said. "Can't promise what condition she'll be in, though."

"You fucking piece of garbage—"

"Save your breath," Max said. "I need you cognizant, and if the boys have to hit you again, I'm afraid they may cause permanent damage."

Cold Pacific air howled in his ear and whipped though his clothes as Bo was hustled up a gangway and shoved onto the deck of a boat. He smelled a particular bright cedar scent and had a good idea they'd boarded the *Plumed Serpent*. While they crossed the deck, he wondered if Mr. Haig at the radio station had anything to do with him and Astrid getting captured, or if someone at the dance hall had recognized them. Maybe Max himself had been upstairs, looking down the peephole, when they'd visited the carousel booth. That thought made him feel a little sick . . . or perhaps that was only his head injury.

"Step up," one of the thugs told him, but not soon enough.

He stumbled up several stairs, crossed a threshold, and was pushed into a cabin.

His arms were wrenched back painfully. Hands bound with rope. And then he was tied to what felt like a pipe on the wall and left in silence. Bo tried to pull himself loose, blindly feeling out his environment with his knees, feet, elbows, searching for anything. All he found were a couple of walls, a chair bolted to the floor a few feet in front of him, and the boat rocking beneath him. They hadn't left port, and from the layout of the cabin—a small room, up a set of stairs—he was almost certain they'd stuck him in the boat's pilothouse.

He ignored his instinct to call out for Astrid. Never show weakness around people who can hurt you. That's what Winter had taught him. Bo didn't want them torturing Astrid to get a rise out of him. And he couldn't let his brain think about what they might do—*what they could be doing to her right now!*—or he'd go mad. He felt the raving panic battering his mind already. Sweat bloomed across his back and beaded his forehead. He wouldn't be any good to her if he allowed himself to crack.

She would fight back, he told himself. That wasn't much, but it was something. She was smart and savvy, and she didn't fall apart under pressure. He heard her voice saying *I am a Magnusson*, chin high, foxlike eyes narrowed, and willed her to summon that defiance now.

The only thing that gave him peace was the dark confidence that he would kill every last one of these people the second he got free. Bo was not clean of spirit. He'd taken life before, twice, in self-defense. The most recent one was a bootlegging deal that went sour—the man had pulled a gun on him—but the first time when he was spying for Winter. When he was sixteen. That was a savage killing, and he'd been an animal when he'd done it. No matter that he'd known in his heart that he would've been dead himself if he hadn't, the weight of it had taken months to purge from his head.

Maybe he'd never really gotten over it completely.

But he knew what he was capable of. And he would do it again. To get her back. To protect her. To avenge her. He would do it without hesitation. And focusing on this made the panic manageable.

A door slammed. Bo sat up as two sets of footfalls approached.

"We're going to untie you now," a British-accented voice said. Mad Hammett. "If you try anything funny, it'll be taken out on the girl. Understand?"

"Where is she?" Bo demanded.

"Close enough that if I press a button, she'll be harmed—and that's all you need to know right now. And in case you haven't noticed, that's a gun on your head."

Blood rushed to Bo's hands as the rope was cut. He was hauled to his feet and pushed forward before being told to sit. The blindfold was removed. Bo blinked into the light.

He sat in front of the ship's wheel. An L-shaped wooden dash with a radio and navigational instruments curved around to his right, and before him, slanted windows looked out over the yacht's bow.

He tried to gauge where they were docked—somewhere on the northern shore of the city—but it was hard to concentrate when a gun was prodding the back of his head and a man with half a face was coughing up blood at his side.

Max leaned against the ship's wheel. "This is what's going to happen. You will pilot us to this location," he said, pointing to a map on the dash. A spot in the ocean was circled, and next to it, a pair of coordinates written in dark ink. It took Bo's eyes time to focus, but he shortly comprehended the location. It was north of the city, off the coast. Near the Magnusson's Marin County warehouse and the lighthouse . . .

Where Captain Haig had taken the yacht the night of its disappearance a year ago.

"Why do you need me?" Bo asked. "I thought pirates were sailors. Or has it been so long, you've forgotten your way around a boat?"

Something like surprise flickered over Max's peeling face, but he looked too weary to care. "Start the engine before I change my mind and throw you overboard."

Bo considered his options. Astrid was on the boat. That was all that mattered right now. She was here, and he would get to her. Somehow. He just needed to get his hands on the gun prodding his skull.

After flipping on the blowers, he managed to start the engine and get his bearings. He also sneaked a look around the pilothouse. It was a cramped space, hardly big enough for all three men to stretch out. Apart from the dash and the wheel, there was a narrow berth to his left and, next to it, the door they'd entered, which led down to the deck. Nothing that could be used as a weapon. He eyed the headset hanging from a hook on the dash. He could radio the Coast Guard.

"Cord's cut," Max said, nodding to the dangling wire

that wasn't connected to the transmitter. "So don't get any Mayday ideas. Just get us moving. The lines have been cast."

"I want to see Astrid."

Max tapped the map. "You pilot us here, I just might let you do that."

Bo checked the gauges, turned on the fog lights, and pulled past a line of buoys, away from the dock. The yacht was big and moved like a slow beast as it cut through the Bay. It would take a half hour or more to get to where they were going. And once they got there, then what?

"How old are you?" Bo asked.

Max coughed into his hand. "I was born in 1491 in Cornwall," he said, his accent changing—sounding awfully close to Mad Hammett's. "I see that doesn't shock you. I'm not sure how you found out about us, but it doesn't really matter. Once I get my vigor back, you and Goldilocks will no longer be my problem."

"How are you going to get it back?" Bo asked.

"The Sibyl will pull it out of her."

"Sibyl?"

"Our priestess."

"Mrs. Cushing," Bo said.

Max didn't confirm or deny it. He just peered out across the water, where the fog lights shone over the surface as they headed away from the northern coast of the city. Bo could navigate this route in his sleep. His eyes flicked around the pilothouse, still looking for something—anything—to use to his advantage, and settled on the radio headset and its dangling cord.

He continued talking to Max, less out of curiosity, and more to keep the man's attention occupied. "If your turquoise idol is Aztec," Bo mused, thinking back to the Wicked Wenches' story, "and you were a Cornish pirate, then I'm guessing you were under the French pirate's command—Jean Fleury?"

"Very good," Max said, sounding genuinely impressed. "Attacking those galleons changed my life. I could've died that day. Instead, I had the fortune to raid the hold where they were keeping the Sibyl. Freeing her turned Max Nance's destiny around."

"How did you end up here in San Francisco?"

Max shrugged. "We settled in France until the Revolution. Things became too dangerous. Fleury was nearly killed by a mob."

"The closest you all ever came to dying, wasn't it, Grandfer?" Mad Hammett spoke up for the first time, his voice floating over Bo's head.

Grandfer? "Are you related?" Bo asked, not seeing the resemblance.

Max's gaze connected with Bo's. A wariness behind his eyes softened to apathy. "You won't be around to tell anyone," he said, more to the view outside the Bay than to Bo. "And who would believe you anyway? No, this is the closest we all came to dying. Because if I go, we all go. Stand or fall together. So thanks to you and your girl snooping around in matters that didn't concern you, we're all here tonight."

"If you touch her—" Bo started.

The muzzle of the gun dug into his scalp.

"I just want my vigor back," Max said. "And if you want to speak with her again, you'll keep us on course and do it with your mouth shut. Because—"

A muffled scream sounded from somewhere on the deck below. *Astrid!* Bo's pulse doubled. He pushed out of the chair without thinking, only to be pistol-whipped on the back of his head. Lights blurred in his vision as pain lanceted through his skull. He fell against the dash and was hauled back into the seat.

"Try it again, and I'll pilot the yacht myself," Hammett warned.

"Please do," Bo said, touching the back of his head and wincing. The pain was almost unbearable. But further shouting from below sharpened his will.

Max cursed under his breath and flicked an uneasy glance out the windows. "Make sure he keeps his hands on the wheel and drops anchor at the coordinates," he told Hammett. "I'm going to check on them. If I'm not back

when we get to our destination, bring him down. Shoot
him in the leg if he doesn't obey," he added with a wry
smile as he exited the pilothouse.

Bo felt the gun pull away from his head. Hammett took
up Max's place near the map while keeping the weapon
pointed at Bo, and smiled at him beneath his heavy mustache. "You heard the man. Stay on course."

He'd heard, but didn't much care. All he was thinking
about right now was that Hammett was holding Bo's own
gun against him. This made him furious. It also made him
wonder where Hammett's two flintlock-wielding thugs
were. Down in the main cabin? Or had they left them
behind on shore? How many guns were on board?

"You don't look young like the others," Bo said, mentally measuring the distance between them. "So I assume
you aren't one of them. Been working with them for long?"

"What's that? Oh sure. Twenty-one years now. Nance
came to Cornwall and tracked me down. Eight generations
back, he had a son before he went on the voyage and met
the Sibyl." Hammett smiled to himself. "Imagine finding
out your ancestor is still alive. I didn't believe him at first,
but he showed me the family tree."

"I suppose the fact that he didn't age was convincing,"
Bo said.

"Not at first. The time difference to travel between the
planes takes a year, you know." Travel between planes? He
supposed the man was referring to the yearlong stretch of
time during which the yacht had disappeared. "And when
they come back in their new bodies, they're confused. So
the first time he switched bodies, I didn't believe it was
really him. Of course, that body had been female. You try
looking into a strange woman's eyes and believing the man
you spoke to a year ago is beneath the skin."

Bo stared at Max while the engine hummed. "They . . .
switch bodies."

"Every decade. Well, all but the Sibyl, of course."

Astrid's vision. She'd said the priestess in red was old.
Mrs. Cushing was young. Was she the only one who was

actually extending her life? The rest of them were . . . what? Hopping from body to body? That would mean . . .

Not a sacrificial ritual, but an exchange.

The people in the burlap sacks weren't being killed. They were the Pieces of Eight members. He thought of what Little Mike had told him outside Mrs. Cushing's house—about Kit Manson, the heroin addict. The Pieces of Eight club had offered him wealth beyond his wildest dreams. Had they told him the catch?

Max had taken Kit Manson's body.

"Heaven," Bo said. "That's where they pick out new bodies."

"I'd give anything to choose my own body," Hammett said. "The Sibyl's six are the only ones who can do that, but hopefully tonight will change things a little for me. When Nance gets his vigor back, the Sibyl is going to give me a little taste of the runoff."

"Runoff?"

"A little shot of the blond girl's youth. And maybe a shot of yours. If you do exactly what you're told, you might even live through it."

Fear knotted Bo's stomach. Not for himself, but for Astrid. He eyed the radio headset. One second. That's all he needed. He waited for Mad Hammett to look away.

TWENTY-SEVEN

"TAKE YOUR HANDS OFF ME, OR I PROMISE YOU'LL REGRET IT."

Astrid took in labored breaths as two of the survivors restrained her arms while standing in front of the piano in the yacht's main cabin. Her previous captors, a thin woman and a dark-haired man, now had a scratched eye and bruised balls. That left one strange man who wouldn't stop laughing . . . and Mrs. Cushing. Max was somewhere; she'd heard him earlier but hadn't seen his rotting face since the yacht began moving.

"Miss Magnusson," the laughing man said. He wore his dark hair a bit longer than fashionable, hadn't shaved, and spoke in a foreign accent. He also seemed to rank higher than the rest of them; he hadn't left Mrs. Cushing's side. "Sibyl," he'd called her several times. Astrid wasn't sure if that was the woman's given name or an honorific. "If you do not settle down," he said, "I will put you back inside the sack."

Her skin chilled at the thought of being thrust back into breathless darkness, unable to move or think. She'd nearly lost her mind inside that sack. She wasn't sure if she'd survive it a second time.

A door banged shut.

"It is well?" the laughing man said to the person circling out of sight behind her back.

"We should be there any minute." Max. His voice sent a fresh wave of rage coursing through her limbs. "What in hell is going on down here?"

"Your girl will not behave," Mrs. Cushing said. Her blond hair, which was pulled tightly into a crown of braids, gleamed under the cabin lighting as she removed her crimson coat and laid it atop the bar. "Fleury was suggesting we bag her up again."

Fleury. Astrid looked at the laughing man as the Wicked Wenches' tale of pirates flashed inside her head. Jean Fleury. She'd found a dark oil painting of him inside a book in Winter's study—one before he was supposedly hanged for piracy in 1527. The man in that painting had looked nothing like the one standing before her now.

"Tie her arms to her sides and bag her up to the waist," the man she'd kneed in the balls said from his curled up position on the floor. "I will break her."

"You can have her after we're done," Mrs. Cushing said. "Nance will need to be physically connected to her during the ritual. Your seed will only muddle the energy."

Max coughed. "Can you even get it up, Bechard? It looks like she got you in the stones pretty good."

"Won't stop me from swiving *you*," the man said with venom.

"Enough!" Mrs. Cushing barked and pointed a finger at Max. "You losing your turquoise is the reason we're all here right now. She's your responsibility. Restrain her. We haven't survived together over the last four hundred years only to be disbanded over one small girl."

Max said something under his breath and limped over to Astrid. His chest rattled with every breath; sweat gleamed on his skin. The open sores and peeling flesh that covered one side of his face smelled putrid.

"I don't think I've hated anyone so much as you," he said a few inches from her face. "I am going to hurt you so badly, you'll beg for death."

She fought the shudder that fanned through her bones. "Where's Bo?"

"He'll be joining us soon enough. We need blood to open up the passage, and unfortunately, the Sibyl says it can't be yours or my vigor might slip out. But after I have it back . . . you *will* bleed."

"What passage?" Astrid said. "If you hurt Bo—"

"I will do more than hurt him, Goldilocks." Max pulled a knife out and held it in front of her face. She recognized the ivory handle; it was the one he'd held to her throat in the elevator. "I will cut him open so wide, his entrails will spill onto the floor."

His free hand moved toward her neck to hold her in place. She saw the blue of his ring, twisted loosely around to face his palm—as if it were too big for his hand—and tried to jerk away, but the men who were holding her tightened their grip. The moment the ring touched her neck, the same terrible electricity she'd last felt in Gris-Gris's restroom suddenly shot through her nerves.

The cabin fell away.

The vision began.

This time, she didn't see the ritual. Didn't see the body sacks in the water, either. She saw another ritual. Another time . . . another boat.

She was inside the wooden hold of an old ship. The dark belly was filled with crates and penned animals, along with the reek of urine, shit, and death. Armored conquistadors lay slaughtered, their bodies stacked against the walls. The ship rocked severely, groaning as wind lashed the ship and thunder rolled. Sputtering lanterns swayed from rafters. And in the middle of the ship's hold, the old priestess in the red robe stood inside a chain of blue symbols. Spread around her, lying on the floor, fanned out in imitation of spokes on a wheel, were five long-haired men and one woman.

All naked.

All covered in blue paint and blood.

All clutching turquoise idols to their chests.

And each of those idols generated a fine white line of light that pierced the dark air of the ship's hold and connected to a carved pendant of turquoise that hung around the priestess's neck.

The vision sputtered. Astrid saw the ritual overlapping with the current yacht. It blurred and rotated, and she thought she might be sick.

"Do you hear me? What's wrong with her? Help me, Sibyl!"

Astrid was sagging in the grip of the two survivors who restrained her. Max slapped her—struck her across the face. His ring made contact with her cheek and the room disappeared again.

Now she was on another ship, in a Victorian-looking parlor. Ornate lamps, chairs, and china had been stacked against the wall in a heap, along with a rolled-up rug. Portholes framed flashes of a roiling ocean when lightning streaked across a night sky. The red-robed priestess stood in the center of a blue circle, guiding a ritual that looked identical to the one Astrid had seen on the *Plumed Serpent*. Six young people with the priestess inside the circle, six old people wearing iron boots lined the outside. Only, Astrid recognized none except the priestess. They were all different people.

Where was Max? Fleury?

"Move!" a feminine voice commanded as Astrid's world spun. "It's your vigor, man. Your touch is interacting with it . . . doing something strange to her. If she dies, you die. And if you die, this entire coven goes with you."

"Aye," another voice answered sullenly. "Stand or fall together."

"I told you the drug fiend was a poor vessel," a third voice said. The laughing man—Fleury. "He was too intoxicated to even hold on to the turquoise. That's what got us in this mess in the first place. If he hadn't dropped it—"

"How many times do we have to talk about this?"

"Feel that? The yacht's stopped. Are we at the passage? I can't tell. Do you detect the Beyond, Sibyl?"

"I think so . . . Go upstairs and check, Nance. We need to be sure."

"What if she dies before I get back? I want my vigor! Go ahead and do the siphoning ritual now. Hammett will bring down the Chinese man after the anchor's dropped."

"Just move and let me see her," Mrs. Cushing said. "Pull her up and let me see what's happening to her."

Astrid was hauled to her feet and saw the crowd around her, silhouetted in her vision like cast shadows behind a flame. *It's the turquoise*, she tried to tell the dark shape that looked like Mrs. Cushing, but Astrid's mouth wasn't opening. *Not Max's touch, but the turquoise around his finger.* How did they not understand that it was contact with his idol that started all this? Astrid's knees gave out and she sagged in her captor's arms.

"Hold her still," Mrs. Cushing said as she leaned over Astrid's lolling head.

Astrid saw the silhouette of the woman's hand moving slowly toward her. Mrs. Cushing tried to pry open Astrid's eyelids, and when she peered closer, a bright blue shape escaped her shadowy breast.

On a chain hung the turquoise pendant Astrid had seen in the vision. It was big as a silver dollar. Big as the gold doubloon that had adorned Max's idol.

The turquoise pendant swung toward Astrid and struck her chin.

Once again, blackness transported her out of the yacht. It was night again—and humid—but she wasn't on a ship. This time, it was a large, round raft—a giant wooden tea saucer with a canopy of woven dried grass. It floated in the middle of a great lake surrounded by mountains and step temples. A circle of candles flickered violently around the edge of the raft, wax melting into the wood, and as the wind blew drops of warm rain beneath the canopy, the candles' flames threatened to extinguish.

Twelve Aztec men and the old priestess stood on the raft in the same way as before: six on the inside of the circle, six on the outside. No burlap sacks and iron boots, though. This time they kneeled inside giant woven baskets weighted down by rocks. Each of the kneeling men held a turquoise idol.

Thunder rolled. The men in the baskets handed the turquoise idols to the six in the center of the circle. The priestess called out an invocation. White light flared around her. It surged from the pendant of turquoise hanging around her neck and grew tendrils that extended like tentacles toward the six in the middle. The light pierced each one of them and kept going, until each tendril pierced the men in the baskets.

The men in the baskets gasped, shuddered, and fell limp.

The raft shook as if it were being hammered by an earthquake while the tendrils of light retracted into the middle six; they gasped, shuddered, and struggled to stand—all of them clinging to the turquoise idols. And on the priestess's command, they all left the circle to stand by the baskets.

The priestess . . .

Light from the tendrils poured into her open mouth. As if she were drinking it. Eating it. Consuming the vigor that Max had spoken about? Or consuming the souls of the men who now lay unmoving in the baskets? Whatever she was doing, it changed her dramatically. Her skin tightened. Cheeks plumped. Hair curled and turned blond . . . until she was no longer old. Until she was Mrs. Cushing.

The light sparked. She lit up like a bonfire, hair whipping around her head, and rose several inches into the air. Beneath her feet, a pool of blue light opened. It swirled and undulated, and Astrid couldn't tell if it was water or clouds or something else entirely, but it was the same color as the idols. And the six who were holding those idols? They pushed and heaved and shoved the baskets overboard. One by one, they fell into the lake and sank.

But there was no time to dwell on that monstrous act, because several things happened in quick succession. Mrs. Cushing exploded in a ball of white light—so bright, Astrid couldn't see her floating anymore. Where was she? Gone? Before Astrid could figure that out, lightning struck the raft, and everything was sucked inside the pool.

The six men.

The idols.

And the raft itself.

It all just . . . disappeared.

The survivors on the raft didn't change, Astrid thought. The ritual only restored youth to the priestess. The old bodies were drowned, but they weren't sacrificed. They were . . . discarded.

The six old men had swapped bodies with the young men.

Time unwound. The vision changed, and Astrid's perspective shifted. She now stood on the shore of the lake as rain pelted the surface. Nearby, Mrs. Cushing stood, a loose white skirt and red feathers around her waist, watching the lake intently. The turquoise pendant hung between her breasts.

A few yards away, lightning struck the water. The raft reappeared—its canopy, candles . . . and the six men with the idols. Cushing made a triumphant noise and spoke in a language Astrid had never heard. She began stripping off her skirt, continuing to intone indecipherable words, until movement in the nearby brush caught her attention.

A conquistador in armor knelt in the brush, a crossbow propped on one shoulder. He released a bolt that shot through the air and pierced Cushing's stomach with a fleshy ripping sound.

Cushing barely faltered. She grabbed the bolt and yanked it out of her body, tossing it aside with a dark smile. The wound began healing, even as the blood dripped down her leg. She shouted something at the man and began marching toward him as he reloaded the crossbow.

She can't be killed, Astrid thought in horror.

Perhaps the conquistador realized this, too, because

before Cushing made it to him, he shot another bolt in a different direction. It sailed across the water and struck one of the men on the raft in the chest.

Mrs. Cushing screamed. The man fell off the raft into the water. She dove into the lake and swam madly toward the raft as the conquistador loaded a third bolt in his crossbow. But as she was swimming, the man who'd been shot bobbed to the surface, unmoving. White light shot out of his chest . . . and out of the chests of the remaining five men on the raft.

A few moments later, all six bodies shriveled up, cracked into pieces, and blew away. And in the moonlight reflecting off the lake, Astrid spied Cushing's hair change from gold to silver.

"Is she dying?" a voice said from a distance as the vision scattered and disintegrated. "What's the matter with her?"

"I don't know," Cushing answered.

"The six are weak," Astrid mumbled. That's why Cushing recruited the pirates—because she had to find new men. That's how she stayed young. Immortal.

"Did she say something?" Fleury asked.

"Her mouth moved," someone else confirmed.

"I don't give a damn, just do something!" Max shouted. "She's got my vigor. I feel my soul drying up. Do the ritual. Now!"

TWENTY-EIGHT

❦

BO SLOWED THE YACHT AS THEY APPROACHED THE MAP COOR-
dinates. Mad Hammett had only stopped talking long
enough to scratch his ass, but he'd slowly relaxed his stance
as the yacht cut through the water. Unfortunately, he hadn't
relaxed enough, and had kept the gun trained on Bo the
entire time. But now he perked up and straightened.

"We're here?" Hammett said, squinting out the windows in snatches.

Bo couldn't wait any longer. If the man wouldn't give
him an opportunity, he'd have to invent one himself. "I
think so," he said, trying to sound unsure as he stopped
the boat.

"You think so? Not good enough. It has to be exact
before we anchor."

"I'm almost positive. Is that a four or a nine?" Bo asked,
nodding at the map.

Hammett frowned at him and leaned closer. "Where?"

"Here," Bo said, tapping one finger on the map while
he reached behind him for the radio headset.

"The last number? That's a three, you—"

Rising out of his seat, Bo wrapped the radio cord around the man's neck.

And he pulled.

Hammett made a horrible gargling sound as Bo swung around his back and tightened the cord.

Hammett was big. Beefy. Heavier than Bo. But Bo had learned long ago that speed and daring went a long way. And as the big man rotated wildly, trying to point the gun at Bo while grasping the cord around his neck, Bo lodged a knee in the man's back and doubled his efforts.

The cord cut into his hands, but that was good, because it was cutting into Hammett's windpipe, too. The gun fell from Hammett's hand and thunked against the floor as Hammett reached over his shoulder, scrabbling to pull Bo off of him, stumbling backward. The man was filled with wild fury.

But Bo was filled with vengeance.

Bo's back hit the wall of the pilothouse. Hard. The impact shattered the dangling headset on one side of the cord and nearly knocked the wind out of Bo. He didn't let go. He dodged Hammett's flailing fist, only to be elbowed in the side. Pain knifed through his ribs, but he was too far hell-bent to care. He choked Hammett as if his own life depended on it. He choked Hammett for Astrid. And as his hands went numb and the big man slammed into him again and again, he hung on.

And on . . .

Whether seconds or minutes passed, he wasn't sure, but he felt the moment Hammett stopped crushing him. The man tried to wedge his fingers between the cord and his throat. In vain. His muscles slackened, and his weight shifted.

Dead.

Dead or passed out. Bo didn't really care which. He shoved the man's limp body aside with a loud grunt, crawled to the gun, and snagged it off the floor. After checking the pistol's magazine for bullets, he left Hammett and the pilothouse behind and raced down the outer deck stairs, coat blowing open as wind ripped across the ocean, only slowing when he approached the door to the main cabin.

He flattened himself against the cabin's wall and peered inside the framed glass doors. The lights were on. No one guarded the door. Hard to tell, but it looked as though everyone was crowded in front of the piano. How many? Five? Six? *The survivors*, a voice inside his head said. They were all here together. For a moment, he thought Mrs. Cushing's blond head belonged to Astrid, until his brain rejected the body. Not Astrid.

Where was she? His heart slammed against his aching ribs. He pushed hair out of his eyes and said a small prayer, and then he opened the door.

The wind betrayed him, howling into the cabin. Heads lifted. He registered the alarm on their faces, but his eyes were scanning for weapons. And for Astrid.

"Sibyl!" someone cried out as the crowd parted.

Bo was aware of the doors at his back and the wind gusting through them. He didn't want Hammett coming downstairs and surprising him, so he quickly sidled toward the bar to get a better angle, and that's when he finally spotted Max leaning against the piano—as if he could barely stand on his own. And in the center of the crowd, Mrs. Cushing was bent over the piano stool.

Over Astrid's limp body.

"What have you done to her?" Bo shouted.

Mrs. Cushing finally looked up. Her eyes blazed with anger when she saw him. "Nance! Hammett has failed."

"Astrid!" Bo roared, pointing his gun from head to head, unsure who he should target. Seven rounds in the Colt. If he didn't miss . . .

"She's not conscious," Mrs. Cushing said. "And if you want her to live, you'd better put that away." The woman snatched up Astrid by her hair and roughly jerked her until she sat up on the piano stool to make her point. "See."

"What have you done to her?"

"Sibyl, the ritual!" Nance rasped, blood spattering as he coughed.

Mrs. Cushing's face softened. She smiled at Bo. "Allow me to perform the ritual and the girl will live. Kill any of us, and she'll die. She's connected to us, and you know this, otherwise you wouldn't have been looking for the symbol."

Bo aimed at Cushing.

"Bo . . ."

"Astrid!" Bo shouted, stalking forward.

"Not her," Astrid mumbled as her eyes fluttered open. "Max."

Cushing gripped Astrid's hair tighter, making her groan. "I'm warning you. If you harm anyone here, the girl will die. Don't be foolish."

Bo hesitated. What if Cushing was right? Astrid *was* connected to them. She possessed something of Nance's energy—Velma had seen it. *Stand or fall together.* That's what Nance had said in the pilothouse.

But when his gaze met Astrid's, he saw something there that he knew as well as his own name. Magnusson confidence mixed with Magnusson temper. Her tired eyes said: *If you don't trust me now, Bo Yeung, I swear to God, I'll die just to spite you!*

And that was all the confirmation he needed.

He'd wanted to kill the son of a bitch, anyway.

He rotated his aim to Max, closed one eye, and fired.

The thunderous shot echoed around the cabin. Max's body flew backward as the bullet struck his chest. Bo fired at him again, just to be sure, and watched him collapse on the floor.

Cushing's scream circled the room and blocked out the howling wind as a white light rose out of Max's body and shot through the yacht's ceiling. Bo struggled to train the gun's sight on the other five, who were scattering around the room, crying out as if in pain. One by one, they all teetered mid-step, seemed to dry up, and burst into clouds of dust.

Cushing released Astrid's hair, and as she stood, Astrid's hand shot up and grabbed a chain around the woman's neck. It broke free, and Cushing jumped as if she'd been struck.

"Catch!" Astrid yelled, and tossed a necklace toward Bo.

He saw the turquoise sphere and chain sailing toward him, but Astrid's throw was weak, and he had to dive forward to reach it. Inches from his fingers, the turquoise crashed against the floor and shattered into bright blue shards.

Astrid gaped.

Cushing froze. Strands of her hair changed from blond to white. Her skin began wrinkling. But Bo's gaze flicked to the spot below her feet, where the floor opened up and a bright blue circle of water swirled like a waterspout, crackling with electricity.

"Bo! The yacht—"

She didn't need to finish. Something terrible was happening. The air was breaking down around them, getting heavier. He gasped but couldn't seem to inhale anything into his lungs.

He didn't think, just raced to Astrid and snatched her around the waist. Cushing rose up in the air over the blue funnel as Bo dragged Astrid toward the cabin's open doors. He didn't care enough about what happened to the woman to look back.

There was no time to lower a lifeboat; the yacht's floor was melting. The wind whipped up Astrid's hair as they came to a stop on the deck. She looked at him and understanding passed between them. She grabbed his hand, they vaulted over the railing together . . .

And jumped.

For a long, suspended moment, there was nothing but cold and darkness as they plunged into the ocean. His body was too shocked to react. To move. To do anything but wonder if he'd never stop sinking. But he did, and when he regained control over his limbs and floundered in the icy water, he'd lost Astrid's hand.

He couldn't see. Couldn't feel. Couldn't call out for her. All he could do was hope.

His lungs felt as if they might burst. He despaired and pushed himself up through the water—was this up? He couldn't tell anymore—fighting against the cold and the friction that longed to pull him back down. Up, up, until he exploded through the water's surface and gasped for breath.

He gulped air and paddled as he called for her. "Astrid!"

It was so dark. So black. So cold. He twisted around, waves crashing over his head, until he saw the yacht silhouetted against the dark blue sky. But no Astrid. Where was she?

Out of nowhere, a bolt of white lightning streaked across the night sky and struck the yacht. The sound was explosive. Waves radiated from the boat like a bomb had been dropped. And as they reached Bo and lifted him higher in the water, he watched in awe as the yacht simply vanished.

Gone!

Captain Haig had told them at the radio station that he'd seen the same phenomenon, but to witness it with his own eyes was startling. The radiating waves lifted him, dropped him, and when he was able to ride their undulating path and look around, fresh panic turned his stomach to stone.

The yacht was gone. Where was Astrid?

Stand or fall together.

He refused to believe Cushing. Refused! Astrid was still here. Had to be. But where? Was she under? He took a deep breath and urged his muscles into action, preparing to dive, when he heard a distant shout across the water.

"Bo!"

His heart leaped. He swam toward her voice, arms cutting through the briny waves, until her shouts flooded his ears and he crushed her in her arms.

I've got you, he told her with his body. *I've got you, and everything is all right.*

TWENTY-NINE

———✦———

ASTRID COULDN'T HAVE GUESSED WHETHER THE SWIM TO SHORE
took thirty minutes or hours, but she was at times almost
certain she wouldn't make it. The water was shockingly
cold, the waves rough, and she was too weak to tread water
and had to rely on Bo to pull her along. The pounding surf
towed them ashore toward a sandy stretch of land between
a break in the cliffs, where neither of them moved for a
long while. It was only because their bodies were wracked
by intense shivers that they got to their feet and hiked up
a trail bounded by coastal scrub, which gradually ascended
until they spotted the dark lighthouse. Bo still had the keys
to the cottage in his pocket—"Thank Buddha, Osiris, and
Jehovah," he exclaimed upon realizing it, though, at that
point, they would have gladly broken a window to get
inside—but they'd lost other things in the ocean, like his
gun and the inner workings of her wristwatch.

"It's ruined," she said once Bo had stripped off their
salty, wet clothes and wrapped them in a blanket near the
wood-burning stove. She tapped the face of the watch, but
it was no use.

"Maybe it can be repaired. We're still alive, and that's the most important thing, yes? They're gone. All of them. They're gone and we're still here. That's enough for now."

She nestled closer, unable to get warm. Of course she was relieved to have survived that ordeal, though she worried that the taint of Max was still with her and wished Velma could confirm it was gone. But Bo was right: they'd won. Bruised and beaten, but still standing together.

At least until they'd have to telephone someone in the city to come get them. Would they slip back into their old lives? Sneaking around. Praying for a stolen moment alone when no one was watching or listening. Hiding.

"It's not enough," Astrid said. "I don't want to merely survive."

"Sometimes that's all you can you do," he said as he tightened his arms around her. "You survive as long as you can and wait for the right conditions to bloom."

But what if those conditions never came? How long could they wait? She wanted an answer. Something definitive. A deadline when the waiting would end. But she knew Bo couldn't give her that, so she just held on to him. She held on until the fire had warmed the ocean out of her bones. Until he lifted her into the small cottage bed. Until exhaustion pulled her into sleep. And when morning sun slanted over their faces, she woke with a clear head.

Yesterday's nightmare was over. It was time to move on. She would tell him her new plan for the future. *Their* future.

"Happy New Year," his voice said near her ear.

"Happy New Year." She turned over to see his handsome face and curved a hand over his cheek. His hair was still matted with dried blood above his ear. "Does it still hurt?"

"My head's killing me."

"We should have called someone to get us last night. You need to see a doctor."

He shook his head and ran a hand through her hair. "I wanted one more night with you."

All they had done was sleep, but she understood. She wanted it, too. This togetherness. To wake up and feel his arm around her.

He propped himself up on an elbow and looked down at her. "I think we need to talk about what happens next. About us." Had he been reading her mind? Before she could agree, before she could even open her mouth to speak, he asked, "Do you love me?"

Her voice caught in the back of her throat. "So much."

"Do you want this?" He didn't explain, but she understood. This. "Knowing how hard it will be for both of us. Knowing . . . I can't marry you. Do you still want this?"

"More than anything."

He nodded briefly and blew out a long breath. "Then I want you to go back to school."

Her hand stilled. "Back to school?"

"The semester starts in three days, so you'll probably need to get on a train tomorrow or the next day."

The heaviness that had lifted from her chest settled back inside as if it had never left. She sat up in bed, angry and hurt. "How can you say that? Did the last few weeks mean so little that you can just send me off with a pat on the back?"

He grabbed her shoulders, brow lowering severely. "Do you even need to ask me that? They mean everything, Astrid. They've turned my world upside down."

"Then why do you want me to go?"

Brown eyes studied hers. His face softened. "Because I want you to be sure that school isn't what you want."

"It isn't."

"I want you to be *sure*," he repeated. A plea. "And if it turns out that you change your mind, then we'll find a way to make it work. It doesn't change us. It's not one or the other. Not us or school."

This wasn't her plan. Wasn't what she wanted at all. She started to tell him what she had in mind. "But it's not the only option. If—"

"Listen to me," he said in a voice that brooked no

argument. "If we're going to do this, legally married or not, I need to be able to take care of you. I can't do that from the basement of the Queen Anne. I need time to put things in order, to stand on my own. I need . . . to talk to Winter."

"He'll have to accept us, and that's all there is to it."

"I know that. But he's my family, too. And after everything he's done . . . well, I at least owe him honesty."

"I could tell him with you."

He shook his head. "No, Astrid. Allow me my pride. This is my job, my home—there's too much on the line for me. It's my entire world. And my burden, too. I know you think that Winter will have to accept us, but have you seriously considered that he might not? And what would we do then? How would we live with no job and no home?"

"Did you ever consider that I can work, too? Plenty of women work."

He picked up her hand and held it between both of his. "A man still must be able to take care of a woman, even if she can stand on her own. I want to be that man for you. I'm asking you to let me do that. Asking you to have faith in me. Give me time to sort this out and secure our future. Go back to Los Angeles."

His words rang in her head. And as they did, it finally sunk in that this wasn't about her going back to school at all. This was about Bo and Winter. Bo and his pride. Urging her to return to the university was convenient for him. That wasn't his only reason for wanting her to go, of course; she had no doubt that he truly believed school was important and a privilege she'd be throwing away carelessly if she quit now. He'd made that clear before tonight.

It took her a handful of seconds to change her mind about telling Bo her bold new plan—one that didn't involve school. He'd only shoot it down. And the thing of it was, she understood exactly what he was feeling, this need to stand on his own feet and prove himself worthy. She wanted that, too. Because in her mind, going back to college wasn't independence; it was giving in and bending to pressure. It was conforming to an ideal that her brothers had wanted—not her. And she hadn't failed at academics because it was too hard or because she wasn't serious enough.

She'd failed because it just wasn't the right path for her.

"Will you give me time to take care of things?" Bo asked, eyes pleading.

"I will," she answered. Not in the way he wanted, but she didn't tell him this. After all, he wanted her to have faith in him, but he needed to have faith in her, too.

She would give him a reason to do precisely that.

THIRTY

———— ⚜ ————

THE FIRST THING THEY DID WHEN THEY GOT BACK INTO THE CITY was to head straight to Gris-Gris. Velma confirmed that the shadow on Astrid's aura was gone. She was free and clear of cursed magic. But after everything they'd been through the night before, Astrid felt that this was less a cause for celebration and more of a consolation prize. Strange to think that dealing with body-thieving pirates and ghost ships was almost preferable to facing the mountain that lay ahead: her future.

Their future.

After they'd made their way back home and given her family a summary of their harrowing experience on the yacht—leaving out several details that came before and after—Astrid spent the day making preparations. Telephone calls and telegrams, secret conversations and whirlwind packing. And throughout it all, her frantic emotions vacillated between panic and excitement.

Please don't let this be a mistake.

The following morning, she said her good-byes to Bo

in private, and that was her demand: that he let her leave on her own, the way she arrived. She hugged everyone else good-bye outside the Magnusson house, nearly breaking down when she saw Greta's stoic face soften. And after all her luggage was loaded onto the family's silver Packard, she slipped into the front seat next to Aida.

"Do you remember teaching me how to drive in this car?" Astrid asked.

"Who could forget?" Aida answered with a grin as she started the engine. "We scared the living hell out of the entire household."

Astrid smiled back at her and glanced at the line of people waving at them from the Queen Anne's porch. "In a way, you're helping me to do that again today."

"Here's to taking risks," Aida said as she backed out of the long driveway.

It took them half an hour in traffic to drive to the train station, where Aida pulled up to the passenger drop-off area behind a dark limousine with whitewall tires. A slender woman with a straight black bob and a black fur coat stepped out from the backseat.

"Everyone here is a witness," Aida said cheerfully as they met the woman on the sidewalk. "I dropped Astrid off at the train station."

"You can say it with a clear conscience," Hadley agreed as her uniformed driver hurried around to the Packard to transfer Astrid's luggage between the two cars.

"It's really not a lie," Astrid said. "It's an omission of pesky details."

Aida waggled her eyebrows. "Every woman should have a few secrets."

"Sure you haven't changed your mind?" Hadley asked Astrid.

Astrid glanced up at early evening fog that rolled over the top of the train platform and considered the question, but she was sure. She'd already mailed the university her withdrawal. She was ready to enact her grand plan for the future . . . with a little help from her sisters-in-law.

"No, I haven't changed my mind," Astrid answered. "I'm ready."

Aida hugged her firmly. "Okay, then. I'm going to head back. I'll collect any mail that comes and telephone you tomorrow, but if you need anything—"

"I'll be fine."

Aida nodded and raised her chin to Hadley. "She's all yours."

"Let's get you settled before it gets too dark," the curator said, and put her arm around Astrid's shoulders to lead her into the limousine.

It was, of course, absurd, to drive back the way they'd come, but Astrid didn't care. She pretended that she was seeing the city for the first time and watched as lights twinkled on in the tall buildings lining the hilly streets. And by the time they got to Nob Hill, she really felt that it *was* new, because for the first time in her life, she'd be spending the night alone. No roommate, no servants, no family . . . no Bo. It was bittersweet, but the excitement she felt outweighed any lingering sadness or doubt.

Tendrils of evening fog clung to columns flanking the driveway of the French-Renaissance apartment building at Mason. The elegant nine-story high-rise was only a couple of years old and very exclusive—across the street from the Wicked Wenches' building. Hadley had been living there when she met Lowe almost a year ago. And though Lowe had renovated a looming Victorian on Telegraph Hill for them and little Stella, Hadley hadn't yet been able to sell her apartment.

"Everything's been cleaned and dusted," the curator informed her as they breezed through the small lobby. She introduced her to the attendant and the elevator operator, and once they'd ascended to the ninth floor with her luggage, unlocked the door.

It was a swank apartment. High walls. Marble floors. The windows looked out over the bright lights of the Fairmont Hotel and the steady clack of the cable cars braving the steep hill.

"What do you think?" Hadley asked. "Not bad for temporary accommodations."

"It's marvelous."

"It can get lonely up here, but hopefully you won't have time for that. The refrigerator is stocked, and anyone in the building will help you find your way around the neighborhood. Otherwise, you're on your own—except for Friday night, that is. Maria and Mathilda have invited you for dinner at eight."

"Oh good," Astrid said. "I have a *lot* to tell them about that idol."

"Well, I better get back home before anyone notices me missing. Here are the keys. You know where to find me if you need anything."

"Thank you," Astrid said, gripping her in a tight hug. "For everything."

When Hadley pulled back, her cheeks were flushed. "It was nothing. We're family," Hadley said. "Besides, Aida's right. A woman should have a few secrets. Do well with yours."

"I'll try," Astrid promised her. "I'll try my best."

Astrid spent the night unpacking and getting used to the sounds of the strange apartment. And though she got little sleep—having spent too much time staring out the window, fighting the urge to telephone Bo and tell him everything—she rose at a decent hour, dressed in a smart outfit, and took a taxi to Hale Brothers department store. On the sixth floor, she walked into KPO Radio's front office, wished the receptionist a Happy New Year, and asked to speak to the station manager. Then she waited until she was ushered into his office.

"I remember you," Mr. Giselman said when he saw her.

"Astrid Magnusson," she said, extending her hand. "You told me you liked my voice and said to come see you if I ever I wanted a job. And, well, I do."

"I do like a gal with gumption. Have a seat," he said. "And tell me about yourself."

"I'm a fast learner, I have some college education"—never mind that it was a disaster—"and if you take a look at my references here"—she handed him typed and signed letters from both Aida and Hadley—"you'll see they're from a director at the de Young Museum and a woman who used to do nightly performances on stage at a dinner club. She says I'm 'gifted with a performer's grace.' "

That was Astrid's phrase. She was quite proud of it.

Mr. Giselman sat down behind his desk, donned a pair of eyeglasses to read the letters, and then looked her over. "Magnusson . . . Why does that name sound familiar?"

Dammit. "Maybe you've heard of my brother?" she said quickly. "He's a well-known professor at Berkley." Well-known to her, at least.

The manager shook his head, but it was enough to steer his thoughts away from the bootlegging. "Well, Miss Magnusson. I did say we're hiring voice actors for radio melodramas—that means you do a dramatic reading from a script, following the director's suggestions. Four hours, three days a week, and the pay is basic."

"I'll do whatever it takes to prove myself. But I think you'll find that my skills are best suited to situations in which I'm able to speak freely. I heard KFRC is doing more talk shows across town that appeal to female listeners. I have some ideas about how you could compete with them."

"I'll bet you do," he said, a look of amusement on his face.

He glanced at her letters again, and while he did, Astrid fiddled with the knob on her wristwatch. It had never recovered after her swim in the ocean that horrid night on the yacht, but she wore it nonetheless, and continually tried to wind it to no avail. It was perpetually stuck on twelve o'clock. But now the knob moved, one turn, and another. She quickly looked at the face. Ten after three. The wrong time, but the hands were moving. *A sign*, she thought. A very good sign.

Stars. The station manager was saying something.

"Pardon?" she asked, looking up from her wristwatch.

"I said, how about we start out testing how you read on a melodrama and see how it goes?"

"I can read today, if you'd like," Astrid said with a bright smile.

He folded up his eyeglasses and set them down on his desk. "Let me introduce you to the programming director and she can tell us whether you'd be a good fit."

THIRTY-ONE

———— ❦ ————

THE DAY AFTER ASTRID LEFT, BO CARRIED HOME THREE PACKING crates from the warehouse. Enough to hold all his things, he thought. Greta spied him before he could sneak the last one inside his room, and though he wanted to be packed and ready to walk out the door before he talked to Winter, he knew the gossip would spread through the house before he finished packing, so he left the crates and hunted down Winter, finding him upstairs in his study.

Afternoon sun beamed through the windows of the third-floor room, which, like Astrid's turret, looked out over Pacific Heights and the Bay. The study had belonged to Winter's father before he passed, and still housed the old man's library, as well as a carved dragon from the front of a Viking longship. And it was here that Winter stood in his shirtsleeves, holding his infant daughter while talking in a hushed, intense voice to his wife.

Aida looked up and smiled at Bo, but her expression changed when she saw his face. Did he look *that* miserable? Probably. "Sorry to interrupt," he said to Winter. "But I was hoping to talk to you."

"I just remembered something," Aida murmured and held out her arms. "Here, let me take her."

Bo wished she'd leave Karin with Winter. Would be much harder for Winter to hit Bo while holding a baby. But he handed the child over, and Aida left the room in a hurry, giving Bo a pat on the arm as she passed.

"What's on your mind?" Winter asked, gesturing to a sofa in front of the unlit fireplace.

Bo declined. He was too nervous to sit. "I need to tell you something, and you aren't going to be happy about it."

His boss's brow lowered. "Well, go on, then. Don't make me guess."

Bo's stomach churned and his breathing quickened. His dazed mind had retreated from reality and floated in some kind of in-between space. "I'm in love with your sister."

Winter didn't move.

Bo exhaled and corrected his first statement. "Astrid and I are in love," he said, and then added, before he could stop himself, "I've slept with her."

Winter blinked his mismatched eyes. Once. Twice. If Bo didn't know any better, he'd think the man's mind had gone to the same place Bo's seemed to be, because he looked just as dazed as Bo felt. And after a long moment, Winter finally said, "Did you get her pregnant?"

"What? No. No," he repeated, shaking his head. Hopefully not. "We've been . . . cautious. Every time." Might as well get it all out in the open.

"*Helvete*," Winter murmured.

"I'm sorry. Not for that. I'm not sorry at all for that," he said a little too fiercely, and forced himself to show some humbleness. "But I *am* sorry we kept it from you. I know this is upsetting, and I know it's probably not what you wanted for Astrid. You've trusted me with her, and I betrayed that trust. And I wish I could say that it will never happen again, and ask for forgiveness, but the truth is that I can't do that." He took a deep breath and finished. "So I'm moving out. And if you don't want me working with you anymore, I understand. I'll find other work. But I won't give her up. I just won't."

"Christ alive," Winter mumbled.

"It will be hard for her," Bo said. "And I wish like hell I could change that. But she knows the risks. She's not a child."

No response.

"We want your blessing," Bo said. "But I won't beg for it."

Winter flew toward him like an enraged bull. Bo faltered, body telling him to flee. But he stood his ground and braced for a punch in the face, praying that the man didn't hit him hard enough to kill him. He'd survived the cursed pirate's blows, but he wasn't entirely sure he'd survive Winter's.

Beefy arms shot toward him. Giant hands covered in sinews hovered in front of Bo's throat. *Choked to death*, Bo thought, resigned. Poetic justice for what he'd done to Mad Hammett, he supposed. He stood his ground, even as Winter's scarred face scowled at him with satanic rage.

A string of Swenglish curses left Winter's mouth. Unfortunately, after living with Swedes for a third of his life, Bo knew what all of them meant.

"*Bo*," Winter finally pleaded and dropped his heavy hands on Bo's shoulders and squeezed but did not release. A pomaded lock of dark hair fell over a brow etched with lines. "I trusted you."

"I know," Bo murmured and met the man's intense gaze. "But I am not ashamed. I love her. And I will take care of her."

Winter sighed. "I trusted you," he repeated, "because you are the most honorable person I know. There are a thousand men in this city who would use Astrid for her looks or her name or her money—and twice as many who would look down at her for those same reasons, too. Who would I trust with her happiness?"

Bo stilled. He was very confused. His body kept telling

him to brace for violence, but his brain was misinterpreting what Winter was saying. What *was* he saying?

"I won't even ask if you're certain," Winter continued. "I've seen how you look at each other for years. And the past weeks? Christ. I knew when she came back home, Bo. I'm no fool. And I won't lecture you on the hardships you'd be facing. You and her. And if you had any children . . ."

"I know," Bo said, swallowing hard.

"Yes," Winter agreed softly. "I expect you know more than anyone. It's not an easy choice."

"And I haven't come to it lightly. I know I can't marry her. Not legally. But we aren't the first couple to face this. If the laws aren't fair, do you blindly obey them?"

Those were Winter's father's words, and Bo knew he was pushing things, throwing them back in Winter's face; his hands squeezed hard enough to leave bruises on Bo's shoulders . . . and then loosened. He turned and walked toward the windows. "You said you'd find other work. What would you do?" He didn't wait for an answer. "You'd just leave me in a lurch, knowing damn well I need you?"

"You'd get by without me."

"Would I? While you did what?"

Bo had thought about it. Quite a lot, actually. "I'd try to get work fishing. Maybe sell the Buick and buy a small boat. There's more out there than crabs. Good money in tuna. Canneries opening up everywhere. There's decent money to be had. Not bootlegging money, but it's honorable work. And I read the news—Volstead won't hold forever. Every day there's more talk of repeal. What happens then?"

Winter crossed his arms over his chest. "You don't think I know that? Forget repeal. It's getting goddamn dangerous. Too many people killing each other over liquor. I got one baby and another one on the way. I think about it all the time. In fact, Aida and I were just talking. She's . . ."

"What?"

Winter gave a dismissive shrug and then scratched the

back of his neck. "I mentioned this before, but it's getting worse. She's been hearing the same message repeated in different séances for different people. Something bad is coming—something to do with the economy. Spirits are warning their relatives to pay off their debts and get their money out of the bank before the end of the year."

Bo temporarily forgot his own troubles. He remembered Winter mentioning this back when the yacht first crashed into the pier. "You believe it?"

"People downtown are talking about the stock market and how buying on margin can't last forever." Winter shrugged. "And Aida believes it, so that's good enough for me. Got me thinking about spreading out our interests. Maybe some legitimate shipping. And like you said, picking up more fishing, too. We've got no debt, and I've got enough in savings to keep us afloat for years." He shook his head, as if to clear it. "But we aren't talking about me. We're talking about you. Where will you live?"

Though he was feeling more optimistic about his chances of escaping a right hook to the jaw, Bo was still wary about saying too much. "I'll move back into my old apartment tonight. I asked Astrid to go back to school until I figured everything out. I have some ideas about apartments. People who might be persuaded to rent me a place outside of Chinatown. It won't be here, but I'll make sure it's safe."

"Bigots won't leave Ju's Russian Hill house alone."

"I know," Bo said. "I have something in mind that might be less of a risk. I just need to find a way to make it work financially."

"You could stay here."

Bo stilled, unsure he'd heard right. Maybe he'd mistook Winter's meaning. "I can't. Not downstairs." He wanted to say more, but he couldn't. His pride wouldn't let him, and if Winter didn't understand, so be it.

"You could have the half floor. The top of the turret. We could convert it into an apartment."

For a moment, Bo imagined this. Living upstairs. But no, he couldn't. Independence is what he wanted. Freedom to be with Astrid. He stuck his hands in his pockets and dared to ask what he was thinking. What he was hoping, but at the same time, didn't dare to hope. "The turret . . . Do you mean just for me? Or for Astrid, too?"

Winter strode back across the study and stopped in front of Bo. "You are both my family, her by blood and you by choice," he said in a low voice. "There isn't a thing in the world I wouldn't do for either one of you. And there's also no one I trust more with her happiness than you. So if you both want my blessing, you have it."

An old, uncomfortable weight sprouted wings and lifted from Bo's chest. He wanted to weep. To collapse. To fall to his knees and thank every deity in the world. He managed to keep himself together and extended a trembling hand. "Thank you, *dai lo*." Big brother—and a term of respect.

Winter accepted and shook, formally, and then heartily. They both chuckled, a little nervous. Winter exhaled a long breath and added, "You've also got my protection, because on the trail the two of you are about to blaze, you're damn sure going to need it."

At eight o'clock the next night, Astrid waited for two workers in overalls to carry a leather sofa past her before stepping into the elevator of the Wicked Wenches' apartment building. She instantly recognized the handsome operator in burgundy uniform—the Jack Johnson look-alike who had helped them when Bo was stabbed. His eyes widened at the sight of her.

"Hello, again," she said. "Mr. Laroche, isn't it?"

"Miss Magnusson."

"Don't worry. No one's chasing after me today," she said. Then added, "He's dead."

He considered this for a moment and said, "That's good news."

"Someone moving out?" she asked, nodding toward the men hauling the sofa.

"The Humphreys," he confirmed.

"The state senator and his wife?"

He nodded and gave her a knowing look. Yes, he remembered her altercation with the nasty woman, too. "It was all very sudden. Divorcing, I hear. Top floor?"

She grinned. "Yes. Top floor, please."

When she got to Maria and Mathilda's penthouse, they were waiting for her in the living room, smiling in their sparkling evening gowns and drinking champagne. Magnusson stock, Astrid thought as she eyed the black bottle. Had Lowe been here, delivering them booze?

"Darling girl!" Mathilda said and hugged her neck.

"We were so happy to hear that you're staying in Hadley's old apartment," Maria said. "We're practically neighbors, at least for a little while. Hadley swore us to secrecy, but you must tell us everything. Where's the dashing Mr. Yeung?"

Astrid's heart fluttered inside her chest. "He doesn't know I'm still in town, actually. It's a very long story . . ."

"And we have a *lot* of champagne," Mathilda assured her with a wink. "Let me pour you a glass and you can tell us all about it."

THIRTY-TWO

———— ❦ ————

NEARLY THREE WEEKS AFTER ASTRID'S DEPARTURE, BO STROLLED into Pier 26 and tipped his hat to Old Bertha the shark. As he hung up his coat, Winter's dark head popped through the doorway.

"How did it go?"

"Signed the lease."

Winter grinned. "Excellent."

Nob Hill. He didn't belong there. Or maybe he did. He wasn't sure, but he damn well didn't care. He was too busy being buoyed on a mix of excitement and queasiness. He'd done it, and there was no going back. When he'd first turned down Winter's offer to live in the turret of the Magnusson house, they'd argued bitterly. But Bo wouldn't concede. He had to stand on his own, even if it was a more difficult path.

And though he could afford the lease—mostly due to the Wicked Wenches offering him the state senator's former cozy one-bedroom apartment on the floor below theirs for an impossibly low rent that no amount of arguing would change—he wasn't used to plunking down that much money every month to live. Or any money at all, frankly.

Selling his old apartment in Chinatown gave him a small cushion, but there were other expenses to consider, not to mention a dozen unknowns, which were busy churning up anxiety in his gut.

He slipped a hand inside his pocket and fingered the new apartment key, dazedly thinking of everything that was now his. A parlor that overlooked Huntington Park. A cozy dining room. A bedroom—spacious enough for a very big bed. A newly remodeled kitchen with electric appliances. And, best of all, a small library. An actual library! All of Bo's books would fit on one bookcase, but he could buy more.

"It's four blocks from Dr. Moon's apartment," he told Winter, thinking of the gray area between neighborhoods that Astrid had talked about their first night in the lighthouse. "And only a fifteen-minute walk from Aida's shop."

"Aida will be eager to see it," Winter said. "Hadley stopped by the house earlier and they were talking about it. The two of them are getting awfully chummy, if you ask me," he said with a lowered brow, as if that was something to be suspicious about.

"Probably just discussing Lowe and Hadley's trip to Egypt," Bo said. The couple was leaving by train tomorrow, heading out to the East Coast, where they'd board a ship bound for an Atlantic crossing. "Hadley's unusually bubbly these days."

"Maybe," Winter said, but he didn't seem convinced as he headed back out into the warehouse.

Bo was too happy to care. He needed to write Astrid a letter. Maybe a telegram. A long-distance telephone call would be too expensive, and he was afraid if he heard her voice, he'd be tempted to beg her to come home today. He wanted that to be her choice. Besides, there were too many other things that needed doing. Moving his things. Buying furniture.

A letter. That would be the best. He could suggest she send a telegram in return when she received it. That would give him a couple of weeks to get things settled.

He dumped the pile of delivered mail he'd been carrying onto Winter's desk and sat down behind it, his mind abuzz with Too Many Things, when the warehouse receptionist knocked on the doorframe.

"Miss Fong to see you," she said.

Bo's hands stilled over the pile of mail. What in the world was Sylvia doing here? Before he could guess, she was escorted into the office.

"Hello, Ah-Sing," she said brightly as she breezed beneath the stuffed shark.

"Sylvia," he answered, standing up. "What's wrong?"

She tugged on the tips of her gloves and sat down in a chair in front of the desk. "Why would there be something wrong? Can't an old friend just pay a friendly visit? I heard you sold your apartment. You could have at least stopped by and told me."

"I did stop by, actually," he said, sitting back down behind the desk. "You weren't home."

"Liar."

Well, yes. But he'd seen Amy walking up the stairs and didn't much feel like visiting both of them, so he'd taken the coward's way out. "I sold my apartment," he said. "Now you know. How are you, by the way? You seem more cheerful than usual."

She flashed him a dazzling smile and pulled off her left glove. A small jewel glittered on her ring finger. "I'm engaged."

"To—?"

"Andy Lee."

"Your boss at the telephone office? That's the boyfriend you've been talking about?"

"Jealous?"

Bo chuckled. "A little. But mostly happy for you. I mean, are *you*? Happy?"

"Very much. What about you? Are you and—"

He nodded. "She's in Los Angeles right now. Back in school." He told her a few details, about the apartment and the fact that her family knew about them. "How it will all work out, I don't know. But I never thought it would go this far, and that's something."

"How far do you want it to go?" Sylvia pulled a newspaper clipping from her handbag. "Because I saw this at Andy's place and thought of you."

He breathed in the scent of ink as he unfolded the newsprint. It was from Seattle. *The Northwest Enterprise.* A social activism newspaper.

"Andy's a member of the Chinese Chamber of Commerce," she explained. "They have affiliations with organizations up the coast. Look at that headline."

Couples Travel Long Distances to Wed in Washington

"The only state in the West that will allow different races to marry. They talk about how couples are getting around the laws in other states—a Caucasian woman claimed to have Filipino blood in order to marry her minister in Nevada. But you don't have to lie in Washington to get a license. Did you know that?"

Bo shook his head. His throat tightened.

"Whether they honor that license here is another story, but you've always had a knack for outrunning the police." She closed the clasp on her handbag and waved the newspaper away. "Keep it. Anyway, I've got to get to work, and I'm sure you're busy. I just wanted to stop by."

He walked around the desk and grabbed her hand as she stood to leave. "Thank you."

"Thank me by coming to my wedding."

"I wouldn't miss it."

She kissed his cheek. "Good luck, Ah-Sing. You deserve it."

He saw her outside and watched her black bob swing as she slipped into a waiting taxi, and after it drove off, he then made his way back to the office, slightly stunned. If he thought his head had been filled with Too Many Things before, it was in a state of all-out chaos now. But by the time he'd reread the article and sat back down at the desk, he'd decided that a letter to Astrid wasn't good enough. He'd send a telegram, caution be damned. They had

Western Union forms around here somewhere. As he forced open a drawer that often stuck, the pile of letters slid across the desk, and he spied a familiar slant of handwriting.

Astrid.

Temporarily abandoning his search for the telegram form, he snatched up the letter. It was to him, no return address. He grabbed a letter opener and sliced through the flap. The scent of rose petals drifted up. Inside was an unusually short message, though she hadn't failed to include her typical dramatic underlining, he thought with a smile.

My dearest Bo,

Please be sure to listen to KPO Friday at 2 P.M. It's <u>*very important.*</u>

All my love,
Astrid

He reread the message in a daze—twice—and flipped over the envelope. A San Francisco postmark. How in the hell . . . ? And KPO? Today was Friday. He glanced at his wristwatch. 2:05 P.M. Dammit!

He reached across the desk, spilling the rest of the letters, and switched on the waist-high old radio that sat on the floor nearby, turning the knob until he found the KPO transmission, already in progress, and listened to the familiar voice that crackled over the speaker.

"If you're a regular listener, you've probably heard my voice on KPO's other programs, such as the melodrama *Murder in the Fog*, or maybe announcing the Fairmont Orchestra's midday performances, but today is the first time you'll hear me really *talk*."

Bo nearly knocked the radio over trying to turn up the volume.

"Every Friday at 2 P.M., I'll be bringing you a unique perspective from the top of Hale Brothers department store. My new program is called *Girl Friday*, and it's a half-hour program for women in San Francisco—all women, from housewives to working gals to the students in college. I'll be giving you the latest updates about fashion, events, and even some juicy local gossip. Whatever you need to know, I'm here to help. Have a question about where to find the best deal on stockings? Telephone our station operator and let her know. Need advice about how to find out if your husband is cheating? Send a letter to *Girl Friday*, in care of KPO at Hale Brothers, and I'll answer it live on air. Tell your friends, sisters, and coworkers to tune in every Friday at 2 P.M., and we'll start the weekend together."

Osiris, Buddha, and Jehovah. That little schemer . . .

He laughed, utterly delighted and twice as proud. She rambled on, brightly talking about how there were no radio programs for women on the other local stations, sounding like everyone's best friend, natural and easygoing and funny—like herself—and halfway through the program, he realized with a start: *She's broadcasting live. She's here. Right now.*

Bo didn't listen any longer. He raced around the desk to grab his coat and hat, and then jogged through the office. "Tell Winter I'll be back," he shouted at the receptionist and jogged to the Buick.

A couple of miles. She'd be there until two thirty, at least. He could make it if he hurried.

He sped out of the warehouse and onto the Embarcadero, cutting down Folsom. When traffic slowed, he honked his horn and shouted at a delivery truck, whose driver flashed him a middle finger, which Bo returned with gusto. He just wanted to get there. So badly, in fact, that as he waited for a police car to help a stalled car blocking the road, he almost considered abandoning his car and running the rest of the way.

By the time he finally made it to Market Street and found a parking space, it was 2:45 P.M.

Please don't let her be gone. He raced down the sidewalk,

dodging pedestrians, and came to a sudden stop in front of the department store entrance.

There she was.

Blond curls. Foxlike eyes. Stubborn chin. Devious smile. Scent of roses.

His.

He was the scholar, and she was the girl running up the road to meet him, and he caught her and crushed her in his arms, kissing her hair and face and mouth, holding on as tight as he could, uncaring what anyone thought about the spectacle.

You are mine, he told her with his body. *Mine, and I will never let you go.*

EPILOGUE

Ten years later, Chinese New Year, February 1939

"THERE IT IS!" ASTRID SHOUTED, LEANING OVER THE BALCONY of Aida's spiritualism storefront on Grant Avenue, where thousands of celebrants thronged the sidewalks beneath painted banners and red lanterns to watch the annual parade in Chinatown.

It was the largest Chinese New Year's celebration in years—aided by an organized effort in Chinatowns across the nation to raise money for the war in China—and the San Francisco police projected that more than a hundred thousand people would stand along the parade route to watch acrobats, lion dancers, and hundreds of Chinatown's residents festively clad in traditional attire. Astrid's family had gathered here in the apartment over Aida's shop every year, but this was the first time they'd done more than just watch the parade.

"Daddy! It's your float!" Astrid's daughter said. May had just turned eight, and was unusually tall for a girl. Unusually pretty, too. She stood on the balcony's bottom rail and peered over the top, grinning Astrid's grin—a smile that went all the way up to eyes that looked just like her father's.

And the man who'd given her those eyes now stood next to her, hoisting their five-year-old son in his arms. "Look, Ty," Bo said. "Do you see it?"

Pulled by a truck, the float trailer was covered in ferns and flowers that spelled out MAGNUSSON AND YEUNG FISH COMPANY around the sides. And in the center was a giant papier-mâché representation of the company logo: a nine-tailed golden fox with a fish in its mouth. The tails moved up and down on sticks held by company employees, who walked behind the trailer.

"It looks good," Winter said over Bo's shoulder.

"Damn near majestic," Lowe agreed, slinging his arm around Hadley as the children whooped and cheered around him—a lot of children. In addition to Astrid and Bo's two, Winter and Aida had four, Stella was in her teens now, and Dr. Moon and his wife, Le-Ann's, two girls were here, too. All of them were crammed into the small space, bobbing and jumping to see over the railing. Astrid held a Brownie camera above all the bouncing heads to snap a good photograph.

"All right, I took five shots," she shouted as the giant fox slipped farther down the street and a new float took its place. "Hopefully one of them won't be blurry."

"Can we have our red envelopes now?" May asked, tugging on her dress.

A traditional Chinese New Year's present. The red envelopes—red for luck—held money. Bo and Astrid gave them out to the entire Magnusson clan every year. Red envelopes for their Chinese side, and *semla* cream buns on Shrove Tuesday for their Swedish side—made by Greta and Lena.

"No envelopes until the parade's over," she told May.

Astrid hadn't been able to catch her breath. She'd come straight from a meeting at the radio station that morning, but the parade route had blocked off the street and parking was a nightmare, forcing her to walk several blocks from their apartment to get here on time. And only barely. Now she pulled May closer and grinned at her husband.

"The float looked wonderful," she said loudly.

He pointed to his ear and grinned back, but there was a question behind his eyes. She knew why, but they hadn't been able to talk privately yet. And as she leaned over May's head to kiss her son's cheek, making him squirm with delight, Bo wrapped a hand around the back of her neck and spoke into her ear. "Downstairs."

She nodded. "Stay here with your cousins," she told May as Aida held out her hands for Ty.

"Auntie will hold you so you can see better," she told him, and he didn't hesitate to jump into her arms.

Astrid mouthed *thank you* to Aida and handed the camera to Stella before Bo grabbed her hand to lead her out of the family gathering.

Strains of music from an approaching marching band floated over the roar of the crowd as they descended the stairs into Aida's shop. It was much quieter here. The intense punch of the parade's din was slightly muffled by the locked door, and afternoon sun silhouetted the bodies of revelers pressing against the windows through the shades.

Bo stopped in front of a bookcase filled with titles about spiritualism and coping with bereavement, and then he turned to face her, dropping her hand to cross his arms over his chest.

"So," he prompted.

"You know, I haven't seen you in two days. I was hoping for a 'Hello, dear wife. I've missed you while I was upstate buying a new boat.'"

"I did miss you," he said, looking unfairly handsome in the slatted light spilling in from the shades. He'd returned from his trip while she'd been in her meeting that morning, and was still dressed casually for travel in slacks and an argyle sweater vest, the brim of his cap pulled down tight. But when she reached up to straighten the necktie peeking above the vee of his vest, he grabbed her hands. "Tell me what Girl Friday decided. I haven't slept the entire trip."

She hadn't, either. Over the past ten years, she'd gone from the girl who broadcasted out of Hale Brothers department store to one of the highest paid voices in the NBC studios on Sutter Street, heard all over the West Coast every week. Her sponsor paid dearly for their corporate name tacked to her show. Her face was on the cover of *Radio Stars* magazine a few months back. And that was what caused all the trouble.

A rival station in Los Angeles wanted her. They offered her a considerable pay raise and a guaranteed coast-to-coast broadcast. A tempting offer, to be sure. But she'd have to move to take it—not an option for Bo. He and Winter had survived the worst years of the Depression and turned the fishing company into a success that rivaled their bootlegging days. He couldn't leave that. His blood and sweat were in that business.

Which meant that Astrid's only option, if she took the job offer, would be to spend a great deal of time away from her family. And though she and Bo had spent days talking over the pros and cons, he'd left the matter in her hands. Her career, her choice, he'd said. But word of the offer had leaked out, and her station manager had called a meeting in the studio that morning, forcing her to give them a decision sooner than she'd anticipated.

"Stars, Bo," she murmured. "The last time I was in Los Angeles, I spent my days pining away for San Francisco instead of attending class. You think I'd really want to go through that again?"

One day, three autumns. All she had to do was look at her wristwatch and she remembered it all.

"No?" he asked.

She shook her head. "I'm not leaving. I signed a new three-year contract here in San Francisco. So you're stuck with me."

He briefly squeezed his eyes shut and pulled her against

him, sighing into her hair as she wrapped her arms around his back. "Are you sure?" he asked.

"Very sure," she said. "I'm not dragging my beautiful babies across the state, and I'm not leaving you here. I can't sleep when you're not in the bed."

"Me, either," he admitted. "The shipbuilder made fun of me. He said I've either been married too long or not long enough."

"Ten years." He felt warm and solid beneath her arms, and his thumping heart picked up speed when her hands skimmed a path down his back.

"Ten years tomorrow." His nose grazed her ear as he placed one warm, lingering kiss on her neck. "But if you can't wait, we can start the celebration a little early."

"Here?"

"The shop's bathroom has a lock on the door." He lifted his head to glance out the front window. "The marching band's still playing. That means Gum Lung is at least ten minutes away."

Gum Lung: the Golden Dragon, star of the parade. It took a hundred men and women to move the big festive dragon down Grant.

"Ten minutes?" she complained.

"Fifteen, if we're lucky," he whispered, kissing her neck with more fervor and sending a waterfall of goose bumps over her skin. He followed their path with his mouth until it met hers.

"*Gung Hay, Fat Choy,*" Astrid murmured the popular Lunar New Year phrase against Bo's lips. *Congratulations and be prosperous. Good luck.*

"I don't need luck," he said, cupping her face in his hands. "I already have you."

TURN THE PAGE FOR A PREVIEW OF THE FIRST
ROARING TWENTIES NOVEL FROM JENN BENNETT

BITTER SPIRITS

AVAILABLE NOW FROM BERKLEY SENSATION!

JUNE 2, 1927—NORTH BEACH, SAN FRANCISCO

AIDA PALMER'S TENSE FINGERS GRIPPED THE GOLD LOCKET
around her neck as the streetcar came to a stop near Gris-
Gris. It was almost midnight, and Velma had summoned
her to the North Beach speakeasy on her night off—no
explanation, just told her to come immediately. A thousand
reasons why swirled inside Aida's head. None of them
were positive.

"Well, Sam," she muttered to the locket, "I think I
might've made a mistake. If you were here, you'd probably
tell me to face up to it, so here goes nothing." She gave the
locket a quick kiss and stepped out onto the sidewalk.

The alley entrance was blocked by a fancy dark limousine and several Model Ts surrounded by men, so Aida
headed to the side.

Gossip and cigarette smoke wafted under streetlights
shrouded with cool summer fog. She endured curious
stares of nighttime revelers and hiked the nightclub's slop-
ing sidewalk past a long line of people waiting to get

inside. Hidden from the street, three signs lined the brick wall corridor leading to the entrance, each one lit by a border of round bulbs. The first two signs announced a hot jazz quartet and a troupe of Chinese acrobats. The third featured a painting of a brunette surrounded by ghostly specters:

WITNESS CHILLING SPIRIT MYSTERIES LIVE IN PERSON!
FAMED TRANCE MEDIUM MADAME AIDA PALMER
CALLS FORTH SPIRITS FROM BEYOND,
REUNITING AUDIENCE MEMBERS WITH
DEPARTED LOVED ONES.
——PATRONS WISHING TO PARTICIPATE SHOULD
BRING MEMENTO MORI——

One of the men standing next to the sign looked up at her when she passed by, a fuzzy recognition clouding his eyes. Maybe he'd seen her show . . . Maybe he'd been too drunk to remember. She gave him a tight smile and approached the club's gated entrance.

"Pardon me," she said to the couple at the head of the line, then stood on tiptoes and peeked through a small window.

One of the club's doormen stared back at her. "Evening, Miss Palmer."

"Evening. Velma called me in."

Warm, brassy light and a chorus of greetings beckoned her inside.

"The alley's blocked," she noted when the door closed behind her. "Any idea what's going on?"

"Don't know. Could be trouble," said the first doorman.

A second doorman started to elaborate until he noticed the club manager, Daniels, shooting them a warning look as he spoke to a couple of rough-looking men. His gaze connected with Aida's; he motioned with his head: *upstairs.*

Wonderful. Trouble indeed.

Aida left the doormen and marched through the

crowded lobby. At the far end, a yawning arched entry led into the main floor of the club. The house orchestra warmed up behind buzzing conversations and clinking glasses as Aida headed toward a second guarded door that bypassed the crowds.

Gris-Gris was one of the largest black-and-tan speakeasies in the city. Social rules concerning race and class went unheeded here. Anyone who bought a membership card was welcome, and patrons dined and danced with whomever they pleased. Like many of the other acts appearing onstage, Aida was only booked through early July. She'd been working here a month now and couldn't complain. It was much nicer than most of the dives she'd worked out East, and to say the owner was sympathetic to her skills was an understatement.

Velma Toussaint certainly stirred up chatter among her employees. People said she was a witch or a sorceress—she was—and that she practiced hoodoo, which she did. But the driving force of the gossip was a simpler truth: polite society just didn't know how to handle a woman who single-handedly ran a prosperous, if not illicit, business. Still, she played the role to the hilt, and Aida admired any woman who wasn't afraid to defy convention.

Though it was a relief to work for someone who actually believed in her own talents, all that really mattered was Aida was working. She needed this job. And right now she was crossing her fingers that the "trouble" was not big enough to get her fired. A particular unhappy patron from last night's show was her biggest worry. It wasn't her fault that he didn't like the message his dead sister brought over from the beyond, and how was she supposed to have known the man was a state senator? If someone had told her he preferred a charlatan's act to the truth, she would've happily complied.

Grumbling under her breath, Aida climbed the side stairs and sailed through a narrow hallway to the club's administrative offices. The front room, where a young girl who handled Velma's paperwork usually sat, was dark and empty. As she passed through the room, her breath rushed out in a wintery white puff.

Ghost.

She cautiously approached the main office. The door was cracked. She hesitated and listened to a low jumble of foreign words streaming from the room, spoken in a deep, male voice. Beyond the cloud of cold breath, she saw a woman with traditional Chinese combs in her hair, on which strings of red beads dangled. Bare feet peeked beneath her sheer sleeping gown. She stood behind a very large, dark-headed man wearing a long coat, who stared out a long window that looked down over the main floor of the club.

Aida's cold breath indicated that one of them was a ghost. This realization alone was remarkable, as Aida had only encountered one ghost in the club since she'd arrived—a carpenter who'd suffered a heart attack while building the stage and died several years before Velma came into possession of Gris-Gris—and Aida had exorcised it immediately.

In her experience, ghosts did not move around—they remained tethered to the scene of their death. So unless someone died in Velma's office tonight, a ghost shouldn't be here.

Shouldn't be, but was.

Strong ghosts looked as real as anyone walking around with a heartbeat. But even if the woman with the red combs hadn't been dressed for bed, Aida would've known the man was alive. He was speaking to himself in a low rumble, a repeating string of inaudible words that sounded much like a prayer.

Ghosts don't talk.

"Is she your dance partner?" Aida said.

The man jerked around. *My.* He was enormous—several inches over six feet and with shoulders broad enough to topple small buildings as he passed. Brown hair, so dark it was almost black, was brilliantined back with a perfect part. Expensive clothes. A long, serious face, one side of which bore a large, curving scar. He blinked at Aida for a moment, gaze zipping up and down the length of her in hurried assessment, then spoke in low voice, "You can see her?"

"Oh yes." The ghost turned to focus on the man, giving Aida a new, gorier view of the side of her head. "Ah, there's the death wound. Did you kill her?"

"What? No, of course not. Are you the spirit medium?"

"My name's on the sign outside."

"Velma said you can make her . . . go away."

"Ah." Aida was barely able to concentrate on what the man was saying. His words were wrapped inside a deep, grand voice—the voice of a stage actor, dramatic and big and velvety. It was a voice that could probably talk you into doing anything. A siren's call, rich as the low notes of a perfectly tuned cello.

And maybe there really was some magic in it, because all she could think about, as he stood there in his fine gray suit with his fancy silk necktie and a long black jacket that probably cost more than her entire wardrobe, was pressing her face into his crisply pressed shirt.

What a perverse thought. And one that was making her neck warm.

"Can you?"

"Pardon?"

"Get rid of her. She followed me across town." He swept a hand through the woman's body. "She's not corporeal."

"They usually aren't." The ghost had followed him? Highly unusual. And yet, the giant man acted as if the ghost was merely a nuisance. Most men didn't have the good sense to be afraid when they should.

"Your breath is . . ." he started.

Yes, she knew: shocking to witness up close rather than from the safe distance of the audience when she was performing onstage. "Do you know what an aura is?"

"No clue."

"It's an emanation around humans—an effusion of energy. Everyone has one. Mine turns cold when a spirit or ghost is nearby. When my warm breath crosses my aura, it becomes visible—same as going outside on a cold day."

"That's fascinating, but can you get rid of her first and talk later?"

"No need to get snippy."

He looked at her like she was a blasphemer who'd just disrupted church service, fire and brimstone blazing behind his eyes. "Please," he said in a tone that was anything but polite.

Aida stared at him for a long moment, a petty but sweet revenge. Then she inhaled and shook out her hands . . . closed her eyes, pretending to concentrate. Let him think she was doing him some big favor. Well, she *was*, frankly. If he searched the entire city, he'd be lucky to find another person with the gift to do what she did. But it wasn't difficult. The only effort it required was the same concentration it took to solve a quick math problem and the touch of her hand.

Pushing them over the veil was simple; calling them back took considerably more effort.

After she'd tortured the man enough, she reached out for the Chinese woman, feeling the marked change in temperature inside the phantom's body. Aida concentrated and willed her to leave. Static crackled around her fingertips. When the chill left the air, Aida knew the ghost was gone.

She considered pretending to faint, but that seemed excessive. She did, however, let her shoulders sag dramatically, as if it would take her days to recover. A little labored breathing was icing on the cake.

"Your breath is gone."

She cracked open one eye to find the giant's vest in front of her. When she straightened to full height, she saw more vest, miles of it, before her gaze settled on the knot of his necktie. It was a little annoying to be forced to tilt her face up to view his. But up close, she spotted an anomaly she hadn't noticed from a distance: something different about the eye with the scar. Best to find out who the hell this man was before she asked him about it.

"Aida Palmer," she said, extending a hand.

He stared down at it for a moment, gaze shifting up her arm and over her face, as if he were trying to decide whether he'd catch the plague if they touched. Then his big, gloved hand swallowed hers, warm and firm. Through the fine black leather, she felt a pleasant tingle prickle her skin—an unexpected sensation far more foreign than any ghostly static.